Dark Angel

Book 9, Jon Spicer Series

CHRIS SIMMS

Other novels by Chris Simms:

Psychological thrillers
Outside the White Lines
Pecking Order

Supernatural Thrillers
Sing Me To Sleep
Dead Gorgeous

Jon Spicer series
Killing the Beasts
Shifting Skin
Savage Moon
Hell's Fire
The Edge
Cut Adrift
Sleeping Dogs
Death Games
Dark Angel

DC Iona Khan series
Scratch Deeper
A Price To Pay

Copyright © 2021 Chris Simms

The right of Chris Simms to be identified as the author of this work has been asserted by him in accordance with the Copyright, Designs and Patents Act 1988.

All rights reserved.

ISBN: 9798712137817

To Danny: thanks for giving me a glimpse of what sleeping rough is really like.

PROLOGUE

The soft night breeze carries the sounds of the city up to him. A sudden clatter as empty bottles cascade into a bin. Clop-clip-clop of heels striking pavement. Single coughs. Muffled conversations. Raucous bursts of laughter. A name shouted over and over. Lee! Lee! Fuck's sake, Lee! And, behind it all, the low drone of car engines that never fade. Not even in the dead hours before dawn.

He opens his eyes and gazes at the massed lights beneath him. By letting his focus drift, he transforms the city centre into a distant, hazy galaxy. A constellation floating in the vast darkness of space.

When a life ends in this world, where does the person go? He knows the answer: somewhere better.

A scraping of cold stone against his cheek brings him fully back. He must have sagged forward, head tipping to the side. He becomes aware of how tightly his fingers grip the ornately carved surface. In the spring, when he'd first copied the key to the clock tower, he'd been told no one was allowed up here – especially when the peregrine falcons were nesting at the top.

Back then, a CCTV camera had been trained on the nest; images available to view online. Three chicks, clad in comedy suits of white feather. That summer, he'd sit on the benches in St Peter's Square and watch the adults scoring the sky in their hunt for prey. Targeting weaker, slower birds. Helping them on their way.

Was that, he wonders, when I first thought I could do the same with humans?

He stares across the jumble of dark rooftops. Chimneys and skylights and air vents. The silhouettes of small plants sprouting from clogged gutters. In the gaps where he can see down to the street, there are people. Their little lives being played out. None comprehends how fragile things are. That person – staggering along, phone before his face – a minor stumble and the car accelerating along Princess Street will hit him. Or maybe the driver will swerve and plough into the huddled group smoking outside The Oak. Death is so much closer than any of them knows.

His chest begins to buzz. Short and regular. Moving back from the windowless arch, he reaches into the pocket of his black coat. That same number on his phone's screen. The person calling doesn't realise, but it's his turn to die next.

He clears his throat. 'Hello, you're through to Manchester Veterans' Helpline. Is that Wayne calling? It is, isn't it? Recognised your number, mate. How are you feeling tonight? Don't worry. Take your time. I'm listening. I'll listen as long as you want me to. It's all right, Wayne. Let it out. Just let it out. No one's judging you. Remember, I'm here to help you. That's all, just help.'

CHAPTER 1

DC Jon Spicer killed his car's engine. As things went quiet, he looked through the windscreen towards his house. The curtains of every ground-floor window were closed; thin cracks of yellowish light showing around their edges. His eyes travelled up to the smaller window above the living room. That one glowed orange. The sight filled him with a warm feeling as he pictured his family inside the terraced house.

Duggy must still be getting ready for bed. Alice would be up there, too. Probably watching to make sure he was actually brushing his teeth. Holly would definitely be downstairs, relishing having the telly room to herself. He felt his smile slip. Recently, they'd both noticed a change in their daughter. Flashes of hostility when asked to do something. A scowl marring her smooth skin. Alice said she was ready to leave primary school, that was all. Outgrown it.

And Wiper? Stretched out in front of the fire or, if Alice wasn't looking, trying to worm his way under Duggy's bed. They'd got the boxer a month before Alice realised she was pregnant again. Once Duggy was born, it hadn't taken long for the family pet to adopt the newborn baby as his special companion: now they were inseparable.

Jon yanked the car keys out, prompting the vehicle's interior light to come on. A brief glimpse of himself in the rear-view mirror as he dragged his briefcase off the passenger seat. Square face and a heavy brow. A slightly crooked nose and a left eyebrow bisected by a neat scar. Sometimes, he wished he looked a little less like a bouncer. His eyes returned to his son's bedroom window and he speculated which book would have been chosen for his bedtime story. Please, not *Little Owl Learns To Fly*. The book was starting to do his head in.

Halfway to his front gate, a voice came out of the dark. 'Spicer, you're still ugly.'

The gruff tone caused a mix of emotions. Happiness at seeing his old rugby coach. Unease at why he'd been lurking outside his house. He turned. A stumpy figure stepped out of the shadows. Sloping shoulders and no neck. Arms hanging straight down.

'That was good timing.' The gnarled old man gestured behind him. 'Just got here as you pulled up.'

Jon stepped towards him. 'Senior. Nice to see you, mate.'

They shook hands in silence, the other man's grip as crushing as ever. Jon searched for clues in his eyes. 'How's things down at the club?'

'Same old, same old.'

He thought about how it was Senior who marked out all the pitches each week, Senior who made sure meals were laid on for visiting teams, Senior who tidied up after everyone had left. The bloke must be well into his seventies by now. 'You mean it's still you doing all the work at that place?'

'You know what they say: no mugs, no clubs.'

'Why don't you get someone in part-time? The club's got enough bloody money stashed in the bank.'

'One day, mate. One day.'

'That's what you always say. So ... you coming in?'

Senior grimaced. 'Got a favour to ask, Jon. Remember Wayne? Thick as pig-shit, played prop for us a good ten years back? Went off to join the army?'

Jon let his hand drop. Bollocks. This didn't sound good. 'Not sure. Action Man haircut? That guy?'

'Yeah, him.'

'Surname began with an N ...'

'Newton.'

'That's it. Wayne Newton.' Jon recalled an amiable lad, even when the opposition were trying to wind him up in scrums. He'd liked him. Loyalty stirred. A teammate. Jon struggled to remember a specific match, but it didn't matter: they'd have supported each other out there, on the pitch. That's the way it worked. 'Always smiling, wasn't he?'

Senior's single nod revealed regret. 'He's not doing so well since he came out. Lost his job, missus slung him out. Drinking and stuff. He's ended up homeless.'

Letting the 'stuff' bit slide, Jon said, 'That sounds unfortunate. He's properly on the streets?'

'Well, he gets to use the odd sofa at mates' houses. But not every night.'

Jon was aware that time was ticking on. Duggy might well be climbing into bed by now. The chance to read him a story was slipping by. 'Where do I fit in?'

'He remembers you. Remembers you were a copper.'

'OK.'

'I bumped into him the other day.' Senior's eyes shifted and Jon sensed the untruth. 'Saw him begging,' he stated. 'We went for some food and a catch-up.'

Typical Senior, Jon thought. Bought the guy a meal and probably gave him all his cash, too.

'So he mentioned you, asked if I was still in touch. Told him you'd fucked your career and got busted back down to detective constable.' Senior's eyes glinted as he gave a quick grin.

Jon lifted a middle finger. 'Twat.'

'Said you were building things back up. That you'd been moved to the Counter Terrorism Unit. His ears properly pricked up at that.'

Jon wanted to sigh. Detective constable was right; he was just a grunt now. He carried no weight. 'Not sure how—'

'Two people have died recently, Jon. Homeless, like him. He knew both of them.'

Jon was surprised; Senior was also ex-forces. Had done a stint in the SAS. He wasn't ignorant. 'That's regular police stuff, Senior. I'll happily check who's handling the cases, but other than—'

'He knew them because they'd both been in the army, too. Apparently, they tend to stick together a bit. On the street.'

Jon cocked his head. Now things made more sense. 'Were their deaths suspicious?'

'The police think not.' His eyes touched on Jon's house. 'Can you just speak to him? Listen to what he has to say?'

Jon looked along the road. Spotted Senior's ancient red Volvo parked beneath a tree. 'Where is he?'

'Not far.'

Jon sighed. 'Come on, then.'

CHAPTER 2

As he reached the Volvo, Jon noted the smattering of leaves littering its bonnet and roof. He wondered how long Senior had really been waiting for him to arrive home from work.

'Do you not want to tell Alice what you're doing?' Senior asked, as he opened the driver's door.

'I'll call her. Tell her I'm still at work.' He caught Senior's raised eyebrow as he climbed in. 'It'll be a lot easier than poking my head through the front door, only to head straight back out, believe me.'

Senior was silent and Jon knew he'd be wondering how things were with Alice. The job's erratic demands were a permanent niggle in their marriage. A few years back, she'd tried to split up with him. The months he'd spent on his own had been the worst of his life. Eventually, she'd had a change of heart. Accepted police work was all he'd ever wanted to do. All he was capable of doing. She could live with that, she'd said – as long as he was always honest with her about what was going on.

Jon couldn't help looking towards the house as his call was answered. 'Hello, you. I'll be a little bit yet. Yeah, me too. Something came in. I know. Kiss the kids for me, can you? And see you later.'

Once he'd pulled out, Senior glanced across. 'How's that little bruiser of yours?'

'Duggy? He's great, cheers.'

'Holly?'

Jon decided to skim over that. 'Growing up fast, she is.'

'And Alice?'

'Yeah, good. Still working part-time. Enjoys it.'

'And they're happy with you looking like that, in the Counter Terrorism Unit?'

Jon glanced down at his battered jeans and old corduroy jacket. Beneath that, he was wearing a faded sweatshirt. Ancient Adidas trainers on his feet. 'Need to blend in, Senior. That's what it's all about.' He knew the other man was ribbing him; Senior had served in Northern Ireland. A plain-clothes unit whose job was to go in and snatch IRA suspects out of their communities. That would have been a bit hairy.

'Blend in? A big lunk like you? That's funny.'

Jon looked Senior up and down. He was wearing a tracksuit. He was always wearing a tracksuit. Some horrific beige anorak over the top of it. White socks and black leather shoes. 'Says him with the fashion sense of an asylum seeker.'

Senior chuckled and they drove in silence for a while. Jon could see they were heading into the city. Before them, the single red warning lights of motionless cranes hung in the night sky like frozen fireflies. 'I've never seen so much building work going on.'

'Luxury flats though, isn't it?' Senior said glumly. 'Big money pouring in from abroad. I don't like it.'

There was a lot of similar talk at work. How the council was eroding the city's character by approving so many prestige apartments. Jon wasn't so sure; Manchester had never enjoyed a gently paced, orderly evolution. It had developed at breakneck speed, powered by profits from the cotton industry. Mills, warehouses, the canals and railways. The grand civic buildings like the town hall, the cramped terraces and the massive merchant's homes on the outskirts. All of it had sprung up in a hectic rush. The world's first industrial city.

They were now on the A6, heading towards Levenshulme train station. Not one of Manchester's more affluent areas. 'Where are we going, anyway?'

'Just up here on the left. A mate of his has let him stay these past few nights.'

A few minutes' later, Senior turned down a side street. When he got to a large house at the intersection of another road, he pulled in. 'This one.'

Jon examined the overflowing bins fighting for space in the front yard. Multi-tenancy, by the looks of it. Like most big houses, it had been split up into smaller apartments. Senior got to the front door and pressed a button.

A metallic voice spoke a few moments later. 'Yeah?'

'It's Senior.'

'The rugby club guy?'

'That's right. Come to see Wayne.'

'Hang on a sec. I'll be down.'

Jon caught Senior's eye. Something was up. A hazy form soon came into view behind the frosted window panes. The door clicked open to reveal a bloke in his mid-twenties. Messed-up hair and bare feet. He peered out, caught sight of Jon and had to lift his chin to make eye contact.

Jon nodded hello.

He mirrored the gesture, then turned to Senior. 'He's not actually here.'

'OK,' Senior replied.

The man glanced towards the stairs. Jon could see a grubby hallway, peeling wallpaper and the usual spread of junk mail littering the floor. 'My girlfriend showed up. Had some holiday she had to take. Wayne knew the score ...'

'Where'd he go?' Senior asked.

The man looked awkward. 'Not sure. He said the city centre. Usually, when he sleeps out, he picks this place on Stevenson Square.'

Senior glanced at Jon.

'I know it. It's in the Northern Quarter. Whereabouts in Stevenson Square?'

'There's this office building with an overhanging porch-thing at the front. It was a printers? Went bump during the first lockdown. It's next to the building with the basement club called the Tiki Bar.'

'I know the Tiki Bar,' Jon said to Senior. A work do and hollowed-out pineapples full to the brim with rum cocktail. Memories were vague after they'd staggered out.

'And he'll just be in the doorway, will he?' Senior asked.

'He used to have a pop-up tent, but the council banned them. So, yeah, I suppose.'

'Cheers,' Senior said, now turning fully to Jon. 'Is it OK if …?'

Jon shrugged. 'Of course.'

The man had begun to close the door. 'Are you the one who's in the police?'

Jon looked at him. 'That's right.'

The man grinned. 'Wayne was talking about you the other night. Said about this time playing rugby with you. A fight where you laid out two from the other team? One punch each, he said.'

Senior erupted in laughter. 'Yeah! Liverpool Collegiate, it was. Cracking match.'

Jon grinned, enjoying the memory. 'I'm not like that now. Well,' he added, giving the bloke a wink, 'unless they're Scousers.'

It was now almost quarter past eight. Jon realised Holly would be in bed, asleep, by the time he got home. Damn it. Senior found a place to park on an adjacent road and they set off towards the square. Away to their left was the start of Ancoats, the latest part of the city being targeted by investors. Jon could see the tips of more cranes, clustering around the place like praying mantises. He remembered reading something about vacant land where a Toys-R-Us store used to be. Locals wanted it transformed into a community space; developers were converting it into another car park.

Stevenson Square had become quite a venue for the type of off-beat bar that thrived in the Northern Quarter. For a Wednesday night, the place was busy with drinkers. And, where drinkers went, so did those who asked for spare change. They soon passed the first person sitting on the pavement, legs swaddled in a sleeping bag, empty cup before him.

Jon pointed out a small neon sign with yellow lettering. 'That's the bar. Wayne's mate must have meant the place next door. Looks like a commercial premises.'

Senior grunted a reply. 'I doubt he'll have kipped down for the night already. Let's hope he isn't too far away.'

But as they neared the deeply recessed doorway, two figures came into view. They were on a flattened layer of cardboard, bags and food packaging around them. One was sitting up, the other was on his side, seemingly asleep. Senior made a beeline for them both. The one with his eyes open watched their approach from beneath the rim of a battered flat cap. After holding up a hand in greeting, Senior stooped down. 'Wayne, wake up, you lazy tosser! It's me, Senior. We're doing pyramids tonight. Pyramids until you puke.'

Jon couldn't help smile at the memory of Senior's brutal fitness sessions. Hated them at the time, he thought. But, weirdly, quite miss them now.

The bloke in the flat cap was now lighting a cigarette. 'He's out of it, pal. You got no chance.'

Senior looked to the side. 'I'll fucking wake him. With my shoe.'

The bloke shook his head. 'He's had Spice.'

'Great,' murmured Jon. The synthetic version of skunk that was rife among the city's homeless community.

Sometimes, the stuff left people temporarily paralysed, even while standing up. The sight of their swaying forms had become depressingly familiar in the city centre. 'When?'

The man squinted at Jon. 'Few hours ago? Should be round soonish.'

Senior crouched down. 'You give it him?'

That caused a glare. 'No. Don't touch it, me. Who are you, anyway?'

'Old friends,' Senior said. 'He played rugby with us, before the army.'

'What's your name?'

'Senior.'

The man nodded. 'You're that coach? He said you two had chatted.'

'And this is Jon. Wayne wanted a word with him.'

The man had to tilt his head right back to see Jon's face. 'Sit down, will you? I'll be putting my neck out at this rate.'

Jon glanced down, found a relatively clean spot of space on the cardboard and sat, trying to ignore the strong scent of piss coming from the doorway. 'Cheers,' he said. 'Where did he get hold of the Spice, then?'

'Some fucking scrote was doing the rounds before. Even gave it him on tick.'

A freebie, Jon thought. So Wayne was in his debt. How scummy could you get? 'You know Wayne, do you?'

'Yeah, we two-up.' He caught Jon's questioning look. 'Sleep as a pair. Safer that way.'

'Were you in the army?'

'I was.'

Jon held out a hand. 'Jon Spicer.'

'Alright.' After they shook, the man dragged deeply on his roll-up, held it down for a second then exhaled. Tobacco smoke wafted across Jon.

'So, Wayne wanted to speak to me about a couple of—'

'Jim Barlow.' The man pointed to the right with his cigarette. 'He went off the top of the NCP on Tib Street two weeks ago. Then Ryan Gardner: he was found in an abandoned building over on Bendix Street. At the bottom of the central stairwell. Fell from the top floor.'

'When was this?'

'About a month ago.'

'And they were both army?'

'That's right.'

Interesting, thought Jon. 'What do you think happened?'

He gave Jon a look. 'Who can say? Sleeping rough: it's risky.'

As the silence stretched out, a group of people strolled past. Jon could tell they'd sensed people were in the doorway, but none of them actually looked.

It's different down here, Jon thought. Like being invisible. 'You reckon someone else was involved?' he asked.

The other man pinched his roll-up out and slipped what was left back into a packet. 'I can't say I saw anything.'

'But you've heard something?'

He sighed, then looked across at Wayne. 'I wish that fucker was awake.'

Jon sensed that was the way to get the other man to talk; get him to give Wayne's story. 'What sort of stuff has Wayne heard?'

He bit at his thumbnail for a second or two. 'Some bloke who dresses totally in black, apparently.'

The man's voice had dropped so low, Jon could hardly hear him.

'Just appears,' he continued. 'No warning. Then vanishes again. I don't know ... there's always bullshit rumours flying about, isn't there?'

Jon draped his forearms over his knees. 'Is there something to suggest this person targeted the two who died?'

The man scratched at his armpit. 'Well, they were in the army ...'

I'll need more than that, Jon thought. 'Had either said someone was after them? Anything like that?'

'No.'

'How many people knew they'd both been soldiers?'

'Couldn't really say. But we don't spread it around. The ones who do that are usually full of shit. "I was in the paras, five tours in Iraq, don't fuck with me." That sort of crap. Soon sniff those types out.'

'Yeah?' Jon asked. 'How?'

'Just ask them their number. You never forget your number, isn't that right, Senior?'

Senior smiled briefly. 'That's right.'

'So, you haven't seen this person who wears black?' Jon asked.

'No. I haven't. But ...' His eyes cut to Wayne, who now seemed to be coming round.

CHAPTER 3

Wayne let out a long series of coughs. Lay there for another minute, the fingers of one hand rubbing away at his ear. A few more coughs and, slowly, his head lifted. Several blinks later, he managed to get a word out. 'Senior.'

'Wayne. You all right?'

'Yeah.' He raised himself onto one elbow and rubbed his face with the palm of his hand. 'Cracking. Got any smokes on you, Senior?'

'No, not tonight.'

'Greg, lend us a smoke, will you?' He reached a hand over his shoulder, unaware that Jon was sitting alongside his companion.

So that's your name, Jon thought, watching as Greg shoved the rolling materials in Wayne's hand. With trembling fingers, Wayne struggled to extract a cigarette paper from the pack. Next, he pulled a straggly pinch of tobacco from the pouch. Half of it fell on his sleeping bag, but he didn't seem to notice.

'You were asking about Jon,' Senior announced. 'The other day, when we spoke.'

The cigarette was now between Wayne's lips and he started clicking on a lime-green lighter. 'Fuck's sake.'

'Well,' Senior continued, 'he's sitting right behind you.'

Wayne's chin lifted and his head slowly turned.

Jon was now able to see his old teammate's face properly. You've aged, he thought. Bloated out. He could see that the man's pupils were heavily dilated. Still off his head. 'Wayne. It's been a while.'

'Jon Spicer! Jon fucking Spicer.' Both his front teeth were missing. A lower one, too. The unlit cigarette bobbled in his mouth. 'Fuck me. It's you. Fuck.'

'Good to see you, mate.'

'Yeah, you too. You too.' He remembered there was a cigarette hanging from the corner of his mouth and got it lit. Smoke wreathed his face as he shuffled back into a sitting position. 'I still remember those matches with you. That fat blob from the team out near Runcorn? Remember that match? He was trying to gouge me in that ruck and you,' he let out a croaky laugh, 'you got hold of his throat and did something with your thumb.'

Naughty me, Jon thought. Using a pressure point in a rugby match; the player must have been going for Wayne's eyes.

'He let out that strangled noise and his legs went. Just went. Dropped to his knees like he was begging you to stop. Remember it?'

Jon couldn't, but he nodded anyway. 'I think so.'

'I reckon he would have blinded me, the bastard.' Wayne dragged on his crooked cigarette, head shaking. He looked about, as if remembering where he was. 'Listen, this – where I am now. Look at this.' His eyes were filling with tears. 'I don't really know how the fuck it happened. I'm sorry.'

Jon leaned forward, squeezed the guy's shoulder. 'Don't apologise, Wayne. It's not necessary.'

'Yeah.' He wiped at his eyes, took another drag.

'Wayne,' Jon said. 'You had something to tell me – about the two people who died recently.'

He looked nervously past Jon to the square beyond, gaze lifting to the rooftops on the far side. Checking what might be up there. 'I know it sounds mad, but I saw him.'

'What did you see?'

'I saw him up on the roof that Jim went off. The bloke with the wings.'

'Hang on: wings? Who had wings?'

'The one who's doing it.'

'You're talking about the person who wears black?'

'Yeah,' Wayne replied. 'Whenever he appears, someone dies.'

Jon glanced over at Senior, who had now crossed his arms and was avoiding eye contact. 'Who else has died?' Jon asked.

'Ryan, of course. In that building over on Bendix.'

'And you saw the same person when that happened?'

'I didn't, but others did.'

'Who?'

'This pair. They'd all been there, up on the top floor. It was a decent place to go.'

'To take drugs?'

'And to sleep. A crash pad.'

Jon thought for a few seconds. This gets worse. Whenever this person appears, everyone's heavily under the influence. 'Talk me through the time you saw him.'

'So, Jim and me had gone up to the roof of the NCP for a wee smoke.'

'Spice?'

'I don't really do it anymore. But Jim, he had some and was offering.'

Yeah, right, Jon thought. 'What time was this?'

'About midnight?'

'OK.'

'At some point, I kind of half woke. Could hear talking nearby. Jim's voice and someone else. They were off to my left. Couldn't really move, so I just lay there on my side. He crosses my field of vision as he walks by.'

'Jim?'

'No – the guy in black. And on his back, he had wings. Black wings. That's what I saw.'

'And after that?'

'I fell asleep again, but not properly. Drifting in and out. No sign of Jim. Then I heard the sirens. When I realised they weren't going away, I got up. Peeped over the roof and there are ambulances and police cars surrounding the benches below me. Found out later that's where Jim had landed.'

'You didn't see him leave with the person you saw?'

Wayne shook his head.

Jon didn't want to ask about the wings. It only risked making the other man look ridiculous, but he had to. 'How big were these wings?'

'Only little. Like things a kid might wear for dressing up.'

'And they were black?'

'Black as a crow's.'

'How ... how do you think this person got down from the roof?'

Wayne looked at him, eyes widening as he started to laugh. It was a shrill sound. Not far from hysterical. 'I don't think he flew! Fuck me, is that what you thought I thought? Jesus, that's funny.' Then, just as quickly, his mirth disappeared. 'He was heading towards the stairwell. I know what I saw, Jon.'

That's a relief, Jon thought. If you'd said the man had flapped away into the night ... 'How far away from you was he?'

'Twenty, no, thirty metres, probably.'

'Can you describe him?'

'You mean like they do in TV programmes?'

'Yeah.'

'A bit under six foot tall. Slim build. Anywhere between twenty and forty.'

'Hair colour?'

'Dark. But I think he was wearing a black beanie hat. And he had gloves on, too.'

'Black?'

'You guessed it.'

'What about ethnicity? Could you see the colour of his skin?'

'Oh, he was white. Definitely white.'

Interesting, Jon thought. 'You sound sure of that.'

'He's in black from head to foot. I couldn't see what he looked like, but his face was white.'

'Did he know you were awake?'

'Doubt it. My eyes were only just open.'

'The other two you mentioned. The ones who saw him that second time, when Ryan Gardner died. Did it sound like the same person?'

'Yeah.'

'Including these, er, wings?'

He glanced at Jon, aggression sparking in his eyes. 'You really don't like the wings, do you?'

'Wayne,' Senior said softly. 'Don't be a dick. He's trying to help out, here.'

Wayne's head dropped. 'Sorry. The wings, as well.'

'Did they give any sort of statement to the police?' Jon asked.

Wayne snorted in reply.

'Who reported it?'

Greg spoke up. 'I heard he was found by the building's owners. They'd gone to secure the doors.'

'So the two who were with Ryan didn't give a statement?'

'I doubt it,' Greg replied.

'Do you know who they are?'

'One of them.' He turned to Wayne. 'It was Dan, wasn't it? The Brummy?'

Wayne nodded. 'And Big Ian, I heard.'

Jon frowned. 'You're not sure exactly who was in the building that night?'

'I was told it was Dan and Big Ian,' Wayne said. 'That's what people are saying.'

'But you didn't actually speak with them?'

'No.'

'Are they around? Can I find them?'

'Haven't seen either in a while.'

Greg adjusted the blanket draped over his legs. 'I think they may have moved on.'

Great, thought Jon. Everyone who's seen this winged man was off their heads, and two of them aren't even around. 'Wayne, did you give a statement?'

He smiled. 'I didn't put things together. Not until I heard about Ryan.'

'So you've not given a statement?'

'No fucking point.'

'Regular police aren't interested,' Greg explained. 'You give a statement and nothing happens. Last year, I woke up to find two blokes kicking the crap out of me. In A & E, this copper takes a statement. But what then? We've got no address, so they don't follow anything up. That's even if they wanted to.'

Wayne pointed to his missing teeth. 'That happened in Piccadilly Gardens. There's CCTV all over Piccadilly Gardens. The guy who stamped on me was with two women. The police could have got the CCTV of that, no problem. Did they? Did they fuck.'

Jon scratched at his jaw. 'OK. Let me have a look at what's on the system. Maybe have a word with the officers working the cases. I can also see if there are any other reports about a person who wears black.'

Wayne was rolling another cigarette. 'I knew he'd come good. Didn't I say, Greg?'

Jon got to his feet. It was time to go, but he felt guilty. 'Do you need anything? Food or something?'

Greg pointed to a carrier bag. 'It's one thing you're never short of, sleeping rough. Folk shower you with fucking sandwiches and that. You're all right, mate. Thanks anyway.'

'Yeah, cheers Jon,' Wayne added. 'And Senior. I appreciate it.'

'You take care, you hear me?' Senior said, stepping back.

Once they were round the corner, Senior let out a sigh. 'What do you reckon?'

'I reckon if I go into work and repeat that story, I'll have the piss taken out of me for months.'

Senior nodded. 'Yeah. Thought so. Sorry I wasted your time.'

'He's not in a good place, is he?'

'No,' Senior replied.

'Emotions all over the place. I thought he was going to cry at one point, poor fucker.'

'What'll you do, then?'

Jon stopped walking. Eyes closed, he took a deep breath. He thought about the last time he'd let himself get dragged into something like this. Using his police powers as a favour to someone. 'Shit, Senior. This sort of thing: it's why I'm a detective constable at forty-six.'

Senior gave a glum nod. 'I understand. I'll let him know you've had to go and do a job down in London or somewhere. Maybe he can report it to the nick on Bootle Street.'

Jon knew that would be futile. If his colleagues would find the story amusing hearing it from him, they'd wet themselves hearing it from someone like Wayne. 'No, don't do that,' he said. 'I'll look into it.'

CHAPTER 4

Alice's voice broke the calm of the breakfast table. 'Duggy, stop it!'

Jon looked up to see a naughty grin on his son's face. Wiper was swiftly snuffling some cereal that his son had accidentally dropped on the floor.

'Jon?' His wife was giving him a look.

He put on a stern voice. 'Oi, you little monster, you know that's not allowed.'

'Seriously?' Alice's voice was incredulous. 'That's it?'

He pointed a finger. 'Duggy, we don't want a dog that begs. No one likes a dog that skulks about the place begging. He gets his food in his bowl, understand?'

'Okay.'

'I mean it.' Jon held his son's eyes for a moment longer then glanced at Alice. There you go. Sorted.

She didn't look convinced.

Holly walked in, poured granola into a bowl, added some milk and attempted to carry it straight back out.

'Where are you going?' Jon asked.

She stopped, but didn't turn round. 'My room.'

'I don't think so, my little sugarplum. No food in your bedroom. Like you'd forgotten.'

She twirled on her heel, stomped across to the last empty chair at the table and flopped down.

Jon looked about. Duggy was shovelling the last of his food in like it was a race, Wiper tracking every movement with doleful eyes. Holly had an elbow either side of her bowl, head bowed, fringe hiding her face. Alice was busily tapping something into her phone, even though they weren't allowed at the table. 'Well,' Jon announced cheerfully. 'Aren't we one big happy family?'

No one replied.

Once Duggy and Holly had left the room to get ready for school, Alice pointed to the shelf above the radiator. 'Oh, there's a letter there from Miss Jennings.'

'Who?'

'That adult who is always in your daughter's classroom. Her form teacher?'

'I thought it was a bloke. Mr Roberts?'

'You mean, Richards? That was last year, Jon. Miss Jennings is the one you would have met the other day when I arranged that meeting. If you'd been able to leave work in time to get there.'

Ouch, Jon thought. 'This about Holly's behaviour?'

Alice was looking pleased with herself. 'She said not to be worried. Apparently, Holly's all sweetness and light when she's in school. And her grades are all good. More than good, in fact.'

'So it's just us two getting the special treatment?'

'Seems to be.'

'I told you, Ali: she's a premature teenager. Got there three years too soon. She'll grow out of it.'

Alice groaned. 'Yeah, but when? I can't take years of her current attitude.'

He smiled. 'She'll be all right.'

'What's going on at work, then?'

'How do you mean?'

'Last night, when you had to stay back.'

He was about to fob her off again, but a little voice stopped him. Do not start snaring yourself in lies. You know it never ends well. 'Actually, it was Senior. He wanted me to meet with this lad who used to play at Cheadle Ironsides. He's homeless and two people he knew have both died recently.'

'Other homeless people?'

'Yeah.'

Alice looked sad. 'It's a disgrace what's going on. I read this article in the *Manchester Evening Chronicle* – it was about how many are ending up back on the streets now government money for Everyone In has ended.'

Everyone In, Jon thought. A scheme to bring the nation's homeless into temporary accommodation while the pandemic was bad.

'So,' Alice said. 'He thinks there was something suspicious?'

He stood, took the car keys off the shelf and nodded. 'That's right. They both were in the army. That's why he wanted to chat with me.'

Alice looked uneasy. 'Jon – don't do anything silly, will you? This job you've got now, the Counter Terrorism Unit was—'

'I know: the only place that would take me. Don't worry, I'll mention everything to my boss. Get his permission before I do anything.'

Her smile disappeared as her eyes went to the clock. 'Shit, I've not done their packed lunches. Before you go, make sure they're dressed and have done their teeth, can you?'

'Will do.' He reached across the table for her hand. 'See you later.'

She squeezed his fingers. 'Later.'

At the bottom of the stairs, he called out as he started to climb. 'You two fungus-breaths? If those teeth aren't clean, I'm going stick your heads down the toilet, add some mouthwash and press the flush.'

CHAPTER 5

Radio Manchester brought him out of a sleep that had been swirling with visions of Claire and Sophie. Waking up was a relief, even if the apartment now only had him in it. He turned onto his back, kicking about to unsnarl his legs from the twisted duvet. One pillow was half off the bed, the other squashed up against the headboard. He checked the backs of the fingers on his right hand for fresh bruises; lately, he'd been waking up with them. It had taken him a while to figure out he was flailing his arm in the night. The edges of the bedside table were unforgiving.

The news was just coming on. Long tailbacks on the approach roads to Manchester Airport. People protesting about the proposed extra runway. A stabbing in Hulme. A factory in Swinton that supplied plastic drums for chemical storage was closing. Forty-six people to join the jobless count. Manchester United had lost again.

He reached across and turned the radio off. It wasn't like he was going to fall back to sleep. The bedroom's plain walls seemed to press in on him. With one smooth movement, he swung his legs off the mattress and stood. Peering round the edge of the curtain, he surveyed the drab street. Early afternoon and most people were hidden away indoors. Two flimsy scraps of blue; a couple of discarded face masks on the pavement. The phone mast on the roof of the old warehouse opposite his flat seemed to be reaching for the grey clouds scudding across the dull sky. Trying to snag them on its stiff metal fingers.

The flat would have been almost unrecognisable to anyone who'd visited when they were a family. When Claire had run the show, her touches made it feel like a home. Things like wallpaper. Framed pictures. A rug with cheerful colours running through it. After they'd gone, he'd got rid of everything. Tore the wallpaper down. Threw the pictures away. Rolled the rug up and left it outside a charity shop. The only room he hadn't touched was Sophie's. He wasn't sure why. Just had shut the door and never gone in it again.

Now all there was in the living area was an armchair positioned squarely in front of an old-fashioned television. A single bookshelf, devoid of books. Beside the kitchenette was a small table with four chairs. Three too many. The walls were as bare as the bedroom's except for one item: a pair of black wings. Measuring barely more than a metre from tip to tip, they had been carefully mounted at eye level.

He padded across the bare floorboards to a foam mat, unrolled it and lay down. Abdominal crunches and leg raises. Onto his elbows to do a plank. Down onto his front. Press-ups. Arms wide, then together. Squat thrusts followed by a hamstring stretch. It was the best thing the army had taught him: the importance of staying in shape. Sometimes, he thought it was the only thing keeping him together.

By the time he sauntered round to the kitchenette, he felt a slight distance from the sense of desolation that always followed him. Exercise always did that. Got him ahead of it. For a bit. Some cereal while the kettle boiled. Standing there, bowl in hand, his mind wandered to the phone call from the day before. Wayne. The man was so close to being ready. In fact, yesterday, the time had seemed right. He'd almost asked to meet him, but then something had happened to make Wayne end the call. No matter. He'd ring again, soon enough.

The calendar pinned to the cupboard door caught his eye. Soon, it would be time to turn to the next sheet. Pinch punch, first day of the month and all that. He lifted the page and his eyes moved across to the 4th. On that day, two names were written.

Claire and Sophie.

After that, the entire month was empty. As was the next month. And all the ones after that. Every single month that would ever pass.

It didn't seem possible the 4th would mark an entire year since they'd left him behind. All the plans he'd formed with his wife during the time he'd been over in Afghanistan on tour. The hours he'd spent searching the Internet, plotting their route. Sleepovers in rooms above isolated Scottish pubs. Bed and breakfasts, lodges and farms. Sometimes car parks if they overlooked a beach or a loch.

Everything destroyed in one night.

He approached the wings on the wall. He'd loved to watch Claire as she'd carefully constructed them in the evenings after Sophie was in bed. Threading each snow-white feather into place on the gossamer-light frames. He'd helped her with the tiny hinges so that, with a pull on the line at the back, the wings extended out to full stretch. It had been their daughter's dream. To have wings. To be able to fly. To spread happiness. Her voice echoed in his head. *'Every angel has wings, Daddy.'*

He studied the feathers – now spray-painted black – and lifted a finger to smooth some filaments of a larger one back into place. Six more days and they would all be together again. Forever.

CHAPTER 6

Jon had his ID ready as he reached the barrier into the car park. 'Morning, Terry. Getting a bit chillier, isn't it?'

The old boy nodded. 'It is sitting in here. Does my piles no good.'

Jon grinned as the barrier lifted. The CTU building that he worked out of was located on the edge of an industrial estate at Trafford Park. Chest-high hedges screened off the outside area from prying eyes. After parking, he crossed to the main building, electing to enter via the interior garage. Surveillance vehicles lined one side of the flooring: a variety of cars both new and old, commercial vans picked up from auctions with the previous company's lettering still faintly visible beneath the paintwork, a couple of lorries and even an ice-cream van.

Michael, the weapons inventory officer, was waiting by a dark-blue saloon as two firearms officers checked the armoured box in its boot contained everything the inventory said it did.

'Morning, lads,' Jon announced as he went by.

At the top of the metal stairs, he had to lean down in order to press his card against the reader. Over a year into the job, and he still hadn't got round to finding a longer lanyard.

Immediately beyond the door was a long room known as the foyer. Seats and wall-mounted mirrors provided an area where officers could check their appearance before going out on surveillance jobs. Something Jon was rarely called on to do: anyone over six-feet tall wasn't ideal as their height was likely to draw attention. He proceeded straight through to the main office, spotting Iona at the desk beside his.

So many sheets of paper were spread out, they covered her keyboard. Her head was down, glossy black hair hanging forward. My daughter, he thought, sits like that at every meal. Very unsocial it is, too. 'Morning.'

Her head didn't move.

'Iona, I said ...' A thin white lead trailed across the desk to her computer. She was plugged in, listening to something. He picked a paperclip out of the little pot by his monitor and tossed it across.

She looked up, bright blue eyes taking a moment to refocus. 'Hi.' She smiled, pressing a button on her keyboard before slipping the earpieces out.

'Hello. What are you so busy with at this time of the morning?'

She sighed. 'Earwigging. Endless earwigging.'

'Waiting for that magic phrase?'

'Correct.'

Jon couldn't imagine anything more tedious than listening to recordings of bugged phone conversations. Someone suspected of no good. Chats that, to the casual ear, were entirely innocent. Mundane, even. But, in reality, might contain a code or reference or hint of something ominous. Maybe just a certain word popping up too often. He didn't know how she did it. 'Is that what you're on today?'

'Probably the week. These are just the first of a new tap. The bloke talks more than my gran used to. What about you?'

When he first joined the CTU, Jon didn't like the fact it took a silo approach to jobs: officers were brought together in groups dictated by what the job needed and the particular skill-sets officers possessed.

Iona was brilliant at analysis: studying columns of figures, scanning records, listening for patterns. Stuff like that. Me? Jon thought, I'm better at the ... hands-on stuff. Like punching people. One job, they might be working as a pair, the next they'd be part of a thirty-officer team. Other times, they worked separately. If nothing else, it ensured variety. 'Not sure. We have a briefing at half nine.' He dumped his phone and keys in his top drawer, shrugged his jacket off and then asked, 'Need a brew?'

But her head was already back down, wire vanishing behind her fringe. No use talking to you, he thought, hanging his jacket on the back of the chair and heading back towards the stairs.

DCI Weir's door was partly open. 'Sir, do you have a minute?'

'Yup, in you come. Take a seat.'

His senior officer had wispy blonde hair, lips that were too wide and eyes that were too far apart. Frog-face was the name he was known by. Jon wondered how to start. 'Sir, I got a tip yesterday evening about a couple of deaths within the last month involving homeless people. The reason it reached me was because both victims served in the army. The person I spoke to saw someone suspicious at the time one of them died. A male figure, dressed completely in black.'

'Anything else?'

No way I'm mentioning any bloody wings, Jon thought. 'Average height, slim build. Anywhere from twenty to forty in age. White.'

'Definitely white?'

'As sure as he could be. It was at night on the roof of a car park. I'm thinking if the skin wasn't pale, he wouldn't have been able to notice.'

'So what are you asking for?'

'Permission to dig around on the system. Perhaps speak to the investigating officers. A few hours' work, maximum.'

Weir considered this. 'You know how many homeless people are veterans?'

Jon shook his head, not sure which way this was going.

'About one in five,' Weir stated.

Jon raised his eyebrows. 'That many?'

Weir nodded. 'And their mortality rates are far higher, too. Suicide, mainly.'

Surprised at the other man's level of knowledge, Jon glanced to the side wall and saw a photo of a younger-looking Weir in army combats. Ah-ha: that's why.

'Were these two recorded as suicides?' his senior officer asked.

'Haven't had a chance to check yet.'

'What are you down for today?'

'Not sure. There's a briefing about something at half nine. Operation Flyer?'

'That'll be the delegation arriving from the States. One of the party merits an armed response unit being in attendance.'

'What's the visit about?'

'The proposed airport expansion. They'll be offering expertise or money. Or both. Your guess is as good as mine. Anyway, there are a load of visits lined up: council bigwigs, the mayor, that crew. You're on the team escorting them about.'

Which, Jon thought, means sitting on my arse, waiting around for bloody hours in a car. Great.

CHAPTER 7

'Those airport security boys are seriously close to losing their shit,' chuckled Detective Constable Kieran Saunders, his Welsh accent adding a sing-song quality to his words.

Jon glanced up from his phone and peered through the windscreen. Beyond the restricted area where they were parked, the group protesting about the airport expansion were causing chaos. As soon as the security personnel succeeded in clearing one of them from the road, another would lie down to take their place. Placards bobbing about bore slogans like: 'There is no plan*et* B.' 'Plane Stupid.' 'One World, Last Chance.' 'Planet before Profit.' Traffic was backed up towards the roundabout; drivers had started beeping their horns, passengers had started climbing out of stationary cars and approaching the terminal on foot, dragging suitcases behind them. Like the protestors, most of them were wearing face masks.

'Surprised they're not just arresting them,' Jon stated. 'There are special measures in place for airports, aren't there?'

Kieran regarded the nearby police van with hopeful eyes. 'If they get the green light, shall we go over and lend a hand? Cuff 'em and stuff 'em. It would be nice to haul their crusty arses out of here, wouldn't it?'

Knowing they would never be allowed out of their vehicle for simple crowd control, Jon went back to studying the information on his phone. His Internet search on homeless deaths in Manchester had brought up a long list. Topping it were news articles by the likes of the *Manchester Evening Chronicle*, the *Guardian* and the *Independent*. Next were reports from organisations that included the Rowntree Trust and St Mungo's. The entry for a Manchester-based drug and alcohol service caught his eyes. New Dawn – working since 2016 to help young people and their families affected by substance abuse.

Shame, he thought, you weren't around for my younger brother.

Further down, various website entries for homeless charities that operated in the city began to appear. He scanned their names: Mustard Tree, Barnabus, the Booth Centre.

The third name on the list sent his mind racing back to when he'd been trying to find Dave. His younger brother had been thrown out of the family home by their dad while he was still in his teens. He'd ended up living an unorthodox life that, sometimes, involved dropping into the Booth Centre to get a free meal.

Jon remembered visiting the place: back then, it had been located in some cramped rooms beside the city's cathedral. The address now showing was different. Wondering when it had moved, his finger hovered over the screen. But he knew visiting the charity's website would only stir stronger memories of the sad sequence of events that led to his younger brother's murder.

Needing to think about something else, he ran over the events from earlier that morning. His DCI hadn't categorically said he couldn't look into the homeless people's deaths. So, before the nine thirty briefing, he'd accessed the records for both. Jim Barlow had been found on the 15th of September. It was as Wayne had described: the body had been spotted shortly before dawn by a delivery driver dropping off supplies on nearby Turner Street.

The uniforms attending had reported that there were no apparent signs of life and duly cordoned off the scene. A Home Office pathologist had stated what was probably obvious to everyone – the nature of Barlow's injuries suggested he'd fallen from a considerable height. There was a bit from a detective who'd conducted a search of the car park's roof. A fair amount of drug-related detritus was up there, but none close to the point from where Barlow had fallen. Jon thought back to Wayne's account; the man had stated how the voices he'd heard weren't particularly close. And, when the figure had passed him, it had been over twenty feet away.

Barlow's corpse had then been packaged and removed for autopsy. Cause of death was severe impact trauma to the front of the head: he'd probably been more-or-less horizontal in the air when he'd connected with the ground. Toxicology had shown he had a decent cocktail of drugs in his system, but not enough to render him unconscious. Stomach contents showed he hadn't eaten anything more than snack foods in the hours before death.

With the death being suspicious, the coroner had opened an inquest which was ongoing. That meant the body hadn't yet been released. Jon had flicked through the rest of the report, searching for the property inventory. Not surprisingly, the list was extremely short – aside from some small change, a ring and a cigarette lighter, it was just his clothes.

The circumstances of Ryan Gardner's death were extremely similar. The landlord of the building, having heard it was being used by homeless people, had gone to inspect how they were getting in. In the main hallway, he'd immediately discovered Gardner's body, lying at the base of the stairs. There were some additional injuries caused as he'd bounced off the banisters on the way down but, again, cause of death had been given as trauma to the head. Both deaths would probably end up as unexplained, but everyone would be assuming suicide.

As the briefing for Operation Flyer was being called, he'd had time to do two things. First was to ask Peter Collier – one of the civilian support workers – if he could check the system for any other recent deaths involving homeless men who'd served in the army. Second was to go on HOLMES to leave a flag in case of a lone male being seen in the vicinity of any subsequent cases of what appeared to be a homeless person's suicide. The system let him enter some search parameters for the lone male: 'Approximately six foot tall', 'Slim build', 'Caucasian, twenty to forty years of age', 'Black clothing'. At that point, he'd paused. After a moment of indecision, he added a final one: 'Fancy dress – wings / superhero'.

The radio on Kieran's vest gave a two-tone beep. 'Delta Tango, they're going to use a rear exit for leaving the terminal building.'

'Wise choice,' Kieran replied. 'There's a right kerfuffle going on out the front here.'

'Be advised that you'll meet us at the top of the access road that's about forty metres in front of where you're parked. See it?'

Jon pointed to a narrow turning that was cut off by a barrier and several large no entry signs.

'Got it,' Kieran replied.

'We'll be about five minutes. Stay where you are until I give you the word.'

'Will do.' He waited a second to make sure the convoy commander was really gone. 'What a shit-show.'

Jon didn't bother glancing across. 'The protest or this op?'

'This fucking op.'

Jon had to agree: in the briefing, the operational firearms commander had made it clear that the escort was purely a cosmetic measure, put in place only to make the visiting Americans feel important. Or, more accurately, the particular high-worth individual among them. It was the sort of decision hatched in high-up offices that made those on the ground resent their superiors.

Kieran sat back, attention on the protest once again. 'Really? They're just going to let them do this? I bet it's affecting the M60, by now.'

'You don't reckon they have a point?' Jon asked. 'I mean, the planet is fucking melting.'

Kieran shrugged. 'Come on, pal, they're breaking the law.'

'Peaceful protest: they're not being aggressive.'

'But this?' He gestured at the queue of cars. 'Causing ordinary people to miss their flights isn't doing their cause any favours. Proper channels: that's how they need to do things.'

'Proper channels aren't working,' Jon murmured.

Kieran shot him a glance. 'Not turning all alternative on us, too?'

Now it was Jon's turn to shrug. 'I've got kids, mate. Have to think about the world they'll end up living in.'

'And when you turn up for your cheap week in the sun to find you can't get to your flight because of this lot?'

He was considering his reply when a taxi jinked to a stop directly before their vehicle, even though the whole area was a mass of yellow hatching.

Kieran flashed the lights, but the driver's hazards went on. A portly man wearing a jumper with an argyle check got out. 'Fuck's sake.'

'I'll handle it,' Jon said, pulling on a police baseball cap as he opened the door. 'You need to move, sir! This is a no-stopping area.'

The driver was too busy scanning the terminal building's doors to even turn his head. 'They are here. I got a text. They are already through baggage reclaim.'

Jon stepped right up to him and dropped his voice. 'Sir, move. Now.'

The man looked to the side. Jon was in the full uniform of an authorised firearms officer: combat boots, dark military-style cargo trousers, black short-sleeve top. Over that was a police vest, with tool belt and sidearm hanging off it. It was a look intended to deter and, if necessary, intimidate.

'I'm not fucking around,' Jon continued. 'Block us in, we just ram you out the way. And then bill you, too.'

That did the trick: the taxi driver retreated to his car and quickly drove off.

'What did you tell him?' Kieran asked as Jon climbed back in.

'Warned him there was a sex-starved Welshman in the vehicle who was getting quite turned on by his woolly jumper.'

CHAPTER 8

The convoy that emerged from the service road beyond the protest consisted of a lead vehicle with a specialist escort driver at the wheel and, beside him, the convoy commander. Next were two black Jaguars – the second of which was the oyster vehicle, nicknamed that because it contained the principal, along with a close protection officer. Kieran and Jon formed the rear sweeping vehicle.

'Here we go at last,' Kieran said, accelerating across the yellow hatching to slip in just behind the bumper of the oyster vehicle as the road curved round, away from the airport buildings.

Jon eyed the fast-receding protest in the car's side mirror with a sense of relief. It didn't matter that the risk to the principal was negligible; any heaving mass of people could be used as cover by some proper bad pixies.

'Who is she, again?' Kieran asked.

Jon sighed. He really liked Kieran, but the bloke's attention span could be put to shame by a toddler with a bellyful of blue Smarties. 'Did you tune out for that bit of the briefing?'

'Probably.'

'She's the daughter of a senator. Her dad was high up in the Bush administration. Almost ran for president one time. And she's high up in the outfit that's offering to help fund the third runway – if airlines from America get the best slots.'

'They said all that in the briefing?'

'Most of it. One of the analysts was also explaining that the only places ready to put cash on the table are America and China. And China's not so popular right now.'

'Too right. Any soy sauce with your bat?'

Jon closed his eyes. 'You don't have a filter, do you?'

'Nope. So, it's big bucks stuff. Movers and shakers.'

Jon smiled. The man's Welsh accent always made him sound like he might just be taking the piss, even when he wasn't.

As the convoy joined the M56 towards the city centre, Jon noted the traffic crawling along on the other side of the barrier. Kieran was right; the airport protest was snarling everything up. Ahead of them, the upper parts of Manchester were coming into view: the high-rise developments and accompanying cranes that were so dramatically transforming the skyline.

'Which hotel are they in?' Kieran asked.

'Guess,' Jon replied.

'I know Weir said it's one of the five-star ones,' Kieran replied. 'The Hilton?'

Until recently, the tall glass building had been the highest in Manchester. But now its crown had been taken by the Deansgate Square South Tower. Jon had heard that would soon be eclipsed by a monstrosity that construction was due to start on next year. Where, he wondered, is the money pouring in from? 'Something a bit more Manchester, mate.'

Kieran frowned. 'That one where the politicians stay when they have their conferences? With all the fancy brickwork: that one?'

'The Midland?' Jon shook his head. 'That's not five-star, is it?'

'Well, it's bloody flash,' Kieran countered.

'Not there,' Jon said. 'Last try.'

Kieran lifted a forefinger. 'I know: The Lowry! Got to be.'

'Give that man a leek,' Jon said. 'But that's not where we're going first.'

'No?' Kieran glanced across the schedule balanced on Jon's knee. 'Not even dropping off their bags?'

'They're being delivered by some minion. We're going straight to meet the reception committee.'

'They don't even get to wash their pits?' Kieran sounded outraged.

'Seriously?' Jon said. 'You've never heard of business class? Never turned left when you board a plane?'

Kieran increased the vehicle's speed to close the gap. 'Left? What the fuck are you on about now?'

'They'll have been seated in the posh bit,' Jon said. 'Seats as big as sofas. Restaurant service, shower rooms, a bar.'

'Fuck me,' Kieran replied. 'On a plane? There's me thinking I'm royalty by paying twenty quid extra for an aisle seat on easyJet.'

Jon suspected the other man was now joking, but he still couldn't tell.

'You've been there, have you?' Kieran glanced at him. 'Where you end up by turning left?'

Jon laughed. 'Of course. Then straight into a limousine which took us to the Sheraton International. Like fuck.'

The convoy made its way clockwise round the M60 for a couple of junctions, coming off on the A56 and following the road past Old Trafford cricket ground and Manchester United's stadium. Soon, the Ship Canal was on their left. Jon looked at the wide expanse of sluggish brown water, always amazed that the thing had been dug out with spades. An army of Irish navvies, his great-grandfather among them.

Puzzled by the route, Jon got on the radio to the convoy commander. The reply came back that they were going on a roundabout route so the American delegation could see a bit of the city.

They crawled along Deansgate for a bit, then cut right. Soon, the circular structure of Central Library and, directly beside it, the Town Hall, appeared.

Jon had to admit the pair of buildings was bloody impressive. The dome-roofed library was built from ghostly white stone. With its heavy front portico supported by five pale columns, it resembled something from Ancient Rome. The Town Hall was a different matter. Dark and imposing, its style was Neo-Gothic, complete with gargoyles perched on parapets and tall stained-glass windows.

'Shame the thing's being refurbished,' Jon commented. 'It's the sort of thing the Yanks would bloody love to look round.'

'What's that, then?' asked Kieran.

Jon realised his eyes were firmly fixed on the vehicle in front. 'The Town Hall, you numbnuts.'

'Closed, is it?' he asked nonchalantly. 'How long for?'

'Oh, only about four years.'

Now Kieran's head turned. 'Really? What are they doing? Building another one inside it?'

'Not far off, I think.'

Kieran shot a glance at the chipboard barrier that had been erected round the base of the building. 'Fuck me, Acorn. Used to work for them, I did.'

'Who?' Jon asked.

'See the leaf-shape logo on the hoardings? Them. When they were restoring Victoria Baths.'

'You were in construction before doing this stuff?'

'Nightwatchman. Easiest job to get when you come out the army. They trained you up for reading the various sensors, like for heat and smoke, but that wasn't hard. Never watched so much porn in my life. Happy days. Well, nights.'

They were now approaching an access point that had been opened into Lincoln Square. The vehicles filed down it before coming to a halt at the ornate entrance of an old red-brick building. Waiting there was a group of smartly dressed men, all wearing face masks. Behind a temporary barrier to the side were a few people in more casual clothes, one with a camera mounted on his shoulder.

Needing to stretch his legs, Jon climbed out of the vehicle. A few curious passers-by had slowed to a stop and were looking at the parked cars to see who was getting out. Probably hoping for a footballer. Jon scanned the windows of the office building on the far side of the square. He could see faces gathering at some of the windows. Something to briefly break the monotony of work.

'Clever,' commented Jon, leaning down to the car's open window and pointing to the statue of a gaunt-faced man in a long overcoat who was standing on a plinth in the middle of the square. 'Abraham Lincoln – the American president.'

'Go on,' sighed Kieran. 'What's he doing here, then?'

Jon could still remember the school history trip. 'Because of Manchester supporting the Union in the American Civil War: refused to buy cotton from the southern states.'

'No doubt that will be stressed heavily to our visitors.'

'No doubt it will.'

The front door of the second Jaguar was now opening. Jon recognised the close protection officer who got out. Lazy twat who, if he didn't lose a bit of weight, was going to get floated from the role. Two uniformed officers had also appeared from the rear of the lead vehicle. Security personnel were twitching about closer to the building's entrance.

DARK ANGEL

Now the rear door of the lead Jaguar began to open. First to emerge was a statuesque woman in her mid- to late-thirties. Long, platinum hair hung over a tailored ice-blue suit jacket. The matching trousers were perfectly smooth. As she appraised her surroundings, Jon thought she didn't look like she'd just flown across the Atlantic. Her eyes turned in his direction and, for a second, her gaze lingered on him. Even though she was about twenty metres away, he felt a jolt at the lasciviousness of her look. Did I just imagine that? he asked himself. It was more suited to a nightclub. Not that he'd been in one for years.

Her eyes swept the remainder of the square before she set foot on the cobbles. The reception committee edged forward. First to extend a hand in greeting was the city's youthful mayor, Ed Farnham. Not long ago, he had been a prominent politician down in Westminster.

'That's the bird, then?' Kieran called from inside the vehicle. 'The one with the rich and powerful daddy?'

Jon realised his colleague couldn't have noticed the look she'd flashed across the small square. He'd have said something, if he had. Which means, he concluded, it was all in my head. 'I think so.'

Once everyone had been introduced, Farnham led the way toward the entrance. But, before taking them in, he paused to gesture at the statue. All the Americans turned, their faces showing polite interest as they listened to the spiel. Jon realised Farnham had positioned himself so he was half-facing the journalists. The man really had learned the media side of things during his time in London.

With Farnham's speech over, a journalist lifted an arm. 'Mayor Farnham, I've seen the recently released proposal for Redgate Towers – the development which would create an impressive 1,520 new flats for the city.'

Farnham paused. 'Yes: another part of the regeneration process that's sweeping our city.'

The journalist's tone switched. 'And the fact that none of the three towers have any affordable housing planned, whatsoever?'

Farnham was clearly caught by surprise. 'Well, as I said, negotiations are ongoing.'

'And Section 106 money, how much of that will be provided by the developers for community projects?'

'Thank you,' Farnham replied, now turning his back on the reporters.

'Is the character of Manchester being ruined by these overseas investment opportunities, Mr Mayor?'

Farnham was now trying to usher the Americans ahead of him.

'What about the companies funding these projects who are based in secrecy jurisdictions? Any comment on that?'

Seconds later, the building's doors swung shut and the smirking journalists began to disperse.

'How long are we here for?' Kieran asked, unclipping his seat belt as Jon got back in the car.

Jon consulted the schedule and groaned. 'Two bloody hours.'

CHAPTER 9

The television was mounted high enough on the wall so no one could reach it. Watching it from a plastic seat in the corner was a young woman. Her thick mop of hair was long and straggly. The beginnings of dreadlocks. The folds of a scarf poked out of the neck of a thick army-style coat. She was bending forward as if cold, even though the room was pleasantly warm. Every now and again, she sipped from a mug of tea.

There were other people in the room. Some chatting to each other. Several were also on their own, flicking through newspapers or, like her, staring at the screen. The posters that adorned the walls either addressed health-related issues or gave information on citizens' rights. Housing benefits, emergency social payments, the bedroom tax.

She knew the two ladies that worked there were watching her. Soon, one would come over, try and start a conversation. She just wanted to drink her brew and watch the telly. The presenter started talking about the visit of Alicia Lloyd, daughter of Bill Lloyd, one of the key figures from when the Bush administration had been in power.

That bunch of fucking crooks, she thought. The arseholes that had wrecked Iraq, then doled out the construction contracts to companies they had interests in. The ones who were still in charge, behind the scenes. They didn't give a shit about the environment, or the welfare of farm animals or, for that matter, people. Not ordinary people, anyway.

Her thoughts were like balloons, jostling about in her skull as she listened to the presenter describe the purpose of their visit. Typical, just fucking typical. Like the planet needed another runway so more aeroplanes could be flying about! She reached up and rubbed at her temples. It made her feel ill just thinking about it. Made her want to curl up and cry. Just stop breathing and have done with everything. What was the point? What was the point in anything?

The pressure in her head was increasing. Growing more intense. Had been for days now. Ever since—

'Hello, there. Everything OK?'

She kept her head bowed. Didn't want to look at where the voice was coming from. See those concerned eyes directed at her. The questions that were certain to follow.

'Yeah. Fine.'

'Well ... we haven't seen you in here before. I wanted to make sure you're feeling welcome.'

The TV presenter was now going on about the visitors' arrival in the city centre. Then she heard her father's voice. No. Please, no. Those well-regulated tones, with a gritty touch of the north. He never sounded like that at home. The prick was the only person she knew who coarsened his accent whenever he spotted a camera.

She opened her eyes and lifted her chin, but the woman was blocking her view. 'I can't see?'

The woman glanced behind her. 'Oh, sorry. Yes. The news.'

There he was, filling the screen. Some crap about the long history of support and cooperation that stretched back between America and the city of Manchester. Oily words designed to get only one thing moving: money.

'Mind if I sit down?' the woman asked, starting to move a chair back.

She half-nodded. Her tea was almost finished. For all she cared, the woman could have the whole bloody table to herself. She watched as the gaggle of smartly dressed people on the screen were ushered into a building.

'So ... are you living here in Manchester?'

As she swigged the last of her tea down, the baby let out a little mewl. Fuck, she thought. The little sprout sleeps for hours and then, of all places ...

The woman's eyes had widened. She'd heard. Her gaze was moving downwards. 'Have you ... is that a ...?'

She needed to be out of this place. Another little mewl, longer this time. Christ, this couldn't be happening! Now she'd stood, the little lump beneath her coat was more obvious.

The woman's mouth was open. Her hand was half-raised. 'Please, there's no need for you to—'

But she was already hurrying out of the room.

CHAPTER 10

The glow in the western sky was starting to fade. Streetlights had come on about twenty minutes ago. Time, he thought, I left for work.

He'd prepared his holdall earlier, carefully placing his pair of wings in at the top. Jogging down the flight of stairs, he spotted the stoutly built woman somewhere in her late twenties who lived in the flat below. She was standing outside her front door, struggling with the zip of a cheap-looking coat.

There was a shopping bag beside each foot. From his position higher up, he could see each bag was full of white cartons. Long-life milk, by the looks of it. He guessed there must have been ten in each.

She heard his footsteps and turned round. From beneath a low fringe he suspected she'd trimmed herself, she glanced up. Eye contact was made for a second before she guiltily glanced down at her bags. He knew that, the previous month, the landlord had discovered she'd been keeping cats in her flat. It turned out they were strays. She'd been forced to ring a rescue centre and have them all collected.

He'd seen her a few times since and had recognised the look of desolation on her face. He knew what it was like to lose the things you loved. The problem was, she'd recognised it in him, too.

'You won't tell, will you?' she asked, sounding like a naughty schoolchild searching for an ally.

'What's that, then?' He came to a reluctant halt on the landing.

'About this,' she whispered, pointing discreetly at her shopping, even though no one else was about.

'Have you been getting more cats?' He realised he was whispering, too.

She tried to suppress a smile but failed. Deliberately, he suspected. 'Maybe—'

'Well, I haven't seen a thing.' He went to carry on, but she addressed him again.

'Do you want to?' She was holding up a key. It was attached to a lanyard which went round her neck. 'You can if you want.'

He hesitated. The woman clearly had some issues. And the last thing she should be doing was inviting some bloke she'd never even spoken to into her flat.

'Quickly,' she said. 'Before someone comes.' She got the door open and beckoned to him.

Before someone comes? He didn't think there was much chance of that; the people in the only other flat on this floor had been evicted the previous month. His neighbours on the floor above had sold up and moved out to Cheshire in the early days of the pandemic.

She grabbed both bags and dragged them inside. 'Close the door behind you!'

The flat was the mirror image of his: a short hall with a door immediately on the right that gave access to a storage cupboard. At the end of the corridor, another door into the living area. Unlike his hall, hers was filled with stuff. Shopping bags bulging with magazines. Flattened cereal boxes. Piles of coats and shoes. Boxes with cups, bowls and saucers stacked inside. Charity shop treasure, he guessed. With dainty little steps, she walked quickly to the far door and clicked the fingernails of one hand against the frame. 'I'm home!'

She looked back at him, eyes shining with delight. He smiled uncertainly as she opened the door.

He was waiting for a sea of starving cats to rush out, but nothing happened.

'Hello, my little lovelies, I've brought someone to see you!' She walked into the room, making little kissing sounds.

He followed her in, eyes sweeping the room as he searched for movement. Whatever she was keeping in here, it was staying hidden behind the piles of crap she'd collected.

'Dinky, what's happened to you, my poor love?' She picked her way towards a sofa laden with cushions, pausing to pick a soft toy off the floor. Placing it carefully on the arm of the sofa, she said, 'That's better. Can't have you lying on the cold carpet, can we?'

He realised Dinky was the toy. A furry ginger cat with glass eyes and a tuft of white in the middle of its chest. The rest of the sofa wasn't piled with cushions, it was covered in toy cats. Same as the windowsills, the shelf units, the top of the telly. Cats of all shapes and sizes. Some lifelike, others with over-sized eyes and unnatural colours. Pinks and purples and luminous greens.

She was smiling at him now. The smile was a proud one, but there was a slight wariness in her eyes. Like she knew the situation was, to anyone else, bizarre. 'These are my little darlings.'

'Right.' He nodded, looking around the room as he tried to think of something to say. 'You've got quite a few, haven't you?'

Seeing her proud smile, he thought: how come people are always so happy to chat with me? To open up. Is it how I look? What I say? He couldn't fathom it.

'Don't ask me for all their names!' She laughed. 'I sometimes get the odd one wrong. But they all get on, don't you?' She turned her head from left to right. 'They are all so well behaved.'

He saw the line of bowls on the floor of the kitchenette. Six or seven, all half full of milk. She must be tipping it all away and replacing it with fresh stuff each day. You, he thought, are barking. Absolutely barking. 'Well ... um, I don't know your name.'

'It's Miriam. They are the best company you could ask for,' she added, blushing slightly, but with just a trace of defiance in her voice.

In that instant, he understood her. You're just lonely, aren't you? Another lonely, lost soul. 'I bet they are, Miriam. And thanks for introducing me to them all.'

She looked relieved at his answer. 'Oh – I don't know your name, either!'

'Gavin.' He took a step back towards the door. 'I live on the next floor up.'

'I know. Flat nine.'

'Right. Flat nine. So ... I really should get to work.'

'OK, Gavin. Call round any time you like. I'm usually in.'

CHAPTER 11

Jon could hear Wiper through the front door. The dog would have heard his footsteps outside and was now waiting in the hallway, its wagging tail striking the wall or radiator. 'You'll snap that in half one of these days,' he announced, searching for his key. The name had been Holly's idea: Punch, their previous boxer, had a docked tail and when Wiper arrived with a long thing that switched back and forth with excitement, Holly had laughingly said he had a windscreen wiper stuck to his bum. All previous names on the shortlist were immediately cancelled: Wiper, it was.

The moment the door opened, the dog was like a wriggling seal, excitedly worming its way around his shins, between his ankles and across his shoes. Jon leaned down to scratch behind the animal's ears. 'Hello, pea-brain.'

He found Alice in the front room watching telly. 'Hi there. How's things?'

She hit the mute button. 'Not so bad. You?'

'Yeah, good. Spent most of the day on my arse in a car.'

'How come?'

'Escorting this group over from the States. They're here about pouring cash into the airport.'

Alice looked confused. 'The proposed new runway?'

He nodded.

'That's meant to still be at the consultation stage.'

'Is it?' He sighed. 'You know how these things work. It will probably have been already decided behind closed doors.'

'I bloody hope not,' she murmured. 'We don't need more planes passing overhead and we certainly don't need the motorways to be any busier.'

He noticed the fire was on full and turned it down a notch before removing his top. 'How are the little monsters?'

'Asleep. Holly wasn't herself, again. You know, it occurred to me today: I wonder if anyone's picking on her?'

'Holly?' Jon found it hard to believe. She had her mother's fiery temper. He remembered how they'd first met. Someone in the rowdy group he'd been part of had bumped into Alice's table, spilling all their drinks. She hadn't hesitated to confront them. Immediately drawn to her feistiness, Jon had rushed to the bar to buy replacements, knowing it would be an opportunity to get chatting.

'You never know,' she said. 'Girls that age can be such little bitches. And with social media, they can all pile in on someone. Be really cruel.'

Jon glanced at the sideboard where Holly had to leave her phone each night before going to bed. 'Have you checked it?'

'No. I want to ask her first.'

Jon was still looking at the device. Bloody things. 'I'll nip up and look in on them.'

Duggy was in his usual position – on his back with arms and legs stretched out. The duvet was a crumpled dune of pale blue at the end of the bed. Jon couldn't help smiling as he pulled his son's pyjama top down over his fat little belly. A brief wriggle, and then the boy's deep breathing resumed.

Holly was also in her customary position – she consisted of a minor disturbance in the corner of the bed, covers neatly across her, pillow barely dented by her cheek. He gazed down at her, acutely aware that seeing her caused waves of concern to swirl about his skull. He could barely hear her breathing, it was so light. What's up with you, little mouse? Whatever it was, he hoped it would soon go away. Stories of kids with eating disorders and anxiety – once issues that were barely on his radar – now seemed to catch his eye with disturbing regularity.

'So, what was this free food that meant you didn't need tea?' Alice asked as he slumped down on the sofa beside her.

'This group. There was a flashy function for them in a grand old building on Deansgate. It's where parts of the council have been relocated while the Town Hall's shut. They're inside shovelling canapés down their throats. We're outside, sitting in a car, sniffing each other's farts—'

'Who are you with?'

'Kieran.'

Alice wrinkled her nose. 'Ugh. I can imagine.'

'This delivery guy arrives with a massive platter of sarnies and it's been sent by the Americans. Well, actually, by Alicia Lloyd, the daughter of that senator, Bill Lloyd? She'd arranged it.'

'She's with this group?'

'I think she's in charge. She's got some senior position in a big corporation who are offering to stump up the cash needed for the expansion, in return for prime positions for their aircraft. That's the score, apparently.'

'And part of this schmoozing is an armed escort?'

'Yup.'

'How does she seem?'

'Only seen her from a distance. A bit too perfect. You know that way American politicians appear?' He didn't say anything about the way she'd looked across at him in Lincoln Square. Like someone who'd spotted their next meal.

Alice lifted a forefinger. 'Wasn't it Hilary Clinton who can remember the first name of everyone she's met? Probably teach them all that stuff in college over there. How long is the job for?'

'A few days. I think they fly back next Sunday.' He noticed how Wiper was skulking around in the hallway. 'Did you manage to walk the mutt?'

'Afraid not.'

'No problem. I'll take him for a quick leg stretch.'

Out on the street, Jon contemplated which way to go. A short one round the surrounding streets, or the longer one across Cringle Fields Park, where they sometimes went with the kids for a Sunday afternoon stroll and a play in the woods.

The direction Wiper was pulling decided it for him. The longer one. At the end of the road was a short row of shops. A newsagent's, laundrette, Chinese takeaway place, bookies and, more recently, a Tesco Metro in what had been a branch of Barclays.

As he neared its sliding doors, he saw a figure hunched down on the pavement. A bloke, with his feet and legs swathed in a blanket. Propped in its folds was a paper cup. Wondering how they managed to sit on the freezing pavements for so long, Jon automatically started to drift to the far side of the pavement.

'Spare some change, please?'

Jon was about to continue on by when he remembered sitting in the doorway of the building in Stevenson Square; the way the passers-by pretended not to have noticed him had been a shock. It had been made him feel dirty, somehow. He patted his pocket, but realised it was empty. 'I'm sorry, pal.'

The man half-smiled. 'You have a good evening, sir.'

'And you.' As Jon carried on, he recalled how Wayne's emotions had veered so quickly from gratitude to hostility. The drugs would have worn off by now, he thought, hoping the man's head was now in a better place.

He strolled along an empty corridor, shoes crackling slightly as they made contact with the protective sheeting laid over the intricately tiled floors.

The walls in this section of the Town Hall consisted of wooden panels, and these had also been covered over with a layer of plastic. Coils of cabling were stacked in a recess that, once, had been home to a bust of some prominent civic figure.

When the building had closed for its refurbishment programme, the first thing workmen did was start preparing all the statues and paintings for going into storage.

He'd got the job as a nightwatchman within two months of leaving the army. It was the sort of work that – for people like him – was easy to pick up. Most treated it as a stop-gap while planning something more permanent. But he quickly realised that he liked the solitude. And he knew that the contract for this particular building wasn't ending anytime soon.

A three-man team did the night shift. They were meant to alternate between roles: one based in the CCTV room, one keeping a check on radio communications and the door-lock circuits, one patrolling the building itself. But Gavin always volunteered to do the patrols and the other two were more than happy to have a radio playing on low with smartphones within reach. That gave Gavin the opportunity to explore the less-visited parts of the building and, if necessary, leave it completely.

He poked his head into the Council Chamber. Like every other room in the building, it was partway through the process of being stripped bare. The carpet had been rolled up, as had the underlay. Both now looked like a pair of long sausages stretching across the middle of the floor. At some point, the floorboards would be taken up and the cables and pipes beneath it replaced. He made a cursory check of the smoke detector then proceeded to the stairs, where he checked his watch. Almost one in the morning. Bhav and Jamie – his co-workers for the night – wouldn't be expecting him to reappear for another hour or so.

He trotted up successive flights of stairs until he reached the sixth floor. Most of the doorways here led into rooms where council employees used to work. But halfway along was a smaller door set deep into the wall. Unlike the flimsy white panelling of its neighbours, this was made of solid, varnished wood. It had a small sign in its centre that simply read: 'Fire Door. Keep Shut.'

Gavin wondered if any of the people who used to pass it every day realised where it led. He removed a key from the inside pocket of his jacket and inserted it into the brass keyhole. The door opened on well-oiled hinges to reveal a steep set of stone steps that curled sharply round a central pillar. Anyone who climbed all the way to the top would emerge on to a narrow balcony directly above the faces of the building's clock tower.

Even though he knew no one else was up here, he checked left and right before stepping through, swinging the door shut and locking it behind him.

As he scaled the stone steps, he wondered how soon Wayne was going to call. It was now the small hours of the morning; the time when people who were at their lowest often reached out, needing someone – anyone – to break their sense of desolation.

The construction work didn't include the main tower. Some work had been done on the roof at the very beginning, but the rest of the edifice was being left. After all, there was no need to upgrade any heating or plumbing as none had been laid. No lighting or Internet network. He trailed his fingertips across the cold stone, thighs beginning to ache slightly with the exertion of climbing. A narrow window to his side let him glimpse how high he'd come. A few minutes' later, he reached the first landing.

A small door to the side was marked, 'Mechanism Room'.

He listened for a moment to the clicks, ticks and whirrs of the rotating cogs and tipping levers beyond it. The sounds had no discernible rhythm, which he thought strange.

On a flat area of a lower roof nearby was the small wooden platform, placed there to encourage the peregrine falcons to nest. Now, the sad remains of the nest were deserted, but next spring the birds would be back, rebuilding. Of course, he wouldn't be around by then. He would be with Sophie and Claire, all of them together once more.

He got to the next landing. This one was smaller and draughtier, but the views through the windowless arches were far better. He liked to check the dark skyline to the north. On a clear night, it was possible to make out the twinkling red lights on the Winter Hill transmitting mast. Tonight was murkier and nothing was visible. He surveyed the city below, imagining what was going on that very second. How many people with nowhere to go, no one to be with. Tucked away in nooks and crannies. Places where the wind and rain didn't reach.

Time was ticking on and he decided he couldn't sit around hoping Wayne might call. That might take ages, or never happen. He continued up, past the door marked 'Dial Room' that gave access to the four clock faces and their ten-foot-long hands. He'd looked in once and noticed the inscription on the wall: 'Teach us to number our days.' For someone with only a short time left on earth, the message struck him as particularly profound.

Moments later, he stepped out onto the balcony itself. Up here, exposed to the elements, the stone was stained with lichen and speckled by white bird droppings. This was where the peregrines settled to disarticulate their prey and strip away the flesh; the scattered remains of pigeons were littered at his feet. Claws, wing bones, beaks. Clumps of bedraggled feathers. A severed wing lay in the furrowed dip of a gargoyle's bunched shoulders. He removed his phone.

Wayne had been the last person to call him, so he tapped on the number at the top of his list.

The phone rang for about thirty seconds before the answerphone kicked in. Damn it! He wasn't going to leave a message. Not yet. Maybe the man just hadn't heard the phone ringing. He tried the number again.

Four rings and success.

'The fuck's this?'

He sounded high on something. Words slow and slurred.

'It's Gavin from the Manchester Veterans' Helpline.'

Nothing.

'Wayne? Are you there? Can you hear me?'

'Who?'

'It's Gavin.'

'Gavin?'

'From the Manchester Veterans' Helpline.'

'Gavin! What's happening, bro?'

Definitely off his head. Probably not sure who he's even speaking to. 'Wayne, how are you?'

The other man sighed. 'Surviving, just. You know what I mean?'

'Things not so good at the moment?'

'Not so good, no.' The semblance of a laugh. 'But that's life, hey? Ups and downs. Got to ride them both.'

'Have you taken anything, Wayne?'

'Taken anything? Wooh, yeah, mate. I'm fucking ... I'm fucking fucked. That's what I am.'

'Wayne, can I come and see you?'

'Say again?'

'I want to come and see you.'

'Yeah, you do? Have a smoke with me? Sound idea.'

'Are you on your own?'

'That I am. Come for a wee toot with Wayne, hey?'

'Where are you Wayne?'

'Me? Oh ... shit, let me see now, where am I?'

'Are you inside somewhere? You sound like you're inside.'

'Yeah, I'm inside.'

'Remember where it is?'

'The old pub, the one that closed down. You and me, mate. Smoke.'

'Where's this pub, Wayne?'

'Out back of Piccadilly.'

Gavin pictured the area. There was one boarded-up pub he could think of. 'The Star and Garter?'

'Yeah, that's it, The Garter.'

'You sure, Wayne? That's the one you're in now?'

'Yeah, go round the back. The door at the top of the fire escape's been forced.'

'Stay put, OK? I'll be there in a few minutes.'

CHAPTER 12

As soon as the morning briefing with the operational firearms commander was over, Jon hurried back to his desk. At eight forty-five, they were due back at The Lowry Hotel; him as the approved firearms officer in the rear sweeping vehicle, with Kieran at the wheel. They would be escorting the delegation back out to the airport, where they would be stationed for most of the day.

Jon checked the time: seven thirty-three. That gave him a good hour to continue looking into the deaths of the two ex-soldiers before they needed to set off.

While his computer was booting up, he surveyed the open-plan office. A smattering of detectives was already at their workstations. Iona would be in any minute, he was sure; she always got in early. Jon could never remember which days Peter Collier worked from home. If he was coming in, he never showed up much before half eight – which meant it would be a while before he'd know if the bloke had unearthed anything interesting.

The first thing he saw once his screen settled down was a message that Peter Collier had left him the previous evening. The message was short, but significant. Two other deaths in the last three months matched much of the criteria. He'd left links to the case files for each fatality.

A tingle started playing along Jon's spine as he read the details of the first one. Luke McClennan's body had been discovered beneath a viaduct close to Piccadilly Station almost eight weeks previously. He had been lying behind a fenced-off area, hidden from view by vegetation. Levels of decomposition suggested he'd been there for about a month. Jon scrolled down to the sections on the person's identity: thirty-two years old, born in Llandudno, served in the Royal Welsh Infantry between 2005 and 2018. On leaving, it appeared he'd drifted about: social security records revealed he'd spent a few months in London, some in Reading and the rest in the Greater Manchester area.

The second fatality was a Roy Jarratt. Twenty-six-years old, his body had been found by construction workers ten weeks ago in the rear car park of what once had been a mill in Ancoats. The building was currently undergoing renovation work and it appeared he'd climbed up some scaffolding, either slipping from that or jumping from the walkway at the top. He'd been dead no more than six hours, which meant he'd hit the ground in the early hours of the morning. Roy had served in the Duke of Lancaster's Regiment.

So, Luke McClennan probably died a week or so before Roy Jarratt, Jon thought as he sat back in his seat. Interesting. No witnesses had come forward for either death. Both had died from injuries consistent with having fallen from a considerable height. Both had high levels of chemicals in their bloodstreams. Jon scanned the list: alcohol, opiates, amphetamine, synthetic cannabinoid – otherwise known as Spice.

In the coroner's report, the family of McClennan had reported that he'd been struggling with life after leaving the army. Joblessness, mental health issues – including

PTSD. The verdict had been left open, but it was obvious what everyone had concluded.

Jon agreed that suicide would seem the most likely scenario – if you hadn't factored in the other recent deaths, along with rumours of a darkly dressed figure being seen at the time of the third and fourth deaths. The problem, as Jon was only too aware, was the fact everything was rumour. Talk on the street. And the source of the rumours couldn't have been worse. Wayne had been using a drug recognised for the unpredictable nature of its effects, included among them hallucinations. The other two, if they could be found, were probably the same.

What I need, Jon thought, clicking hopefully through to HOLMES, is a credible witness. No response to the flag he'd left. Bollocks. He returned to the files and began printing off the sections he'd need to show Weir. Surely, his senior officer would agree there was a possible pattern emerging.

He was on his way back to his desk, printed sheets in hand, when he heard his mobile phone ringing. Increasing his pace, he made it back before his answerphone kicked in. His screen was displaying a single name: Senior.

'Morning, pal. And to what do I owe this pleasure?'

'Jon, it's Senior.'

Bless him: the bloke still hadn't got the hang of caller ID. 'What a lucky guess by me. What's up?'

'Junior's just done a call out.'

Junior was the name the rugby coach's oldest son was known by. He was with Manchester Fire and Rescue Service. Jon didn't bother sitting back down. 'OK.'

'There was a body reported. A homeless guy out back of this derelict pub by Piccadilly. Junior recognised him; it's Wayne.'

Jon was almost tempted to sit, after all. 'What happened to him?'

'Junior said he was being loaded into the back of an ambulance when they arrived. They were all saying he'd gone off the top of the fire escape stairs behind the building.'

'You said ambulance. He's alive?'

'Apparently. But they weren't sure for how long. He'd been lying there a while.'

Jon's mind was racing. The attending officers would no doubt be writing it off as attempted suicide, not realising the whole area needed to be treated as a potential murder scene. 'How long ago was he found?'

'An hour or so.'

Shit, he thought, reaching for his car keys, people would have been tramping to and fro, lessening the chances of any evidence being found. 'Which pub?'

'The Star and Garter. On Cresbury Street. Near The Pits?'

The unofficial name for the spread of five-a-side soccer pitches close to Piccadilly Station. 'I know it. Is Junior still there?'

'No. He's on his way back to the fire station.'

That isn't good, thought Jon. It means people are already wrapping things up at the scene. 'I'm on my way.'

It took him just over fifteen minutes to get to the abandoned pub. The building was in a sorry state: all the windows were covered over with chipboard, on which ugly crawls of graffiti and tattered posters for gigs around town vied for space. Two metal rods jutted out above the front door where, at one point, lamps had probably hung. He spotted that a large section of tiles was missing on one side of the roof. Rain would be getting into the building's upper floor.

Directly behind the property was the main railway line into the city. A train was sliding past, another heading the other way. The area had probably been a residential neighbourhood, once. But the terraced houses would have been demolished years ago. Probably as part of the slum clearances back in the 1930s. Now, the only thing near the pub was a newly built car showroom. Beside that was a kitchen appliance store.

He'd called ahead and requested that the attending officers stay at the scene. A single car was parked in the side street. Dark-blue Volvo. Standard vehicle for detectives in the Major Incident Team, the unit where he used to work. He wondered if he'd know them as he pulled to a stop behind their vehicle.

They all emerged from their vehicles at the same time and Jon grinned at a familiar face.

'Spicer! Fuck me, still struggling on then?'

'Whitey,' Jon replied to the overweight bald man beaming in his direction. 'Watch I don't kick that lardy-arse of yours.'

The detective turned to his younger colleague, a finger pointing at Jon. 'Meet the legend himself.'

The junior detective was extending a hand, his eyes bright with eagerness. 'Detective Constable Platt. Andrew.'

Reminds me of Rick Saville when he was starting out, Jon thought, shaking the other man's hand. 'Detective Constable Jon Spicer.'

He frowned. 'DC?'

Jon nodded. 'That's right.'

Platt threw a questioning glance to his partner.

Whitey sighed. 'You're thinking, if he's so good, why is he a DC? Check the end of his nose, Platt. You'll observe it's not covered in a brown substance.'

Jon waved the comment aside. 'No CSI van?'

'Been and gone, mate,' Whitey replied. 'We were almost on our way, too. Until your request that we stay pinged up.' He glanced up at the sky; spots of rain had started coming down and the strengthening breeze carried a chill.

Jon looked toward the open gates into the pub's car park. Crime scene tape had been stretched across the gap, but there was no inner or outer cordon.

'How come CTU are sniffing about?' Whitey asked. 'This guy on your radar, is he?'

'Sort of,' Jon replied, moving towards the entrance.

'What for?'

'Almost dying.' That's confused them, Jon thought. Just as I hoped. The car park was strewn with a variety of rubbish. A metal wheelie bin in the corner. Empty plastic crates that once held beer bottles. A few wooden pallets. What looked like a bedraggled pair of jeans lying beside the bin. The usual assortment of bottles and cans, probably lobbed over the wall by passers-by.

'Passengers in a couple of trains saw him,' Whitey stated. 'See it, say it, sorted.'

The mantra for if anything suspicious was spotted on the rail network. It was meant for bombs or terrorist activity. But, Jon thought, it obviously worked well enough for a body, too.

'He'd landed half on a pallet,' Whitey added. 'Maybe that saved him. But probably only a temporary reprieve.'

'How so?'

'They thought his back's broken. Multiple fractures, punctured lung. Hypothermia, too. I should think pneumonia is on the cards.'

Christ, thought Jon, ducking under the tape. He realised they weren't bothering to follow him towards the metal steps of the fire escape. 'This one?' He pointed to the nearest pallet.

'Yup.'

'No one moved it?'

'Nope.'

Jon looked to the top of the steps. The pallet was more or less directly below the landing at the top. Maybe a foot or so out. 'No witnesses come forward?'

'Not as yet.'

'Do you think he was up there alone?'

Whitey's laugh was grim. 'Hard to say. The place is a horror-fest, mate. Part drug-den, part knocking-shop. Maybe at the same time. You're welcome to have a peek.'

'Don't want to join me?'

He directed a forefinger straight up. 'I reckon it'll be pissing down, soon. I'll be in the car. Oh – and someone's taken a shit in the corner. Enjoy!'

Turning his collar up, Jon climbed the stairs. Nothing caught his eye on the rusty steps. The door at the top had also been nailed over with chipboard at one point. Someone had got a tyre iron in. Some kind of lever, anyway. The board had been ripped off, then they'd dug away at the frame, tearing chunks out before finally prising the lock. Using the toe of one shoe, he hooked the door open.

What was probably once a bedroom lay beyond. Bare wooden floorboards, speckled with bird shit. Walls stripped of paper, empty plug sockets dangling wire. A mattress lying on the far side. More plastic crates. These ones upturned to act as stools. Debris littered the floor: cans, bottles, wrappers of food, plastic bags. A trainer.

Jon stepped inside. The place had a damp and musty aroma. He looked into the blackened fireplace and saw syringes. Stuff was on the mattress and he had to cross the room to make it out. A pair of heavily stained boxer shorts. A few crumpled condoms beside them. How. Fucking. Grim.

He stuck his head out to check the landing. The bedroom on the opposite side was open and daylight was pouring in through the hole in the roof. A couple of pigeons cautiously regarded him from the top of a wardrobe that had no doors. More of their crap stained the floor. Stairs led down to the first floor that was swathed in darkness.

Back out on the fire escape. The rain was coming down harder now. He saw Whitey watching him from inside his patrol car. Jon lifted a thumb then examined the fire escape railings. They were waist-high. To topple over them accidentally would take a serious loss of balance. Not impossible, if you were heavily under the influence. How about a shove? Again, it would have to be a powerful one to send you over. He made a note for the pathologist to check for any bruising to Wayne's chest or back. Leaning forwards, he examined the pallet below. A nasty drop, especially to land on your back.

A gust of wind caused the door to begin swinging shut. Saves me the trouble, Jon decided, vaguely disappointed to not have found anything. From the corner of his eye, he registered small, rapid movements near the top of the door. Something fluttering. His head turned properly. Holy shit. A feather. Large and black, its upper edge caught in the heavily splintered wood.

CHAPTER 13

The evidence bag dangled from DCI Weir's fingers. 'You knew what the arrangement was, Jon. You ignored that and did your own thing. Which is the issue that keeps repeating itself, isn't it?'

Spicer sat perfectly still, hands folded in his lap. 'I was anxious to get to the scene as soon as possible, sir.'

'Clearly. And that decision fucks up my entire allocation of officers.' Weir gestured impatiently at his monitor, agitation tightening his voice. 'I had to pull an armed response officer in from somewhere else and put him on the airport job with Saunders.'

'Who'd you send?' Jon asked.

'Meredith – who was down for the Lynex job. And now what do I do with you?'

Send me to the Lynex job? Jon held back with his suggestion. 'Well,' he nodded at the feather safely sealed inside the evidence bag, 'I hoped this might mean priorities would change, that we'd allocate more resources—'

'This?' Weir swivelled his wrist so the bag swayed gently to and fro. 'You didn't mention wings, did you? A male figure who dressed exclusively in black was what you told me. Not someone with fucking wings sprouting out of his back!'

'I thought, given the source of the description, it wasn't something to emphasise.'

'Emphasise,' he said, sneeringly, letting the evidence bag fall to his desk. 'You didn't even mention it, Jon. And who could blame you?'

Jon kept his head bowed. This wasn't going like he'd hoped it would.

'This derelict pub, with the hole in the roof. Would you say that, maybe, it's the sort of place that might attract pigeons?'

Jon glanced up. There had been a couple of birds in the other bedroom. But they were a pale grey. 'The feather's jet black. I wouldn't have thought—'

'What, you've never seen a pigeon with bits of black on it? They come in all fucking colours: white, black, grey, brown, blue. Mixtures of the lot. Christ, Jon.'

'The bigger picture, sir, with these other two deaths. Taken as a whole, it—'

'This isn't some kind of spike, it's pretty much consistent with expected levels! Four in as many months.'

'Five, if Wayne Newton doesn't survive.'

'I told you veterans make up the majority of deaths among the homeless.'

'But all of these have died in similar circumstances. They've not overdosed or hanged themselves or stepped in front of a train – they've all fallen from a height. In secluded spots, away from potential witnesses. They're not choosing places where anyone might see them, try to persuade them down.'

'Which – if you're after topping yourself – would make sense. Don't you think?'

Jon kept silent. He couldn't argue with his senior officer's reasoning. But the sense of something not being right persisted.

'Listen,' Weir said more softly, 'if you reckon I wouldn't act if I thought someone was targeting ex-soldiers when they're at their most vulnerable, you couldn't be more wrong. But this isn't holding together. Not so that I'm going to allocate resources to it.'

Jon nodded. 'What should I do, then?'

'Rejoin DC Saunders at the airport. Send Meredith back. The schedule said you're there until five.'

'And outside of the schedule, I can continue looking into these deaths?'

DCI Weir leaned back and gave Jon a long look. 'Are you trying to take the piss?'

Jon spotted a tiny twinkle of something in the other man's eye. Keep pushing, Spicer. You're nearly there. 'No, sir. That was the arrangement we had. Before I got over-excited.'

'Over-excited.' Weir was smiling as he flicked his hand. 'Go on – get out of here.'

Jon stood. 'So that's a yes?'

Weir sighed. 'Jesus! Do you ever let up? So long as it's in your own time.'

'Of course. And is it OK if I rope in Iona to help out? On the same basis.'

Weir shook his head in exasperation. 'Yes. If it means you bugger off and give me some peace.'

Jon reached down and retrieved the evidence bag. 'I'll be taking this, then.'

Saunders looked up as the van's passenger door opened. 'Fuck me, it's the Lone Ranger. Weir tear you a new arsehole, did he?'

'Had a pretty good go.' He nodded to Meredith. 'You can hop it. Weir wants you back at base.'

'Hop it? That's some thanks, that is, you cheeky fuck.'

Jon grinned as he tossed him the keys to the pool car he'd come in.

Meredith jabbed a thumb over his shoulder as he climbed out. 'You haven't smelled what's coming out of his arse. The Lynex job is heaven compared to that, trust me.'

'Cheers for the warning,' Jon replied.

'OK, pal.' The other officer jangled the keys as he walked towards the nearby car.

Jon turned to the vehicle with Kieran in and swung the passenger door back and forth a few times. 'Let some air in first, I think.'

Saunders was slumped behind the wheel. 'That's enough. It's safe now.'

'What's the scores on the doors, then?' Jon asked, sitting down beside him and closing the door.

'They're in that building for a bit longer. Then it's a visit to where the extra runway is planned.'

'Which is?'

'East. Going towards Knutsford. So, what kicked off this morning that had you flying out the door?'

Jon sighed. 'You were in the army, right?'

'First battalion, the Royal Welsh.'

'Same as one of the victims. A fair bit younger than you, though. And don't ask me which section, either.'

Kieran rolled his eyes.

'What's your take on the amount of veterans who end up sleeping rough?' Jon asked.

'The armed forces attract its fair share of nutters, right? The army does, anyway.' He raised his hands briefly. 'Take me, for instance.'

Jon smiled. The first time he'd met Kieran was in the gym at work. They'd had a little spar in the boxing ring and got on straight away.

'Kids who didn't do so well at school,' Kieran continued. 'Maybe were getting themselves in trouble. Army's a great place for them. The trouble starts when they come out.' He tapped the side of his head. 'A lot of those boys on the street, they're not right up here. PTSD and all that. And the mental health support is shite. But then, it is for everyone. What can you do?'

Jon nodded. 'I've been looking into something. There's been a few suicides recently that might be iffy.'

Kieran glanced sideways. 'Ex-army?'

'Yup.'

'How many?'

'Four. Could be five with the one from this morning.'

'Why iffy?'

Jon shrugged. 'They've all fallen to their deaths – off buildings, mostly. I don't know, it just doesn't seem right. The other day, I spoke to this person who reckons someone dodgy was at the scene of one of the incidents. That person then went off the top of a fire escape.'

'When?'

'Last night. It's why I shot out earlier; I wanted to get to where it happened as soon as possible.'

'Really? And Weir isn't biting?'

'Said I can follow things up – but only during any downtime I have.'

'And the one from last night. Is he conscious? Have you spoken to him?'

'I wish. He's in intensive care. I spoke to a doctor over the phone, and she said they're keeping him unconscious while his head injuries are sorted out.'

Kieran's handset beeped.

'Delta Tango, we're due to exit the building any minute. Be ready to depart.'

'Roger that,' Kieran replied, starting the engine. 'You know what you need?' He shot Jon a swift look. 'Some other fuckers to die. Maybe then, they'll take it seriously.'

Two cars emerged from the office's underground car park – one of the Jaguars and a white Range Rover with the airport logo on its side and a revolving roof light.

'Who's on this little tour?' Jon asked.

'Just the blonde bint and a couple of lackeys,' Kieran replied.

Jon shook his head.

'What?' Kieran asked.

'Blonde bint.'

'What is she, then?'

'Earning about a thousand times more than you, I should think.'

He pulled in behind the Jaguar. 'Still a bint.'

They passed through a security gate and then joined an access road. The orange light on top of the Range Rover began to flash. A plane was taxiing along on the other side of the security fence beside them. Jon took in the size of it; the wheels alone were the size of a garage. It swung sharply to the right and Jon got a momentary view of the engine beneath its wing. An elephant could have stood in the opening and still not filled it. 'How much fuel does it take to get something like that in the air? Enough to fill a swimming pool?'

'You're asking me?' Kieran said. 'Fucked if I know.'

The access road led to a double gate that was topped with barbed wire. Beyond it was only fields. The Range Rover pulled over on the verge; the Jaguar pulled up on the asphalt.

Jon looked around. 'How the hell can there be any need for an armed escort out here? We're inside the secure area of a frigging airport. Can't believe we've been given this detail.'

'All for show,' Kieran stated. 'Make the Yanks feel important.'

Jon watched the close protection officer climb out and open the Jaguar's rear door. She wore a lilac padded jacket tailored at the waist. Hair tied back in a ponytail, gunmetal grey trousers which were tucked into what appeared to be brown riding boots. Or really posh wellies. Jon wasn't sure which.

The group moved nearer to the fence and some bloke with a roll of paper began pointing stuff out. Conversation bounced back and forth for a while. Jon watched a plane making its descent. It passed them with a thunderous sound, touching down about four hundred metres away.

'More chance of being killed by one of those bastards,' Jon muttered. In the distance, he could see another plane already making its approach.

One of the assistants tapped away at a phone, talked briefly, then handed it over to her. She moved away from the rest and spoke for about two minutes. She rejoined them. More things were discussed. The second plane passed them and Jon began to scan the sky. There was another tiny speck. 'It's just a procession,' he stated. 'All day bloody long.'

Now the group began returning to the cars. He watched as she regarded their vehicle for a moment. Then, to his surprise, she altered course towards them. The close protection officer started to follow, but she waved him away.

'What the hell is she doing?' Kieran murmured.

'Not sure,' Jon replied.

Soon, it was obvious she was approaching his side of the car. He started to lower the window and clear his throat. 'Whatever you do,' he whispered, 'don't call her a bint.'

'Hi there!' Her voice was clear and confident. Close up, he could see her eyes were a greyish blue. She brushed a stray strand of hair away from her lips. 'Windy out here. So, you're armed back up, I take it?'

'That's correct, ma'am,' Jon replied in a formal voice. 'Pleased to meet you.'

His answer seemed to amuse her. She leaned down for a better view into the vehicle. 'What are you packing?'

'Erm, our sidearms?'

'Yeah.' There was a playful note in her voice. 'Us Yanks, we're obsessed with guns. Is that a Glock?'

'It is.' He shifted slightly so she could see the weapon strapped to his thigh more clearly. 'Fifteen rounds in the clip and another magazine in my vest.'

'Nice.' Her eyes travelled to the rear of the vehicle. 'Weapons box, too?'

'Of course.'

'What do you carry in there?'

'Lots of goodies.'

'I bet,' she narrowed her eyes. 'Carbines?'

'A Sig Sauer MCX.'

'Nice!'

'But don't ask to look, because it's not allowed.'

She pushed her bottom lip out. 'Not just a little peek?'

He smiled. 'Sorry.'

'Too bad. Well, it was nice meeting you.' She looked past Jon to Kieran. 'I'm Alicia, by the way.'

'DC Kieran Saunders. And cheers for sending those sarnies out the other night.'

'Sarnies?'

'Sandwiches.'

'Ah, yes. I hope you enjoyed them.' Her eyes turned to Jon. 'And you are?'

'DC Jon Spicer.'

'Jon.' She seemed to be tasting the word in her mouth. 'Nice to meet you, Jon.' Then she straightened up and sauntered away.

Jon was still staring at her back when he heard Kieran's whisper in his ear. 'Mate? I think you might be in there.'

CHAPTER 14

Gavin trotted down the stone stairs to the landing below, where he paused to listen outside Miriam's door. The faint sound of music was coming from inside. The tune was familiar. A song from a musical. Was it *Annie*? His wife and daughter used to enjoy watching the film version. He continued down the stairs, anxious to leave those thoughts behind.

Once on the main street, spots of rain were starting to come down. He turned right towards the bus stop. Before he reached it, he had to pass a cashpoint. Sitting on the pavement beside it was a homeless person. They were definitely spreading out further from the city centre, where competition for the best spots was fierce. That's what one had told recently told him during a phone call. The bloke had been going on about the steadily increasing numbers, and how many of the newcomers were youngsters. Lads in their late teens or early twenties who didn't care about the informal systems already in place. The sense of community among them was being eroded. And it was a hostile enough environment without your fellow rough sleepers being aggressive.

'Got any spare change?'

He ignored the request and took his place beneath the Perspex shelter, beside a back-lit poster that advertised £29 flights to Turkey. Another airline battling to entice passengers back. The sky was turquoise, the sea awash with sparkles. But this close, he could make out the clusters of white dots that made up each pinpoint of light. It was all an illusion. The promise of happiness, of escape.

A half-empty bus arrived. He put his mask on and made his way towards the back where some free window seats were available. He gazed out at the dreary street passing by. Boarded-up shops. Charity shops. Second-hand furniture shops. A closed-down garage with a fenced-off forecourt. On the ground beneath the overhanging roof he could see items strewn about. Clothing. Flattened out cardboard. A foil blanket. Even a pillow. The homeless: there was evidence of them everywhere, if you knew where to look.

Up ahead, tips of cranes were trying to puncture the grey and bulbous sky. As if they wanted the city to be drenched in rain. He counted seventeen. Six within touching distance of each other. There was something peaceful about the way they slowly rotated, silently going about their business.

He passed a massive poster advertising a TV show that appeared to be set on an island. Handsome men and glamorous women in beachwear, lounging beside a pool. They were clutching drinks and grinning at the camera with rows of white teeth exposed.

He jumped off just before the Shudehill Interchange and made his way to the narrow side street where the office for the Manchester Veterans' Helpline was located. It was in a building that was owned by the Co-operative Bank. Now the company leased cheap space to any business that could show it had ethical considerations at its heart.

Gavin said hello to Ann, the receptionist, before signing in and then climbing the wide stairs to the first floor. He wasn't sure why James had asked to see him. The man in charge of the outfit was the type who, if at all possible, preferred face-to-face conversations. Which was odd, Gavin thought, for someone who ran a telephone helpline service. It hadn't been a problem to call in; from here, it wouldn't take him long to get into work. Not if he walked quickly.

The office consisted of a single room with three tables. James Pearson's at the top, then two others for those volunteers who liked working alongside other people. Gavin didn't. He kept the phone the charity had provided on him at all times. He was happy to take calls day or night. His answerphone message said that, if they left a number, he promised to ring back the moment he could. No call ever went unanswered, that was his solemn promise.

Three people were in, all of them male. He recognised the nearest one. Fergie McLagan – had been a paratrooper who lost his left leg to an IED out in Afghanistan, the other to sepsis from a dirty syringe. He was now drug-free and, just four months ago, had rowed the length of Loch Ness to raise money for the charity.

'Ah, Gavin – good to see you!'

It was James, calling from his desk. Gavin nodded hello to the others, then approached the man in charge. 'Hello, James. You're looking well.'

'Really?' He smoothed a hand over his side parting. Oxford shirt and chinos. Gavin knew he'd be wearing battered brogues, too. A Barbour jacket hanging in the corner. The man meant well, but Gavin couldn't quite work out why he'd chosen this type of job. The wage couldn't be much.

'It's been a bit frantic recently. We missed another. Did you hear?'

Gavin wasn't sure which person James was talking about. Had word already got to him about the one from the fire escape, the night before? He gave a little shake of his head.

'Ah, sadly a man called Ryan Gardner. Seems he fell down the central stairway in an empty building near Piccadilly Station. Sometimes, you feel you're making a difference, and then something like that happens.'

'That's ... no, I hadn't heard. I tend not to follow much news.'

'I understand.' He gestured. 'Sit down, please. It's good to see you, Gavin. You're looking well. How's the world of night-watching?'

'Fine. It's fine. The building work seems to be coming along – though they've still got masses to do.'

James nodded. 'And you're OK? Working nights isn't for everyone.'

He'd lowered his voice and Gavin sensed he was building towards something. 'It's no problem. I sleep just as well during the day.'

'Evidently.' He smiled briefly then licked his lips. A tiny indication of nerves. 'I was checking the calendar the other day, actually.' James gestured to the wall chart behind him. Coloured bars denoted who was available to take calls on which day. 'You've been with us over ten months, and you haven't had a single week when you've not been on call.'

Gavin shrugged. 'No need. I enjoy it.'

'Right. That's good. But I think, maybe, you're due a break. Don't you?'

He closed his eyes for a moment, as if conducting a swift internal assessment of his tiredness levels. 'No, not really. I'll let you know when I do want one.'

James let out a forced laugh. 'We actually have two people who've recently volunteered. I was going through the process of providing them with a temporary phone for their probationary period, when it occurred to me that one of them could have yours. If you were to take a little downtime.'

This was disastrous. He couldn't have anyone else using his phone. He needed to be available to answer anyone who called it. How else would he find the ones who needed help in leaving this world? 'I don't want to take a little downtime.' He realised he'd sounded abrupt, and attempted a smile. 'Honestly, I'd ask if I felt that was the case.'

James leaned forward slightly, voice lowered so no one else could hear. 'Gavin. You do realise we're now almost at the anniversary ... when you lost your wife and daughter?'

He gave a stiff nod. 'Of course I do.'

'So is that not a good reason for you to ... you know ... step back from helping others. Commit some time to yourself, for a change.'

'I won't lie. It's not been easy. Sometimes, I ...' He sighed, eyes cutting to the window. The rain was falling steadily, now. 'You know what Winston Churchill said? "When you're going through hell, keep going." I need to be busy, James.'

'But is that just so you can avoid your feelings? I'm a bit concerned, Gavin. To be honest, I am. The grieving process is something that shouldn't be avoided. We,' he gestured to the room, 'of all people realise that.'

'I don't know what to say.' He glanced up. 'Other than I think it's better I continue.'

James held his eyes. It felt like the man was peeling away layers, gazing into his head, seeing the night skies, the rooftops, the lost souls as they finally buckled, giving way to despair, their sobs of anguish, their bodies tumbling into the dark ... Gavin had to break eye contact.

'Are you OK, Gavin?'

'Yes.'

'You're absolutely sure? You know you can tell me anything. Christ, we've all been through things. That's why we choose to do this. To help.'

He shook his head.

'So I can't persuade you to have a break? To give yourself time to think – and reflect.'

'No. I appreciate your concern. But there's really nothing to be concerned about. Honestly.'

'You know, I could just put a stop on that phone? If I felt that it was for your own good.'

He had to grip the undersides of his legs to stop from kicking out. 'That's not ... please don't do that, James.'

'I wouldn't, don't worry. But have a think about this, OK? We'll be fine. There are enough people to cope if you have a break.'

He got to his feet. 'I will. I'll have a think. Is that all?'

'Yes.'

'OK. Bye.' He turned around and, head down, made for the door.

There was a look of concern on James Pearson's face as he watched Gavin go.

CHAPTER 15

'And just pop me a little autograph there,' the WIO said from behind the protective grille. He turned the clipboard in Jon's direction before picking the Glock off the counter and sliding it into the rack behind him.

Pop me a little autograph. Jon wondered if the man would ever tire of saying the line. Probably isn't aware he's even using it, he thought, as he signed the form and pushed it back through the hatch. 'Cheers, Michael.'

'Right,' Kieran said next to him. 'A cheeky snifter before heading home?'

'Tempting,' Jon said. 'But I need to meet someone. I'll catch you tomorrow, yeah?'

Kieran was smirking. 'Yeah?'

Jon glanced at him. 'What?'

'Meet someone? Who might that be, then?'

Jon took a moment before the penny dropped. 'Oh, right, I'm hot-footing it over to The Lowry Hotel and asking reception if they can tell Alicia Lloyd I've arrived.'

Kieran laughed. 'And she'll say, scrub him clean and send him up to the penthouse suite. There she'll be, waiting in a silk dressing gown with nothing on underneath ...'

'You've really thought this one through, haven't you?' Jon retorted, tapping his temple. 'Safely stashed it up here for later?'

'Absolutely,' Kieran said. 'Oven-ready, it is.'

Sitting at the wheel of his car, Jon stared at his phone for a second before calling home. Answerphone. Which meant Alice was probably upstairs with Holly. 'Hi, babe, I've just got some last bits to sort out at the office. I reckon an hour. If my tea's in the dog, ping me a text and I'll grab something en route. Otherwise, see you soon. Love you.'

He cut the call, but continued staring at the screen. Why did you do that? Why didn't you just tell her the truth? Because, he thought, she would go off on one if I did. And, what's more she'd be right. What am I doing going on forays among the city's rough sleepers? I should be going home to tuck in my kids.

He pocketed his phone and reached for the seat belt. I will, he said to himself. Before I get any deeper into this, I'll tell her what's going on.

He parked on the same side street close to Stevenson Square and walked round. But the doorway to the printing business was empty. Jon scanned the surrounding pavements. No luck. He could see why the police struggled to follow-up incidents involving street-sleepers: you never knew where the hell they'd be.

Deciding that Piccadilly Gardens might be worth a look, Jon set off through the narrow back streets. He emerged by a bus stand where a crowd of people waited. Among them was a couple of kids, neither more than six years old. Jon checked his watch. Almost nine at night. The mum was on her phone, face mask tucked beneath her chin, lit cigarette in her spare hand. One of the kids asked her something.

'Stop fucking mithering, me!' she snapped, not taking her eyes off the screen. 'Doing my head in! Seriously. Both of you.'

The harshness of her words had no visible effect, other than to make them both look even more bored. The surrounding people seemed oblivious to her outburst.

Jon checked for anyone sitting beside the row of cashpoints to his right. Two blokes: neither was Greg. A woman encased in a mound of blankets outside the Wetherspoons pub. Remembering people often asked for change near the pedestrian crossing at the approach road to Piccadilly Station, he set off in that direction. He'd almost reached the twenty-four-hour Spar when he saw Greg step through its doors. The man immediately turned left, and left again, onto a dim side street leading back towards the Northern Quarter.

Jon broke into a jog. 'Greg!' he called, rounding the corner. The other man's stride slowed and he looked back.

Jon lifted a hand. 'Greg: it's Jon — we spoke the other night?'

He came to a stop. He looked like he needed a good sleep. Shadow formed an unbroken ring round each eye.

Jon came to a stop beside him. 'You walk fast, mate.'

'Went to try and see Wayne earlier,' Greg said.

'How did he seem?'

'They wouldn't let me in. Intensive care ward.'

'Yeah, he's not great. What do you know?'

'That an ambulance took him from behind a pub near Ardwick.'

'Word gets around, then?'

Greg nodded.

'Look, can I get you a coffee or something?'

His shoulders lifted a fraction. 'OK.'

Greg led him towards the Burger King at the far end of the Gardens, explaining that the staff were very laid back about who came through the doors — and the upstairs seating area was large and usually quiet. On the way, they passed four more people positioned with empty cups on the pavement before them. Jon noticed the perfunctory way Greg nodded at most of them. Like you would on passing a colleague at work.

They found two stools at the large windows which overlooked the public space. Except for the tram tracks curling across it, the entire area immediately below them was pedestrianised. Puddles glistened everywhere. Everyone was picking their way around them, heads down, shoulders up.

'Good spot, this,' Greg stated. 'For seeing what's going on.'

Jon watched as he emptied five sachets of sugar into his tea. The big video screen on the side of the building away to their left was flashing up an ad for a new make of rum. A low-ceilinged bar in what was probably meant to be a Cuban back street, full to bursting with a young crowd partying away. Sultry couples with glistening skin doing the tango or something. Old guy bashing away on the piano. Smouldering looks passing between people as they sipped from tall glasses. Pile of bollocks.

'When did you see Wayne last?' Jon asked, taking a sip of his black coffee.

Greg stirred his drink for a bit longer before saying anything. 'Yesterday, about four. Half-four, maybe. He thought he was getting the sofa back – at his mate's flat. But then the girlfriend decided to stay on. We'd planned to head for that pitch on Stevenson Square, but then that little toerag came by and Wayne ended up scoring. That's the last I saw of him.'

'The dealer?'

Greg nodded.

'The one who sold Spice to Wayne the other night?'

'Yeah, him. He had some other stuff, too. Don't ask me what; I can't be doing with it. Wayne spent all his money on it, though. Stupid twat.'

Exactly the sort of thing my brother would have done, thought Jon, sadly. 'What's the situation with services to help people get out of using? I saw a website for one called New Dawn—'

'Good bunch at that place. But the building they're in – I heard the landlord is hiking the rent. Knock-on effect of all these bloody skyscrapers going up, isn't it? They can't spend time helping people and raising the money they need for rent.'

'What'll they do?'

'What other outfits have had to do: find somewhere outside the city centre that's cheaper. But then they won't be near the people who need their help. Shit situation, it is.'

Jon looked briefly out at the rooftops. The cranes that lurked behind them silently going about their business. 'What happened next with Wayne?'

'He disappears in the direction of Piccadilly saying he'll be back about nine. Yeah, right, I thought. I ended up in Stevenson Square on my own. And I never can sleep if I'm on my own. Wayne didn't come back, obviously.'

'Who told you about Wayne going off in the ambulance?'

'There was a few chatting.'

'What were they saying?'

'Just that someone had seen a load of emergency vehicles parked up. Word is, it was Wayne.'

'Did they say if anyone else was there with him in the pub?'

'No. I can try and find out. Did he overdose or something?'

Jon turned to look at him. 'He fell. From the top of the fire escape.'

Greg looked genuinely shocked. 'Jesus. No one said about that. He fell?'

'That's why I need to know if he was there with anyone else. Maybe that dealer you mentioned?'

Greg shook his head. 'That little parasite doesn't stick around. Once he's made his sales, you don't see him again. He's got a flat of his own nowadays, out Eccles way.'

'He was homeless?'

'Yeah. Once.' He sipped at his drink. 'You think that this could be another suspicious one?'

'It's a bit early to say. But falling from a high place? I don't like the sound of it. How did Wayne seem to you yesterday afternoon? Was he feeling down?'

'Oh, yeah. He was really pissed off when he realised he wasn't going back to that mate's place. Really pissed off. That's why he scored.'

'Did he ever mention not wanting to carry on? Anything like that?'

'Not carry on?'

Jon gave a nod.

'You mean suicide?'

Jon thought of the young man he'd once played rugby with. Always smiling, always positive. He inclined his head.

'It had crossed his mind, in the past. But he's been much steadier lately. Of course, throw in the drugs and who knows.'

Jon lifted his Americano and turned his attention to the Gardens. On the grassed area near the fountain were a few benches. Two men were in a heated discussion about something. One kept waving an arm towards Mosley Street; the other didn't seem happy. Eventually, he sat on the bench and crossed his arms. The one still standing kicked the other's sleeping bag and rucksack over and started remonstrating once more.

'Right, I need to go.' Greg announced, gulping back his tea. 'Got an offer on somewhere for the night.'

'You mean a hostel bed?'

Greg smiled. 'Something like that.' He peered through the windows. 'That dealer I mentioned? He's known as Jay. That's him – hassling the bloke by the benches.'

Jon turned. 'The one who's standing up?'

'That's him.' Greg started to go, then stopped. 'Also, Wayne did say to me once, he'd never jump. Said he couldn't stand the thought of those seconds on the way down. Both us were agreed on that – we said sitting down in front of a train would be better.'

'You'd discussed suicide with him?'

'Not seriously. It was more to pass the time. When you're lying there, looking up at the stars. Like when you discuss what's beyond space. Or if there are aliens.' He shrugged. 'That type of chat. See you.'

Jon watched him heading down the stairs. Seconds later, he came into view below, walking with short fast steps towards Chinatown. Jon checked the benches. Jay now appeared to be taking some money off the man. It was people like him who'd sped his younger brother, Dave, towards his death. Vile parasites who preyed on people's vulnerabilities. Jay, he said to himself. It's time you and me met. He slid off the stool, coffee half-finished.

By the time he got outside, the man over on the benches was alone. Jon spotted Jay about thirty metres away, wandering towards the top of Oldham Street. Striding fast, Jon closed the gap, then slowed down to a safe distance.

He guessed the dealer was in his early thirties. Five-eight, thinly built, shaved head. The brown padded coat looked like it cost a few quid. One of those things with fur lining the hood. Fat trainers on his feet.

Every time he reached a person asking for money, Jay paused for a quiet word. The first few shook their heads, but – outside The City pub – he found a customer. A young lad in a sleeping bag with a filthy deerstalker cap over his head. Jay crouched down in the shop doorway and an exchange was swiftly made.

Jon was thinking about his younger brother again as he shadowed Jay round the corner. A narrow side street led to a small, poorly lit open space. An empty car park. Jay was cutting straight across, trainers crunching on the gravel.

Jon checked for any cameras. None that he could see. He lifted the hood of his own top over his head.

'Jay? Wait up, mate.'

The dealer turned round, a questioning look on his face.

Jon knew he had a few seconds at most before the other man sensed something was up. He kept walking, a hand now in his pocket, as if bringing out money. 'I heard you've got pills.'

Jay's head tilted to the side, a frown forming on his sharp features. 'You what?'

'Pills,' Jon repeated. Four more steps would be enough. 'Here.' He brought his hand out, a ten pound note visible in his fingers. But he allowed his arm to keep rising, a fist forming at the very last second. Knuckles connected with the underside of Jay's nose and his head snapped back. Just a little jab. Not enough to floor him, but it would do for starters. Jon planted his front foot close to Jay's, flexed his knees and swung a meaty fist into the underside of his ribs. That's for my little brother, he thought. The blow emptied the other man's lungs of air and, as he started to drop, Jon caught him in the side of the head with a left. And that's for Wayne.

Before he hit the ground, Jon had him by the hood and was dragging him to the side of the car park where the shadows were deeper. Jay was starting to cough and gasp. Which meant, next, he'd try shouting. Jon brought a fist down on his upturned face. 'Shut it.'

Once he had him by a low perimeter wall, he lowered a knee onto the man's right bicep and reached across to pin his other arm by his side. That left Jon's right arm free. He started going through the man's pockets. Little bags of green stuff. Pills. Dirty yellow powder. Zipped into an inner pocket was a wedge of cash. Easily a grand, Jon guessed. Jay was recovering once again, splutters and whimpers. Bubbles of blood ballooning from his nostrils.

DARK ANGEL

Jon slapped him. 'I said, shut up! And keep your eyes closed.'

Next was a phone and a set of keys. Something metallic and ridged. Knuckleduster. Nasty. Jon reached his arm back and hurled the phone against the wall. It split apart. One by one, he tore the bags open and starting to empty them on Jay's face. 'You sold some gear to the wrong person, you scummy little turd.' Powder was in his eyebrows and eyelashes, across his cheeks, in his hair. Specks of green were sticking in the blood pouring from his nostrils. Pills rolled off his face into the folds of his coat. Jon flipped him onto his front and yanked the fur-lined hood over his head before scooping up the cash, knuckleduster and keys. He jangled them above Jay's head. 'I know where you live. I see you doing the rounds again, I'll come and take your kneecaps off with my hammer. Hear me?'

Jay's head moved.

'Good. Lie here. Have a think about it.'

Duggy's night light filled his room with a soft orange glow. He was beneath his duvet, lying on his front, a thumb nestled in his partly open mouth. Jon traced his fingers through his son's hair then moved next door to Holly's room.

She was in her customary position, back to the wall, curled in on herself. He eased himself onto the edge of the bed and gazed down at her. Whatever was playing out in her head was causing her eyes to move restlessly behind their lids. A tremor went through her lower lip. He reached over to cup the side of her head in his palm. To try and smooth the bad thoughts from her mind. He spotted the dark specks of blood on the backs of his fingers and withdrew his hand before it made contact.

The noise of the bathroom taps masked the sound of Alice coming up the stairs. Before he knew it, she was behind him, arms sliding round his waist. Her voice sounded beside his ear.

'What's that on your hands?'

He paused with the nail brush to examine his fingers. The lie was out of his mouth before he could stop it. 'Must be ink from the photocopier. I had to change the cartridge at work just before setting off.'

She rested her head on his shoulder blade. 'You look tired. Did you eat?'

'Yeah. A crappy burger.'

'With cheese?'

'Of course with cheese.'

He felt her hand move and, next thing, she was prodding the folds of flesh at his stomach. 'Fatso.'

'Only because I'm leaning over the sink.'

Her fingers continued to probe at the folds of flesh. 'Salad-dodging fatso.'

He checked his fingers were clean before straightening up and twisting round. 'You calling me fat?'

'Big fat-fatty-fat-pig.'

'I have to warn you, here. That sort of language isn't called for.'

'Fatzilla.'

Now smiling, he dipped a shoulder and hooked a forearm behind her knees.

'Go on, say that again.'

'Fatzilla. Human fatberg.'

Now her feet were off the floor as he carried her towards their bedroom. 'You're really giving me no other option, here.'

'Good.'

CHAPTER 16

There was a note on his desk from Peter Collier. *When you have time, give me a shout.*

Jon turned his head and saw the civilian support worker was looking over. An office day, then. He picked up the note and headed across. 'Morning, Peter, what's up?'

'I got pulled from your stuff, I'm afraid.' He flicked his eyes ceiling-ward in explanation. 'But not before finding another.' From beneath an open file, he slid out a sheet of paper. 'See what you think. For what it's worth, I had time to go back another three months before that one, but didn't find any others that matched.'

'Cheers, Peter. I appreciate it.'

'No problem.'

Jon read the top sheet as he returned to his desk. This one dated from six months ago. Body found at the base of what had been a block of student flats on Granby Row, near Piccadilly Station. Jon made another dot on his mental map. Another death in that part of town. The flats were earmarked for demolition and empty at the time. Jon could picture the building: it had come down the previous month and the new building was already almost built.

The person was called Frank Kilby. Aged forty-six. My age, Jon thought. Had served in the Royal Artillery for twenty-seven years. Originally from Bury. Peter had highlighted a few things: no witnesses, was known to social services, already signed off as an open verdict by the coroner.

Jon sat down heavily at his desk.

'That was a long sigh,' Iona announced from her side of the workstation.

He looked up. 'Five homeless ex-soldiers in the last half-a-year have suffered fatal falls.'

'Statistically, is that unusual?'

Typical Iona, he thought. Straight to the numbers. 'Not significantly. People who sleep rough are more likely to die. If they're ex-forces, they're more likely to die than anyone.'

Her eyes seemed drift off for a second before she blinked. 'So what's bugging you?'

'How they all died. Times of deaths: all of them during the dead of night. None of them left suicide notes. Plus, there are a couple of people who claim they saw someone else right at the time two of them died.'

'Which people?'

'That's part of the problem. Fellow rough sleepers who, at the time, were heavily under the influence of drugs. One of them was found this morning at the base of a fire escape. Somehow, he'd fallen from the top of it.'

'Really?'

Jon gave a nod.

'So you think suicide's unlikely?'

'Well ... it could be, that's the thing. Maybe. They've not ended up on the streets because life's dealt them a lucky hand. But still ...'

'You need to see what might connect them, surely?'

Suppressing a yawn, he pulled his top drawer open.

'Sorry if I'm keeping you up.'

He gave a rueful smile as he lifted out the files. 'No – I'm just a bit knackered. I've been looking. Nothing obvious, other than they all served in the army.'

'Do you know if they knew each other?'

'When?'

'While they were serving? I mean, there's a good chance they crossed paths while sleeping rough, wouldn't you say? But how about before?'

'Good point.' He checked his watch. Twenty minutes before he and Kieran needed to set off for The Lowry. Not enough time. Never enough time. 'I could try and track down some relatives. See what they say.'

'You still on this armed escort thing?'

'Yup. Another four days. You?'

'Those damned transcripts. Leave the files somewhere I can find them. If I have time, I'll pitch in.'

'You don't need to, Iona. Honestly.'

She gave him her school teacher's look. 'Have you looked in the mirror lately? You need a hand, Jon.'

'Back to the damn airport, then,' Kieran said, easing out and following the two Jaguars.

'Another action-packed morning watching bastard planes take off,' Jon replied, fiddling about for the seat's controls. Not enough room in these cars, he thought.

'What's that?' Kieran asked, nodding at something.

The instant Jon turned his head, he felt a tweak of pain followed by an impact on his right arm.

'Pinch-punch, first day of the month!' Kieran called out triumphantly. 'And no returns to me.'

Jon looked back at his colleague. 'You are such a kid, Saunders.'

They spent the first part of the morning parked outside a sleek looking building on the edge of the airport complex. Jon did a tally of the vehicles in the car park. Audi. Lexus. Audi. Porsche. Range Rover. Porsche. Audi. Aston Martin. Obviously where the big earners had their offices.

Shortly before noon, Kieran shifted in his seat and announced: 'You can have that.'

Jon turned his head, wondering what he'd meant. The putrid smell hit him an instant later. 'You rank dog. Jesus!' He reached for the window button, changed his mind and opened the entire door. 'That is evil. What the hell did you eat?'

'Not sure,' Kieran murmured, a faraway look on his face. 'But the turtle's wanting to poke his head out.' He shot Jon a look. 'I mean really wanting to poke his head out.'

'Fuck's sake,' Jon groaned, waving a hand at the building. 'Go in there and find a toilet, then.'

'I'm not marching through the doors and asking to use their shitter!'

He's got a point, Jon thought. Probably stink the whole building out. He looked over to the main airport. 'You'd better hot-foot it to the terminal building. Plenty of public bogs in there.'

'We can't leave the principle.' Kieran shifted again. 'Oh God, it'll be touching cloth at this rate.'

Jon consulted the schedule. 'She doesn't finish here until lunch. You've got plenty of time. I'll stay.'

'You're sure?' Kieran was already starting the engine.

'Let the OFC know. And don't be long, OK?'

'Don't worry, it'll be over pretty damn quick, I promise.'

Aware he'd be in sight of those in the office building, Jon grabbed an overcoat with the word 'Police' emblazoned across its back: it would hang low enough to conceal his weapons belt. The vehicle roared away and, after putting on a police baseball cap, Jon looked about. Alone among the parked cars, he felt horribly exposed. Apart from a short section of wall either side of the main doors, the exterior of the building consisted entirely of sheets of smoked glass. No way of knowing how many people are bloody watching me, he thought, levels of discomfort rising even further.

Your best option, he said to himself, is beside the entrance. So what if you'll look like a bouncer? Anything's better than being stood out here. Trying to look like this was a perfectly normal turn of events – and he hadn't been dumped out of his armed response vehicle because his driver was about to crap in his own pants – Jon casually set off across the asphalt.

The doors were controlled by a security pad and had a large camera above them. Jon positioned himself with his back to the wall and crossed his hands in front of him. Definitely look like a doorman now, he thought. He surveyed the terminal building, hoping Kieran would have found somewhere to park.

A minute later he heard a shooshing sound as the doors slid open. He glanced to the side and saw Alicia Lloyd step out. He waited for the close protection officer to appear behind her. She was on her own.

'You know,' she announced, looking straight ahead as she stretched her arms out and rotated her wrists. 'These meetings can get so boring.'

Is she speaking into an earpiece? Does she even know I'm here? He wasn't sure whether to say anything. Her coat was beige. That material which looks almost like felt. Cashmere? Expensive, anyway. Her long hair cascaded over the upturned collar.

Flexing her fingers, she turned to look at him. 'I mean, you're in that vehicle for hours on end, but at least you can chat. Listen to music. Can you listen to music?'

So she is talking to me, he thought. She'd seen me out here. He nodded. 'If the volume's on low.'

'Where's your buddy? He took off pretty quick.'

Jon cut his eyes towards the main part of the airport. 'Something came up. He'll be back soon.'

'You know, I didn't know much about Manchester before this trip.' She was staring in the direction of the city's skyline. 'I like it. What's your opinion on all the new developments?'

'My opinion?'

'Yes. I'm thinking of making an investment. An apartment in one of the towers that's being built. They say, if I buy now, the prices are much lower. Do you think the demand is there?'

'I don't know how these things are decided. But smarter people than me obviously think it's a good bet; I've never seen so many developments happening around the city.'

'My thoughts, too. Cranes are always the best sign. It rains a lot here, though, doesn't it?'

'You know, a man once visited Manchester. After three days of getting soaked, he passes this kid on the street. Says to him, "Hey, does it ever stop raining in this bloody city?" The kid looks at him and says, "How should I know? I'm only ten."' He broke into a grin.

She took a moment, then a giggle came from deep in her throat. 'That's excellent. I'll use that for when I'm next in Seattle.'

'Help yourself,' he said, looking towards the airport. After a second, he sensed she was still looking at him. No, he thought. More than that. Examining me.

'Can I ask you something?' she asked.

'Don't see why not.'

'How did you lose the top of your ear?'

He glanced at her. Other than her immaculate eyebrows being fractionally raised, her face was blank. 'Er ...'

'Sorry. Too direct. It's an American thing.'

'No, you're all right. It was an incident.'

'Well, duuuuh! A work incident?'

He thought about the windswept car park in County Galway. How his face had been pressed into freezing tarmac that was peppered with horseshit and hay. The cold grip of the pliers as his flesh was pulled until it finally tore. It would be easier to lie. 'Yes, work incident.'

'So you're trained in hand-to-hand stuff as well as weapons?'

'The full shebang, that's us.'

He could now feel her eyes travelling slowly down him. 'Sounds dangerous.'

Not much I can say to that.

'All that training, it must be frustrating to be sitting in that car for hours on end babysitting someone like me. I mean, I realise this is tedious. You're having to do this because someone up the chain decided it would look good.'

He met her eyes for a second. Thought, she's smarter than I realised. 'Nature of the job, ma'am. We're used to it.'

'Ma'am.' She laughed. 'What is it with this ma'am business? I'm not the Queen.'

'That's just how we address any female senior to us.'

'Am I senior to you?'

Most people are, Jon thought.

'Well, Jon Spicer, I'd better get back to this meeting.' But, rather than step towards the doors, she moved closer to him. 'Here.'

He looked to his side. Oh Jesus. There was a business card in her hand. She was holding it out.

'Take it.'

'Sorry, ma'am. I'm – I'm not sure that's appropriate.'

'Why?'

'There are ... you know ... already communication channels.'

'So?'

'You've been assigned a close protection—'

'Him?' She made a scoffing sound as she slipped the card into the pocket of his trousers. 'I'll feel safer knowing you have my number.'

She walked away without another word. At the doors, she signalled with her hand and they immediately parted. Only when she'd vanished inside did he feel able to breathe again. Did that just happen? He felt like he should check the pocket to see if a card was really in it. But he didn't want to move. The ARV appeared on the feeder road for the car park. Kieran was back. Jon set off for where they'd been parked. One thing I know, he thought, I'm definitely not mentioning this to him. The piss-takes would never end.

CHAPTER 17

'Got some things to show you,' Iona announced as he neared his desk.

'Yeah? What things?'

'I went through the files. Tried to organise stuff into a spreadsheet.'

He saw a message alert was flashing on the phone beside his computer. 'You did? When?'

'I had some time in my lunch break,' she replied breezily. 'Anyway, want to go through it?'

'Of course, thanks. Let me just see what this is.' He sat down and reached for the phone. The message had been left at three forty-three that afternoon. Robin Newton in the forensics department located on the building's upper floor began to speak.

'Hi Jon. Right, this feather you left with me. You thought it was a crow's or raven's. I've taken a look. Turns out it doesn't belong to any member of the Corvus family. Not unless that bird was an albino. It's been spray-painted black, Jon. Originally, it was white. So I think it's highly unlikely it came from a pigeon, either. My guess? Probably a seagull. Maybe, a swan. It's quite large. There are also traces of glue at the base of the shaft, so I imagine it was once stuck to something larger. Maybe formed part of a display. Or a decoration? That's pretty much it. There isn't any chance of fingerprints. I got it under the microscope, but couldn't see anything we could lift for DNA, either, even if you had approval for testing. Which you hadn't. So, I popped it in the internal post. Let me know if there's anything else, thanks.'

Jon replaced the receiver. Not a pigeon feather. Which scuppers Weir's theory. 'Interesting.'

'What's that?'

He sat back and crossed his arms. 'You know, earlier, I mentioned a couple of people were claiming someone else was in the vicinity – when two of the deaths occurred.'

'Yes.'

'Well.' He lowered his voice. 'This is where it gets a bit bizarre. One of those people said the figure he saw had wings on his back.' He saw the look on Iona's face and lifted a hand. 'Not big ones for flying. Little things. Like for – I don't know – a kid's fancy-dress costume.'

'OK. Carry on.'

'Not much else, really. The figure walked to the top of the stairwell and disappeared down them.'

'But he had wings sticking out of his back?'

'Yup. Head-to-foot in black, including a pair of wings.'

'Hang on: the person who claims he saw this is the same one who went off the top of a fire escape last night?'

'It is. And he's now in the intensive care at the MRI. Broken back, massive head injuries. Still unconscious.'

'I see what you mean about bizarre.'

'I haven't finished. Yesterday morning, I went to the fire escape where it happened. It's behind this derelict pub near Piccadilly. Stuck in the splintered frame of the door at the top of the fire escape stairs was a black feather. Weir said it wasn't significant – probably just a pigeon's. Birds had been using the upper floor as a roosting area. But that phone message was from Robin up in forensics. The feather had been spray-painted black; originally, it was white. He thinks it came from a seagull or swan.'

'Someone had sprayed it with black paint?'

'Correct.'

Iona carried on staring at him. 'Almost like this person – who may or may not actually be real – is wearing some kind of outfit. Black everything.'

Jon checked no other detectives were listening in. 'Freaky, isn't it?'

'Just a bit.' She gave a little shake of her head. 'Anyway, this spreadsheet. Have a look.'

Jon went round to her side of the desk and pulled a nearby chair across. 'Christ. You sure this only took your lunch break?'

Each person's name was written down the left-handside of a large grid. Jim Barlow. Ryan Gardner. Luke McClennan. Roy Jarratt. Frank Kilby. 'We should probably add the details for the guy in the ICU as well,' Iona said. 'So, you see the columns? Each one is for an aspect of their lives. First is which part of the armed forces they served in.'

'Got it,' Jon answered, scanning down the column. Jim Barlow: Royal Regiment of Fusiliers. Ryan Gardner: The Yorkshire Regiment. Luke McClennan: The Royal Welsh Infantry. Roy Jarratt: Duke of Lancaster's Regiment. Frank Kilby: The Royal Artillery. Wayne Newton: The Tank Regiment.

'Next column is their place of birth – and you can see there's no common thread there. Then it's each person's age: these vary from Roy Jarratt, twenty-six, right through to Frank Kilby, practically twenty years older.'

Jon's eyes had already gone to the following column: next of kin. Not a lot in that one, so far. 'That could be interesting. For background on each one.'

'I agree. As you can see, I also went into prior convictions. That's a mixed bag. A couple of them had records before joining up; all but Frank Kilby had come to the attention of the police after coming out.'

Jon scanned the offences. All minor stuff: vagrancy, begging, shoplifting. Hardly, in Jon's opinion, worthy of police action He went to the final column. 'And I see you've had a go at when they arrived in Manchester.'

'Seemed to make sense. Roy Jarratt was from Wigan and Frank Kilby from Bury, so they were probably based here from when they came out of the army. For the others, it's only a rough guess. For instance, Ryan Gardner. He's from Wakefield, near Leeds: his date is based on an arrest for shoplifting in the Arndale. But that doesn't mean he hadn't been around for weeks before that point.'

'Something each next of kin might be able to help with.'

'True.'

Jon rubbed his fingers across his chin. 'Sticking with the military thing, we'll need to access the army's records to find out if they all were deployed at the same time on a foreign posting. That might be where they all came across each other.'

'Won't be hard. Not if the request is coming from the Counter Terrorism Unit.'

Jon glanced towards the doors. 'By the way, is Weir still around?'

Iona consulted her watch. 'It's only just after six. Probably.'

'I'll pop up.' He glanced at the next of kin column again. 'And another thing: I hate dealing with relatives. What'll we say? Your dead family member, things are looking a bit murky. You might have been thinking suicide, but we're thinking ...' He shook his head. 'It could open a right can of shit.'

'You're right. That needs to be approached very carefully.'

Jon tapped his forefinger against the sheet as he stood. 'I'll see if Weir is about. Top stuff, Iona. Really helpful.'

'Well, it's only a start. I'm sure there'll more columns to add before we make any progress.'

He was about to stand when his desk phone started to ring. The number showing on the display was zero: reception. 'Spicer here.'

'Hello. We've just had the front desk from the police station on Bootle Street call. A message was left for you there.'

He leaned forward. 'Who by?'

'Someone called Greg?'

'Go on.'

'He asked that you meet him in town later. Regarding, he said, Wayne.'

Jon nodded. 'OK. Did he give a time?'

'Six thirty, Stevenson Square.'

'Got it, thanks.'

The traffic passing above her caused the underside of the bridge to hum. If she got to her knees, she could reach up and touch the metal girders. Feel the metal shiver. But she'd stopped doing that: it only sent the perching pigeons into a mass of flapping wings. And they'd found this place first. It was their home, not hers.

She'd discovered it by squeezing through a gap in the roadside fencing. Then she'd picked her way down the top of a grassy slope that was littered by items that had been lobbed over the fence. Traffic cones and shopping baskets and entire bin liners of rubbish. Where the bridge connected with the slope was a ledge. Compacted earth that was perfectly dry. Beneath it, trains regularly rumbled by. But she was too high up for any passenger to spot her.

Sometimes, she heard people on the road as they walked past. Snatches of conversation. Who said this, who was doing that, what could be going on with him, what did she think she was doing. The usual.

She liked it under here. It was out of the wind and rain. There was the pile of sleeping bags she'd lifted from doorways around the city centre. More than enough to keep warm. And she had the sound of the pigeons. Their gentle cooing was like a chorus. She looked up at them looking down at her with half-closed eyes. Smooth heads resting on curved chests. Content. They didn't need much. Why couldn't people be more like them? Just take what they needed. The planet wouldn't be collapsing if people were more like pigeons. The thought made her smile.

She became aware of a damp feeling. Her breasts were rock hard with milk. So full, they'd begun to leak. She hated the feeling. Raising herself onto an elbow, she folded back the edge of the blanket to look at the tiny form beside her. How could anything sleep so much? Her puffy little face, swollen eyelids and light fuzz of hair. No interest in the world. She remembered seeing what the midwife had jotted down in her red book. 'Failure to thrive.' The woman had talked about a specially enriched formula milk. Olivia wasn't keen: if the stuff her body was producing wasn't good enough, that was what nature had decided. This constant reaching for artificial, man-made alternatives. Shrink-wrapped powders, blister-packs of pills, vaccines and injections and hormone therapy treatments. Pumping alien substances into your body. It wasn't right. It wasn't what was meant to be. The world was spiralling out of control and she wasn't sure she wanted to be part of it anymore.

CHAPTER 18

No sign of Greg in the doorway. Jon checked his watch. Almost quarter to seven. He wondered what to do. A large Aldi bag full of clothing was balanced on a stack of bedding in the corner. Flattened cardboard boxes beneath it. For a moment, he contemplated sitting down. No. He couldn't face the prospect of looking like someone bedding down for the night.

Instead, he walked the few steps to where Lever Street cut across the square. On the other side of the road was some type of cafe bar. The old Soviet logo featured heavily in the signage. On the pavement before it was a cluster of tables and chairs. It was cold, but not too cold for sitting out. He took a seat, ordered a coffee and waited.

His drink was long finished and the bars surrounding the square were getting busy before he spotted a flat cap bobbing its way towards the building's doorway.

Right, let's hear what you've got to say, he thought, ambling across. 'Evening.'

Greg was shaking out the top sleeping bag. He looked over his shoulder. 'There you are. I was worried you'd given up.'

Well, Jon thought, you are over an hour later than you said you'd be. 'You've got some news about Wayne?'

'Yeah – the night he fell. Someone saw something.'

'Who?'

'He's fucked off for now. But I asked him to swing by here when he's ready.'

Jon suppressed a sigh. 'When will that be?'

'Thing is, he's got a good pitch – so he wants to sit tight for the time being. Do a bit of grafting.'

'Why don't I go to him?'

Greg's head shook. 'He wasn't keen on that. Not keen, at all.'

Jon looked about. Shit. It was getting late. 'How long will he be?'

'He's by an entrance to the Arndale. That shuts at eight, so he said he'd come across then.'

Great, thought Jon. That's in half-an-hour. Another evening of not being home to see Alice and the kids.

Greg had slid out some sections of cardboard. He tossed a sleeping bag in Jon's direction. 'May as well get snug, hey?'

Jon hesitated. But Greg was already settling down. In for a penny, in for a pound, he thought, lowering himself on to the cardboard and zipping up his coat.

'Here, put that across your legs,' Greg instructed, draping the sleeping bag over Jon's knees. 'Need a blanket? I got some nice blankets. They were only dropped off last night. Clean.'

'No, you're all right,' Jon said, gingerly tucking the sleeping bag in around his waist, relieved that moving the fabric didn't release the aroma of piss.

'Hat? Got a spare one of them, too.' He waved what looked like a tea cosy. 'Proper wool.'

Jon shook his head. 'This stuff gets given to you?'

'Yeah. The charities, but often from people, as well. I had this one woman give me a twin pack of thermal socks. Put both pairs on straight away. Cushy as.'

The nearby sound of voices picked up. Women, laughing about something. They came into view. A group of six, chattering away, all done up for a night out. Shimmery dresses, heels, little handbags. Jon realised that, down here, you were knee height. It felt weird. He realised he'd have to lift his chin to see their faces, but he didn't want to make eye contact.

'Any spare change, ladies?' Greg called.

Neither the speed of their footsteps or the cadence of their talk altered as they passed by. It really is like being invisible, Jon thought.

'Have a nice night. Be safe,' Greg cheerfully added just as they passed from view. 'Yeah, you get some treats,' he continued. 'Then, other times, you think, really? Tins of soup. Can't even get the bastards open, let alone cook them.'

Jon realised he hadn't eaten. 'Actually, do you want some food? There's a pizza place across the way.'

Greg was rummaging in the Aldi bag. 'No need.' He produced two packs of sandwiches. 'Got ploughman's or beef and tomato. Which one?'

Jon didn't know what to say. To refuse would be plain rude. 'You choose.'

'I don't know. Two of my favourites. Go halves?'

'Sounds good to me.' Jon took a surreptitious look at the use by date as he opened the pack Greg handed him. Two days' time. That's a relief. 'You mentioned before food's not a problem.'

'No one starves on the street.'

'But it's all convenience stuff like this?'

'Mostly.'

'Like being on the job. The amount of crap we end up eating. It's terrible.'

'Sometimes, I just wish someone would hand me one of those ready-made salad things. Or a bit of nice fruit. Still,' he took a hefty bite of his sandwich, 'I'm not really complaining.'

Jon finished his first sandwich in a couple of bites. They swopped packets and, as he leaned back against the door, Greg said: 'I told him you're Wayne's brother, by the way.'

'This bloke we're waiting for?'

Greg gave a nod. 'It's easier that way. People will be more prepared to talk if they think you're his brother.'

'Rather than if I'm police,' Jon said.

Greg nodded again. 'Of course.'

Jon thought about the fact his younger brother, Dave, had also lived on the streets around Manchester for a while. Every now and again, he'd reach out to Jon, ask for cash – just a bit so he could sort his life out. Get straight. Jon got to realise it was all a ruse. Should he have refused? Just cut him off? It was something he wondered about all the time. Might that have saved him?

'It's weird. I keep expecting Wayne to walk round the corner,' Greg suddenly announced.

Jon floated a look at the other man. 'How are you finding it without him?'

'You know – there are other options.'

Really? Jon thought. Is that why you're back in this doorway on your own?

'But I got on with the lad,' Greg added. 'No more news?'

'Afraid not. I suppose you boys who've been in the army have an advantage when it comes to sleeping rough.'

Greg chewed away for a while. 'You'd think. But it often works the other way.'

Jon looked at him questioningly.

'What gets to most ex-servicemen is the loneliness,' Greg stated, his voice more serious. 'When you're in the army, you're part of a bigger thing. You might be sleeping under hedges, but you're being paid for it. And you're with your mates. Once you're homeless, it's a totally different world. A lot of ex-servicemen think they'll cope, but I reckon it's harder for us. The loneliness of it is what really hits you.'

'Was Wayne lonely?'

'Of course. We all are. I think he was scared, too. He'd lost control of his life and that's not a nice thing. Then he started using drugs.'

Jon thought about punching the shit out of the dealer the night before. That had felt good. 'What do you think happened on the fire escape?'

'I don't know. But wait for Colin. Hear what he has to say.'

It was another hour before a gaunt-faced man with a shaved head sidled into the doorway. Immediately, Jon felt his hackles rise. He had the look of a junky, for a start. And the way he'd slid round the corner. There'd been a slyness about the movement.

Avoiding Jon's eyes, he nodded at Greg.

'Colin, this is the person I mentioned. Wayne's older brother.'

Only then did his eyes shift across. 'All right?'

Jon wasn't sure whether to reach out a hand so they could shake. It didn't seem appropriate. 'Yeah. I'm called Jon.'

He sank down into a crouch, back against the wall. 'Getting colder,' he said to Greg. 'This your pad for the night?'

'No. You know where Jamie's Italian used to be? I've got a space in the porch bit there.'

The man thought about this for a second. 'Who with?'

'Baz? Him and his mate, Turbo. Maybe a couple of others.'

Jon could see Colin filing the information away. 'Top of King Street? Posh. I'm off to the Printworks after this. Prime time.'

Greg turned to Jon. 'When the pubs start to close. It's the time people are most generous.'

'Or violent,' Colin added. He looked at Jon again. 'You join the army, too? Like Wayne?'

'No.' Jon could see the other man was waiting for more. He picked the job he used to do before joining the police. 'Construction.'

The other man seemed happy with that. 'Good money in construction, hey? What are we talking about here? I thought a twenty.'

Realisation caused Jon's hopes to plummet. He's after payment. 'What did you see?' He watched the man weighing things up. You're wondering whether to insist on the money first, aren't you? Dream on.

Colin looked away for a second, still making a decision. He sniffed. 'It was about two in the morning. I was walking through Ardwick, back towards town.'

Normally, Jon would have hauled him up on that. Asked what he'd been doing there at such a strange time. But this wasn't a police interview. He stayed quiet.

'I was on the far side of the road, passing the Garter. Was just wondering whether to duck in, see if anyone was about. That's when I saw them both.'

'Both?'

'Wayne and this other guy, who was all in black. He was stood behind Wayne, whispering stuff in his ear.'

'You could hear him whispering?'

'Yeah.'

'But you just said you were on the far side of the road.'

The man wiped at the tip of his nose. 'It was the way his head was tilted towards Wayne's ear. I couldn't hear what was being said, just murmurs.'

'He was taller than Wayne, then?'

'You what?'

'You said his head was tilted. So he was a bit taller than Wayne?'

'Yeah. A bit.'

'Can you describe him?'

'He was wearing black. Couldn't see a thing.'

'Not even skin colour?'

'He had a balaclava covering his face and head.'

Balaclava, Jon thought. That's a new detail. 'OK. Carry on.'

'That went on for a bit then Wayne climbed up on the hand railing. It's like he was hypnotised. In a trance. Then he jumped.'

'The bloke in black: he didn't push him or anything?'

'No. He'd got Wayne in a spell. Didn't need to.'

Jon thought about Wayne's injuries. Most were to his spine. 'Like someone going off a diving board?'

'How do you mean?'

'Face first, arms out. That kind of jump?'

Colin hesitated. 'It was dark, yeah? But, I suppose so.'

He's bullshitting, Jon thought. 'What happened next?'

'That's when I see he's got wings. Once he's on his own up there, I could see them. It was the Dark Angel: he got Wayne like he got the rest.'

Dark Angel, Jon thought. He has a nickname now. That meant the gossip mill had really started turning. Not good. 'I heard something about wings. How big were they?'

Colin stretched his arms fully out and wafted his fingertips. 'Like this.'

You lying twat, Jon thought, suppressing a sigh. 'What he did he do once Wayne had fallen?'

'He ... he just stood there. Looking up at the sky.'

'What did you do?'

'Fucking did one, didn't I? I've got the Dark Angel a few flaps of his wings away? I was off, pal.' He cut the air with his hand. 'Gone.' He turned to Greg. 'You stay safe, bro. Stick close to Baz and his mate. Don't be sleeping anywhere on your own. This fucker is picking us off man. Serious.'

Greg nodded in agreement. 'I will.'

Colin's head turned expectantly in the direction of Jon.

He dug into his coat and removed a twenty from his wallet. 'Cheers for that.'

The money was whipped from his fingers and Colin was on his feet. 'Safe,' he said with a nod then vanished back round the corner.

Greg was blushing slightly. 'Sorry. That was a waste, wasn't it?'

Jon pretended to think for a second. 'Probably.'

'So why did you pay him?'

To not create any shit for you, Jon thought. 'If I'd refused, word would soon get round. Then no one's going to say a thing.'

Greg was looking concerned. 'Yeah – but plenty round here will be happy to spin you a yarn if they know you've got cash.'

'It's OK – I'll claim the money back. He used the words Dark Angel. Is that the name doing the rounds?'

'It is.'

'So word's spreading, then? Among rough sleepers. People are talking about this?'

'They are starting to now.'

The thought made Jon feel uncomfortable. How soon before it spread further? Before it reached a journalist ...

'Oh, I didn't mention. You know last night? Someone took that little scrote Jay by surprise. Robbed all his merchandise and left him quite badly hurt, apparently.'

Robbed all his merchandise, Jon thought as he checked his watch. No surprise Jay had claimed that. It was almost eleven. Bloody hell. 'I'd better be off. Early start tomorrow.'

'It happened pretty soon after I pointed him out to you,' Greg added, looking at Jon with one eyebrow slightly lifted.

He folded the sleeping bag off his legs and, as he climbed to his feet, thought about the previous night. After leaving Jay he'd gone in the direction of Anders Street, dropping the keys and knuckleduster into separate bins en route. New Dawn's premises looked like they'd once been a retail unit. The roller blinds had been spray-painted with the oranges and yellows of a sunrise. He'd found the hinged flap of the letter box, lifted it up and stuffed all of Jay's cash through.

Mirroring Greg's casual tone, he said, 'Well, it's a dangerous game, dealing drugs.'

Greg's mention of the drug dealer had got Jon thinking about Wayne – and the fact he still hadn't been to see him in the hospital. He altered his drive home to go via the Manchester Royal Infirmary.

His face mask made it feel like the air lacked oxygen as he made his way down the quiet, gleaming corridor to the Intensive Care Unit. The nurse on the front desk briskly informed him there was no change, that it wasn't worth him looking in, that the patient would be unresponsive.

Jon lifted his ID back off the counter. 'I'm not here to try and take a statement. I've just come off duty and I'm on the way home. The bloke was a teammate of mine; we played rugby together. I don't suppose he's had any other visitor?'

She shook her head. 'No. He hasn't had anyone.'

'Well, can I be the first?'

She sighed. 'You'll need to wear full overalls, face visor and gloves. And don't touch anything, OK?'

Wayne had been placed in a room with three other patients, all of whom had suffered head traumas. 'He's first bed on your right,' the nurse said. 'I'll be back in a few minutes.'

'Thanks. I appreciate this.' He turned and backed through the swing doors, keeping both hands raised in a surgeon's stance. Extractor fans in the ceiling kept up a low hum. Despite their presence, the room felt close and stifling. Beeps, that in isolation would have been reassuringly slow, even relaxing, combined with those from all the other machines to create something similar to an amusement arcade. One at the far end of the room one of them made a sudden chirruping sound and Jon tensed, worrying it was the precursor to an alarm going off.

Stands and trolleys beside each bed partially obscured the motionless figure which lay in each one. Jon wondered briefly how the other patients had sustained their injuries. Car crashes? Toppling ladders? Tumbles down stairs? Hopefully, nothing as sinister as what happened to you, he thought, turning to where Wayne was stretched out.

Bandages covered the top of his skull. His head was tipped back, a ventilator tube protruding from his partly open mouth. Little scraps of white material were pinned over his eyelids to keep them shut. In the dim light they reminded Jon of the coins people once placed over the eyes of those who'd passed away. Both arms were laid over the sheets. Jon spotted a few tattoos alongside several cuts and grazes as he moved closer to the bed.

His voice was muffled behind his mask and visor. 'Hi Wayne, it's Jon. Jon Spicer. Come to see how you're doing, mate.'

He glanced at the nearest monitor, searching for something among the moving lines that might indicate Wayne knew he was here. Some coma patients were aware of sounds, weren't they? He remembered stories of kids who'd come round when played messages from their idols: footballers, actors or singers.

'Sorry, pal, you just got me. We talked the other day. You were remembering that rugby match we both played in. Out near Liverpool. The one where someone tried to gouge your eyes?' He thought he detected the tiniest of tremors behind Wayne's eyelids. Might adrenaline-fuelled memories spark something? He leaned closer. 'The fat fucking Scouse bastard. I got my fingers round his neck, didn't I? Dropped him to the floor like a sack of shit. Yeah?' He checked the screen again, hoping his words may have caused the man's pulse to pick up, even by a fraction. 'Tough matches back then, hey? Get on the wrong side of a ruck and you got a proper shoeing. Studs down your back, arms and legs stamped all over. I bet you had a few of those playing prop?' The lines on the monitor continued unchanged. He looked down at Wayne's slack features. In your head is the killer's face.

He checked the swing doors were properly shut. 'Wayne, what happened to you?' he asked more loudly. 'Someone else was there when you fell, weren't they?' He extended a hand across the ruffled sheet, slipped an index finger beneath Wayne's left hand. 'Just squeeze my finger if they were. Press down, tap it, anything you can manage. Did someone throw you off that fire escape? Someone who wore black?' He waited for some kind of reaction. A flinch, however faint. 'Wayne, was it the same person you saw on the roof of the car park?'

Nothing happened.

Spicer, he said to himself, sliding his finger back out. That would have been way too fucking easy.

He stepped out of Holly's room and pulled the door almost shut. She had been fast asleep, same as Dug in his room. After brushing his teeth, he stripped to his boxer shorts in the bathroom, leaving his clothes neatly folded on the washing basket in the corner. Less noise in the bedroom when he went through.

Alice was facing away from him, curled on her side. He paused for a moment, guilt washing over him at how much he left her to cope on her own. And, a little voice in his head added, you still haven't told her what you're up to yet. Idiot.

He turned the duvet down and climbed in, doing his best not to disturb her. The bedside clock said twelve fifty-two. In just a few hours' time, the alarm would sound. Christ, he thought to himself, I'm so knackered.

CHAPTER 19

'Oi, Spicer!'

He opened his eyes with a start, not sure where he was. A hand was shaking his shoulder.

'We're here, Scouser-Land.'

He hauled himself upright and looked out the vehicle's window. To the left was a large sign. Welcome to Liverpool John Lennon Airport. Above us only sky.

Last thing he remembered, they were queuing to join the traffic crawling along the M602 over in Manchester. He checked his watch. Quarter past nine. I've been asleep for over an hour.

'You were snoring and everything,' Kieran said. 'Properly out for the count.'

Jon wiped a bit of moisture from the corner of his mouth. 'And dribbling.'

'She been keeping you up late, has she? Alicia. Likes a bit of heavy servicing, is that it?'

Jon shook his head. 'You're such a knob.'

The airport's perimeter fence was suddenly close beside them as they followed a turn-off towards the main terminal. The airport was much smaller than Manchester's. Jon thought back to when he'd last used it. A cheap flight to Barcelona with Alice, before they had kids. Two nights spent wandering from bar to cafe to bar. No worries in the world.

As far as he could remember, back then, both airports had been a similar size. Manchester's must have more than doubled, since. And now it was pitching for another expansion.

'What do you reckon they want to come over here for?' Kieran asked.

'Who knows?'

'Maybe Liverpool are trying to offer them a cheaper deal.'

'Might seem cheaper,' Jon said, 'until they factor in having all the tyres nicked off their airplanes.'

Kieran laughed. 'So, you reckon they're robbing little bastards, Scousers?'

Jon was looking around him with narrowed eyes. 'Yup.'

'You lot hate them, don't you?'

'Us lot?'

'Mancs. You all hate Scousers.'

'Can't trust them,' Jon replied. But he'd let more than a hint of sarcasm into his voice; in his opinion, the rivalry between the two cities was hyped to a ridiculous level. Unless you were a football fan, and then it was probably genuine. But he didn't follow football.

'Maybe they're fans of the Beatles,' Kieran said, nodding towards a sign bearing John Lennon's name.

'Don't get me started on that.' Jon sighed.

'On what?'

'How they try and cash in on the Beatles at every opportunity. Who else does that? Names their airport after a local famous person?'

'Doesn't Nottingham? Isn't theirs the Robin Hood airport?'

'He wasn't a singer: he robbed from the rich and gave to the poor!'

The two Jaguars were now indicating right. A security gate was starting to roll back. Beyond it was a small parking area filled with expensive cars. Kieran pulled into a restricted bay to the side of the main road. 'Isn't there a Nelson Mandela airport out in South Africa?'

'Maybe, but my point stands. He deserves it. What did John Lennon do? Sang bloody songs.'

'I quite like the Beatles,' Kieran said.

Jon nodded at the radio. 'Well, find Liverpool FM. You can be sure they'll be bloody playing them.'

His phone rang shortly before noon: Iona's name on the screen.

'Hi there.'

'Hello. Where are you?'

'Liverpool Airport, sitting in a car, waiting. You?'

'Well done on getting the green light from Weir.'

'He was just setting off home; the bloke was so desperate to get going, he would have approved of anything. So, you've been in touch with whoever you needed to?'

'Yup. But don't get excited.'

'They've got back to you?'

'Yeah – to my surprise. It was the Ministry of Defence, after all.'

'So what did they say?'

'You want the long or short version?'

'Short's good.'

'OK. All the victims had some overseas postings, but not ones where they all overlapped at the same time. There's no common denominator with countries or specific bases, either. Frank Kilby had spent the most time abroad, but he was the oldest. Compare that to Roy Jarratt, say: he had only been to Cyprus and Germany. Neither time when Frank Kilby had been posted there.'

'You're saying it's a non-starter?'

'I'll take another look after lunch, but I'm not crossing my fingers. Anyway, I'd better get back to my transcripts. When are you due back?'

'Late afternoon.'

'See you then.'

'Cheers, Iona.' As soon as he cut the call, he could feel Kieran's gaze on him.

'Sounds interesting. More on the rough sleepers?'

By the time Jon had brought him up to speed, Kieran was looking completely bemused. 'If you're ruling out the army connection, what does that leave? Just their time sleeping rough in Manchester?'

'I suppose so,' Jon replied. 'What are you thinking?'

'If they're being targeted because they're rough sleepers who served in the army, maybe you should be asking how someone found that out. Could they have declared it when signing up for benefits or applying for housing?'

Jon turned in his seat. 'You mean someone working for the council? Like an admin clerk, for instance?'

Kieran shrugged. 'Or do they put that on the forms at homeless hostels, maybe?'

'Good point,' Jon said. 'That's worth checking. I can try and find that out from my contact.'

'Who's your contact?'

'Another rough sleeper – who was also in the army. He's agreed to help.'

The gates beside them started to beep. Jon looked through the narrow metal bars as a group of people started to leave the building. He spotted her towards the rear, talking to a silver-haired man. She was wearing a black suit, the skirt coming down to just below her knees. Black heels, not too high. Her hair was tied up in an elaborate plait and he found himself wondering whether it was something she'd managed to do herself. A childhood skill? A routine so ingrained she could do it by touch alone? He imagined her sitting on her bed in her hotel room, listening to the morning news on CNN or Bloomberg or another of those American channels as her fingers worked nimbly away. Had her mum taught her?

Where did she grow up? Somewhere rural, like a farm in one of those dust bowl states? Or had she lived a city life? If her dad had been some big shot, he doubted it had been poor, wherever it was.

They were now saying their goodbyes, shaking hands and stepping back. The door to her Jaguar had been opened for her and, as she turned to the vehicle, her eyes moved across the car park. Had she spotted them? Had she seen him looking across? He couldn't tell as she ducked her head and vanished from view.

The banners that stood on either side of the plate glass doors of the Bridgewater Hall fluttered slightly. Block letters printed on the upper part of the taut nylon material spelled two words: Northern Powerhouse. Below them was, effectively, a subheading. Where do we go from here? The line at the bottom spoke of a symposium organised by the DBT Foundation.

Removing his face mask as he emerged from the building, Ed Farnham paused on the smooth flagstones; the two aides shadowing him had to alter step so they didn't bump into him. Immediately behind them was an intern with a camera slung round his neck.

'Next?' Farnham asked.

'So,' the aide on his right said. 'We're due over at the Eye Hospital in fifty minutes.'

'That's to do what?' he asked, starting to walk briskly again.

'A new piece of scanning equipment. Part-funded by the university.'

'Manchester?'

'No, Salford.'

'Ah-ha. Then?'

'Diary's clear until this evening.'

'Good.' His mind went back to the speech he'd just given to the assortment of business leaders, charity representatives and academics. They'd seemed to appreciate his positive words and upbeat attitude. As much as a crowd like that could be expected to, anyway.

'Mr Farnham? Mr Farnham?'

A split-second glance told him all he needed to know: a young man approaching from the direction of the metallic globe sculpture to his right. Not carrying anything, on his own, no one recording anything. No threat. Probably some sort of activist. The aide on that side peeled away to deal with him. Even so, Farnham wondered if he should have slightly better security for these public events; attacks on politicians were getting worryingly common.

Only a matter of time before someone decided a mayor was worth targeting, too. And what good would either of his two aides be? They could wield a fountain pen and that was it. But having proper security would detract from his brand. He portrayed himself as a man of the people, bred and raised in the region, not some Westminster would-be. A down-to-earth type, sticking up for the city, not seduced by the allure of London.

He didn't bother slowing down. Clive could deflect the person and then catch them up. He'd got another ten steps before the person started calling his name again. Fuck's sake, Clive, he thought. Take the man's sodding email address and send him on his way.

'It's about your daughter, Liv!'

Farnham's step slowed. Liv. Not Olivia. She only let people who knew her use that version of her name. He glanced back. Clive was trying to prevent the man from getting any closer. The pair of them were crabbing sideways towards a shallow flight of steps that led down to a water feature.

Ed Farnham's eyes swept the immediate area again. A few members of the public were in the vicinity. A tram was approaching from the direction of the Central Library. There was an office block close by with windows overlooking them.

The man called out once more. 'Have you heard from her in the past few days?'

Jesus. Of course I haven't. As far as he could tell, the man really was on his own. It didn't seem like an incident engineered to embarrass him; a photographer hiding somewhere close, ready to start snapping away. He turned round properly. 'Clive, it's OK.'

The aide lowered his arms and stepped aside. Farnham got a better look at the person. Early twenties, straggly hair. Stubble. A fluorescent workman's jacket which, nowadays, was as much of a fashion statement as a requirement of any building site. Baggy combat trousers and heavy-looking boots. He hoped the person wasn't a boyfriend, but suspected he probably was.

'What's this about?' he said, careful to keep his voice low and professionally detached.

'Your daughter, Liv?' He pointed briefly at his chest. 'I'm Ben? I think she may have mentioned ...'

Farnham gave a little shake of his head. Of course he remembered the name, but he wasn't going to reveal that. 'Sorry.'

The man looked momentarily hurt and Farnham knew he had control of this. 'How can I help you, Ben?'

'Me and Liv, we've been together. Sharing a place together—'

He raised a hand. The tram was almost alongside. This encounter needed to be somewhere more private. 'Let's head down here a minute.' He descended the fight of steps at a trot. The expanse of water had a fountain in its middle. Pattering droplets, which was good. Harder for anyone to overhear. At the bottom of the steps was a boarded-up bar. Usual signs of the doorway being used by a homeless person: food wrappers and flattened cardboard. Was there any disused doorway in the city centre that didn't have stuff like that clogging it up?

He turned round, keeping his voice very quiet. 'Carry on, please.'

The man looked back up the steps, clocked the two aides waiting at the top with tight expressions on their faces. 'Er ... OK ... we've been seeing each other for the last year or so,' he whispered. 'She hasn't said anything ...?'

Ed shook his head. 'Ben, you'll have gathered she has issues with me. There hasn't been any contact.'

Ben broke eye contact to look at the ground. 'Right. I wasn't sure if she was telling the truth when she said she wasn't speaking to you. She really isn't.'

'She really isn't.'

'Well, me and Liv.' He now glanced skyward. 'Shit, this is awkward. She ... she got pregnant.'

Ed felt his heart thud a couple of times. Oh Christ.

'She said she wanted it. We both wanted it. But she found it difficult, the pregnancy. I think, basically, she got depressed. Then, once she had the baby, she definitely was.'

'She's had a baby?'

He nodded.

'When?'

'Almost three weeks ago.'

Despite the thoughts whirring in Farnham's head, his face was almost serene. 'I see.' This person before me now counts as family. How much of a liability is that? He looks like some sort of vegan eco-warrior. Not good. He'd said something about depression. More negative potential. 'How depressed?'

'Pretty bad. Sorry. But she couldn't see it. And nothing I said would make her—'

'Hang on. You asked just now if I'd seen her?'

'She cleared out of the place we shared last week.'

'What do you mean, cleared out?'

'She left. I came back one evening from work—'

'You work?'

'I do.'

'Who for?'

'The Seventh Day? The shop on Oxford—'

'I know it. You were saying?'

'She'd gone. Her and the baby. That's why I was asking if you ... I thought she might have gone back to—'

'Where else do you think she might be? You've rung all her friends?'

'No one's heard from her. I've been asking all over. Someone – he works on the market stalls in the Arndale – saw her walking by two days ago. She was carrying a sleeping bag.'

Ed had to shove his hands in his pockets. The temptation to make a fist and punch the bloke was overwhelming. 'What's your surname, Ben?'

'Whitehall.'

'And you're saying you think my daughter and this baby—'

'Amy. We called her Amy.'

'You're saying they're somewhere here in Manchester, sleeping rough?'

'I don't know. I mean, I suppose that, if she was carrying ...'

Ed set off up the steps, leaving the man's words to wither on his lips.

CHAPTER 20

Gavin sat cross-legged on the carpet staring at his copy of *Ascent of the Blessed*. He couldn't remember exactly when, in the dark fog of despair following his wife's and daughter's deaths, he'd come across the old painting. Initially, it had probably been glimpsed on a screen. Perhaps a TV programme aired in the early hours of the morning. At some point, anyway, during those long hours he'd spent stretched out on the sofa, hardly able to summon the will to get up and use the toilet.

He'd now come to believe the image had actually found him. Slipped inside his skull, uninvited.

For a while, it had lurked at the back of his mind, content to wait. Then, slowly, shyly, it had started to announce itself. Allowing him, to begin with, infuriatingly brief glimpses. He couldn't understand why he'd started seeing a radiant tunnel. Then he noticed the naked human figure floating down it, gently steered through the air by a winged presence. He wondered if either figure was him.

Over subsequent days, more of the scene revealed itself. Two other forms, these ones faint and shimmering, drenched in brilliant light at the tunnel's far end. He sensed with ever-increasing certainty, that they were his wife and daughter. They weren't dead! They had just moved to a different existence and were waiting for him at its threshold.

He started to discern more. Other figures floating up from the darkness beneath the bright tunnel. Winged beings lifting other naked humans towards the light. He started to suspect it was a cracked and ancient canvas that his mind's eye was seeing. Something from centuries ago. Internet searches for paintings that involved heaven and paradise and angels revealed hundreds of works of art. But not the one he wanted. Was it just something his dreams had conjured, after all?

Finally, out of sheer frustration, he'd gone in the opposite direction; searched for paintings of hell and demons and torment. The work of Hieronymus Bosch filled his computer's screen. Nightmare imaginings of torture and torment. Hordes of people being gouged and pierced and sliced. Shovelled into burning pits by grotesque demons. It was the peoples' nudity that let him know he was getting closer. Scrolling through everything the painter had ever created, he finally found the image from his dreams. Its purity sang out from the surrounding scenes of suffering and the hope it gave him was like a beam from a lighthouse shearing through the storm.

Lifting his eyes from the image, he gazed at the shrine to his wife and daughter. The collection of picture frames was on a small table that he'd draped in a red sheet. They were arranged in a semi-circle around a single candle. Its flame didn't waver. In front of it were a few precious objects: the engagement ring he'd bought Claire. Her favourite pendant. The wind-up mechanism from the first mobile that they'd hung above Sophie's cot. Sometimes, he'd twist the key at the back and let the tinkle of its tune soothe him. Beside it was a small block of resin that carried an imprint of Sophie's foot at one week old. So tiny.

He studied the photographs lit by the candle's warm glow. Claire up on Kinder Scout, strands of her hair flying in the breeze, Kinder Reservoir like a shard of glass in the distant valley below. Claire and Sophie on a picnic blanket on the grass beside the river at Chatsworth House. Sophie too young to sit up on her own, nappy bulging out beneath her leggings. Sophie again, this time in the local playground. She was sitting in a bucket seat, at that moment of stillness when the swing has stopped travelling upwards but wasn't yet falling back. Her mouth forever open in delight.

As usual, he shut his eyes in the hope that, by cutting himself off from the image, the sound of her laughter wouldn't stop. It echoed for a while in his skull. He let his head hang forward, thoughts drifting to the second-hand camper van he'd bought. The bastard, bastard camper van. The wreck on wheels he thought he could repair. Make good.

He thought he had succeeded. He thought he'd saved them so much money by doing it himself. He thought everything was fine.

A growl of anguish escaped his lips. Kicking a leg out straight, he hammered his heel against the floor. He did the same with his other foot. Anything to stop the thoughts building momentum. A shuddering great sigh leaked from his mouth and, a moment later, the candle flame shrank to the side before slowly righting itself.

He got to his feet and walked towards the bathroom. After a shower it would be time to set off for work. At the calendar on the cupboard door, he paused and did a quick count. Three more days to go. As if he didn't know. He lifted a finger and was tracing it across the grid of days when his phone began to ring. His charity helpline phone. Someone needing to talk? He wasn't sure if he could face it. Not right now.

But rather than a number, there was a name. James P. What did that arsehole want now? He nearly let it go through to answerphone, then changed his mind. 'Hello, James.'

'Ah, Gavin. Hi. What are you up to?'

'About to set off for work.'

'Yes, I thought you might be. Any chance you can swing by our offices? Just briefly.'

'Well, my shift starts at six thirty.'

'I won't keep you, Gavin.'

'This isn't something we can talk about over the phone?'

'I'd prefer not to.'

He didn't like the ominous tone. 'It's important, then?'

'I'll see you here, if that's OK.'

He was on the landing, turning back on himself to start down the next flight of stairs, when Miriam's door opened. 'Gavin! I thought I heard your footsteps.'

He glanced back. There she was, only half of her showing. He thought she must have been waiting behind her door to get it open that fast. 'Yes?'

Her face flinched.

'Sorry,' he gestured to the flight of stairs leading down. 'I'm in a rush. What was it?'

Tentatively, she pointed upward. 'You were banging earlier. On my ceiling.'

He remembered his heels hammering against the floor. 'Oh, yes. I was moving some bits and pieces.'

'I thought you might have wanted something.' Her door opened a little wider and the rest of her was revealed. She was cradling a stuffed cat in the crook of her other arm. Wanting to show it off.

'No.' He moved closer to the top step, anxious to be on his way. 'Everything is fine.'

'My little lovelies, they all turned their big eyes up. Thought the sky was falling in, didn't you?' She reached across and stroked the fake fur.

Jesus, the woman was puddled. 'Sorry.'

'But you would, wouldn't you?'

He stopped again and turned his head. Now there was a coy expression on her face. 'I would ... what?'

'Ask me, if you wanted anything. Seeing as we're neighbours. Sort of.' She risked a smile.

'Of course, Miriam. Now, I'm in a real hurry. See you soon!' He started trotting down the stairs before she could say anything else.

He was told James was waiting for him in one of the side meeting rooms. There was a single manila folder on the table. 'Take a seat, Gavin,' he said with a hint of sombreness in his voice.

As soon as he started easing himself into the other chair, Gavin got up, skirted round the table and pulled the door closed.

Gavin half-turned his head. 'What's going on?'

James reappeared in his field of vision. 'Erm,' he said, retaking his seat. 'How are you today?'

'Fine. Thanks.' The other man was looking tense. Gavin interlinked his fingers and rested them on his lap. He waited.

James retook his seat. He nodded at Gavin's orange tabard. 'Ready to start work, then?'

'Yup.'

'Still at the cinema on the Upper Brook Street?'

Gavin was about to say no. He was about to tell Pearson he'd been transferred across to the Town Hall site. Had been months ago. But something caused him to just nod. Pearson knew enough about him already. Now the nosey bastard knew one thing less.

'Still enjoying those night shifts?'

'I am. What's in the folder?'

He glanced down at it. 'The other day, we were discussing you taking some time off? I mentioned the fact we have a couple more volunteers—'

'I remember. I said I was keen to continue.'

'Yes, you did. It was after our meeting, when I was going over everyone's phone records to calculate costs.

That's when I noticed some activity on the number registered to you.'

Calculating costs. That was a lie. He'd been snooping. 'Activity?'

James looked up. 'There were quite a few outbound calls that you'd made. Often in the early hours of the morning. Some of them were to numbers that had originally called your phone.'

Oh no, Gavin thought. All the trouble I went to gathering their phones in. He saw himself prising open cases, snapping SIM cards in two, tossing handsets into bins. All for nothing. Because I didn't think it through carefully enough. I didn't think of the phone I'd used.

'Gavin, when you started volunteering for this organisation, you signed a code of conduct. You remember?'

'I suppose so.'

'So you recall the key principle about not ringing people who call us for help? How we're a reactive, not a proactive, service — a non-judgemental listening ear, if you will. I presume that's what you've been doing, calling people back?'

Gavin's mind was racing. Of course the phone's records would be available to James, if he wanted to trawl through them. I should have only rung those numbers with my own phone, not the charity's. Stupid bloody idiot! 'Well, we're also meant to signpost to other services, if they're appropriate. Aren't we?'

'Correct — during the call. Not ringing the person back to do it.'

He tried another tack. 'Isn't there something in the code of conduct about breaking that guidance if you think there's a risk to life?'

'If there's an imminent risk to life, yes. Essentially, if someone rings you saying they're about to commit suicide and then hangs up. And in those instances, you're required to complete a contact report detailing your actions. I haven't been able to find any. Were any completed?'

'No.'

'Besides that, you'd received no calls immediately before making your own to those numbers. In fact, there was a gap of over twenty-four hours in two cases.'

Shit, he's really gone through everything carefully. 'I wanted to check how they were doing. That was all.'

James nodded sadly. 'Which is understandable; but not what we do. I'm being honest here, Gavin: I think you've become a little too involved with your work here. It happens. People think that, if they do just a little bit more, they can put things right. But work of this nature will keep taking that little bit more, until you've got nothing else to give. And then no one benefits.'

This all felt pre-prepared. A speech, worked out in advance. 'What are you trying to say?'

'What I suggested the other day: that you take a rest, Gavin. Step back, have a breather. That's all.'

He wanted to explain that there were only three days left before he joined Claire and Sophie. That he needed the phone if he was going to help more to ascend before that time. How else would they get in touch and tell him they were at the end of the road? That they wanted help finding a way out?

'Gavin?'

He realised James was staring at him.

'I asked, when's the last time you saw your doctor?'

'My doctor? I ... I don't know.' The prospect of no one being able to call him, in their darkest hour, needing help. Asking for help.

'Gavin?'

He focused on the other man once more. 'What?'

'Are you on any sort of medication at the moment?'

'Why do you ask that?'

'You seem to me ... fatigued. Perhaps you're doing too much.'

'I need to keep busy. I told you that. And now you're going to stop me from being busy.'

'But why are you keeping busy? Is it to prevent you thinking about what happened to your wife and daughter?'

He looked away. My wife and daughter. It wasn't right him even being allowed to mention them.

'Please listen, Gavin. This isn't permanent. I know you find this work of value – and I find all your effort of value, too. But I don't want you risking your health. You're no good to the people who call us if you're ill. So, if you can give me your phone, I'll allocate it to one of the new volunteers while you take some time out, OK?'

He wanted to shout that it wasn't OK. Not at all. There were so many lost souls out there who needed his help. 'There's no need for this. Honestly, James—'

'Your phone, Gavin.' He held his hand out, palm up.

'How about I do just a few more days? To mentally prepare myself for the time off?'

'That's not a good idea. I can't agree to that.' There was now a firm note in his voice.

Superior rank. Probably like how he used to address grunts like him when he was an army officer. Gavin shook his head. 'You don't realise.'

'Sorry?'

'Nothing.'

'I don't realise what?'

He took a breath in. 'I need this work, OK?'

'This is a way to ensure you can carry on with it. In the future.'

'The future?' He couldn't stop the snort of derision.

James leaned forward. 'What's wrong?'

'Nothing.'

'Something about the future?'

'It doesn't matter.'

James said nothing for a few moments. 'I presume you have the handset with you?'

'Yes, I have it.' He took it from his jacket. For a moment, he considered throwing it against the wall or window. Or at James' face. He weighed it in his hand. Would do some damage to a face.

'Thank you, Gavin. It's appreciated.'

Rather than place it in the outstretched hand, Gavin put it on the table and got to his feet. 'Goodbye, James.'

'I'll call you next week, about when—'

'I said, goodbye.'

'Gavin? Wait a second. I'll call you. Next Friday?'

He kept his back turned. 'Don't call me.'

'Pardon?'

'Don't call me.' He stepped out of the room, gently closing the door behind him.

CHAPTER 21

'You seriously have no idea why he might want to see you?' Kieran asked as they pulled to a stop behind the industrial unit that was their office.

The call from DCI Weir had come as they were returning from Liverpool to Manchester. Report to my office as soon as you're back at base. The sort of terse request that usually presaged something bad.

Jon rummaged in his mind. The only recent thing was the incident with the drug dealer, but there'd been no witnesses – and the scummy little shit certainly would never say a thing. 'No, I haven't. I hope it doesn't take too long, though – I need to be back for parents' evening at Holly's school.'

Kieran unclipped his seat belt. 'Perhaps he's called you in because you're being promoted.' He spotted the look on Jon's face and stifled his chuckle. 'Sorry, mate, couldn't resist it. Listen, I'm sure it'll be fine.'

They were halfway across the car park before he spoke again. 'Or maybe that American bint has filed a complaint because you haven't knocked on her hotel room door yet.'

'Kieran? Shut the fuck up.'

Iona was nonplussed, too. The work she'd put in on the homeless deaths had, as Jon had instructed, been squeezed in around her official tasks. The requests she'd made to the Ministry of Defence had been met cordially and efficiently.

'Well,' Jon sighed, 'I'd better see what it's about.'

His feet felt heavy as he climbed the stairs. All my working life, he thought, it's felt the same. The headmaster wants to see you, Jon. Not far off fifty and I'm still getting that schoolboy feeling in the pit of my stomach. Sad.

He gave two knocks on the smooth wood of Weir's door.

'Come in!'

'Sir,' he said, stepping inside, trying to keep his voice upbeat. Even optimistic. 'You wanted to see me?'

Weir waved at the chair. 'What the fuck have you been up to, DC Spicer?'

Bollocks, he thought, sitting down. The bloke is fuming. 'Today?'

'No, not today. Two nights ago, on Oldham Street.'

Jon immediately knew he'd been wrong. It could only be about the drug dealer thing. How the hell had Weir found out? He frowned. 'Oldham Street?'

Weir's jaw clenched. He held up a hand. 'Don't. I really haven't time for stupid fucking games.' He tossed half a dozen CCTV stills across.

Jon glanced down. It was him. He was emerging from a dark and narrow street. In another he was at the kerb, looking off to the side. He remembered standing there, waiting for the cab to go past before crossing over Oldham Street. Now he was lifting the hood of his top up. Fucking cameras: they were everywhere.

But how had Weir got hold of these precise images?

'A couple of uniforms were checking a parking lot just off Oldham Street,' Weir said, seemingly aware of what was going through Jon's mind. 'Recently, several vehicles have been broken into, in that exact area. So they'd stepped up their presence. They come across a badly injured individual making his way out of the parking lot, heading towards Ancoats. They realise this person is a known peddler of drugs. He's obviously been the victim of a very recent assault, though not keen on discussing it. Which rouses their curiosity. So, once back at their desks, one of them takes a peek at the footage from the nearest CCTV cameras. Lo and behold, who did they find?'

One of the uniforms must have recognised him and passed it onto his senior officer, who would have passed it onto his boss, who'd quietly passed it to Weir. Jon sat back and crossed his legs. This would be interesting. He knew that Weir knew that he'd done it. But, so far, he wasn't treating this formally. And nothing could be proved. Not without the drug-dealer's involvement. They were in a stalemate.

'I'm not getting into a question-and-answer thing,' Weir announced. 'Because I know you'll just play dumb. Or lie. It's part of the homeless thing you've been looking into, is what I'm guessing. Who the fuck cares. But tell me this, how much time have you been spending on it?'

'On what?'

'Wandering around that part of the city. Approaching the dregs of humanity who congregate there.'

Dregs of humanity? Jon suppressed the urge to challenge his senior officer over his choice of words. 'A few evenings.'

'And what's it involved, exactly?'

'Just asking questions. Trying to find out if anything's behind the deaths we discussed.'

'So you still think there is something going on?'

'I'm not certain. But the homeless community is, sir. They've even got a name for the person they think's doing the killing.'

'A name?'

'The Dark Angel.'

'Fuck.' Weir's eyes drifted to the side.

Now it was Jon's turn to guess what was going through the other man's mind. It didn't take much. Weir would be conjecturing on how soon word about the killer was likely to spread beyond the homeless community. Just like he'd done.

He'd also be weighing up the probability of the problem actually being real. And what it would mean if he'd failed to take action when given the opportunity. Jon almost smiled. The joys of being a senior rank.

Weir turned his gaze back on him. 'Iona Khan informs me that there's nothing to connect all the victims while they were serving in the army.'

'So I gather.'

Weir's voice was softer now. 'And you've not found anything that links them, either?'

'Not so far. Other than that they all were in the army.'

'What about this character?' Weir pointed to the sheets. 'How does he fit in?'

Jon stared back.

'Sorry.' The sarcasm was heavy in Weir's voice. 'Hypothetically speaking, how might this character fit in?'

Jon shrugged. 'I don't know.'

'Listen, Spicer. We both know there'll be no comeback from this assault. It's in none of our interests, frankly. But we also both know it was you. I might not take official action but, trust me, stonewall me on this and your career in the CTU will go nowhere while I have any say in the matter. What happened?'

Jon shook his head. 'As I said, sir, I don't—'

'I'm offering you the chance to speak honestly, here, DC Spicer. Off the record and without any comeback.'

Yeah, right, Jon thought. You're just working out if you need to cover your arse. And once you've done that, you'll have no hesitation hanging me out to dry if it's to your advantage. 'As I said, sir, no idea.'

Weir's lips curled. 'That's your position is it?'

Jon nodded. 'It is. I honestly don't know what happened to him.'

Contempt made Weir's voice thick. 'Everything I was warned about you – it's all true, isn't it? You think you know best. So you do what you like, and,' he tapped the CCTV images, 'when it goes wrong, you start to lie.'

Jon stayed quiet. No point in replying to that.

'Piss off home, DI Spicer. The sight of you in my office – in this building – is making me want to vomit. Go on, get the hell out of here.'

Alice placed her elbows on the kitchen table, raised both hands and burrowed her fingers into her hair. She spoke from behind the backs of her hands. 'Does that mean you're sacked? Has he sacked you?'

Jon ran the tip of his thumb across the handle of his mug. 'I don't think so. Not yet, anyway.'

'But what did he mean? "Get the hell out of here." What does that mean? Go home and don't ever come back?'

From beyond the closed kitchen door came the sound of the telly. Duggy and Holly were through there, along with Amanda, Alice's mum, who'd come round to babysit while they were at parents' evening. Not that Amanda will be listening to whatever programme is on, Jon thought. She'll have her ear turned to the door, relishing the fact something is wrong. More proof for the sour-faced cow that her daughter made a disastrous decision, marrying me.

'I'll head back in tomorrow morning and find out,' he said. 'But there are two reasons he can't just boot me out.'

She said nothing.

'If there is someone out there killing ex-servicemen and he shut me down, his career will never recover. And all he's got is some stills of me in the vicinity of an incident. Proves nothing.'

She lowered her hands. 'Why Jon? Why did you do it?'

'What?' He met her eyes. 'Filled in a nasty little scrote who preys on people who are in the depths of despair?'

'No. Why do you get involved in these things?'

He'd asked himself the same question plenty of times while driving home. In fact, he'd been asking himself that question for years. Even as Senior had asked him if he could help out, he knew it was a bad idea. And still he'd said yes. Was he missing a bit of his brain? Some kind of switch with a label that read 'sensible'?

Alice sighed. 'Is it some pathological need to prove you're a good person? That you're ready to help out? That you're ... oh, forget it. I don't think you have a clue. It's like a compulsion. You know what really pisses me off?'

Jon stared down at his tea. I knew this was coming.

'It's the fact that you didn't tell me. You promised to tell me and ... you didn't. Those evenings you said you were working late. That's what I hate, Jon – the fact you bloody lied. Again.'

He pursed his lips. Of course, she had homed straight in on the crucial thing. 'I was going to, Alice. Honestly, I was. I should have said straight away. I don't know why I kept quiet. I wish I—'

'Because you knew I would have said to not be so such a bloody idiot. To stop trying to be some ... I don't know ... saviour? The person who rides in, wanting to put everything right, but does the opposite. What happens if you're out? You've already told me you can't do anything other than this job. Oh, Jon.'

He looked up. She was close to tears, staring at him in despair. He hated to see her like this. 'Alice, it's not that bad. I've got another boss who now thinks I'm a tool. Nothing new there. I'm used to that.'

'Tell me about it.' She gave a sniff.

Tentatively, he reached out, praying she'd take his hand. 'I know. I'm a fucking idiot. I know.'

She looked down at his fingers. Then, with a little shake of her head, she placed a hand over his. 'You got that right. Fucking idiot.'

Relief mixed in with his embarrassment and regret. 'Maybe he'll sleep on it and feel a bit differently tomorrow.'

She lifted her other hand and used the tip of her little finger to wipe at the corners of her eyes. 'Yeah. And maybe we'll win the lottery and move to the Seychelles, you massive dickhead. Come on, we need to be at Holly's school.'

As they both stood, he leaned across the table and whispered, 'What are the odds your mum is just outside the door?'

'High,' Alice muttered.

Amanda was hovering in the doorway of the living room. 'Oh, I was just coming to find you. You need to be going ...'

Jon watched the woman's eyes roving across her daughter's face. She'd have clocked Alice had been crying. And now the need to know why would be like a swarm of ants beneath her clothes. He gave her the sweetest of smiles. 'Thank you, Amanda. We won't be long.'

'Mr and Mrs Spicer?' The staff member's voice rang out across the school hall. 'You may proceed to classroom two.'

Jon contemplated how the hell he was going to get to his feet. He and Alice were sitting on a little bench. The things had been arranged in widely spaced rows across the wooden floor. He glanced about: several parents perched on their own little benches were watching. Some even had faint smiles on their faces.

'Sorry: no dignified way for me to do this,' he announced, sliding forward and placing one knee on the floor. He then planted a hand on the bench and, with a groan, hauled himself to his feet. 'Ta da!'

'Should have been a ballerina,' Alice observed, the grey tray that held Holly's schoolbooks in her hands.

One of the other dads gave a little clap. 'Can you give me a pull up when it's my turn?'

Following the red markers taped to the floor, they headed down the left-hand side of a corridor to classroom two. A bottle of hand sanitiser was mounted on the wall beside it.

Alice passed him the tray of their daughter's books as she floated him a look.

'Really? Jon muttered. 'Again?'

She was already rubbing gel into her palms. 'Again.'

They made their way into the classroom where Jon almost groaned again. Two plastic chairs designed for people no bigger than munchkins were positioned opposite the teacher's desk. Here we go again.

Miss Jennings looked like she'd had a long day. Which, seeing as it was almost seven in the evening, was to be expected. She was taking a few hurried sips from a thermos mug as they approached.

'Is this the contortionists' class?' Jon asked, gesturing at the chairs with a smile.

She looked bewildered for a moment, then both embarrassed and amused. 'Not the biggest in the world, are they?'

Jon imagined he was readying himself for a set of squats. As his behind made contact with the seat, he hoped the thing wouldn't buckle. Once settled in, he looked about. My knees, he thought, are almost level with my ears.

'Well,' Miss Jennings said. 'Have you had a chance to look through some of Holly's books?'

Alice immediately responded. 'She seems to be getting lots of ticks for her written work.'

The teacher nodded. 'I think that's what she enjoys most. And she has such a lot to say about whatever we're looking at. All the work on ancient Rome particularly fascinated her. She has great spelling and a very good vocabulary. She reads a lot at home, I take it?'

'Always,' Alice replied.

'That's good to hear.' The teacher ran her finger across the print out before her. 'Maths, she hasn't scored quite so highly in – though well within her targets.'

Alice produced the relevant workbooks from their daughter's tray. 'I noticed she's struggling with fractions.'

'We'll be revisiting that topic; most of them find it hard at first.' She cupped her hands together. 'She's a pleasure to have in the class. Always kind and considerate. Anything you wanted to ask me?'

Alice shifted. 'We spoke recently about her moods at home. How she's a bit more distant with both of us. Staying in her room as much as she can. You don't notice anything ... negative in class?'

Miss Jennings looked down at her printout once more, as if a response might be there among the numbers. 'No. I mean, she's getting to that age when they start showing some independence. It's not unusual for you – as parents – to sense that distance and be concerned.'

Jon smiled to himself. Parental advice off someone in her early twenties, at most. Someone whose own kids were probably a hazy plan, somewhere far off in the future.

'But with her peers, she's fine,' Miss Jennings added. 'She's popular. I don't see her isolating herself or getting into disagreements.'

Jon nodded. That was nice to hear. He placed his hands on his knees, readying himself to stand. Beside him, Alice turned the page of Holly's exercise book. 'This method you're using for long division: it's so different from the way I learned.'

As the teacher started to reply, Jon reached over and took the uppermost book from Holly's tray. The page he opened it on revealed a very striking picture. It was of a volcano erupting. Streaks of fire filled the blackened sky. His eye was drawn to the impressive detail in the foreground. People fleeing the scene, mouths howling in anguish. Possessions littering the roadside. He felt himself frown. Was that an infant, lying abandoned? He looked up. 'You've covered Pompeii, then?'

Miss Jennings broke off from replying to Alice and glanced at the image. 'We have. They do seem to enjoy the more dramatic elements of what happened.'

As the discussion about long division resumed, Jon examined the picture more carefully. Some of the people, he thought, are wearing modern-day clothes. That one has a phone in her hand. I'm pretty sure that's the back of a car poking out of the ditch. And there, in the field beyond: surely that's an electricity pylon?

He realised the room was silent; Miss Jennings was now smiling at him. Their five minutes were finished and she still had loads more parents to see. He closed the book and passed it back to Alice. Now wasn't the time to mention the picture depicted a modern-day apocalypse, not an ancient one.

CHAPTER 22

Gavin slowly made his way along the deserted corridor. Renovation work in this area was still at the preparation stage. He pushed through the double doors of the Great Hall. The chandeliers had been lowered from the vaulted ceiling and their ornate metal frames were now lined up in the centre of the vast floor. Orange and white barriers had been arranged round each one. He paused to look at the fretwork that curled and twisted above each empty light fitting, all of it converging on a wide circular band. They looked like the abandoned crowns once worn by a race of giants. Some lost time of history celebrated in this cavernous and dusty room.

The murals along each side wall had been made ghostlike by films of semi-opaque paper. Beneath the protective layers, phantom figures sat astride watery horses that were trailed by the shadows of dogs and children. Dots for eyes, suggestions of open mouths.

The meeting with James Pearson had left him in a daze. The feeling carried a faint reminder of when he'd first been told about Claire and Sophie. That sense of the world lurching uncontrollably beneath your feet. Knowing things had been torn beyond repair.

He trudged across to the far corner and began to peel back a section of the padded sheeting that was protecting the end wall. Behind it was a small door. It was built into the wall's wooden panelling and, as a result, was almost invisible. But he knew it was there. And he knew where the catch was to get it open.

The steep stairs beyond were unlit. He removed a torch from his pocket and turned it on as the door closed behind him. He directed the beam upward. The steps took him to the cavity above the Great Hall's ceiling. He loved places like this. Secret areas. Vast wooden beams stretched across the floor area. In the gaps between them were unvarnished planks covered in a layer of fine dust. Above him were the arched support struts of the roof itself, then the slate tiles of the roof. It was colder up here, like in most attics. The sounds of the city leaked in. Muffled two-tone beep of a van reversing. The faint screech of a tram's wheels scouring the rails.

He followed a well-trodden line of his earlier footprints to a point on the far side. Here, the regular symmetry of the timbers was marred by a foreign object hanging from one of them. Rather than smooth linear curves, it was bobbly and misshapen. Almost alien in design. A closer look had revealed a surface that was as flaky as papier mâché. When he'd first realised he was looking at an abandoned wasps' nest, he'd gawped in wonder. The thing was enormous. So strange to think it had been painstakingly constructed by a hoard of flying insects. The swirling patterns that ran across its dry surface a result the result of countless tiny regurgitations of wood pulp, each little drip deposited there by a wasp before being smoothed carefully into place by the insect's mandibles.

A section near the mid-part of it had been damaged; something had gouged out a large chunk. This was the part of the structure that fascinated him the most. It was a glimpse into the colony's inner workings, like an illustrated cross-section from a book. He shone the torch in. A honeycomb of hexagonal cells. Rows and rows and rows of them separated by winding corridors. A use of space as efficient as any warehouse or factory. He gazed in, imagining the adult wasps that would have crawled along the interconnecting corridors, attending to the hundreds of larvae that were gradually taking shape in the cells.

When he'd first found the nest, the missing section had been lying on the floor directly beneath it. He wondered if it had been ripped away by the person who'd wielded the canister of gas that must have been used to kill off the insects. There was no doubt they'd been slaughtered; he'd spotted the corpses of adult wasps among the debris on the floor. And, looking closer, he'd also found dead larvae. Nothing more than dried out little white pellets.

He reached a hand into the ragged crater and, using the nail of his forefinger, prised open the papery cap of an undamaged cell. Snuggled inside lay the tiny corpse of a baby wasp, its wings, legs and eyes yet to form. So delicate. So vulnerable. The sight always made him think of his wife and daughter. How they'd both suffocated in their sleep. The pair of them side by side in the fold-down bed of the mobile home. He imagined their sleeping faces. His wife's arm, draped over Sophie's little form. Hugging her close.

He used the tip of his finger and thumb to lift the little body clear of its resting place. He held it before his face, moving his hand fractionally to the side so it was lit by a thin spike of light lancing down from the roof above. My Sophie. You were so perfect, so full of potential. He swivelled his wrist to make the corpse rotate. You never got to grow your wings, to spread them and fly. He replaced the brittle husk before wiping the tears from his eyes.

He tried to imagine how many cells were contained in the bulbous structure. It was the size of a small beanbag. The endless rows, forming layer after layer. Thousands. Tens of thousands. More than the number of rooms in any tower block. An immense catacomb. A city of dead insects.

Somewhere nearby, a lorry's horn blared. His attention went to the sound, as it bounced around the canyon-like street below. The echo allowed him to picture the sheer variety of buildings that rose up from the ground to form the city centre. The office blocks, shopping centres, theatres, banks, hotels, pubs and restaurants. The library, art galleries and cathedral. The car parks, warehouses and mills. And, suddenly, he knew there was still hope. Still a way to help people.

How could he not have thought of this? They didn't need to phone him; he would find them. He knew the type of place they sought out when needing to end it all. The quiet bridges and silent rooftops. The darkest corners of the city. The places that others avoided. He would come to them in their hour of need, just like he'd been doing. Yes. He would be there for them. He would be there. When they needed him, he would be there. Yes.

CHAPTER 23

The main room felt subdued. No one's looking at you, Jon said to himself, as he approached his desk. That's promising, surely? But the feeling of being a trespasser wouldn't leave him.

A detective coughed lightly as Jon passed. Another took a sip of tea, eyes idly drifting in Jon's direction. Neither seemed shocked to see him there.

See, Jon thought. Weir was just mouthing off last night. He wasn't serious about kicking me out. Jon began to relax a bit, nodded a good morning to another colleague and stepped into the aisle that led to his desk.

To his right, the office manager was hanging up his phone. He spotted Jon and clicked his fingers. 'You're wanted upstairs. Weir's office.'

Jon changed course so he didn't need to lift his voice. 'What's he want?'

'Not sure. I gather he's in there with a couple of others.'

Shit, Jon thought. 'Now?'

The office manager nodded.

'Who are they?'

'Best you head up, mate. Said I'd send you up soon as you appeared.'

'Tell him I'm on my way.' Jon continued to his desk, wondering if it was worth even taking off his jacket. He might be back in two minutes, collecting it on his way out. Iona was there, anxiety clouding her face.

'You heard that?' he muttered.

'Yes.'

He found himself checking the display of his desk phone for any messages. He wanted to turn his computer on, take a seat, do what he'd normally do. Instead, he draped his jacket over the back of the chair. 'I'd better go.'

'Good luck,' Iona whispered.

When he reached the top-floor corridor, the first thing he saw was Weir standing outside his office.

'DC Spicer,' he glanced at his watch. 'You're late.'

Jon wanted to say he wasn't sure if he was even meant to show up for work.

'Come on, DCI Pinner's expecting us.'

Pinner, thought Jon. The other manager of their section of the CTU. It was serious. You didn't get to sit with the two of them if it wasn't. Weir had already walked ahead of him. He was knocking on the door three further along and pushing it open. 'He's here.'

Jon heard Pinner's voice from inside. 'OK. This is the person we mentioned.'

We? Jon frowned. Who else is in there? Someone from human resources? An arsehole who knew what protocols to follow when someone needed to be jettisoned.

Weir stepped back from the doorway and held his hand out. 'After you.'

Waving me to my execution, Jon thought, stepping past him without a word.

Pinner was over on a soft chair beside his desk. The man sitting next to him was turning round. Farnham, Jon thought. That's Ed Farnham. The bloody mayor of Manchester. Why the hell did he need to be here?

'Take a seat, Jon,' Pinner announced softly, in a businesslike way.

First name? Now feeling totally confused, Jon chose the seat furthest from the two men. The door clicked shut and Weir settled into the last empty chair. There was silence for a moment.

'This,' DCI Pinner stated, 'is Ed Farnham, our mayor.'

Jon inclined his head. 'Sir.'

Farnham lifted a hand and let it drop. 'No need for that; Ed's fine.'

'There's an ongoing situation,' Pinner said, 'and when I described it to DCI Weir, he mentioned that you're in a position to help.'

Jon turned to Weir. But the man's face showed nothing.

Pinner gave a cough. 'We gather the assignment you've been on over the past few days involves working among the homeless community?'

Now, he thought, it's an assignment? Tearing his eyes from Weir, he decided the safest thing was to just nod.

Pinner turned to the mayor. 'Ed, perhaps it would be easiest if you ...?'

Farnham crossed his legs. 'Are you married, Jon?'

'Yes.'

'Kids?'

'Yes.'

'How many?'

'Two.'

'What are their ages?'

'Ten and six,' Jon replied, wondering if the man's next question would be to ask their bloody names.

Farnham gave a wistful smile. 'Nice ages. After that, not so nice. Make the most of it.'

Jon returned the smile, even though he was finding the man patronising.

'I have just the one daughter,' Farnham continued. 'She turned eighteen in March. We don't really get on, unfortunately.' He studied the end of his shoe. 'Her name is Olivia, though most people know her as Liv. She dropped out of school last year, left home shortly after her eighteenth birthday and moved in with her boyfriend – in what I think was a squat.' He quickly lifted his gaze, checking Jon's expression.

Jon looked straight back, eyes steady.

Farnham's attention moved back to his shoe. He reached down to adjust a lace that had become twisted. His voice grew harder. 'Yesterday, I was approached by the boyfriend. It transpires my daughter now has a newborn baby. Add to that post-natal depression. Now she has disappeared from the place they shared. She's somewhere in Manchester, it seems, sleeping on the streets.'

Jon had to make an effort not to sound appalled. 'With a little baby?'

'I believe so.'

'How young are we talking?'

'I'm led to believe, about three weeks.'

Led to believe, Jon thought. Surprised you didn't say, 'allegedly'. That's the word arseholes normally chose. He flicked his eyes quickly to Pinner for confirmation; the man's head was bowed. Weir was keeping his mouth shut, too.

'Well,' Jon stated cautiously, 'she shouldn't be hard to locate if that's the case. There is a definite community among the rough sleepers. I'm surprised none of them have approached the emergency services already.'

Pinner drew air into his nostrils, readying himself to speak. 'I gather that you've fostered a useful contact. An ex-serviceman who knows what's happening.'

That had to have come from Weir, Jon thought. Had to. What's the shifty little bastard been saying? All three men's eyes were on him. Fuck me, this is like tiptoeing across a field of landmines. 'That's correct.'

'Would this person be likely to mention to you if he had knowledge of ... Olivia's whereabouts?' Pinner asked.

'I reckon he would.'

Pinner sent a pleased glance in Weir's direction. The look said, you were right. Well done.

Weir sat forward. 'What I want you to do, DC Spicer, is continue with your assignment, but with a shift in focus. Olivia and the baby need to be located, quickly and without any fuss. That is the priority now. I want you on it full time, with Iona providing all the support you need back here. We'll set you up with comms, so she's in your ear whenever you need her.'

Jon sat back. So, there we have it. Weir had been given an opportunity to shine and now the deaths of the veterans were being shunted aside. What a greasy bastard. Clever, too, though. There's a newborn baby out there, somewhere. And her mum in no state to take care of her. Resolve this and be in the mayor's good books.

'What were you working on, if I may ask?' Farnham enquired.

'A cluster of suicides—'

Weir cut in. 'It wasn't going anywhere.'

Jon was glad one of his hands was cupped over the other: none of them could see how deeply his fingernails were dug into his palms.

Farnham regarded Jon. 'You think you can find my daughter?'

'Can you give me a photo of her?'

He reached into the jacket of his suit and passed Jon a glossy photo. He glanced down. Christ, she would have fitted in at the airport protests the other day. He screened out the half-formed dreadlocks and nose piercings. Studied her actual face. Tried to get a sense of the person beneath. She had fragile features and a slightly haunted look. He wondered if she'd had episodes of depression in the past. 'How tall is she?'

'Five feet four.'

Jon guessed, with Farnham's position in life, there was a good chance his daughter had been privately educated. Although the mayor proudly flew a set of socialist credentials, it wasn't totally certain the values extended to his offspring's education. 'Where did she go to school?'

'Altrincham Grammar.'

Private, then. 'Does she have an accent?' Farnham's eyes narrowed. 'If she sounds posh, she'll stand out even more,' he explained.

'She doesn't sound like she's from some Salford comprehensive, if that's what you mean.'

The type of place I went to school, Jon thought. He let the arrogance within Farnham's statement pass. 'I should think finding her won't be hard. But how come we're doing it this way? Surely uniforms, community support officers, social services: all those channels would be more efficient?'

Pinner lifted a finger. 'Discreet enquiries have been made and, in fact, are ongoing.'

'And the only thing from all that,' Farnham said in a sour voice, 'is a single possible sighting of her on Tuesday in an outreach facility for homeless women on Oldham Street.'

Pinner sent the mayor a placatory look before turning back to Jon. 'The staff in the Daisy Centre reported someone matching Olivia's description had dropped in – and it appeared she had a newborn baby concealed beneath her coat. But she left before they could offer her assistance. Jon: what we need is someone out there, with their ear to the ground. That's what we in the CTU can deliver, without creating any ripples. This all needs to be handled sensitively, is that clear?'

'Certainly is.'

'Good.' Pinner sat back.

Seeing Weir stand, Jon realised his time was up. He glanced at the mayor. But Farnham had already turned away and was speaking to Pinner in a low voice. Weir got the door open and gestured urgently to Jon.

Once they were a safe distance along the corridor, the DCI looked back. 'You're clear on this, then?'

Jon shook his head. 'Not really. Your office or mine?'

Weir looked taken aback. 'Pardon?'

'Your office or mine? Not that I have an office, which leaves discussing it out here.'

The DCI pushed his door open and stepped through. 'Yes?'

Jon moved past him and waited until the door was closed. 'What's the link with Pinner and Farnham?'

'The link?'

'Come on. The CTU on a missing person? Why's Pinner agreed to it? Mates, are they?'

'I believe they went to the same university.'

'Same Masonic lodge, too?'

Weir crossed his arms. 'DC Spicer, are you forgetting our talk yesterday? I'm giving you a chance, here. Don't fuck things up at the first hurdle.'

'From here, it looks like my chance is your chance.'

'Meaning what?'

'Last night, the sight of me was making you want to puke. Now, this time I've been spending on the streets has suddenly become an assignment of yours. Something you can simply repurpose to solve Farnham's embarrassing little problem.'

Weir reddened. 'As I said, it's a chance for you, Spicer. Get it sorted and you're back in the game. As far as I'm concerned, the incident from that parking lot never happened.'

'And if things fuck up? God forbid, but if Farnham's daughter is found floating in the canal, the baby at the bottom, is all still forgiven then?'

Weir was moving towards his desk. 'We'll see.'

'In the meantime, what if more ex-servicemen show up dead?'

'I seriously doubt that will happen, DC Spicer,' he replied, sitting down and reaching for some paperwork. 'But, while finding Farnham's daughter and her baby, keep your ears open.'

'And Iona has official time to pursue things this end?'

He looked up. 'You really like to push things, don't you?'

'Listen, I'll find that baby and her mum. But I need to know that Iona can continue with what we were doing.'

'As long as it doesn't impinge on the prime concern here, yes.'

I'll settle for that, Jon thought.

'And Spicer?'

Jon paused in the doorway to look over his shoulder.

'Remember DCI Pinner's words: no ripples.'

CHAPTER 24

'Greg, how's it going?'

The ex-soldier looked up from his doorway. He took in Jon's appearance: dirty jeans, battered trainers, old coat and woollen hat. Frowning, he asked, 'What the hell has happened to you? Wife kicked you out?'

Jon hitched the shoulder strap of his battered little rucksack a bit higher. 'Can we go somewhere and talk?'

Greg looked across Piccadilly Gardens to the Burger King on the far side. 'There's always my office.'

Jon nodded. 'Sounds good to me.'

Greg removed the blanket that was covering his legs, emptied the change from the cup before him into his hand and pocketed it. He then climbed stiffly to his feet, placed the empty cup onto the ruffled blanket, rolled it all up and stuffed it into a massive a shopping bag that, Jon spotted, already contained a few items of food.

Once they were back on the first floor, sitting on the same pair of stools overlooking the Gardens, Jon scratched at the stubble on his chin. 'There's been a new development.' He pictured Farnham's daughter, somewhere in the city with a tiny baby. 'It's not a good one, but – even so – it works to our advantage.'

Greg was busily tipping sachets of sugar into his tea. 'Go on.'

'I've been given the go-ahead to be out here full-time.'

'Out here?'

He tipped his head toward the window and city beyond.

'Yeah? And what does "full-time" mean?'

'Knocking about during the day, finding somewhere to sleep at night. The whole thing.'

'Which is why you've got the rucksack,' Greg murmured. 'What's in there?'

'Sleeping bag, blanket, a couple of T-shirts, some thick socks, gloves. Not much else.'

Greg looked faintly amused. 'You're going to try roughing it, are you?'

'Well, I thought I'd stand a chance if I could find someone who knows the ropes.' He slid a look at Greg. 'A seasoned pro, so to speak.'

'You did?' He smiled.

'This development – it means my boss has given permission for all this. Actually, he ordered it.'

'So what's changed?'

'This can't go any further than us, OK?'

Greg tipped his head to the side. 'Think I don't know how to keep my mouth shut?'

Without revealing exactly who Olivia was, Jon told him what was going on. Once he'd finished, Greg shook his head with disgust. 'So, the deaths of five – six, if Wayne doesn't pull through – homeless ex-servicemen count for nothing. Then a rich and powerful man's daughter ends up on the street and everything changes.'

Jon took a sip of coffee. 'You've hit the nail on the head.'

Greg's smile was grim as he peered out the window. 'And she has a baby with her?'

'Looks that way, yes.'

'Jesus. You can't be hiding a baby. The things cry all the time, don't they?'

'Yup.'

'Someone must know something. Unless she's keeping it hidden away somewhere.'

'That's what I thought. Here's what I reckon: the baby needs to be found. No question of that. And whatever the hell's happening with these deaths, it needs to be sorted, too. We can do both, don't you think? What do you reckon? Shall we give it a go?'

Greg's lower lip bulged as he ran his tongue across his teeth. 'And you've got a colleague following up on stuff back at your office?'

'Yeah – she's sharp as a tack, too. It's a proper investigation now, Greg. But I really need your help.'

He turned his head. 'And we're saying you're Wayne's brother.'

'May as well, seeing as you've told a few that already. I thought we could say that I've run now out of money. I've got nothing better to do, so I'm sticking around until I find who killed him. Would that work?'

'I've heard from folk with crazier schemes than that.'

'So are you up for it?'

'Aye, I'm up for it.'

Jon reached over and squeezed the man's upper arm. Beneath the bulky coat, he was painfully thin. 'Nice one, Greg. Thanks.'

'No problem. No problem at all.'

'What do you reckon, then? Where should we go first?'

He jabbed a thumb at the glass. 'Down there. There's no place like the Gardens for a flavour of what's going. Just sit and let the city come to us, Jon. That's all we have to do.'

On leaving Burger King, Greg cut left towards a row of shops that included Boots, McDonalds and a Halifax. He nodded at an empty doorway beside the bank's glass doors. 'This'll do.'

Three steps led up to a large wooden door that was padlocked shut. Graffiti tags lacerated the dark surface. In the corner was a piece of flattened cardboard. Greg tore it in half and handed a piece to Jon. 'Park your arse on that.'

'That's the secret, then?' Jon asked. 'How you sit on cold steps and pavements for as long as you do?'

Greg flashed him a grin. One of his molars was missing. 'That's one of them. You can do a lot with cardboard to keep warm. But if you're going to be grafting for a while, you get yourself a shopping basket. Tip it upside down, lay some card across it, or a free newspaper. They work fine. That's your seat.'

'Clever.'

'I know all the tricks, me. If you're sitting there in your sleeping bag, which you want to be doing come the winter, you don't want your dirty shoes on, do you? So you put them under the shopping basket where they'll be safe. But now you're in your socks. Toes'll get cold. Fold up more cardboard and put it at the end of the sleeping bag. Inside it. Your feet go on that. Nice and warm. Great stuff, cardboard.'

'I've seen it used it for signs, too. Propped up before the person.'

Greg shook his head. 'Begging signs are shit. Hungry and homeless, please help. You'll end up with far less. Got to clear your throat, speak up for yourself. Get vocal. But always be nice. You be nice and people will be nice. Watch.' He turned his attention to a woman who was walking past. 'Hello! Any spare change, love?'

Her step slowed and she smiled apologetically. 'Afraid not. Sorry.'

'You take care, thanks!'

'And you.' She continued on her way.

'See?' Greg asked. 'Just a sign and people might be like, oh, poor bloke. But they'll sail straight past, thinking they'll leave it to the next person to reach in their pocket.'

'How many times do people actually give you anything?'

'Depends on the time of day. And where you are.'

'But, on average, one in ten, one in twenty?'

'Somewhere posh, you'll only get one or two giving you anything. But it'll be a good amount. Notes, even. Somewhere ropier, you get much more people happy to give, but it'll be small coins. In the end, it probably adds up to about the same. Unless it's pub closing time. Friday nights.' He let out a whistle. 'Best time of the week by miles.'

A scrawny man of about thirty appeared. 'Greg, can I poach a ciggy, pal?'

'Sit yourself down, Sammy. I was just going to have one myself.'

The man perched on the edge of the bottom step. Once he'd rolled a cigarette, he gave Jon a questioning look. 'Who's this?'

'You remember Wayne? It's his older brother.'

The man's eyes widened. 'I heard you were round and about. Searching for the Dark Angel, yeah?'

Jon met the other man's eyes. 'That's right.'

He looked Jon over. 'Fucking size of him, Greg! It'll be the Dead Angel, soon.' His dry chuckle came to a stop as Greg lit his cigarette, then his own.

'Have you spotted this lass about?' Greg asked. 'She has a wee one with her?'

Sammy cocked his head. 'What's that?'

'A couple of boys down at the Booth Centre said they'd seen this young lass begging with a little baby. A newborn.'

'Romanian or something like that, is she?'

'No, local they said.'

'Always spot the Romanians,' he said. 'Dresses like patchwork fucking quilts.'

'None of that, they said. Local. You've seen her?'

'Nope.'

'Me neither.'

'She'll be in the centre top of Oldham Street. That one's for girls and that.'

'Yeah,' Greg replied. 'Probably right.' He lifted his chin. 'Can you spare some change, please?'

The passing woman sailed on past without showing she'd heard.

Sammy flicked the end of his roll-up across the pavement and stood. 'Got to go. See you about.'

'Cheers, Sammy.'

'Cheers.' He glanced towards Jon. 'Good luck.'

'Cheers.' Once they were alone, he leaned his head towards Greg. 'What's that place he mentioned called?'

'The name's something to do with a flower,' Greg replied. 'Spare some change?'

The man patted his trouser pocket to demonstrate it was empty. 'Sorry, mate. Only got contactless.'

'Have a good day, sir. Thanks. It only opened recently. Dandelion, maybe.'

'Daisy?'

'That's it.'

'Colleagues of mine have already made contact.' Jon adjusted his position, trying to get comfortable in the doorway. Watching the steady flow of people moving past in both directions meant tilting his head back. After a few minutes, his neck began to ache, so he let his chin sag forward. Now all he could see was legs. He observed the variety of footwear. The mind-boggling array of trainers. Laces, no laces, side laces. Fat soles. Thin soles. Heels that flared out. Tongues that lolled over. Every pair seemed like it had hardly been worn. The money people spend, he thought. Every now and again, a coin or two was dropped into Greg's cup.

After a bit, Greg sighed. 'A warm day like this; it isn't so bad.'

Jon shuffled back so he could lean against the chipboard that had been nailed over the door's lower half. 'What isn't?'

'Being here, watching the world go by.'

Jon glanced at the throng out on the pavement. 'Suppose so.'

'Sometimes, I just listen to their footsteps. Hurrying this way, hurrying that. Us? The last thing we're short of is time.'

Greg had a point, he had to admit. People looked so hassled. So put upon.

'You got a mortgage?' Greg asked.

'Of course.'

'I haven't. No gas bills, electricity bills, water rates, council tax, either. Nothing.'

Jon regarded the other man. 'I hadn't thought of it like that. You feel you've got less to worry about?'

'I've definitely got less to worry about.' Greg grinned, gesturing to his carrier bag. 'Fuck all, in fact. Things can't get much worse, can they? I mean, they could. I could get my head stamped on by a bunch of pissed-up blokes. Get frostbite or pneumonia this winter. But no point worrying about that, is there?'

'That's what they say. Don't worry about things beyond your control. So, if you were offered a little flat somewhere, you wouldn't take it?'

'Course I fucking would, you daft twat.'

Smiling at the comment, Jon tipped his head back. Greg's point about a lack of bills had got him thinking about home. When he'd explained to Alice what was happening, her reaction had been mixed. Firstly, relief that he still had a job. Then trepidation about what keeping it involved.

'Out there, on your own, sleeping rough?' she'd asked. 'For how long?'

'It's not going to be more than a few nights. You can't be wandering the city with a newborn baby and not get noticed.'

Alice had looked sad. 'She must be in a terrible state – and the poor baby ...'

'Exactly.'

'But they expect you to do this with no support?'

'I'll be linked to Iona back at the base.'

'What about at midnight, when someone decides to mug you?'

'Mug me?' He'd laughed. 'What would they hope to get? My spare socks?'

'You know what I mean. Being homeless: you're so vulnerable.'

'I'll be OK. I've been trained, don't forget.'

'What about when you're fast asleep? Have they thought about that?'

'I have. I'll two-up – that's how they do it.'

'Two-up?'

'You find another person to share your sleeping spot with. Safety in numbers. This bloke who was in the army used to do it with Wayne. I'll ask him.'

'Any more news on Wayne?'

Jon shook his head. 'Nope.'

'It's not looking good for him, is it?'

'Nope.'

She'd reached up to embrace him. 'Just make sure you come back in one piece, Jon Spicer.'

He wrapped his arms round her and pulled her in close.

'And you can tell the kids Daddy's off on a work trip,' she murmured. 'Say it's a nice hotel in the Lake District or something. Not a bloody pavement in Manchester.'

They'd only stood like that for several seconds before Wiper spotted them. He rushed over, reared up on his hind legs and started desperately thrusting at the back of Jon's knee.

Alice looked down. 'Ah look, he's giving you one of his special hugs.'

'Bloody dog. Off!'

By the time a couple more hours had crept by, Greg had been handed two packs of sandwiches, a pasty, a pint of milk and a carton of apple juice. His cup had a few more coins in it as well. 'Time for a bit of lunch?'

Jon rotated his shoulders. His lower back felt numb, his arse frozen off. 'What are you thinking?'

'It's serving time at the Booth Centre.'

Booth Centre. Jon almost shuddered. The two words were like cold breath across the back of his neck.

Greg must have spotted the impact of his words. 'Something wrong?'

Jon toyed with the idea of saying no. But he didn't want to start bullshitting his companion, however painful the memories. 'I had a younger brother. He was called Dave. He was murdered a few years ago.'

Greg paused in the act of standing, one hand seemingly glued to the step. 'Really? Here, in Manchester?'

'Out in Haverdale, in the Peak District. But he'd been drifting around the city for a while before that. Living in squats, that kind of thing.'

Greg sank onto his haunches. 'That's a shocker. What's the Booth Centre got to do with it?'

'He hung about there, sometimes. For meals. Feels really bloody odd to be doing the same.'

'This was when it was based by the cathedral?'

'Yeah.'

'Oh, you're alright then. New place now. Bigger. You don't have to go back there.'

Before they set off, Greg took his blanket back out of the shopping bag. He placed both on the lower step, with the empty cup visible in the blanket's folds. 'Don't want to lose my spot, now.'

*

DARK ANGEL

The organisation's new premises were tucked away on Pimblett Street, behind Victoria station. The area looked like a small industrial estate; high fencing with sharpened spikes enclosed the nearest units. Beyond it, Jon spotted the upper part of Strangeways prison's watchtower jutting into the sky.

An effort had been made to brighten the exterior of the Booth Centre. The gutters and window grilles had been painted purple and hanging baskets had been attached high up the walls. Above the door was a sign: Edward Holt House.

Greg led the way through the door. On the wall just inside were a variety of notices: Activities Week, Respect Policy, The Manchester Sleepout and other information sheets.

Jon found himself thinking of school. He looked about, wondering why. The smell, he realised. School canteen. The aroma of frying mince. Tinge of grease.

The main room was filled with low voices and long tables, each one the required distance from its neighbours. A piano in the corner. Artwork on the walls. At the far end of the room was a large hatch, beyond which was a kitchen area. Two women and a man were dishing out food. Greg nodded towards the list of dishes on the blackboard. 'Lancashire hotpot. Get in!'

They made their way across. Jon saw several people glance in their direction. Quick looks. The type you might do in an unfamiliar pub. Jon waited until they were in the queue before scanning the room for any females. Out of the forty or so people dotted about, he counted three. Olivia wasn't among them. Once they'd been served, Greg surveyed the room looking for a space. 'Jesus, look who's over there,' he announced. 'The one in the corner with the green and white bobble hat. See him?'

Jon's gaze settled on a large man with a huge beard. He was busily shovelling food into a mouth that was missing most of its upper teeth. 'Who's that?'

'Big Ian. He was up in that building on Bendix Street the night Ryan Gardner died.'

CHAPTER 25

Even though Big Ian looked like he could rip a lamp post out of the pavement with his bare hands, Jon quickly spotted the anxiety in his eyes – especially when Greg moved the talk about the recent deaths.

The man began to nervously smooth his beard, beady eyes repeatedly bouncing off Jon. 'Terrible thing. Terrible. Sorry to hear about your brother, there.'

Jon shrugged. 'Thanks. Greg said you were with Ryan Gardner the night he died.'

'I was, yes.' He ran his fingertips through his beard once more. 'That was also terrible.'

'The person you saw that night, what did he look like?'

'Well, it was only a glimpse, you realise?'

'A glimpse will do if it helps me find him.'

'Normal height, nothing unusual – except for those wings on his back.' His eyes dropped to the empty plate before him, as if he couldn't quite believe his own words.

'And his clothing ...?'

'Black. All black. Same as what Wayne said. Can't believe he got to him, too. He's in intensive care, I heard. Is that right?'

Greg nodded. 'Not getting out any time soon.'

Jon sat forward slightly. 'Nothing about his face you can tell me?'

Big Ian lifted his chin. 'He's a white fellow, that's all I can say.'

Jon dragged his fingers along the line of his jaw. 'I'm probably being thick here, but how did he get Ryan to the top of the stairs?'

'Don't know. But they were talking, the two of them. Only quietly, but I heard their voices as they went past the doorway of the room me and Dan were in.'

'This was when they were heading towards the stairwell?'

'That's right. It was weird because neither of us had heard him come up the stairs.'

'Did you hear what they were talking about?'

'The bloke in black, all I heard was him say to Ryan, "Yes, I can help you." He said it as they went past.'

'"Yes, I can help you." Is that all?'

'Yeah.'

Jon glanced at Greg, who just hunched his shoulders.

Jon considered the comment. It was an answer to something. A confirmation. Yes, I can help you. What was the person offering that Ryan wanted? 'How did he seem that night?'

'Ryan?'

'Yes.'

'Well ... same as usual.'

'Which was?'

'Getting by. Sleeping rough: some days are better than others.' He looked at Greg who nodded in agreement.

'Had he ever mentioned wanting to die?'

Big Ian's face flinched. 'Suicide?'

'Anything like that.'

The man's eyes started to glitter. 'He didn't kill himself. That bloke made him jump or pushed him or something.' He brought his palm down on the table with a bang. 'You think your brother was trying to kill himself? Why are you asking all these questions if you think he wanted to kill himself? If they all killed themselves? It's this person, the Dark Angel – he's the one doing this!'

Greg lifted both hands. 'It's all right, mate.'

The anger seemed to vanish as quickly as it had appeared. The man slumped lower and his hand slid off the table to land in his lap. 'Sorry.'

Jon could see a lot of heads had turned to watch. He hunched forward, keeping his voice quiet. 'No, I'm sorry, mate. I just can't get this straight in my head. That's all.'

Big Ian took in a big breath and stroked at his beard for several seconds. Slowly, he breathed out and started speaking again. 'There's this big crashing sound. I poke my head out the door. Ryan's gone and it's just him. He's stood there with both his hands on the bannister, looking down – and he's got wings sticking out of the tops of his shoulders.'

'They weren't there when they went past the doorway?'

'No. He was normal, then. I ... I knew the noise had been Ryan falling. I just knew.'

Jon was thinking of Wayne. How he'd landed on his back beneath the pub's fire escape. 'You think the bloke flipped him over?'

'Maybe. He stayed that way for a little bit longer then he sets off down the steps, with those wings sort of bouncing up and down. Soon as we heard the front door shut, we were out of there.'

'And you saw Ryan at the bottom?'

He closed his eyes for a second. 'Yeah – he was lying there. Dan took a closer look, said he was definitely dead.'

When they got to the doorway they had been in earlier, they found a young-looking bloke – nineteen at most – sitting there. He had a pinched face and a shaved head. Grimy fingers were holding an upturned baseball cap that was nestled in the folds of Greg's blanket. Jon had seen his type many times before; usually in the back of a police vehicle after he'd arrested them.

'Hey pal,' Greg announced in a kindly voice. 'That's my spot.'

He looked off to the side. 'Empty when I got here.'

'And that's my blanket, too.' Greg peered behind him. 'Been eating my scran as well, have you?'

He reached back, picked up Greg's shopping bag and let if fall to the pavement.

Greg looked at Jon. 'This is the thing nowadays. These youngsters are showing up and they don't give a shit about how things are done.'

The lad yawned, seemingly oblivious to Greg's comment. Jon knew there would be no reaction from him while things were just verbal. Only the threat of actual violence got through to people like him.

Maybe sensing that, too, Greg shook his head as he retrieved his bag. 'You've got some learning to do, son.'

'Do I look like your fucking son?' he shot back, still staring off to the side.

Greg floated a pained glance at Jon. 'Come on, we'll go down to Deansgate. See what's doing there.'

Jon let Greg get a couple of steps in front before turning back and leaning into the doorway. 'Want to stop me taking this?' He started to pull the blanket off the lad's legs.

The fingers gripping the cap immediately uncurled. Jon saw his other hand start bunching into a fist. He bent lower, bringing his lips close to the lad's ear. 'Please try it, you scummy little turd.' He moved back, giving the lad space to swing, if he wanted to.

A second of eye contact passed. The lad's fist relaxed and he scowled at something off to the side. 'Have it, like I give a shit.'

Jon reached down and gathered it up. 'Good decision, fucktard.'

The youngster seemed to slump in on himself as he announced in a whining voice, 'What's your problem? Christ.'

Jon walked off, always amused at how quickly they could switch from aggressor to victim. 'Here you go.'

Greg turned round, eyes flicking momentarily to the doorway then back to Jon. 'I won't ask what you said,' he whispered, stuffing the blanket into his bag.

They walked in silence along Portland Street for a while. Across the road, Jon could see a small group sitting among a variety of bags. They'd congregated beneath the overhanging roof of a large music shop. 'What did you mean when you said, this is the issue nowadays?'

'The issue? I meant the new lot who're now showing up on the streets. They're so young – and they're so full of attitude. They don't get it.'

'How you help each other out?'

'Yeah – we play by certain rules. Not stealing someone's spot, for a start. They're young, though. Teenagers, some of them. I was talking with someone who works at the Booth Centre. She said for every one person they manage to find housing for, another three are being made homeless.'

Every twenty metres along Deansgate there seemed to be someone on the pavement, begging. Greg stopped to chat briefly with almost every one of them. Jon kept his distance, happy to let the other man do the talking.

'Nothing,' Greg stated as they reached the turning into Saint Ann's Square. 'No one's seen her. I need a ciggy. Come on, I'll show you something.'

He led Jon past a section of cobbles, then across ancient slabs of stone to the little church at one end. 'Seen this?' he asked, pointing to a bench beside the building's main doors.

Jon realised it was actually more of a sculpture; three quarters of the sitting area was taken up by a horizontal figure almost entirely hidden beneath a blanket. Only a pair of bare feet stuck out. The entire thing looked like it was cast from bronze.

'It's a statue to us homeless folk,' Greg announced cheerfully, sitting down and tickling its toes. 'See those?'

His forefinger was moving between twin holes in the flesh of the feet. Clever, Jon thought, realising the sleeping figure was, in fact, Christ.

'Homeless Jesus,' Greg said proudly. 'There are more of them in other cities. America, Canada, Rome, Australia and Dublin. Some other places I don't remember. It was offered to London, first. But they didn't want it. Their loss, I reckon.'

Jon felt a commotion beneath his left armpit. Two brief vibrations, then a pause. 'Got work ringing me,' he said, tapping his side before moving quickly round the corner to be less in view. Iona's name was on the screen. 'Hi there.'

'How's it going?' she asked anxiously.

'No luck with finding the mayor's daughter.' He sank into a sitting position beside what looked like a stone crypt. Judging from the smell, someone had recently taken a piss against it. 'Can you contact a place at the top of Oldham Street? It sounds like an outreach centre for homeless women. I think the name is something to do with a flower.'

'Will do. Is that where you are now?'

'No. St Ann's Square, by the church.'

'Is that where you'll be sleeping?'

'Iona, I've no idea where I'll be sleeping tonight.'

'Can't believe Weir's got you doing this. Are you on your own?'

'No, I'm with the one I told you about. Greg. He's just round the corner, sitting next to Jesus.'

'Did you just say Jesus?'

'Yeah, he's smoking a roll-up. Greg, not Jesus. What's up, anyway?'

'Sure you've not been smoking something?'

Jon smiled. 'Come on, have you got good news?'

'No, afraid not, Jon.'

Shit, he thought. That probably meant all her enquiries with the victims' families had come to nothing. 'I'm listening.'

'Word just came in from the MRI. It's Wayne. I'm afraid he died.'

'No. When?'

'About an hour ago. The hospital just phoned it through.'

Jon let out a long sigh. The one person who might have been able to help them crack this. Now he was gone. Jon couldn't believe it.

'You still there, Jon?'

'Yeah. Yeah, I am.'

'What do you want to do?'

'I'd better come in. Weir wants a daily update anyway. Shit.'

'How long do you reckon you'll be?'

'Give me an hour or so.'

'OK, see you soon.'

He approached Greg with a sense of trepidation. The man was snubbing out his half-smoked roll-up against the sole of his trainers. Carefully, he put the remains back in his pouch. Catching sight of Jon, his face broke into a smile. 'There you are. Ready to go again?'

'Actually, Greg ...'

When he told him, Jon was shocked to see the other man start to cry.

CHAPTER 26

Iona looked perplexed. '"Yes, I can help you?" He was sure that's what the person said?'

Jon thought back to Big Ian's recollection of what had happened the night Ryan Gardner died. The bloke had seemed pretty clear about everything. 'He was.'

'Help with what, I wonder,' Iona mused.

Jon was sitting in his chair, legs stretched straight out before him. 'There was one person who could have answered that. He gave her a glum look. 'What was the cause of death?'

'First, he was in bad shape, Jon. A lot of drug use.'

'And?'

'Pulmonary embolism. Probably came from a DVT in his leg.'

'DVT?'

'A blood clot, basically. Broke off, travelled up his leg and lodged in his lung. Caused his heart to fail.'

'He wasn't even thirty, for fuck's sake. You know, when I mentioned it to Greg, he broke down? They had a much stronger bond than I realised, those two.' He pulled his feet in and sat up straight. 'Anyway, how've you done today?'

'Which order do you want it in? The mayor's daughter or the ex-army deaths?'

Jon quickly checked Weir wasn't lurking nearby. 'Better start with the mayor's daughter.'

'Well, that won't take long.' She retrieved a file from beside her keyboard and opened it. 'The three main charities in Manchester working with the homeless appear to be: the Booth Centre, Mustard Tree and Barnabus. The women's outreach centre where Olivia was spotted is a new initiative created by Mustard Tree. With the homeless problem becoming so much worse since the government's austerity measures, they've had to get more organised. Work together as a network.'

Jon thought about Greg's comment: the new flood of people now ending up on the streets.

'It's made things a bit easier for me. Recently, the charities formed The Manchester Homeless Partnership to get some proper coordination going. That has links to the Town Hall, us, mental health workers and such like. I've been making calls all day, but no one knows where she is.'

'Nothing at all?'

'A big blank.'

'Me, too. Greg must have asked about a dozen other rough sleepers if they'd seen or heard of her.'

'Mention what to a dozen rough sleepers?' asked a voice from behind him.

Jon turned to see Weir approaching. 'Sir. I was just comparing notes with Iona before giving you a call.'

'Compare away. I'm all ears.'

As they brought him up to speed with the lack of progress, their DCI made little effort to hide his disappointment. 'When are you heading back out, DC Spicer?'

Jon checked his watch. Coming up on five already. 'Straight after we're finished here.'

Weir rose to his feet. 'What else is there to discuss?'

Jon struggled briefly to control it before, as usual, accepting defeat. 'Oh, I don't know. Just the fact Wayne Newton died earlier this afternoon.'

Weir's eyes hardened. 'You want to correct the tone in your voice?'

Jon spread his hands. 'You want to acknowledge that we could now be on the sixth victim?'

Weir raised a forefinger. 'Keep the focus on Olivia Farnham. Once she's safe, you can try gathering some evidence that supports this theory of yours. Clear?'

Iona announced hastily, 'Absolutely, sir. Thanks,'

Weir's eyes stayed locked on Jon. 'Clear?'

He let the silence stretch for another second. 'Clear. Sir.'

Weir strode away.

From the corner of his eye, Jon could see Iona's head shaking. 'What?'

'You. Is it a compulsion of yours, to piss off your boss?'

'Ah, fuck him. He's only after brownie points with the mayor.'

'That's called fostering friends in high places. You should try it.'

'Kissing arse, more like.'

'Or maybe just being sensible? You know, in terms of a career.'

Jon shook his head. 'I'd rather lick vomit off the pavement.'

Iona gave a curt nod as she reached for another folder. 'Clearly. So, I got through to relatives in three of the families.'

Jon swivelled his seat. 'What was said?'

'I won't lie, Jon. All of them – and we're talking Jim Barlow, Luke McClennan and Frank Kilby here – were struggling with their mental health. I spoke to the mum of Luke McClennan. He'd been diagnosed with PTSD in the months after leaving the army. Plus, he was boozing loads.'

'But had he mentioned suicide?'

'He had.'

'And the other two?'

'Similar. Frank Kilby had visited his GP, described his state of mind and was promptly given a prescription for Citalopram.'

'Antidepressant?'

'Correct.'

'Who told you this?'

'The wife.'

Jon ran a knuckle back and forth across his lips. This was the problem they faced; most people living on the streets had issues. If they didn't arrive with them, they soon developed them. 'Just because they had suicidal thoughts, it doesn't necessarily mean they killed themselves.'

Iona stayed silent. Glancing across, he spotted the look on her face. 'Go on.'

'Luke McClennan had specifically mentioned wanting to end it all. That was in the weeks prior to him disappearing from his home in Llandudno.'

'And that's according to who?'

'The parents. I asked who he'd said that to; they told me he was quite open about it. It would be on his doctor's records. He had been due to see a counsellor, but he missed the first two appointments then took off. Next time they heard from him, he was in Manchester. The mother even said she knew, in the week or so before they were contacted by police, that he was dead.'

Jon closed his eyes, knuckle now motionless against his lips. This was going to make it so much harder to convince anyone they were dealing with anything other than suicides. Especially Weir. 'How did she know? Mother's instinct or something?'

'No. He'd stopped calling.'

'Right.' He murmured, dropping his hand. 'Always go for the simplest option, Jon.'

'Sorry?'

'Nothing. Just reminding myself of something.' He checked the windows. The light outside was beginning to lose strength. 'I'll ring home before I get going,' he announced, reaching for the phone on his desk.

When Alice answered, she sounded slightly harassed. He sat forward. 'Everything OK?'

'Jon, hi. Yes. Nearly feeding time at the zoo, that's all. How are you doing?'

'Fine. I'm sat here with Iona. Just going over things before I head off to my temporary accommodation for the night.'

'Oh, Jon. Where will you go?'

'I'll let Greg decide. He's the expert.'

'I really don't like you being out there.'

'Hey, it'll be fine. Loads of people are sleeping out, Ali. It's not that unusual.'

'Which is bloody tragic,' she replied. 'You want a quick word with the kids?'

'Please.'

'This training course you're on; I've told them you're staying in your own little hotel room, OK?'

'OK.'

'Duggy, it's your dad. Here, say hello.'

His little voice came on the line. 'Daddy! Is your toilet in your bedroom?'

'Hi, little fellow. Is my what?'

'Is your toilet in your bedroom?'

'No,' he chuckled. 'Why?'

'Mummy said it was in your bedroom and that would be really weird. And smelly.'

He heard Alice in the background. 'I said it's an en suite room, Duggy. Ask Daddy what en suite is.'

'What's on sweet?'

'I do have a little bathroom, but it's in another room that's joined to my bedroom. So you call it en suite.'

'Oh. Does it have a door?'

'Yes.'

'So people can't see you pooping?'

'No.'

'Oh.' Silence.

'Are you watching telly?'

'Mmm?'

He's watching telly, Jon thought. 'What are you watching?'

'Here's Mummy.'

'Right. Bye, then.'

Alice again. 'That's your lot with him. You want a word with Holly?'

'Is she there?'

'Well, she's in her room. Hang on. Holly! It's your dad. No, you come down. The phone is on the stairs. Jon? I need to see to these fish fingers. You be careful, you hear me?'

'I hear you. Love you.'

'Love you, too.'

There was a muffled bump as the handset was placed on the carpet. He waited. Faint sounds of telly in the background. The light clatter of plates. Suddenly, he wished he was there, at home, sitting in the warm kitchen with his wife.

'Hello?'

His daughter's voice sounded flat. Sullen. 'Hi there, Holly. How are you?'

'OK.'

'Yeah? What are you up to?'

'Just in my room.'

'Right. On that Insta-tube thing?'

'Dad.'

'Sorry. I meant Whats-chat.'

'You're so embarrassing.'

'Course I am; that's my job. You know, earlier today, I caught someone stealing helium balloons from a shop? I held him for a while, but then I let him go.'

'That's one of your jokes, isn't it?'

'Yeah. I let him go? So he floated away ...'

'Shall I pass you on to Mum?'

Christ, he thought. When did this humourless alien take over my sweet little girl? 'Holly, I know you don't like talking on the phone. But, you're OK, aren't you?'

'How do you mean?' She sighed.

'You're happy, right?' He knew his approach was awful. Not only was he asking closed questions, he was phrasing them to encourage the answers he wanted to hear. 'Things are OK at school?'

'Suppose so.'

'And with your friends? Things are OK with them, too?'

'Yes.'

'Good. But, you know, if they're ever not ... you can tell me. You know that, don't you? You can call me anytime you want if I'm at work. Anytime at all.'

'I know that, Dad.'

'OK. Well, I'll see you soon, OK?'

'OK.'

'I love you, my little berry.'

'Bye.'

'Bye.'

CHAPTER 27

The doorway of the office building in Stevenson Square was deserted. He headed over to the Spar on London Road. A bloke he'd never seen before was sitting by the entrance. Perched in his lap was a little brindle Staffie.

'All right?' asked Jon, squatting down beside him. 'You've not seen Greg about, have you?'

The man glanced to the side, bloodshot eyes touching for a moment on Jon's face. 'Don't know who you mean, mate.'

The dog's stumpy tail was wagging. Jon held out a hand and let the animal lick his fingers. He was missing Wiper. 'What's his name?'

'Deefer.'

'Deefer?'

'D for dog. Deefer.'

Jon smiled. 'Does what it says on the tin, hey? You alright, Deefer?' The animal's eyes half-closed as Jon tickled behind his ears. 'Greg. Skinny bloke. About forty-five. Wears a flat cap.'

'Oh, that's his name is it – Greg?'

'Yeah.'

He shook his head. 'Not since about lunchtime. But if you find him, tell him I might have seen that girl he was asking about.'

Jon masked his interest. 'Which one?'

'About twenty, wearing a big army coat. Woven into her hair were little dreadlocks and that. She stopped to give me some change.'

'Yeah? When was that?'

'Two hours ago?' He nodded in the direction of Piccadilly. 'She was going that way. Her and this other girl who was a bit Paki-looking. Loads of jewellery,' he traced a dirty finger round the outer part of his left ear, 'all along that bit. She called her Anura.'

'The girl in the army coat called the other one Anura?'

'Yeah. She called out Ann to begin with, but she never heard. So then she shouts, Anura! Anura waits until she caught up and they carried on that way.'

'Right, I'll mention it. What was this Anura wearing?'

He shrugged. 'Jeans and trainers? Not those dresses they wear, anyway.'

'OK. Nice dog, by the way.' He got to his feet. Dusk had set in. The flow of people was mostly one way: towards the train station. The last of the city's workforce heading home for the night. Going against the human tide, Jon made his way into Piccadilly Gardens. The row of market stalls selling scented candles, trays of fudge and mementos of the city were packing away.

He stood in the gap between two of them and removed his phone. 'Iona, hi. Listen, can you get me a number for Farnham? Might have a sighting of his daughter in the vicinity of Piccadilly Station.'

'OK – I'll call you back.'

'Cheers.' He slipped the phone out of sight and re-emerged from the two stalls. Burger King was directly in front, and he glanced up at the windows, hoping to see Greg's face. Nothing.

A feeling of unease announced itself at the very back of Jon's mind. The atmosphere of the city centre was rapidly changing as it emptied out. He felt like he was being left behind. Nowhere to go for the night. Exposed. Alone.

He shook himself free of the thoughts, cutting across to the top of Mosley Street and walking purposefully along the pavement. He suspected people were drifting out of his path. He looked more closely and could tell their eyes were avoiding his as they passed. I look different to them, he realised. With my big coat and rucksack hanging from one shoulder. Beginnings of a beard and a woollen hat. I look homeless.

Office buildings rose up on either side. Brightly lit upper floors. Window after window with nothing behind them. Deserted workstations. Empty meeting rooms. So much space and all of it denied to people like him.

Three people were already preparing a sleeping area in the portico entrance of what used to be Jamie's Italian at the top of King Street. Greg wasn't among them. No one had seen him.

A portly man with a bushy beard scrutinised Jon for a second. 'Why are you looking for him?'

'We were going to two-up for the night.'

'Right.' He shook out a blanket and turned away.

Jon hovered for another moment. No space at the inn, he thought. 'If you see him, can you say I'm over in Stevenson Square? He knows the spot.'

'Will do.'

He looked around, realising it was now properly dark. Where the hell had Greg got to? There was a pub opposite. Clusters of office workers lined the bar. A blackboard on the pavement announced that pie, chips and gravy cost eight pounds. There was an emergency twenty-pound note tucked down one of his socks. But he couldn't wander into the place – not in full view of the lot behind him setting up their spots for the night. And besides, the two guys in bomber jackets at the front door probably wouldn't let him in.

Taking his time, he wandered down King Street, passing Belstaff and DKNY. Each had closed for the day, but the interiors were still brightly lit. Spotlights carefully arranged to pick out certain items. He gazed through the thick plate glass at dresses and coats that cost several hundred pounds. Handbags that cost thousands. The gulf between those that had money and those who had none had never jarred so badly. At Cross Street, he turned right. By continuing straight on, he could circle round the Arndale, angle up through Shudehill and reach the Northern Quarter. Twenty minutes, at most, he'd be back in Stevenson Square. What do I do, he wondered, if Greg isn't there?

Security screens protected the fronts of most shops. A figure, swaddled in blankets, lay in the doorway of what was once a bank. In a narrow side street beside Boots was a line of wheelie bins. A stack of flattened cardboard boxes had been placed beside them. He remembered Greg's advice about using the material for an insulation layer to lie on. As he diverted towards them, the temptation to check no one he knew was approaching was strong. Going through bins, he said to himself. Doesn't get much more humiliating than this.

The boxes had been secured with a thick strip of adhesive tape. The ones at the top of the pile had been splashed with liquid. An overturned Caffé Nero cup lay behind them. At least it's not piss, Jon said to himself, peeling the tape back and discarding the damp cardboard. He guessed the rest of the stack consisted of seven or eight boxes. Enough to make some kind of platform to sleep on.

There were a couple of guys positioned at the steps of the Arndale. Jon paused in passing. 'Seen a bloke called Greg around?'

One glanced up. 'Saw him coming out the Booth Centre earlier.'

Jon moved the cardboard to his other arm. 'When was that?'

'Around lunch?'

'Did he say where he was off to?'

'Nope.'

'Did he find that lass he was looking for? The young one with a baby?'

'Not a clue, pal. Got a tab?'

'Don't smoke, sorry.'

The bloke turned to his mate and their conversation resumed. Jon continued round the corner of the giant shopping centre, following the road as it inclined upwards. The garish neon signs of the Printworks were now on his left. A horde of lads in shirts and smart trousers were heading towards him. Jon kept to the side of the pavement, suddenly aware he could be a target to a group like that, especially if they'd been drinking. To his relief, they cut across the road to start queuing outside a bar.

The platforms of Shudehill tram stop were almost deserted. A few couples with shopping bags. A man with a loosened tie, staring at his phone. Everyone heading home for the night. He thought of his own front room. His slobbing-out chair beside the fire with its threadbare armrests. Alice on the sofa, legs curled beneath her. Wiper, crashed out on the carpet, paws occasionally twitching. Duggy and Holly, snuggled down beneath their duvets.

The pubs and bars of the Northern Quarter were busy. People who looked barely in their twenties sitting at tables with brightly coloured cocktails before them. This lot had no young kids to worry about. Wide eyes and loud laughter. Thumping music. No one seemed to notice him as he passed through; just a ghost, drifting on the breeze. A woman who might have been somewhere in her thirties was positioned on the pavement at the intersection of Hilton and Oldham Streets. There were so many blankets arranged around her lower half, she looked like she was melting into the pavement. He realised she'd noticed him. And her expression, while not welcoming, wasn't hostile.

'Alright?' he asked, coming to a hesitant stop.

'Yeah.' A brief smile. 'Bagged yourself some cardboard there?'

He shifted the stack to his other arm. 'Too good to miss.'

Her eyes rotated in their sunken sockets as she studied the street behind him. 'Slow, isn't it?'

He glanced into the cup she was holding. A few coins, some of them silver. He wanted to ask how come she was out begging, on her own, at this time of night.

He wanted to ask what had happened in her life that had led her to this. He wanted to ask if she had somewhere safe when she needed to sleep. But those weren't the type of questions you came out with. Not if you were homeless. Instead, he said, 'Have you seen a lass wandering about? Early twenties. She has a baby with her?'

She frowned. 'Greg was asking about her before. I've not seen her. Don't know anyone who has. Not a lass with a little baby. Why are you asking?'

He shrugged. 'Greg was asking me, that's all. Didn't know who he was on about either.'

'Sounds like he's asking everyone.'

'When did you see him?'

'Oh, I don't know. Earlier today. Around lunch?' She took another look at him. 'Are you knocking about with Greg at the moment?'

'Yeah.'

She nodded. 'He mentioned you. Said you're trying to find out what happened to your brother.'

'That's right.'

She lifted an eyebrow. 'Said you're trying to catch the Dark Angel.'

'I'm just trying to find out what happened to my brother.'

Her other hand emerged from beneath its covering layers. She swigged from a stubby little bottle and let out a sigh. The bottle sank below sight once more. 'Fair enough.'

'Where did you see Greg? Only, we were meant to be meeting and can I find him? Can I fuck.'

'It was here. You tried the Spar? He's often around there.'

'Yeah, no luck. I might try again.'

'So you were in the army, too, then?'

'Me? Nah – building trade's all I know.'

She nodded. 'He prefers ex-soldiers. For when he needs to two-up.'

Jon paused. She said soldiers. Plural. 'Right. Like Wayne?'

'And the other one. Before Wayne showed up.'

Jon looked off down the street, as if something nearby was more interesting. 'Who was that, then?'

'Luke. I liked Luke, cheeky little fuck that he was.'

Jon's head turned. 'Luke?'

'Topped himself. Found his body near the railway arches. Poor bastard.'

'From Wales?'

'Yeah, the Welsh boy. Him.'

She means Luke McClennan, Jon thought. Greg would two-up with him. Why didn't he mention that? He took a step away. 'See you about.'

'You take care.'

'Cheers.'

He left her sitting there with her drink and cup of spare change. Someone had been in the doorway in Stevenson Square; there was an empty bottle of Tropicana, a few crumpled sandwich cartons and a half-eaten pasty lying in the corner. He put the stack of cardboard down in the middle of floor and sat on it.

What the hell was going on with Greg? He was mates with two victims in this, he thought. He trawled back, trying to remember if Luke's name had ever been mentioned. In Burger King earlier on? I didn't use actual names, he realised, but surely Greg was aware Luke had died? After all, the woman who'd been begging knew all about it.

The air was getting colder and he wondered what temperature it would be by the early hours. A few degrees less than this. Will I be warm enough wearing my coat inside the sleeping bag? I'll soon find out, he thought.

He watched the people going past, perfumes and aftershaves trailing in their wake. The thought occurred about his own aroma. He was sure that he didn't smell yet, but he might do in another day. He ran through possible places where he could go for a wash. Two pubs with large disabled toilets sprang to mind. Ones with a sink and hand dryer. If the staff let him into the pub, they'd do nicely.

Passing footsteps came to a stop. He lifted his chin to see a couple of women looking down at him. One of their hands was outstretched, painted fingernails so close to his face, they were out of focus. 'It's only a bit of shrapnel, sorry.'

It took him a moment before he realised she was trying to give him money. 'Oh. Thanks—' He was about to say there was no need, but she carried on speaking.

'You need a cup or something.' Her voice was a bit wobbly and he suspected she'd been drinking. 'For collecting?' Her hand moved up and down. She didn't know where to place the coins.

He raised a palm. 'Cheers. Just getting organised.' The change clinked as she let it go.

'A friend of my sister's, she lives in Bristol, and her neighbour – this guy who had a job at a big warehouse. I met him a few times. Lovely bloke. He ended up losing his flat and having to sleep out. It was terrible.'

Her friend had started moving away. 'Louisa.'

Her eyebrows had a sympathetic tilt. 'I hope things work out for you.'

'That's very kind of you. Thanks.'

She smiled briefly then turned to catch up her friend.

Jon examined the money. About eighty pence. Greg can have that, he thought. When he shows up. He felt his phone vibrate. Iona calling, at bloody last.

'No joy, Jon. Sorry.'

'How come?'

He's giving a speech at an official function and can't be contacted.'

Jon couldn't believe it. The fucker's daughter and her baby are missing and he won't take my call? Unbelievable. 'What official function?'

'A private dinner. In that new restaurant that opened. Mistral.'

'The one in Spinningfields?'

'Yes.'

Jon had seen the newspaper stories: part of a small but very exclusive chain. The first had opened in London. Then Edinburgh. Absurd prices to ensure only the great and good could afford to dine there. 'I'll go and see him myself, then.'

'Jon, do you think that's—'

'Oh, I do. I definitely do.'

The restaurant was nestled at the edge of a lawned square closed in by plate glass edifices to corporate power. The entire development was fairly recent, but with its proximity to the Crown Court, law firms were soon vying for office space. Next in were the big financial sector companies. Posh shops and restaurants soon followed.

Jon was marching past the live-flame torches that formed an avenue to the restaurant's entrance before he realised that, to all intents and purposes, he looked homeless. The door staff had already positioned themselves to block his way.

'Closed,' one of them announced with a stony face.

'Right: so what are all those people doing inside?'

The man crossed his arms by way of reply.

Jon contemplated his next move. It was already gone ten o'clock. Surely it would be winding up soon? He backed off and settled himself on the low wall outside the neighbouring building.

Less than an hour later taxis started aligning themselves on the road that led down from Deansgate. Soon after, people began to step out from the restaurant's doors. Men in dinner jackets and bow ties, women in evening dresses. Jewellery sparked and glinted.

Jon removed his woollen cap and stood just beyond the line of torches. Even though the men closest to him didn't acknowledge his presence, Jon could see their shoulders were just a bit too stiff. Some of the women used the pretext of adjusting an earring or stray strand of hair to partly turn their heads. Nervous eyes brushed him and words started being whispered.

Farnham was making his way along, shaking hands and flashing smiles as he went. He spotted Jon and his face fell for just a moment. Jon lip-read the words 'Over there,' before Farnham inclined his head fractionally to the left.

Jon moved towards the corner of the building, enjoying the bewildered looks from the group. Taxis began manoeuvring themselves alongside the kerb. A flash of pale hair caught Jon's eyes: Alicia Lloyd. She was wearing a plum-coloured oriental-style dress that shimmered in the soft light. Silk, he thought.

'Why are you here?' Farnham asked in a low voice.

'I tried to get through to you on the phone.'

'Really? When?'

'Earlier.'

'No one told me.'

Jon didn't believe him. 'You weren't taking calls, apparently.'

'You couldn't leave me a message?'

'I hate leaving messages. Especially if it's urgent: missing people, babies, that kind of stuff.' Alicia was talking to an old bloke who barely came up to her shoulder. She kept glancing over the man's bald head in their direction. 'Does your daughter have a friend called Anura?'

'Anura? I ... not that I'm aware of.'

'A girl – possibly Indian. Line of piercings in her left ear?'

'I've never seen her with any ... with anyone like that. Why?'

'It was a possible sighting from earlier today. The one called Anura was wearing jeans and trainers. Her companion had on an army coat.'

Farnham was edging away. 'It could have been two students; there's a big block of student flats behind the station.'

'Perhaps you could check with her friends, if it's not too much trouble? See if any of them have heard of an Anura?'

'Will do. I'll get word to you via Trevor. DCI Pinner.' He melted back into the gathering.

Jon watched him go. Leave me a message. Christ. He realised Alicia's eyes were on him again as a silver-haired man stepped forward to speak with her. Jon wandered towards Deansgate, glad to leave the chattering crowd behind him.

He'd got as far as Kendals when a white Range Rover turned into the side street before him and came to an abrupt stop. The rear door opened and a long pair of legs swung out. Alicia. Now straightening her dress, she smiled in his direction. 'I thought it was you.'

Awkward, thought Jon. He checked over his shoulder. No one was near. 'I really can't talk. Not here.'

She stepped closer. 'I wondered what happened. One minute you're escorting me ... your partner, the one from Scotland—'

'Wales.'

'The one from Wales, then. He wasn't saying anything.'

Jon moved round the corner to be out of the glaring lights of Deansgate. 'I was redeployed. It happens.'

'Undercover, by the looks of it.'

He nodded.

'Will I see you again? For the escorting work?'

'You fly home tomorrow afternoon, don't you?'

'That's right.'

'Probably not, then.'

'Are you working now?'

'I am.'

'Until when?'

'It's not a shift. Until the issue's resolved.'

'You look like a vagrant. Is that the intention?'

'Listen, I should be ...' He took a step away.

'Where are you sleeping?'

'Somewhere close.'

She closed the gap again. 'You couldn't use a hot shower? A nice glass of brandy?'

You have no idea how good that sounds. 'Thanks. I really should be going, though.'

'You know where I am.' Her eyes flicked to the side. 'Two minutes to my hotel. You still have my number?'

He wasn't sure what he'd done with her card. 'No.'

'Just mention my name at reception. They know which suite I'm in.' She swivelled on one high heel, smooth calf muscles flexing as she sashayed towards the Range Rover's open door.

He remained where he was until the vehicle was out of sight. Then he stepped back out onto Deansgate and continued towards the Northern Quarter.

He was soon standing in Stevenson Square, wondering what to do. The prospect of sitting in the doorway attracting the odd donation from passers-by didn't appeal. An image of Alicia's hotel room appeared in his mind. Soft lights and towelling robes. Like something from a film. It occurred to him that he hadn't actually visited the places where the others had died: the NCP on Tib Street; the abandoned building on Bendix Street; the viaduct near Piccadilly station. What, he asked himself, are the chances of finding anything useful? About zero. But anything's better than this.

A streetlight up on the road threw a triangle of light into the shadowy ledge beneath the bridge where she lay with her baby. It was bright enough for her to read by. Sometimes she flicked through a copy of the free newspaper that was available throughout the city. The stories about flooded communities, here and in other parts of the world. The droughts that were making swathes of Africa and Australia uninhabitable. The unusually violent storms wreaking havoc in the Caribbean and along America's coast.

The articles were usually interspersed with advertisements for wellness products. Drinks to support the immune system. Powdered organic supplements to increase focus or decrease stress. Online yoga courses to promote inner peace. Anything to help people avoid facing up to what the real problem was.

She found a report about how countries were already squabbling over the mining rights to parts of the Arctic that were being made accessible by the shrinking ice cap.

Was no one else joining the dots? Why couldn't people see what was happening? The planet was being wrecked and no one cared. She should have never had this baby. What hope did her daughter have in such a place?

She threaded the line of cotton through the shaft of the last pigeon feather then knotted it at the other end to form a loop. Lifting it up, she admired the necklace she'd made. Smallest feathers at the top, larger ones at the bottom. As she draped it round her neck, the filaments caressed her face. They felt nice. Why didn't Amy like the feel of them? She'd run the tip of one back and forth across her daughter's cheek earlier, trying to wake her. But it got no response. All the little thing did was sleep. Olivia had come to believe that her daughter didn't really want to enter this world. It was like she could sense the place had been ruined. An instinct only a person with a totally pure heart could possess.

Her own stomach rumbled loudly. She wasn't sure when she'd last eaten. She shook the carton of UHT milk that stood by the back wall. Empty. Sighing, she lifted herself to a kneeling position. Her movement caused a quickening of the pigeons' low chorus above her. Bunched forms shifted in the shadows. But they now knew she was no threat. Should she find food? She probably should. But it was such an effort to get up. Staying here was so much nicer. And more peaceful. The city, with its bright lights and loud noises, gave her a headache.

The long thin blanket was still wrapped round her torso in a rough papoose. Popping Amy into it and zipping her coat up would only take seconds. She visualised walking the concrete canyons with their walls of glass. The echo of voices and the stares of people she passed. Perhaps the two of them could just snuggle down here, drift off to sleep with the soft cooing of the pigeons above and never wake up.

CHAPTER 28

The door at the top of the car park's stairwell scraped loudly as Jon shoved against it with his shoulder. No one would leave their vehicle up here. Not at this time of night. He replayed Wayne's account of when Jim Barlow had fallen to his death. Wayne said he'd been lying on his side while Jim and another man had been talking off to his left. That man – with wings mounted on his back – had crossed his field of vision en route to the stairwell. Jon looked around. Tell-tale flattened cardboard boxes lay there. Plus a few empty cans and a bottle of a brand of vodka he'd never heard of before. An abandoned coat, too. That could be the spot people favoured when they came up here.

He wandered across. A few bits of graffiti scratched into the waist-high wall. A love heart encircling the words 'Adam and Steve'. Jon turned his back to the writing. To his left was the side of the building that overlooked Thomas Street. He made his way along it while peering over the side. There, some fifty feet below, were the benches Wayne mentioned the emergency vehicles had been parked alongside. So this was it. The spot where Jim Barlow dropped to his death. Jon ran his hands lightly along the tip of the wall, rough concrete snagging against his palms. Did Jim climb up onto the edge? That would be hard, especially if the man had been taking Spice. Had he been thrown off? Wayne hadn't heard any sound of a struggle.

Jon tried to imagine how he would scale the wall if he was looking to jump. One hand on the top, then swing one foot over. That meant he'd be straddling it. After that, he just had to swing his other foot over. Once perched there with the top of the wall digging into his buttocks, a quick shuffle forward would be enough ...

A grating noise caused him to glance over his shoulder. The stairwell door was slowly opening. Jon turned properly, his heart now beating faster. A male form in dark clothing began to step out. A bit under six feet tall. Average build. There was a bulky black holdall hanging from one hand and a hood was covering his head. The person hadn't spotted him as he began to turn to the corner where Wayne had been lying. Jon wished he had a baton, or at least a pair of cuffs.

More movement at the door. Another figure appeared, this one smaller. Jon realised it was a woman just as she started to speak.

'Fuck's sake, Darryl. Wait for us, will you?'

'This is it,' he grunted back. 'We're here.'

Her head turned and she spotted Jon standing on the far side. 'Darryl! Someone else is up here.'

The man shuffled unsteadily through one hundred and eighty degrees. He was somewhere in his forties, Jon guessed. White.

The all looked at each other in silence.

'I'm not doing anything with him here,' the woman announced.

The man jabbed a thumb towards the door. 'Do us a favour, pal.'

Jon started to approach them. 'What's in your bag?'

The man gave a tired sigh. 'Get fucked.'

'Yeah – fuck off,' the woman added.

Jon regarded her for a second. She was staring at him with a mixture of fear and hostility. The man plonked the holdall down, bent forward and pulled the zip open. Then he extracted a loosely rolled sleeping bag, followed by a couple of blankets. Next, a large plastic bottle of nasty-looking cider appeared. The woman shifted the shopping bag she was holding to her other hand. Glass clinked.

A romantic night for two, Jon realised.

'You still here?' the man asked, folding the empty holdall over and throwing it to the side.

No wings in that, Jon thought. He glanced at the woman who was still in the doorway watching him. 'You want this place to yourselves?' he asked. 'Then you'll need to let me past.'

The doors to the building on Bendix Street were firmly locked. That meant no assessment of the stairwell Ryan Gardner fell down. Jon walked round the back of Piccadilly Station towards Temperance Street and the railway bridge Luke McClennan had plunged to his death from. The streets in this part of town were flanked by industrial units and work yards with chain-link fences topped by rolls of razor wire. Behind them were piled a variety of materials. Old fridges and ovens. Tyres and car doors. Planks of wood.

He reached the stretch of road where McClennan had died. It was the same stretch made famous by footage from Google Earth. When the camera-car had passed by, it had captured a wasted-looking man leaning with his back to the wall in a narrow recess. Kneeling before him, face level with his flies, was a prostitute. A still of the image had done the rounds on social media before something else popped up to distract everyone.

The railway arches were about thirty feet high. How did anyone get up there? He looked left and right, but could see no obvious place to climb. Perhaps there was an access point closer to Piccadilly Station itself. Or further down the line at Ardwick. Either way this was an isolated spot. How, he wondered, did the Dark Angel ... Jon's chain of thought ground to a halt.

I'm using that name now. Christ. Stick to calling him the killer, he told himself.

How did the killer locate McClennan? How did he know the man was out here? Or did they approach this spot together? Was that it? Maybe, all the victims knew the killer and had been lulled into a false sense of security by him. His thoughts settled on Greg once more. He knew Luke and Wayne. Was he working with the killer? Persuading victims to come with him to these lonely spots where the killer waited?

It didn't quite fit. He was overlooking something. It was like the feeling he sometimes had on leaving the house in the morning. A nagging sense of things being ... not right. Then he'd get to work and realise he'd left his phone on the table. Or his lunch in the fridge. That feeling.

He looked about in frustration then set off for the building where Frank Kilby's life had come to an abrupt end. Work had continued on it during the intervening months. Now, the scaffolding had disappeared. New windows had been put in place; the glass panes crisscrossed with white tape. Jon contemplated climbing over the perimeter fence for a closer look. What was the point? Without the scaffolding, he couldn't get a sense of what had actually happened.

To his surprise, a man came wandering round the corner of the building, torch in hand. The beam of light occasionally swung about, settling momentarily on a row of Portaloos, an orange skip. Eventually, it reached Jon as he peered through the entrance gates.

'Can I help you?'

Jon lifted a hand in an attempt to show he wasn't up to anything. 'Were you working around the time Frank Kilby died?'

The man, who Jon could now see was about fifty, with a large gut, ambled closer on slightly bowed legs. He was wearing a bomber jacket with the words 'Sharp's Security' embroidered on the left breast. There was a look of casual curiosity on his face. 'Who?'

'The bloke who died when he went off the scaffolding?'

'Oh, him.' The man paused. 'The homeless one found in the car park. Why, did you know him or something?'

Jon nodded. 'Actually, I did. But I only just heard.'

The nightwatchman now looked a little embarrassed. 'The contract to patrol this place happened after he died. Something the insurance company insisted on. Can't help you, mate. Sorry.'

'OK.' Jon took a last look at the converted warehouse. Seven rows of windows. It was a long way down from the top. He scanned the freshly laid asphalt of the car park. Immaculate lines awaited the ranks of residents' vehicles. Somewhere, at the base of the building, Frank Kilby had connected with that hard surface. Had it been suicide or something else?

The walk to the Star and Garter didn't take long. He crossed the empty yard at the rear of the derelict pub and paused at the base of the fire escape stairs. People had been here since his last visit; the wooden pallet Wayne had landed on was now a mass of splintered wood. The wheelie bin in the corner was on its side. His eyes climbed the fire escape stairs. The door at the top still hadn't been secured. Or maybe it had, only to be forced again. Either way, there could be people up there. He listened for a while, but heard nothing.

Watching where he placed each foot, he climbed the flight of metal stairs. On the landing, he stopped again. The door was half open. Was that the sound of movement in the darkness beyond? He half-closed his eyes and turned his ear to the doorway. Definitely movement. A faint rustle followed by ... what was it? The noise was soft. Was someone asleep in there? 'Hello? Someone in there?'

Silence for a few seconds, then he heard it again; it was almost like someone trying to clear their throat as quietly as possible. The noise repeated and, suddenly, Jon knew.

It was the gentle coo of a bloody pigeon. Maybe several, roosting in there for the night. He contemplated opening the door, but didn't want a load of panicked birds to come flapping out around his head. Instead, he pushed it almost shut then turned his attention to asphalt below. He tapped a forefinger on the thin metal handrail. Like the NCP car park, it wouldn't be easy to climb up without losing your balance. Wayne had landed on his back, partly on the pallet. Which meant he had almost completed a somersault on the way down. Holding on with both hands, Jon leaned his upper body out into the darkness.

Another faint noise from the room behind him. This one sounded more like a scratch. Probably a bird jostling with its neighbour for a better perch.

The metal rail was now pressing deep into his stomach. If he relaxed his grip on it, he would definitely topple over. It wasn't that far to the ground. Far enough to turn through almost one revolution? Jon thought it wasn't – not unless you'd been propelled over by someone else.

He remembered a time with his brother Dave, when they were younger. A family holiday in North Wales, forced to visit crumbling castles by their mum and dad. The two of them had ended up at the top of a watchtower. He'd been leaning on the low wall, gazing out across the sea, when Dave had crept up behind him, grabbed both his legs at the knees and lifted them up.

Jon could still remember the terror of finding himself being upended: head, shoulders and chest poking out over the edge. The shimmering grass far, far below. There was absolutely nothing he could do to prevent it happening; his terrified bellow had been loud enough to turn heads all along the lower battlements.

Dave had swiftly let go of his legs. Feet back on the ground, he'd whirled round to find his brother doubled over with laughter. It had been one of the few times he'd punched him in anger. A crack to his temple, not his face. But still enough to send him crashing to the cold stone flags.

Nodding to himself, he stepped away from the railing. That's how Wayne died. Someone grabbed his legs and flipped him. He trotted down the steps, more certain than ever someone was out here killing people.

It was almost one in the morning when he got back to the Stevenson Square. It was nice to be somewhere that was properly lit. Music thudded up from the Tiki Bar. There was a lot of people still flitting about. A sell-by-the-slice pizza place further along looked especially busy; folk grabbing something to eat before looking for a way of getting home.

Jon made his way to the shadowy doorway. He was surprised by how much he wanted to see Greg's form nestled there. But, apart from the stuff he'd left there earlier, the recess was empty.

He found himself looking off in the direction of Deansgate. The Lowry Hotel was on the other side of it. Barely a five-minute walk. He shook the thought from his head.

So this is it, Jon said to himself. Your first taste of sleeping rough.

Conscious of people walking past behind him, he laid out the flattened cardboard boxes edge-to-edge. The last couple he opened out completely to form an upper layer that, he hoped, would keep the arrangement below in place. Next, he laid the blanket down. Finally, he unrolled the sleeping bag. For a place to crash, it didn't look too bad. He removed his walking boots and placed them at the foot of the bed. Then he half unzipped the sleeping bag and climbed in. As soon as he'd zipped it back up he realised he hadn't got a pillow. Damn. Reaching forward, he picked up the boots and positioned them next to each other where his head would be. Then he laid his empty rucksack across them to provide a bit more padding and lay down.

The cardboard formed a very effective insulating layer with just a bit of give. Probably not enough to stop my back from aching, he thought, but a lot better than sleeping direct on freezing concrete. He nestled his head into the folds of the sleeping bag. Immediately, he knew that the light encroaching from the nearby streetlamps would keep him awake. That and the constant ebb and flow of noise. Engines revving, vehicle doors slamming, footsteps passing, peoples' voices, the intermittent beep of a pedestrian crossing. How am I supposed to sleep with all this?

Bit-by-bit, the noises seemed to merge. Eventually, they became a relaxing drone. He realised his mind had stopped trying to process what people were actually saying as they walked by. Voices were growing indistinct. Blurred. Fainter. Everything was fainter now.

A siren brought him round.

He opened his eyes. Did I just fall asleep there? He suspected he had. For how long, he wasn't sure. There was definitely much less noise coming from the square. The syrupy presence of sleep hadn't fully receded. He turned his head towards the wall and let it slowly envelop him again.

Next thing he knew, something was pressing down on his head. He felt the soft flesh of his lips being stretched and pulled. His mind struggled to work out what was happening, where he was, if it was a dream. He came fully awake: I am lying in a doorway and someone's hooking their fingers inside my lips. His reflex was to gag. To try and spit them back out. A growling noise rose from the back of his throat as he struggled to free his arms.

The pressure on the side of his head increased and he began to make sense of what was occurring: there was a man leaning over him. One of the person's hands was pinning his head down. He could hear stifled giggling as fingers probed roughly at his gums and against his teeth. More laughter: this from someone else standing slightly further back.

'Get the fuck off me!' Finally, he freed a hand and scrabbled to catch hold of the other person's wrist.

The scathing laughter picked up. Jon cursed: if I could just hold this bastard's hand still, I can bite his bastard fingers off. The hand withdrew and, an instant later, Jon felt his head jerk. Colours bloomed in his head. He's punched me. Or slapped me. Jon wasn't sure which was worse. Anger coursed through him like a rush of bright water.

Cool head, he thought. Think. 'Please,' he whined, letting himself go limp. 'Leave me alone.' He brought his knees out of the crumpled sleeping bag and up to his chest, while curling his hands over his head. The foetal position: the posture everyone instinctively adopted when a fight was lost.

The pressure on his head eased. Whoever was above him assumed they had won. Which was a mistake. A terrible mistake. Jon knew that once the person stood up straight, the stamps and kicks would start. Before the hand lifted completely, he clamped both hands around the person's wrist and yanked with all his strength.

The person just had time to let out a grunt of surprise before his face connected heavily with the doors just above Jon's head. Keeping a tight grip on the wrist with one hand, Jon placed his other palm against the ground and quickly twisted over onto his knees. His shoulders were now beneath the other person's chest. A punch connected with the side of his jaw. But the angle was awkward; it didn't carry much venom and certainly wasn't going to stop Jon as he planted a foot on the ground and, using the powerful muscles of his legs, drove himself fully to his feet. The person was now draped over his shoulders, both trainers clear of the ground, legs kicking about uselessly as his free hand thudded harmlessly against Jon's back.

Jon glimpsed the look of astonishment on the companion's face before he whirled in a tight semi-circle; the head of whoever was over his shoulder connected with the side wall of the doorway. The person cried out with pain. Leaning to the side to keep the person's skull wedged against the surface, Jon ran him across the panelled doors before heaving him against the far wall. He hit it with a dull thud before dropping to the ground. Not pausing to stop, Jon lunged an arm out at the other person. His fingers closed on the neck of the bloke's shirt and, for a moment, they were face-to-face. Just time for a quick smile before Jon slammed his forehead into the person's mouth. The bloke staggered backwards across the pavement, collided with a bin and fell over.

Jon turned back to the doorway, vaguely aware of a sour taste on his tongue and lips. The man who, while giggling, had assaulted him in his sleep wasn't finding things so funny now. He was back on his feet, just. Some kind of gym monkey, with a tight T-shirt to show off his muscled torso. Jeans that shrouded, Jon guessed, legs like a pair of matchsticks. Hair that had probably been in an overly elaborate side-parting, but was now a straggly mess. There was a strip of skin missing from one side of his face. Blood was pouring from his nose, dripping from his lips and chin. He was looking at Jon with wild and desperate eyes.

Yeah, Jon thought, you're cornered. And I'm only just getting started. As he closed in on him, pulses of blue light started bouncing off the pavement and walls around him.

'Stay exactly where you are!' Even though the voice was from the road immediately behind him, the roar of blood in Jon's ears gave it a distant quality. He could just make out a car's doors being opened.

Another voice shouted, this one sounding closer: 'Move and this taser gets fired straight in your arse!'

Two of them, then. Jon raised his arms from his sides and half-looked back. Multi-coloured halos danced around the lights of Stevenson Square. A couple of uniformed officers were beside the kerb. Each one had a taser pointed at him. 'They attacked me.'

'I said, put your hands behind you.'

Jon was amazed by the amount of adrenaline in his system. He'd been in enough scuffles to be familiar with the way the hormone heightened your senses. Made everything super-sharp. But this ... part of him wanted to whirl round and take on the uniforms, too. He felt bloody invincible.

'I said, put your fucking hands behind you!' The voice was angrier this time.

'Why the fuck are you arresting me?' he called back. 'This prick attacked me while I was asleep in that doorway!'

The same voice again. 'Shall I just fucking give it him?'

The other officer spoke up. 'Last chance, mate. Hands behind your back or you'll find yourself flipping about on that pavement like a fish.'

Sighing, Jon touched his fingertips against the small of his back.

A hand came down on his shoulder and he was steered firmly towards the building. 'Face the wall. Now, do I need the cuffs? You going to cause any more trouble?'

It felt like something was shooting a stream of bubbles into his blood. He had to breathe deeply a couple of times before he could speak. 'They attacked me.'

'You were asleep in that doorway, then?'

'Yes.'

'You know that's illegal? Anything in these pockets that shouldn't be? Any needles?' The officer asked as he started to pat Jon's pockets.

From the corner of his eye, Jon saw the man emerging from the office doorway. He had untucked his T-shirt and was using the hem of it to dab the blood from his mouth and chin.

'Are you OK, sir?' the officer behind him asked.

'Yeah, yeah, I think so.' The man glanced uncertainly at Jon.

'An ambulance is on its way. What happened here?'

'Well ... we were just checking on him. Seeing if he was OK.'

'Bollocks!' Jon realised he'd snarled the word. He twisted his head to see a bystander had helped the man's companion to his feet. The one he'd head-butted. It looked like he'd live.

'Who bloody asked you?' The officer behind him demanded, pushing him against the wall. 'I asked if there's anything in these pockets of yours that's going to injure me. Syringes, blades, anything like that?'

Jon had to breathe deeply. 'No.' His heart felt like a piston in his chest. The feeling of sheer power was almost overwhelming. It was like, if he dipped his knees, he could spring up to the window ledge above. Scale the side of the building like Spider-Man. He wrestled the urge back down.

The officer's breath felt warm against his ear as a hand reached into his jacket. 'This your phone?'

'Yeah. Honestly, I didn't start this.'

'Course you didn't.'

'Look, can we speak in the back of your car?'

'Why?'

Because, thought Jon, I need to let you know I'm a police officer. And I don't want to spend the next few hours in a cell. 'Just need to have a quiet word.'

'Of course.'

Jon felt his shoulders relax. Thank God for that.

The officer searching him called to his colleague. 'Rich?'

'Yup?'

'MDV?'
'What about it?'
'Expected, is it?'
'Imminent.'

MDV: mobile detention van, thought Jon. Lying bastard. They weren't about to have a chat in the rear of the vehicle; they were going to arrest him, sling him into a secure cubicle no bigger than a toilet, and probably let him stew there until morning.

Fuck that.

He swept an arm back, spinning on the ball of one foot as he did so. His elbow connected with the officer's chest and – to his surprise, the man fell away like a cardboard cut-out. His colleague's eyes went wide as he began to scrabble for his taser once more. Jon jumped over the stricken officer and sprinted off up the street in his socks.

CHAPTER 29

Gavin tugged gently at the lapels of his long black raincoat. When he had the wings strapped on beneath it, he always worried the feathers were being damaged. Or that they were creating an odd-shaped lump beneath the material.

Three in the morning: the time when the temperature always seemed coldest. He removed a black woollen cap from the pocket of his coat and pulled it on over his head. Just as he was about to step out of the side street's shadows, he heard the thud of rapidly approaching footsteps. He paused. A big bloke in a flappy army coat and no shoes shot by.

Gavin frowned. Odd. He waited a few seconds and, sure enough, a uniformed police officer sprinted past. A snatch of breathless words. 'Lever Street! On foot, towards Ancoats!'

Gavin melted back into the darkness. No point heading into that part of town, then. He turned around and moved quietly in the opposite direction. Seconds later, he was in an area of open ground. An open-air parking lot, flanked by a wide expanse of water. What was once a wharf that connected to a long stretch of canal. He knew that if he took the towpath leading into the city centre, it would take him through a tunnel before emerging at the top of Canal Street. From there, he could bear left to the block of student flats the university were about to knock down. The empty building was tall, and he'd heard several rough sleepers had started sneaking in at night. It would be worth a check.

There was a male figure lurking near the mouth of the first tunnel. Some lonely soul, hoping for a quick fumble with a stranger. Gavin could feel the man's eyes tracking him as he moved past.

'You all right there, mate?' the person asked in a soft voice.

He kept looking straight ahead. 'Not interested, thank you.'

Once inside the short tunnel, his footsteps started to echo. He kept an ear open behind him, but the other person hadn't tried to follow. Soon, a set of steep stone steps appeared on his left. He climbed up them and emerged on to David Street. Perfect: the condemned tower block was on the adjacent road.

Jon reached the intersection with Great Ancoats Street and looked back. The officer was a good fifty metres behind. 'Keep the fuck up!' Jon bellowed in his direction before laughing out loud. This was fucking ace. Which way, now? He toyed with the idea of the Oldham Road. What would it be: seven, eight miles to the moors? He liked the idea of a chase across the hills. Jumping streams, leaping rocks. No bastard would get in touching distance. The sour taste still lingered in his mouth. He patted his tongue against the roof of his mouth. Thirsty. Where to get water? There was a garage on the Cheetham Hill Road that stayed open all night. Yeah, let's get me a little drink there.

Another glance behind. The officer was still about fifty metres back. How could that be? Was he just running on the spot? Felt like he'd been stood here thinking for ages.

'Fucking useless, mate!' He set off along the main road. The headlights flowing in his direction had halos, just like the ones had in Stevenson Square. These were bigger, though. And they were shooting out little sparks of silver. Like silent fireworks. Was it some sort of headlight filter car shops had started selling? Jon drifted to the edge of the pavement for a better look. The nearest car swerved across to the far side of the road. So did the next while letting out a long beep. Don't be like that. Only checking your special effects, Jesus.

Gavin looked across the grassy area to his right. The Vimto Sculpture was just visible across the expanse of grass. A giant bottle, with a scattering of over-sized pieces of fruit at its base. Bizarre.

Before him stood the empty building. Hoardings had been erected around it. Attached to them at eye-level were regular-spaced signs. O'Connell Brothers, demolition.

Gavin followed the path towards the rear of the building. The way they got into these places was always at the rear. Out of the normal world's sight. He soon spotted a section of hoarding where the base had been forced apart to create a narrow gap with the neighbouring panel. He squeezed through the wedge-shaped opening, careful to not scrape his back and the delicate wings beneath his coat.

In front of him, a knee-high line of metal loops emerged from the concrete. A bike rack. One loop had a front wheel chained to it, another just a bike's frame. He didn't bother trying the empty building's rear doors. Instead, he hugged the base of the building, going in a clockwise direction, waiting for some kind of alternative entrance. One that was more discreet. At the second corner, he came across a service door: 'Fire Exit. Do Not Block.' The area before it was clogged with industrial-size bins. But there was a narrow corridor through. He pushed a palm gently against the door. It opened.

The corridor beyond was pitch-black. Once he'd closed the door behind him, he took a key ring from his pocket and pressed its little button. A dot of white light appeared on the floor at his feet. He directed it forward; a short set of steps. Careful to make no noise, he climbed up to the top. A door that probably opened onto a communal area. He turned to the next flight of steps, knowing if he kept going he'd eventually reach the roof. High spots: always the best place to find someone who was ready to leave this world.

Someone shouted at him from across the road. 'Run, Forrest, run!'

Jon turned to where the voice had come from. Three pale faces lit from above by a harsh streetlight. Shadow had pooled in the men's eye sockets. It lurked in their open mouths like tar. They were all laughing at him. One had a bottle in his hand. Drink, Jon thought. I need a drink. He wondered whether to cross over and ask for a swig, but his legs wanted to carry on. The pavement was like a sprung floor. Every time his feet connected it was seven-league-boots stuff. Striding impossible distances with every step. He continued running, parked cars flowing smoothly past like they were on a conveyor belt waiting to be picked. I'll have that red Audi, thanks. But no big pincer came down from the sky to lift the vehicle off. Too bad.

Coke. His eyes were snagged by the bright sign. A nice cold can. That would hit the spot. Stop the rot. What what. He steered himself towards the vending machine. The lines of cans were queuing behind a clear window, all covered in dew. Can after can. A can-can of cans. So close. He delved a hand into his pocket and it came back with coins cupped in the middle. A twenty. A few tens. A five pence, too. He rattled each one down the hungry opening and into the guts of the machine until no more were left. Nothing. Come on, come on, don't be like that. I fed you plenty. He lifted both hands and grasped the thing firmly by its shoulders. Are you and me going to fall out? No response. Not a peep. A gentle shove. I'm warning you. A good shake. No? Maybe there was a button to press. Was there a button to press? He took a step back. There most certainly was: a black one. Coins cascaded into the little tray below it. Down into a crouch for a look. Jackpot! A twenty. A few tens. A five pence, too. Hang on, are those the ones I just put in? He picked out a five pence piece, squinted at the Queen's profile. 'Ma'am, I'm most terribly sorry, but there seems to be an issue with your credit.' The comment made him want to laugh, so he did. He sank to his knees and laughed and laughed until his stomach ached and his forehead was resting against the Perspex.

Something about the building was making him feel optimistic. At the doors to the third floor, he thought he heard music. A metallic hissing from somewhere nearby. He cracked the fire door open an inch and saw a thin glow further along the corridor. Someone was in one of the rooms, then. But could there be anyone else?

He continued with his ascent. Four, five, six, seven, eight. How many tons of steel and concrete did the structure weigh? All of it waiting to be smashed apart. By the twelfth floor, he could go no further. The door before him said 'No Access', but he wasn't so sure. The lock mechanism was missing, for a start. Punched clean out. He crouched at the perfect hole that had once housed it. The cool air flowing in made him blink. Beyond, was a two-tone band: dark-grey and orange-black sky. He tested the door with a shoulder, but it didn't budge. It took him a second to work out why. Pull, not push. He hooked a fingertip into the hole and it swung inwards without a sound.

When the soles of his shoes made contact with the surface of the roof it sounded like rough sandpaper. Away to his right, a red dot hung motionless in the night sky above him. The warning light of a nearby crane. Looking down, he could just make out a cellophane wrapper at his feet. That hadn't blown up on any breeze. People had been here. The next thing he saw was a shopping trolley lying on its side. He shook his head. Why? Why bring that up here? Unless it had been transported up when the lifts still worked. He stepped round it and began a slow survey of the dimly lit roof. Nothing in the shadows directly in front, nothing to either side, nothing behind him. The sense of disappointment was sharp. For some reason, he'd felt sure the place wouldn't be deserted.

He checked his watch. Dawn would be breaking soon. A blackbird somewhere nearby had already started to madly twitter. His last full night on earth and he hadn't found anyone. He quelled his feelings of disappointment by thinking about the next evening and being reunited with Claire and Sophie.

He was turning to go when he heard a delicate whimper. His neck twisted. Where did that come from? It had to be the other side of the brick construction he'd just stepped out of. Careful not to make a sound, he moved round it. A lone figure came into view. A sense of elation surged up; he knew it! And he knew exactly what the person was up here for. He stood still, happy to just watch for a little while.

The figure was leaning against the rail, head bowed forward, totally still. Trying to build up courage, no doubt. I can help you with that. He approached, treading softly. Once closer, he could see the other person was quite small. Thick coils of hair distorted the shape of the head. A slender hand rested lightly on the rail. Rings on two of the fingers. What he could see of the jaw line was soft and round. He realised with a shock it was a woman.

CHAPTER 30

The little window in the centre of the door dimmed. Someone was out there, looking in on him. There was no point asking what was going on: no one was prepared to give him an answer. About an hour or so before, he'd heard the other prisoners being taken, one by one, from the back of the secure van. Jon hunched forward on the little bench and rested his head in his hands. Anything to try and lessen the pounding in his temples. He badly needed a drink which, he appreciated, was ironic seeing as his feet were like two islands in a pool of liquid. The smell filling the tiny cubicle told him the liquid was urine. He had no idea if it was his own, but suspected it was.

A while later, a key was inserted into the lock and the door opened. The face of the police officer looking down at him was filled with disdain. 'Fucking disgrace.'

'How long have I been in here?' Jon rasped.

The officer stepped to the side. 'Long enough to piss everyone off. Go on, shift.'

Jon took his time getting to his feet. Once upright, he tried to assess how bad he was. The inside of his skull felt like someone had crammed it full of drawing pins. Drawing pins that, when he moved, started ricocheting off each other. Christ almighty, this was worse than a whisky hangover. He eyes felt red, raw and itchy, and that sour taste ... it was still on his tongue. Sharp and chemical. The pain at various points across his back told him he'd probably taken a few whacks from an extendable baton. There was a lump above one ear, too. Plus some tender spots down his thighs. Bastards.

Wet socks flopping against the floor, he made his way slowly down the narrow central aisle. If anyone else was still locked up in the vehicle, they were keeping quiet. Outside, it was dusk. No, dawn, surely? He recognised the building the mobile detention van was parked outside. Bootle Street station. At least, I'm still in the city centre.

'Oh, my God.'

He looked down and to the side to see Iona standing by the van. The two uniforms next to her were staring at him intently. He took a deep breath, hoping the influx of oxygen wouldn't make him keel over. 'Isn't it a fine morning?'

One of the officers shook his head. 'Twat.'

Oops, thought Jon. I really must have been a pain in the arse. But enough to warrant them beating me? Not wanting to show he was in any discomfort, he made his way down the ramp. 'This us?' he asked, gesturing to the nearest car. To his relief, Iona nodded.

He ambled past the watching officers. Catching the hostility in their eyes, he paused. 'Gentlemen, it's been a pleasure.'

They didn't reply.

He was about to get in the car, when he stopped. Lifting one foot, then the other, he slid the sodden socks off his feet. His tightly-folded twenty-pound note fell to the ground. After pocketing it, he held the bedraggled socks up to the watching officers. 'Would you mind taking these? They're a bit pissy.'

Iona opened the driver's door while speaking softly. 'Just bloody get in, Jon.'

Realising she sounded slightly worried, Jon dropped his socks into the footwell and climbed inside. Only once the doors were shut, did he let out a sigh. 'I think I'm dying. Please tell me there's some water in here.'

'Glove compartment.'

He got it open. Inside was a litre bottle of Buxton. You absolute beauty. He cracked the top and had gulped half of it down before they were out of the car park. 'Jesus,' he announced, pausing for breath. 'That is the best water I've ever tasted.'

Iona pulled to a stop besides the first bin they came to. 'Sling them in there.'

'Sling what?'

'Your socks!'

'Oh.' He lowered a window and lobbed them in. 'Done.' She continued to look at him. 'What?'

'Is that all you've got to say?'

'What do you expect me to say?'

'Well ...' She broke eye contact to pull the car away from the kerb. They turned onto Deansgate and she headed towards the Mancunian Way. 'What do you remember?'

Looking down at his bare feet, Jon started to shake his head. Instantly regretted it. 'Not a lot after the patrol car turned up in Stevenson Square.'

'How about chucking the member of public about in that doorway like a rag doll?'

'Oh yes – I remember that. How do you know?'

'I've seen the report.'

'Oh. Who else has? Weir?'

'Not as yet, but he will eventually. Once it goes through the system.'

'So did that member of the public make a statement?'

'He did.'

Good, Jon thought. That means the bastard would have been required to leave his name. So long as it's not fake, I'll catch up with him one day. 'I assume he and his mate are choosing not to press charges?'

Out of the corner of his eye, he saw Iona's head turn. 'How did you know that?'

'Because I woke up with that member of the public's fingers poking about in my mouth. He drugged me, Iona. Rubbed something nasty into my gums.'

'I don't ... why would he do that?'

'Why? Because I was lying there, fast asleep and helpless. A bit of garbage to have fun with.'

Her eyes widened. 'Which would explain why you—'

'Exactly. What the hell did I do?'

'Hang on, he can't get away with that. If he drugged you, we should be paying him a visit.'

Oh, he'll get a visit, all right, Jon thought. One day. 'It's not worth it. I'll be OK. I'm more interested to know what I did.'

'Where do you want me to start?'

He drained the rest of the water and lobbed the empty bottle onto the back seat. 'You tell me.'

By the time she'd got to him being re-arrested while kneeling before a soft drinks machine on a petrol station forecourt while talking to a five-pence piece, Jon's head was pounding again. He realised he was clenching his teeth and had to close his eyes while taking a few deep breaths. *What if I'd run into traffic? Or got to a canal and tried to jump across it? One day,* he promised himself, *the man who spiked me will wake up to find himself lying in a hospital bed.*

'You OK, Jon?'

'Yeah. Just thinking things over.' He opened his eyes to see they were now on the Mancunian Way, doing seventy. He wondered why the hurry.

'It gets worse,' Iona announced.

'Really? Can it?'

'It took a few, but they eventually got you in the MDV. Obviously.'

Jon became aware of the throbbing across various bits of his body. 'Obviously.'

'Every other cubicle already had a drunken City fan in it. A brawl down near Deansgate Locks, apparently. Some were singing football songs. Apparently, you started calling them all pansies for liking football.'

Jon shut his eyes again. 'I used that word. Pansies?'

'You did. Which set them off. So then, you bellowed a Sale Sharks song at them – non-stop – for over an hour.'

'Sale Sharks song?' Jon thought of all the times he'd watched the rugby team play. 'But there aren't any Sale Sharks songs.'

'Saaa-le,' Iona crooned softly in a monotone voice, dragging the word out into two syllables. 'Saaa-le.'

Jon closed his eyes. 'No. I shouted that for over an hour?'

'Then urinated over the floor of your cubicle and fell asleep.'

No wonder the officers weren't looking too impressed with me, he thought. 'How the hell did you find me?'

She pointed to a bag of possessions beside the empty bottle on the back seat. 'They took your phone when arresting you in Stevenson Square. I tried ringing it about forty-five minutes ago. Luckily, the custody officer answered. They had no idea who you were.'

'Right. Thanks.' He glanced at the dashboard clock. 'Hang on: why were you ringing me before six in the morning?'

She took a quick breath before answering. 'There's been another death.'

Jon felt his chest tighten. The pain coursing through his body was instantly forgotten. 'Someone has gone off a roof?'

'Correct. Only this time, the whole thing has been captured on film.'

CHAPTER 31

Back at base, they found a pair of trainers for him in the costume box of the departure lounge: the room where officers going out on surveillance operations prepared their appearance.

'You seriously need a change of clothes, too,' Iona said, looking him up and down with a grimace.

'Later,' Jon replied, with a quick point at Iona's bag. 'Got some perfume or anything in there?'

'Yes. Why?'

'Just give us a spray; that'll do for now.'

'That most certainly won't do for now,' she replied, taking out a small bottle and releasing a few bursts of fine mist at his torso. 'Turn round, lift your arms.' She fired a few more at his back and armpits. 'Congratulations. You now smell like the rancid guard dog of the world's worst brothel.'

'Cheers. Where are they?'

'Third floor. Main meeting room.'

Sitting round the table were DCI Weir, a few other detectives and the office manager. Cups of coffee were dotted about and the room smelt faintly of bacon. All their heads turned as the door opened. Weir, halfway through what looked like a breakfast burger, gave Jon a what-the-fuck look.

'Just in time,' the manager said, gesturing to a younger man in jeans and T-shirt who was busily tapping at a wireless keyboard. 'Finn, here, is an analyst with the video unit. He's bringing up the footage now.'

Jon pushed a chair as far from the table as possible.

'Something wrong with us, DC Spicer? Weir asked.

'Not you, me,' Jon replied. 'It's been a bit since I had a shower.'

'Looks it.' Weir shot back, balling up his food wrapper and turning to the table. 'This footage came from where, exactly?'

'A crane operator,' Finn replied. 'There's a construction site on the adjacent street to the building you're about to see.'

'And what is this building?' Weir demanded.

'It was a hall of residence owned by the University of Manchester,' Iona replied, sitting down next to Jon. 'Situated at the top of Granby Row. It's now empty, awaiting demolition.'

'When's the footage from?' Jon asked.

'About three hours ago,' Finn replied. 'Apparently you left a flag on the system for deaths involving falls from high places and the wearing of fancy dress?'

Jon caught Weir's look of surprise. 'I did.'

'Well, nights when the crane operator can't sleep, he heads in to work early. As if things on building sites don't start early enough as it is, Jon thought.

'Once there,' Davis continued, 'he likes to watch the sunrise from up in his cab. Sitting there just before dawn, he spotted a figure on the roof of the university's hall of residence.'

Weir sat back and crossed his legs. 'I get it: he does what ninety per cent of the population do on witnessing something suspicious: reaches for his phone and starts filming. Finn, how are we going, there?'

'Ready. Shall I play it?'

'Please do.'

The footage was dark and grainy. The only thing to break up the different grades of grey was a dim line of yellow splodges towards the edges. Finn immediately pressed pause. 'So, just to orient you, we are looking down at the rooftop area from an elevation of about thirty metres. These glowing points of yellow are streetlights, viewed from above. The square shape filling the central area is the top of the roof. That squat shape to the left is the access point from the stairwell. Directly behind it, you can just make out a person. Very faint. You see? Standing at the perimeter railings of the roof. Continue?'

'Go for it,' Weir immediately responded.

'OK,' Finn replied. 'And the voice you're about to hear is that of the crane operator.'

The footage continued for a few more seconds before there was a sound of a cough. 'Not sure what they're up to, but it don't look good to me.' The man's voice was little more than a murmur and, even though the words were spoken softly, they carried an undercurrent of excitement. Jon was reminded of TV programmes; a wildlife cameraman who'd finally struck lucky.

A moment later, a second figure appeared through the door that gave access to the roof.

'Hey up,' the crane operator whispered. 'Some company's arrived.'

Finn paused the footage once more. 'We can get this footage tidied up a fair bit, given time. But my guess is the newcomer is male. Not quite six foot tall. A few inches under. He's wearing a black hat and long black coat, which is why he's so poorly defined. I'll let it continue.'

The figure stood perfectly still, just the head moving as he surveyed what was around him. A thought suddenly struck Jon. Greg was about five foot ten. Thinly built. And he'd been missing from his usual haunts all last night.

The person took a step back and was in the act of turning round when he stopped. After a couple of seconds, he began to move again. But now he proceeded more cautiously as he skirted round the stairwell. He stopped again.

Jon cocked his head to the side. Could it be Greg? All done up in black clothing?

'He's spotted the other person!' The crane driver's voice. 'Thank Christ for that.'

They watched as the taller figure slowly approached the smaller one at the railings.

'As you can see,' the video analyst announced, pressing pause once more. 'The top railing comes to well above waist-height for the person who was there first. For the newcomer, I'd say it's about level with the thigh. From that, we can surmise the smaller person is about five feet four. The other, just under six foot.' He pressed play once more and, this time, sat back in his seat.

'Some sort of conflab,' the crane driver's voice stated as the taller figure turned slightly and placed an arm round the shorter one's shoulders. 'Go on, son. You're doing well. Now get them away from that bloody edge.'

The two figures stayed that way for a bit. Then the arm of the taller person withdrew. He appeared to be speaking to the shorter one who, after a second's hesitation, began to tentatively climb over the railings. The crane driver's voice was ragged. 'What are you doing? No. No. Stop him, why aren't you stopping him?'

The shorter one had now got both legs over and, keeping one hand on the railing, faced away from the taller person, who seemed to continue talking before holding an arm out, gesturing to the city below, then up to the stars. Shaking their head, the smaller person turned back from the edge and began to lift up a leg, as if to climb to safety.

The taller person suddenly stepped forward and shoved hard with both hands. The smaller one's grip on the rail was lost. Both arms windmilled for a second before the figure vanished.

'Oh, my fucking God.' The picture became unsteady. 'He pushed him! Oh, Christ, he pushed him off. Fuck, fuck, fuck.'

When the image steadied once more, only the taller figure remained. Slowly, he shrugged the long coat from his shoulders.

'This is where it gets weird,' Finn whispered.

They all watched in silence as two thin, elongated shapes extended out from the person's shoulders.

'Holy shit.' Weir's voice had gone up a notch. He shot a disbelieving glance at Jon before turning back to Finn. 'Are ... are those wings?'

'Pause it!' Jon barked.

Finn did as asked. 'I would guess each one is about sixty centimetres long. The shape is definitely that of a wing – or a pair of wings, but it's impossible to say what they're made from. Feathers, cardboard, silk: could be anything.'

Jon's mind was reeling. It was all true! My God: the rumours swirling around the homeless community were accurate. He was wearing a pair of bloody wings! Jon could hardly believe his eyes. 'What happens next?'

Finn looked to the DCI for approval. Weir gave a quick nod.

The wings stayed stretched out as the person's head tipped back. It was almost, Jon thought, like the fucking freak was drinking in a beautiful aroma. Savouring a magnificent sound. Gradually, the angle of the person's head altered as his gaze returned towards earth. He peered over the edge for a second, then an arm moved and the wings folded in, seemingly absorbed by the expanse of his back. He half-turned and bent forward, the action causing most of him to blend in with the shadowy roof.

'He's retrieving his coat,' Finn explained. 'You can see better very soon.'

It was a few seconds before he straightened back up. The balled-up coat was now held to his chest as he strode purposefully back to the access point of the stairwell.

'That's it. He doesn't reappear,' Finn announced, pressing stop.

It was like a room-full of people trying to stir themselves from sleep. A sigh. Someone stretched their arms above their head. Another rubbed at his face. Jon glanced at Iona; she was still staring in shock at the screen.

Weir picked up his pen and made a few notes. 'The victim: we now have confirmation the person is female, correct?'

Jon's head whipped round in Iona's direction; she appeared equally surprised.

'Correct,' the office manager replied sombrely.

'Female?' Jon asked. 'What do you mean, female?'

Weir turned to Jon with a tired expression. 'Officers at the scene reported the body was that of a female.'

'Was there any ID? Do we know who she is?'

Weir shook his head. 'Not as yet.'

'But ... surely there's a strong chance it could be Olivia Farnham?' He thought back to the faint image of the person in the phone's footage. 'Whoever it was on top of that roof, she had a lot of hair, practically dreadlocks; you could see it piled on the head. And she's about five foot—'

'Ed Farnham's on the way to the hospital now,' Weir snapped. 'DCI Pinner is meeting him there. You think we haven't considered that?'

'Was there a baby with the body?' Iona asked in a small voice.

'Apparently not.' Weir sighed. 'And before you ask, no, the officers checked: there was nothing on the roof. So, first thing we'll need to do is gather in CCTV from the adjoining—'

'What did he pick up?' Jon asked.

Weir closed his eyes for a second. 'What?'

'He picked something up from the roof. After the wings folded back in, he bent down for a bit.'

'Yes – that was his coat,' Finn responded, a hint of uncertainty in his voice.

Weir clicked a finger at him. 'Back it up.'

The footage went into reverse.

'Stop,' Jon almost shouted.

They were looking at the moment the person came back into full view. Shadow meant all fine detail was lost, but something black was balanced across his forearms.

'Whatever that is,' Jon said, 'he's not carrying it: he's cradling it.'

CHAPTER 32

Gavin Conway didn't know what to do. He stood at the door with the tiny thing in his arms. It seemed barely alive. More than once on the walk home, he thought it had stopped breathing. Only by pausing, bringing the little mouth close to his ear and listening, was he able to hear the faint sound of breathing. Miniscule little pants. Mouse-like. Easily drowned out by any passing car.

When he'd got into his flat, he'd stood in the middle of the room for a long time. His mind went back to the rooftop. The girl he'd found up there was already on the edge. She'd been so ready to go. That's why she'd gone up there in the first place. At first, he hadn't been sure whether to leave her be. He'd never assisted a woman before. But then he'd seen the feathers round her neck. A necklace of feathers and he knew it was a sign. She wanted to fly. They had a bond. A connection. Whatever pain she was in, he would help her leave it all behind.

And when he'd done that and she'd left this world, he'd felt happy. Doubt sometimes crept into their mind at the last second. It was fine. To be expected. Her cry of terror as he'd shoved her off the ledge had quickly faded in his mind. He'd felt calm. He'd felt content. Then came the faint noise at his feet. Something was down there. He'd crouched and gingerly parted the dirty blanket lying on the floor, wary some kind of animal might scuttle out. But the little face turned up to him was human. Puffy eyes tightly closed. Was it real? A living baby? He'd touched the back of a finger against the cheek. Warm.

He repeated the movement now, holding a finger to the smooth skin. All the times he'd held Sophie, just like this, cradled in his arms as he shifted his weight from one foot to the other. Left to right, left to right, gently rocking her to sleep. Except this baby was already asleep. It had never really been awake.

The moment, less than half an hour ago, when he'd opened the door to Sophie's bedroom came back. It was the first time light had spilled into it since she and Claire had left him behind. Stale dead air. The high-sided bed, the duvet and pillow with underwater creatures. Seahorses, starfish and hermit crabs. There was a pale-blue blanket and a pack of wet wipes. He'd peeled back the flap and pressed a finger on the top one: still moist. Cuddly toys and a night-light that sent moons and stars gliding across the ceiling.

But it only took moments to realise the place wasn't right. The bed was too big and the baby too small for any of Sophie's stuff. The infant would be dwarfed by the cuddly toys. Memories came back: when babies were this little, they needed special nappies. Cream when they got a rash. Dummies. Tiny little socks for their feet. Had they kept none of those from when Sophie was this size?

He'd placed the infant on the bed. It tensed its arms and legs for a moment, miniature fists momentarily raised before everything went floppy once more. He approached the chest of drawers and slid the bottom one out. Inside it were some dungarees and a swimsuit. Several dresses and pairs of shorts in pastel colours. Unworn trainers. Things for the coming summer that Claire would have spotted in sales and bought, knowing that when the weather got warmer once more, Sophie would be the right size. Except Sophie never got to see another summer. And neither did Claire. He picked one of the trainers up and smelled the pristine rubber sole. A little sticker said, 'Half Price'. Below that, '£3.49' been written in red biro. Through his tears, he smiled. Claire. Always planning ahead.

He put the trainer back and returned to the bed. The infant hadn't moved. Then he remembered the box on top of the wardrobe. The collection of items Claire had hung on to. Mementos of their daughter's first years on this earth. He reached the box down and placed it on the carpet. So light. It took an effort before he was able to remove the lid. But this is necessary, he thought, blinking back tears. It needs to be done. The cardboard shuddered slightly as he slid the lid off. Nestled inside were several objects wrapped in tissue. He couldn't bring himself to fold back the gossamer-like paper shrouding them. Instead, he reached straight for the stubby plastic feeding bottle and took it out. The cap took a surprising amount of force before there was a click and he could remove it. The teat still felt soft and rubbery. Maybe the cap had protected it from the air. He went through to the kitchenette. All he needed was a splash of milk in the bottle and then, what was it? About twenty seconds full power in the microwave. Yes, that was it. Test the temperature by releasing a drip against the inside of your wrist. That's how he used to do it. Funny, he thought, how just holding an object – its feel in the hand – released a stash of memories.

He opened the fridge and immediately saw there was no milk inside. His palm slapped against the side. Shit! Back in the bedroom, he gazed down at the tiny sleeping form. 'I'm sorry,' he whispered. 'To not be more use to you, little thing. But don't worry. Because I've thought of something.'

Footsteps were now approaching and he focused on the door directly in front of him. The handle turned and

Miriam looked out to see him standing on her landing. She was in a dressing gown and slippers. Puffy eyes immediately dropped to the blanket. 'What have you got in there?'

He glanced over his shoulder, even though he knew they were alone. 'Can I come in, please?' he whispered.

Both her eyebrows lifted. 'Er ... it's very early. What is it?'

'Please, Miriam.'

'OK.' She stepped back, obviously intrigued. 'Is it for me?'

'Well ...' He edged into her hall. 'Let's go to your front room and I'll show you.'

She clapped her hands. 'Is it a kitten? Have you brought me a kitten?'

He pushed the front door shut with his heel. 'After you.'

She couldn't stop herself from looking back over her shoulder. 'Where did you find it?'

The fire was on in her front room. A dozen toy cats were arranged before it on a rug. 'Off, please!' she said, plucking several from the sofa and placing them on the floor. 'That's better.' She sat at one end and patted the space next to her. 'Here.'

He stayed standing. 'Miriam, what if I told you that it's not a kitten?'

'It's not?' Her smile shrank. 'It's not a puppy, is it? I don't like puppies.'

'It's not a puppy.'

She now looked totally lost. 'But ... what, then?'

'It's a baby, Miriam. A human baby.'

'A baby?'

He nodded.

'Whose baby?'

'A friend's. But she's very poorly. She needs to rest, but has no one to look after it while she does. She asked me and I couldn't say no. Do you think you could help to look after her baby for a little while?'

'Me? I don't know.' Her fingers fiddled nervously with the pendant round her neck. 'I've not looked after a baby before.'

He caught her eyes straying to the blanket. She was itching to see it.

'What if you tried? You're such a caring person. I think you'd be great.'

'You think that?'

There it was in her voice: hope. He nodded, now certain she would agree. 'I think you'll be brilliant. Here, why don't you have a hold?'

She couldn't keep her smile from returning. Wriggling back in the seat, she brought her knees together, patted them and turned her palms up. 'What's the baby's name?'

Name. He looked down. Shit. The babygrow was grimy, but he could see fine pink stitching running through the hems. He said the first girl's name that came into his head. 'Sky.'

'Ooh, Sky? I like it.'

He lowered the blanket onto her lap and then sat himself next to her. Keeping his eyes on her face, he watched as emotions flickered across it. Apprehension, replaced by wonder. A flash of something that could have been joy. Then concern.

'Is she OK?' Miriam asked.

'I don't think my friend has been feeding her very well.' He looked towards the kitchenette, knowing there was one thing her fridge was full of. 'Maybe we could warm up some milk?'

CHAPTER 33

Jon was on his feet. 'I'm going back into town.'

'For what purpose?' Weir's face looked sickly.

'To find my contact. Someone knows what the hell is going on here. I think he's our best bet of finding out.'

Iona leaned back in surprise. 'Jon, you think that's ... don't you need to rest?'

'I'm fine. It makes sense I go. The places where he might be: I know them.' He turned to Weir. 'Sir?'

'Keep in touch, understood? Soon as you hear anything.'

'Understood.' He looked at Iona. 'Fancy giving me a lift?'

She glanced at their senior officer.

Weir's hand lifted. 'Go.'

As Jon and Iona slipped out of the room, they heard the sound of paper being ripped. Jon glanced back to see Weir removing an A1 sheet from the flipchart in the corner of the room.

'Where the fuck are the fat pens?' Weir demanded. 'We need a bloody plan, here.'

Jon marched towards the stairs, Iona having to almost jog to keep up.

'You were keeping something back in there,' she said. 'What?'

He almost smiled. Not a lot got past Iona. 'It's my contact. He vanished yesterday afternoon and was gone all evening.'

They started trotting down the stairs.

'You think it could be him?' she asked after a moment's silence.

'I don't know. Just that he's floating around in town. Put it this way: every night someone's died, he hasn't been far away.' He reached the first landing and stopped. 'The person in that footage was about the right height and build. And I've been thinking about the night Wayne died. It was Greg who told me that Wayne had buggered off to some derelict pub to get wasted. Greg knew which one.'

They carried on down to the doors of the departure lounge. Jon held them open until Iona was through. 'I mean, Greg could have turned up once Wayne was off his head. And I don't think Wayne fell from the top of that fire escape by his own choosing. Not with him landing on his back. I reckon he was thrown and the force of that made him flip over on the way down.'

'Like the woman in the phone footage. How will you find him?'

'It would help if he had a bloody phone. I'll just have to do the rounds, keep asking people. It's how things seem to work.'

Iona veered off to the line of cupboard doors on their left. Throwing open the first, she removed a beaten-up coat and a pair of battered jeans from the line of garments hanging inside. 'Here.'

'No time, Iona. I need to find him.'

She threw the items at him, while pulling the adjoining door open. A faded sweatshirt landed at his feet. 'I'm not getting in a car with you while you smell like that. I assume you've got some socks and pants in your locker?'

Jon's eyes cut to the male changing room. 'Think so.'

DARK ANGEL

'Good. I'll get us a coffee while you sort yourself out.'

'Can you get my warrant card from the top drawer of my desk?'

'You're taking it with you?'

'Yeah. Just in case.'

'In case of what?'

'I bump into some over-eager uniform again. There's no time to be pissing about.'

DCI Pinner scanned the other two vehicles parked outside the mortuary at the Manchester Royal Infirmary. Neither car belonged to his friend. At least I got here before him, he thought, turning his engine off.

It took a few minutes for someone to respond to him pressing the buzzer. But this was outside official hours, so he kept his irritation in check. When the door was finally opened, it was by a middle-aged man clad in long white plastic overalls. A blue hairnet covered his head.

Pinner raised his police identification. 'I'm here about the young female that just came in. She was found at the base of the building on—'

'Granby Row. I was told you were coming. I've just been cleaning her up a bit.' He looked beyond Pinner. 'Where's the ...?'

'On his way. Have you been told who he is?'

'No.'

'You may well recognise him – he's the mayor of Manchester.'

The man's face didn't change. 'Makes no difference to me who he is.'

'Right. What ... what sort of condition is she in?'

'She's fine for an ID. Now. There's a lot of damage to her upper-right cranium, but I can wheel her in so that side is facing away. Besides, she has a lot of hair, so we've been able to arrange it to help conceal things. The wider skeletal damage; he won't see that beneath the sheet.'

Pinner closed his eyes for a moment. 'When you say a lot of hair, is it in a particular style?'

'Do dreadlocks count as a style? She has some of them. Bits of coloured cotton woven in. Some beads, too.'

It's Liv, Pinner thought as he heard the sound of a car coming round the corner.

Iona's car had barely come to a stop in the parking area of the Chinese supermarket on the Oldham Road before he was out the door. A few minutes' later, he was back at the entrance of the office in Stevenson Square. The bits of cardboard were still there. No sign of his other stuff. Or Greg. He hurried down to the Spar, where he spotted the person with the brindle Staffie he'd seen the day before.

'Hey, how's things?'

He looked up, took in Jon and nodded. 'OK. You?'

'Yeah.' He crouched down and extended a hand to the dog. 'And how about you, Deefer? Good kip?'

The dog's tail began beating furiously as Jon started to tickle behind its ears. 'Have you seen Greg about?'

'Said he was heading to the Booth Centre.'

Jon glanced at the man. 'Where did you see him?'

'We both slept at St Joseph's last night. You didn't get his note?'

'What note?'

'He left a note stuck to the wall of that porch in Stevenson Square you were using for a pad. He waited there for you, but when you never showed, he headed off.'

Jon searched his memory. He didn't think there'd been anything stuck to the wall. 'Must have missed it. What time was this?'

'Just before six. You have to get there at six before all the places go.'

When I was back at the base, Jon thought. Shit. 'I ended up sleeping there on my own.'

'You did?' The man looked concerned. 'Go alright, did it?'

'So, so. Greg never mentioned St Joseph's. Is it a church?'

'Yeah. They turn the hall next to it into an overnight place. It's very strict, but that makes it quieter than the main ones.'

'Where is it?'

'Bengal Close, Ancoats.'

'I'll have to remember that. Right,' he patted the dog on the head before standing up. 'I'll try and catch Greg up. You take care.'

'And yourself. Laters.'

Jon waited until he was out of sight of the Spar before taking a sharp left and making his way quickly through the narrow streets of the Northern Quarter. Could he trust the owner of the Staffie to be telling the truth? Greg might have left instructions for him on what to say, if anyone asked about the previous night. After decades in the job, Jon knew better than to take anyone's word about anything.

Bengal Close was the other side of Great Ancoats Street. The church was at the top end; a soot-stained building with a stubby tower. Beside it was a much newer building with a corrugated roof. A silver-haired man with a stoop was coming out of the front door, dragging a large laundry bag behind him. There was a Renault Scenic with its boot open parked near the steps. 'Morning,' Jon announced. 'Is this the place that's used as a refuge?'

He glanced at Jon. 'It is, but we're closed now. Doors open six tonight.'

Jon could see the bag he was struggling with was full of sheets. One was partly hanging out and Jon noticed it had elasticated corners; the sort they used when Holly was first learning to sleep without a nappy. He lowered his voice. 'Actually, I was hoping to have a quick word.'

The man looked round once more. This time, Jon's warrant card was raised. 'Oh. Now?'

'If that's OK. I won't be long.'

Jon slipped it back in his pocket and nodded at the laundry bag. 'This lot going in the boot?'

'It is.'

'I'll give you a hand.' Without waiting for a reply, he took a looped-handle from the man and lifted the bag clear of the wet steps. Together, they ferried it to the people carrier and slung it in the back.

'Thanks,' the man said, slamming the hatch and then rubbing his hands. 'So ... a quick word?'

'In private, if that's OK.'

'You'd better come in.'

A loud two-tone beep sounded as he opened the front doors. Beyond them was a reception area: a row of soft seats either side of a counter with a glass window. The walls were covered by posters that detailed a variety of services: Manchester and Salford Samaritans. Turning Point: Smithfield Detox. The Manchester Veterans' Helpline. Jon glanced through the next set of doors that led into the main hall: rows of narrow tables occupied the large, open floor. 'Where does everyone sleep?'

'In there. We serve an evening meal until eight. At ten, the people staying here collapse the tables away and stack the chairs. You see the blue plastic rectangles lining the walls? Those are mattresses. They're unclipped and laid out across the floor. Each person gets one of those sheets we just put in the car, a pillow and a sleeping bag. There's a screened-off area in the corner for any females. We used to sleep forty-two here. But since the Covid regulations, that's gone down to eighteen.'

'I suppose every refuge is similarly restricted?'

'They are.'

'That's a lot of people with nowhere to sleep at night.'

'Sadly, yes. A vast returning to the streets.' He sighed. 'At seven o'clock in the morning, the lights go on and the reverse takes place. Breakfast until eight thirty and then everyone heads off for the day.'

It sounded to Jon like a military operation.

'We also ask those who stay here to help with the washing up and cleaning. Most are happy to do so.'

'Impressive. How come they don't just use their own bedding?'

'No one is permitted to take personal possessions beyond this point. It's the only way we can ensure the hall remains free of drugs, alcohol and weapons. It has to be a safe area and everyone in the building has to know it's safe. So, when people arrive, they place all their things in a bin liner, which is labelled and sealed before being locked away. And they must sign a form declaring they have nothing else on their person. Those are the rules.'

'And it works?'

'For the most part, yes. Everyone knows if you ever break them, you won't be allowed back.'

'These forms. They serve as a record of who was here each night?'

'I suppose they do.'

'I'm trying to ascertain the whereabouts of someone called Greg. He's—'

'Greg was here. He hadn't been in for a while. It was nice to see he was OK.'

'This is Greg who used to serve in the army? About sixty or so, wears a flat cap?'

'Yes, absolutely. He's never any bother.'

Jon stepped towards the front doors for a closer look. He had to be certain Greg really had been here all night. 'What's stopping someone leaving once you've locked-down?'

'Nothing. But they wouldn't be permitted back in. If they leave, they take their bag with them and they don't get to come back. We have to operate a strict curfew.'

'Could someone leave without being noticed?'

He shook his head. 'We have three staff on each night. Once things have quietened down, they are based in there.' He gestured to the side office with its sliding window.

Jon gauged the route from the main hall to where he was standing. If someone was crawling, they could sneak past the office, no problem. 'Is this door locked at night?'

'It's on a buzzer. We have a camera and intercom to see who is outside ... oh, you mean sneak out?'

'Either.'

'No, I can't see that happening. A beeper sounds whenever this door is opened. You heard it when we came in.'

Jon nodded. 'Rear fire escape?'

'If that's opened, a proper alarm sounds.'

'How about windows?'

'What's this about, if I may ask?'

'I need to be certain everyone booked in here last night remained on the premises until morning.'

'I see. The windows are on a latch system. You couldn't climb out of one without unscrewing the mechanism. And you'd need a stepladder and tools to do that.'

'Were you working last night?'

'I was.'

'And nothing unusual happened?'

'No. Nothing.'

'OK, thanks. I might need to send a colleague or two to check the building and your CCTV, if that's alright.'

'I don't see why not.'

'And last thing. Could I take a quick look at the form Greg signed?'

'One moment.' He returned with a sheet of paper in his hand. Jon checked the bottom. The name Greg Scott was written alongside yesterday's date. Win! Now I can supply a surname to Iona. Get her to thoroughly check this person out. He used his phone's camera to take a snap. 'Thanks. That's a great help. And I'd appreciate it if you don't mention I was ever here.'

DCI Pinner moved towards the Audi as Farnham climbed out. 'Edmund.'

'Trevor.'

Briefly, they shook hands.

'Are you OK?' Pinner couldn't recall ever seeing his friend looking so strained.

'Shitting myself, if you want to know the truth. I really am.' He looked fearfully at the nondescript building. 'Christ. Is ... do you think it's ...'

Edmund placed a hand on his arm. 'I think you need to assume it is.'

Farnham blinked a couple of times. 'Why? Have you been in already?'

'No, I haven't.' He glanced back to the door. The man in white was still holding it open. 'Shall we?'

Farnham nodded. 'OK.' He breathed deeply. 'That big detective showed up last night – the one who's meant to be finding Olivia.'

'Spicer?'

He nodded. 'I was at the farewell dinner for the delegation over from America. Wasn't good to have him lurking outside. Tell him my daughter knows no one called Anura.'

'I will.'

'Can't say I warm to the man, Trevor.'

'He has his own way of doing things.'

'You're happy with him working under you? Not sure if I would be.'

Trevor bowed his head. 'Understood.'

'Come on, then.'

Once they'd put plastic overshoes on, the mortician keyed in the entry code for the inner door. A stark corridor lay beyond, white walls and a shiny floor. 'If you wait in there,' he pointed to the right-hand door, 'I'll just be a minute or two.'

He set off for the double doors at the other end of the corridor, soles of his white boots squeaking with each step.

Pinner led his friend into a small room. The far wall had a window at its centre. The room it looked through to was in darkness. 'It's a viewing, only, Edmund. With circumstances as they are, we have to consider forensics. Sorry.'

Farnham was staring at his reflection in the glass. 'Forensics, Jesus Christ. I don't think it's her. She can't have been ... no. What if I can't recognise her, Trevor? I'm not sure I can do this. I mean, if her face is—'

'There's no damage to her face, Edmund. It's OK.'

The window transformed as strip lights flickered to life in the room beyond. The mortician backed in through a swing door, pulling a gurney draped in a sheet. He eased it to a halt the other side of the glass and, without looking at the window, turned the top of the sheet back and retreated a step.

Liv's profile was as Pinner remembered. The same button nose and tiny ear. He'd seen that face so many times. Birthday parties, cinema trips, walks in the Lake District. Beside him, Farnham's breathing had sped up. He turned to see tears coursing down his friend's face.

The canteen area of the Booth Centre was almost empty. Jon noticed the serving hatch doors were shut. To his relief, Greg sat on the far side of the room, a mug in one hand, his head bowed over a newspaper.

Jon waited until he was a table away before announcing his presence. 'Greg.'

The other man looked up and immediately grinned. 'There you are! What the hell happened to you?'

Jon sat down. Greg was appraising him with an expression of concern and curiosity. 'I couldn't find you,' Jon said. 'Looked everywhere.'

'I left word with a few people. And there was a note in the entrance – I stuck it to the wall.'

'Maybe the wind blew it off? I didn't see any note.'

'So what did you do in the end?'

'Slept in that doorway, of course. I didn't know if you might turn up.'

Greg blushed slightly. 'I had to get myself to St Joseph's. I'm really sorry we missed each other.'

'Why?' He kept his eyes on Greg, searching for anything that might suggest deceit.

Greg's look of embarrassment deepened. 'Once you'd gone, I thought I might get myself in trouble. St Joseph's was the best place for me to be.'

Jon knew you had to be an exceptionally good actor to blush like that on demand. 'I don't get you.'

'When you told me about Wayne dying, it was ... the old switch clicked. In my head. I wanted a taste of something strong. I haven't drunk in almost three years, but I wanted to last night. I really wanted to.' He stared down at the paper for a moment. 'He was a good kid, Wayne. I liked him a lot.'

Jon recalled the tears that had started streaming down Greg's cheeks when he'd told him Wayne was dead. Those had looked real enough, too. 'What is St Joseph's?'

'A place where nothing can tempt you. A lot of folk won't go there. They say it's more like a prison.'

'You slept there?'

He nodded. 'Aye. And I'll probably go back again tonight.' He lifted his hand. 'It's been a long time since I've been like this.'

'So, booze was your thing?' Jon asked, observing the tremors running through Greg's fingers.

'Booze was my thing,' he repeated. 'It's what I chose. No one wakes up in the morning and says, I reckon I'll be an alky. It comes down to choices, Jon. Ultimately, it's choices. I don't blame anyone but me for my life. I made those choices.'

Jon shifted his gaze to the other man's eyes. 'You got family, Greg? I never asked.'

'Yeah, there's a boy back home. But he's got his own life. I'm not dragging him down into my shit. Best we stay apart.'

'How old is he?'

Greg's smile was sad. 'Twenty-six.'

More or less Wayne's age, Jon thought. Do I need to worry about you, Greg? Are you scouring the city at night, luring people to places where the Dark Angel can make a kill? 'More happened last night. The girl we were trying to find is dead.'

Greg's hand, that had been holding the paper, contracted into a fist. Paper scrunched and then tore. 'For fuck's sake!'

Jon looked about. All the tables surrounding them were empty. 'You OK, Greg?'

His head nodded. 'The streets. They cost so many bloody lives. How did she die?'

'It looks like she fell from the top of a building.'

He shoved the crumpled paper away from him. 'So the Dark Angel is killing women now? And the baby, did he …?'

'There was no sign of the baby. We think he may have taken it.'

Greg shook his head. 'He took her baby? Jesus Christ, why?'

'We don't know. But I don't think we have much time. Which means I can't afford to not be able to find you. So, after this, we're going to a phone shop. I'll get you a handset, OK? Then I'll put my number—'

'I've got a phone.'

Jon frowned. 'You have?'

'I never use it.' His hand burrowed into his coat and re-emerged clutching an ancient Nokia. 'I doubt if it's even got any charge.' He pressed the power button. 'Oh, looks like I'm wrong.'

Jon sat back. 'Greg, I can't believe you've got a phone. Why the hell didn't you say?'

'Did you ever ask?'

'No, but I could have just rung you last night – actually, no I couldn't. You don't even have it turned on!'

'No. Hate the little bastard, if I'm honest.' He saw something on the display and a sadness filled his eyes. 'Last person to ring me was Wayne. See?' He turned the phone round.

Jon squinted at a screen with so many scratches, he could hardly make out the number beneath. 'Can I?' He held out his hand.

Greg plonked the device in his palm.

'Wayne had a phone,' Jon murmured, tilting it so he could read what was on the screen. He couldn't recall anything about a phone being among Wayne's personal possessions. In fact, he wasn't sure if a phone featured in any of the victims' lists. Had Olivia Farnham owned one? Surely she must have. He took his own device out, selected the camera function and took a picture of Greg's screen. The list of digits making up Wayne's phone number was just legible. 'While I'm at it, what's your number, Greg? I'll put it in mine now.'

'No idea. It's in there under my name.' He took the Nokia off Jon and pressed a few buttons. 'Here you go.'

Even better, thought Jon. Now I've got your surname and phone number. Once he'd taken a snap, Jon got to his feet. 'I need to head back, Greg. But I shouldn't be long. Get some more charge on that museum-piece, can you? I'll ring you in a bit.'

'What are you going to do in such a hurry?'

'Get hold of some records.'

CHAPTER 34

Jon and Iona found Pinner striding back and forth in his office. 'Leave the door open, DCI Weir's on his way,' he said, waving them to the meeting table in the corner. 'Before we start, I have a message from the mayor: Olivia had no friend called Anura.'

Jon blinked. Bit late now.

'And I don't think your method of asking him was appreciated,' Pinner added.

'Tell him I'm sorry if my attempts at finding his daughter caused him any inconven—'

'Sir,' Iona cut in. 'We've made some progress with the phones.'

Pinner continued glaring at Jon for a moment longer. 'Go on.'

'Jon?' Iona asked.

'I found my contact earlier this morning, having lost track of his whereabouts last night.'

'This is the one who used to serve in the army?' Weir demanded, slipping through the door.

'That's right,' Jon replied taking a seat. He'd already decided to hold back with his suspicions about Greg – at least until Iona's enquiries were complete. 'I was arranging for him—'

'Where was he?' Weir interrupted.

'A church-run refuge.' He didn't bother adding that Kieran and another colleague were en route to the location to check the building's windows and CCTV. 'I was arranging to get Greg – my contact – a phone so we don't lose touch again. Turns out he has one, but rarely uses it. In fact, he tends not to even have it turned on. But he also let me know that the last person who called him was Wayne Newton; the sixth ex-soldier to have recently died.'

Pinner lifted a finger. 'The empty pub? He was found by the fire escape of ...?'

'The Star and Garter,' Jon replied. 'That's the one.' He turned to Iona, who already had her laptop open.

'I put Wayne's number into the phone system. It's registered with Wiffle on a monthly contract.'

'How fast are they with access requests?' Pinner asked.

'Well, it varies. Obviously, I stressed the urgency—'

'Let me have those details, DC Khan,' Pinner said. 'I'll make sure we get them.'

'We also ran a check on the personal item inventories of all six ex-servicemen to have recently died,' Jon announced. 'With all of them homeless, none had much by way of possessions. Even so, there wasn't a mobile phone found with any of them. Not one.' He checked both senior officers were listening. 'But the family of Luke McClennan had already told us he used to regularly check in with them. In fact, that's how they first suspected something was wrong – when his phone calls stopped. They've now given us his number.' He turned to Iona once again.

'I've contacted the network and—'

'Forward the details to me,' Pinner said quietly.

'Will do,' Iona replied. 'Thanks, sir.'

'So,' Weir said, eyes darting to Jon. 'You're thinking some of them might have owned a phone?'

'I think,' Jon replied, 'that it's worth asking the families or anyone they knew, that question.'

Iona looked at DCI Pinner. 'Obviously, if Olivia Farnham had a phone, it will be a great help if we can access her records, too.'

He nodded. 'I'll see if Ed can help us with that. Anything else?'

Jon shook his head.

'Right,' Weir said, pointing to the door. 'See where the phone angle takes you. And Jon? If it's a dead-end, you get straight back out there and hook up with that contact of yours again. Keep doing the rounds.'

Gavin paused on his way out the door. He knew the question wasn't necessary, but he asked it anyway. 'Are you sure you'll be OK?'

Miriam's head was bowed, all her attention focused on the little baby on her lap.

He tried again. 'Miriam? You'll be OK?'

She raised the feeding bottle and examined the amount of milk inside. 'That's almost an ounce of milk gone. She's starting to do a bit better. Do you think she's starting to do a bit better?'

Gavin wasn't sure: how could a baby drink so little? The tiny thing had been lying there for what seemed ages. And in all that time, she'd managed about a thimble of milk. 'Seems to be.'

Miriam nodded. 'Yes, I think so, too. Is it warm enough in here? Do you want to turn up the fire a little more?'

The place is already like an oven, Gavin thought. 'No need for that, Miriam. I shouldn't be long.' He started down the corridor. 'Call me if you think of anything else!'

Miriam's voice drifted through the doorway. 'You put nappies on the list?'

'I did.'

'When will you be back?'

'Soon. A few hours.'

'OK. If you speak to the mummy, tell her there's no rush, will you?'

He picked his way through the junk that clogged his path. 'Will do.'

'Tell her I'm happy to look after Sky for as long as she needs me to!'

He closed the door of her flat, thankful to be free of its cloying atmosphere. Time, he thought, to carry out a risk assessment. Work out if the police are any closer to finding me.

Jon stretched his arms to the ceiling. Almost two hours of making phone calls and not a thing. Tiredness was catching up on him.

Iona replaced her phone receiver. 'Interesting.'

She'd been on the phone to her contact at the Ministry of Defence for almost quarter of an hour. Jon raised his eyebrows in question.

'Greg Scott,' she announced. 'Scots Guards. Joined in 1973, left six years later.'

'Where after that?' Jon asked, thinking maybe the Parachute Regiment.

'Our man at the MoD was a bit cagey. But he reappeared in the Scots Guards in 1995 and served in it for another fourteen years. Left the army completely in 2009.'

Jon sat forward. 'I don't get it. Where was he for the middle bit? Still in the army?'

'Still in the army.' Iona nodded. 'But that part of his file is restricted access. Basically,' she continued in a lower voice, 'he was recruited into covert stuff. Given his background and the years he was off radar, he thinks it was probably undercover work in Northern Ireland. Better chance than an Englishman of infiltrating the IRA.'

'The IRA? Christ.'

'And this was the Eighties, Jon. He was saying about it being some of the worst parts of the Troubles. Maze Prison escapes, bombing of Harrods, assassination attempt of Thatcher.'

'I remember that; the Brighton hotel bombing. She was lucky not to have died.'

'To quote him, if he was over there, it took balls of steel.' She folded her arms. 'Still not sure about him?'

Shock and guilt vied for supremacy in Jon's mind. Had his view of the man been prejudiced? Just because he slept on the streets and had a shady past? 'Let's see what Kieran says. And if his number features on any of the victims' phone records, if they ever come through.'

'Spicer!'

Jon turned to see Kieran Saunders approaching from the direction of the doors. 'Hey mate, how did it go?'

'That place is organised. I reckon the guy in charge hopes to be promoted to running Strangeways one day.'

Jon smiled. 'Apparently, the regime isn't to everyone's taste. No chance anyone ducked out during the night, then?'

He perched on the adjoining desk. 'Not unless they're related to Houdini. CCTV was good quality. Honestly, once that place goes into lockdown, it really goes into lockdown.'

Jon felt a sense of relief. Looked like Greg was probably in the clear. 'OK, thanks for doing the check. When are you due back at the airport?'

'Straight after lunch.'

'And then that's it?'

'Yup. They're on an afternoon flight back to the Big Apple.'

Jon could see Alicia Lloyd in his head. Had she waited up, expecting him to turn up at her hotel room last night? He checked his desk drawer, wondering what he'd done with her business card.

Kieran was now moving back towards his own desk. 'By the way, Jon,' he pouted. 'Love your fragrance. What is it?'

Jon raised his middle finger. 'Ask Iona: it's hers.'

Kieran turned in her direction. 'Iona, care to share? It's gorgeous.'

She smiled back at him. 'I had you down more as a Brut kind of guy, Kieran. That's from the 1970s, isn't it?'

'Oh, yeah, very funny.'

Iona joining in with the banter, Jon thought, lowering his finger and then lifting a thumb towards her. Nice!

She grinned briefly before her eyes cut to her screen. 'Wayne's phone company has just sent the records.'

A few minutes' later she'd printed out the last three months of his calls. He'd rung three numbers on the night he died. Two early evening, one at nine forty-one. Jon retrieved his own phone and brought up Greg's number. It wasn't among them. Looks like I was wrong about the bloke. 'OK: we've got one landline and two mobiles.'

'He also received a call,' Iona said, finger on a separate column, 'from another mobile.'

Jon noticed the time the call had come through. 'Odd time for someone to be ringing him: gone two in the morning.'

'And,' Iona said, 'he rang that number the day before. Look: eleven forty-six at night. Stayed talking for almost half an hour.' She scanned a few more columns. 'There – the previous week. Wayne rang it again: another late-night call lasting twenty-three minutes.'

'Could be his mate,' Jon said. 'The one whose sofa he kipped on sometimes.'

They looked at each other. Normally, it would be a case of handing the number to the comms team for them to do a discreet trace. But they both knew there was no time for that.

'Who calls it? You or me?' Iona asked.

What, Jon thought, if it's the drug dealer? The one I battered. That would be bloody typical. 'You.'

She regarded him. 'OK. Any particular reason, me?'

'Yes. But you don't need to know. Plus, I've been asking enough questions of people. There's a chance my voice will be recognised.'

She tapped the number in and listened. After a second, her eyebrow lifted. 'Sorry – I've dialled wrong.' She hung up and turned to Jon. 'The person said it was the Manchester Veterans' Helpline.'

Jon frowned. 'A helpline?'

Iona had already started typing at her keyboard. 'Yeah. Here it is.'

Jon moved his seat closer so he could see her monitor. 'Where are they based?'

She selected the 'About' tab. 'Right here. Down near Shudehill.'

Jon scanned the menu that listed the website's other sections. 'Go to "Who we are" can you? Let's see what it tells us about the staff.'

There was only one name and a photo on the click-through screen. 'James Pearson,' Jon murmured. 'Looks like a retired major. What do you think, Iona? Should we pop down to the office for a little visit?'

'Let's see what Weir and Pinner reckon,' Iona replied, printing the charity's details off.

Pinner raked back his hair back while letting out a sigh. 'I agree, it's certainly very interesting. Martin, what are your thoughts?'

Weir was still studying the phone records laid out on the table in Pinner's office. 'But Olivia Farnham didn't call this number, correct?'

Pinner lowered his arms. 'Correct. But in all ways, she's a bit of an anomaly, isn't she? Female, didn't serve in the armed forces, wasn't homeless in the same way the ex-soldiers were.'

'You mean,' said Iona, 'like he's now altered who he's targeting?'

'That would be one interpretation,' Pinner replied.

Jon tapped the phone records with a finger. 'Here's what seems odd to me: this number called Wayne at two nineteen in the morning. Shortly after that – possibly within an hour – Wayne is dead.'

'Forgive me if I've got the wrong end of the stick; are these helplines not there to be a ... last option for people who are considering suicide?' There was a faintly derisory tone in Weir's voice. 'Places like that, I should think the measure of an operator having a bad night is a caller taking their own life. A pretty common occurrence, given the nature of the work. No?'

'But,' Jon countered, 'that number rang Wayne, not the other way round. It doesn't seem right to me.'

Weir was studying the records. 'But you said just now Wayne had rung this number ... when was it? Here you go: the day before. At 11.46 p.m., and spoke for twenty-seven minutes. So, Wayne is feeling particularly low. He rings the number for support. Speaks to an operator or volunteer or whatever they call themselves. That person marks Wayne down as vulnerable, at risk of suicide, etcetera. Whoever is working the following night – possibly the same person, possibly not – follows up to see how he's doing.' He glanced at Pinner. 'I'm not convinced we should be focusing our efforts on this particular avenue.'

The ping of an email arriving came from Pinner's computer. Sighing, he hauled himself out of his seat and went over to his desk. As he read whatever was on the screen, his eyes narrowed. After a moment, he sat down. 'What was that number again?' he called over. 'The one that called Wayne on the night he died?'

Jon read it out.

Pinner regarded them over his monitor. 'I've got the phone records for Luke McClennan. He was found dead on Thursday the second of July, but it's estimated his body had been there for a month. The last activity on his records is a call that he received on Wednesday third of

June at 3.06 in the morning.' He stared directly at Jon. 'And it was from the number you just read out.'

Jon kept his eyes on Pinner, even though he wanted to lean close to Weir and shout triumphantly in his face. 'Sir, can you tell me if another number features?' He removed his phone and read out Greg Scott's mobile.

Pinner checked his screen. 'Nope. Just that one call from the same number that called Wayne Newton.'

That's it then, Jon thought. Greg isn't part of this.

Pinner started tapping a finger. 'We keep talking about this number ringing the victims. Means nothing. Let's stop talking about it being a number that called them; it's a person. We need to know who.'

CHAPTER 35

Jon and Iona were outside the offices of the Manchester Veterans' Helpline within twenty minutes. The street was narrow; tall Victorian buildings rearing up each side. The entrance was on the junction with another road and, before they got to the steps, Jon slowed his pace to check no one was nearby. A motionless figure was lying in a deeply recessed doorway opposite, blankets completely swathing his head. Out for the count, Jon thought, turning to Iona. 'Before we give anything up, let's be totally sure of how this outfit operates.'

'Agreed,' Iona responded. 'And I also think we should assume the guy in charge – this James Pearson – could be involved.'

Jon nodded. 'True, even though he seemed eager to help when I rang.'

'So how shall we play it? You taking the lead, or me?'

'Let's see what sort of a person he is.'

'Fine.'

From a gap in the folds of the blanket draped over his head, Gavin Conway watched the man and woman. They made an odd couple. He was large with closely shorn hair and clothes that looked like he'd just fished them out of a bin. She barely came up to his elbow. Jet black hair tied back in a neat ponytail, small briefcase and office-style clothes. Some of what they'd said was indistinct, but he'd heard enough to learn who they were and the person they were going to see: James Pearson. What he'd feared was going to take place was already happening. The police were on to him.

Once they'd entered the building, he threw the blanket back and sat up. He felt like he'd been poisoned. Sweat had started breaking out across his forehead and down his back. There were pins and needles in his toes. What should he do? He'd hoped to spend the early part of the evening searching for more who needed helping on their way. How long would it take the two officers to get his name and address? What if it had been Pearson who had called them? Other officers might already be at his house. Or watching it. Why had he used his work phone to call back people who'd rung the helpline? Always the little things that messed up a plan.

He took a deep breath. Keep calm, he told himself. No point in panicking. The doorway was in shadow and, with a hood over his head, no one was going to recognise him. Best to wait. See what else he could find out.

The receptionist directed them up to the second floor where they found a tall man in chinos and an Oxford shirt waiting. His presence out on the landing irritated Jon. It was like he'd wanted to surprise them. Take the initiative.

'Detectives Spicer and Khan, I'm James.' A hand was extended.

Iona shook first. Jon delayed a second before lifting his hand. The hesitation caused Pearson to glance up. Jon met his eyes and held them as they shook. The man's grip was firm, but not overly so. Certainly not the vigorous pump of a military man.

'I hope you don't mind us chatting out here,' he said. 'Only, the office is very modest – and open-plan. I don't have a room of my own.'

'Well,' Jon replied, 'we can't talk out here.' He dipped his head to see through the window of the door. Two rows of tables, three people sitting around chatting. Immediately, Jon sensed a shoestring operation, probably relying on a few generous donors and a load of volunteers. Like most small charities.

'Right, yes,' Pearson said, sounding a little flustered. 'There are breakout rooms which we're meant to book. We could chance it, if we can find one that's empty.'

The man seemed so ... nice. Almost vicarly, Jon thought. 'After you.'

He led them along the corridor to a pair of red doors. 'Ah – we're in luck. This one.'

The room had a circular desk in the middle surrounded by four chairs. The window looked directly out at other offices across the narrow street. Jon could see a lady behind the nearest window gesturing at a whiteboard. He slid out the chair on the far side.

'Always can tell a policeman.' James smirked. 'Never sit with their back to a door.'

Iona nodded. 'That's DC Spicer. He'll walk out of a pub rather than sit somewhere he can't see everything.'

So this is how we'll work it, Jon thought. I'll be the quiet suspicious one. Fine with me. 'Old habits,' he murmured.

Pearson's laugh was brief and polite. 'Nothing wrong with that.' Once they were all sitting, he looked from Jon to Iona and back again. 'How can I help?'

'I think,' Iona answered, taking out a pen, 'it would be best if you could start by telling us how your organisation works.'

'Sounds a bit ominous.' He tried a grin, but just got a tight smile back from Iona. Jon's face didn't move. 'Right. We're here to offer support to ex-servicemen who find themselves struggling. It could be that they get in trouble with the police or behind on their rent. Issues with drink or drugs. Sometimes relationships break down. Whatever the reasons, many end up homeless and often in a very fragile mental state. We are here to listen and, if we can, give advice and support.'

'Like the Samaritans, then?' Iona asked.

'Yes, but with a focus on the particular issues those coming out of the armed forces might face. Often that's post-traumatic stress disorder.'

Iona was jotting things down. 'And the people who work with you, they all served, themselves?'

'Yes. That's a prerequisite. They need that perspective. Often, they've been through similar situations themselves. Of course, that isn't anything unusual among volunteers.'

Jon wondered what Pearson had been through. What thing had motivated him to set up a telephone helpline?

'How many do you have in at any one time?' Iona asked.

'That varies. But not all our volunteers are based in the office. Some of them keep a phone with them at home. I'd say, in all, the team averages about fifteen.'

Jon placed an elbow on the table. 'How does it work, then? When someone calls?'

Now he was addressing two people, Pearson adjusted his chair slightly. 'There is a central number – the one that appears on all our literature. When someone rings it, the switchboard routes the call through to a line that's free. I try to make sure we have three people available to take calls at any one time. Demand rarely exceeds that. Perhaps in the early hours of a weekend.'

Jon was thinking about when Wayne had rung the number. And when that number had rung him. 'That's a peak time for you, is it?' he asked. 'The early hours?'

'Yes. If your thoughts are keeping you from sleep, it can be particularly bleak.'

Jon nodded. 'So when you say "line", you actually meant someone with one of your phones?'

'Yes. The telephones here in the office are connected to the switchboard. It routes calls to them first, but if the volunteers here are all busy, that call goes to one of the mobile phones. For the person calling, there's no difference. The call is free, whoever they end up speaking to.'

'And the people with a mobile phone – they can be living anywhere in the country?' Iona asked.

'In theory, yes. But this is a Manchester-based service. All of them live locally.'

'How many mobile phones have you handed out?' Iona asked.

'Currently? Eleven, including mine. Phone bills are by far the charity's largest overhead.'

'We're going to need the name and address of each person who's currently in possession of a phone registered to this organisation,' Iona said. 'Do you have a list?'

'I do.' His face was sombre. 'I take it this is something I have no choice in handing over?'

'Not at all,' Jon said. 'You could refuse. Then we go away and come back in a bit with the necessary authorisation to obtain that list. And what have you achieved? Apart from pissing us off big time, you'll have probably contributed to the death of at least one person. Maybe more. We can work out exactly how many later and let you know.'

'The death of ...' Pearson looked crestfallen. 'How? I don't follow.'

'Just get us the fucking thing,' Jon growled. 'We don't have much time.'

They were leaving the building with the list in under ten minutes. Jon waited for the front door to click shut behind him. He was about to start speaking, but there was an office worker off to the side smoking a cigarette. No way of knowing which company she worked for.

He gestured to Iona and they moved across the street. 'Is it there?'

'Is what there?'

'Come on, Iona. The number that called Wayne on the night of his death.'

'Oh, that number.' She grinned up at him. 'Yes!'

He came to a stop and pumped a fist up and down. 'So, we have a name and address, then?'

'We do.'

He set off again. 'Right, let's get back and run a full check on him. I should think we're going to need an architect's plan of where he lives, too.'

'It'll be treated as a hostage situation, then?'

'If he has someone else's baby in his bloody house, yes.'

Jon saw a hand holding a cup rise from the shadows of the doorway they were passing. The cup waggled from side-to-side. The homeless person had woken up, then. Remembering how it felt to be sitting down there, Jon patted his pockets. Nothing in the tracksuit bottoms. 'Sorry mate.'

Down in the doorway, Gavin waited until their footsteps had faded. So, he had a little time before they came for him. That was useful to know. At least now, he could make some sort of a plan for his final hours on earth.

CHAPTER 36

Jon was surprised to find that, apart from DCI Pinner, the third-floor meeting room was empty. He'd been expecting a team of detectives waiting for a brief. No sign of Weir, either. He looked at Pinner questioningly.

The other man shook his head as he started to move aside some paperwork. 'There's been a bit happening since you left. Sit down.'

Jon gave Iona a wary glance as they settled into the nearest chairs. His phone went off and he slid it from his pocket and checked the screen. Alice. Of all the times to ring me, he thought, diverting her to answerphone.

'The death of Olivia Farnham is being treated as murder,' Pinner announced. 'Inevitable, given the footage shot from the cab of that crane.'

Jon immediately knew where this was going. He sat up straight. 'But he's our suspect – likely to be behind the killings of at least six ex-servicemen.'

Pinner sighed. 'You were in the MIT, so you know how it works: murders are their responsibility. The Counter Terrorism Unit is here for sneaky-peeky stuff, not catching killers.'

'Those deaths weren't even on MIT's radar. They'd written them off as suicides. It was only the work we did here that proved—'

Pinner's hands went up. 'No need to persuade me of that. But this has already gone up the chain. DCI Weir is on his way to a meeting with the ACC. They're working out the best way for everything to be handed over to MIT. It's just a question of how soon.'

Jon leaned back in the chair and crossed his arms. 'Bollocks.'

'However,' Pinner added, 'there's a decent chance we won't be entirely shut out. DCI Weir is going to argue that we provide support.'

'Great.' Jon snorted. 'So we sit in the office and wait for them to call us with the odd question?'

Pinner sighed again. 'DC Spicer, would you mind closing the door properly? Thanks.'

Jon got to his feet and swung it shut with a bang. Once he was back in his seat, Pinner sat forward. 'You'll be aware I was at the mortuary earlier. My involvement in this has a personal angle.'

Jon nodded slowly.

'Edward Farnham is someone I've known for over twenty years. We have been on family holidays together. When Olivia was younger and less,' he stared sadly off to the side, 'troubled.'

Watching him, Jon saw another side to the man. The DCI was someone who was trying to support a friend the best way he could. He regretted his earlier flippant comment to Weir about Masonic lodges.

The DCI cleared his throat. 'You know Weir isn't your biggest fan, DC Spicer?'

'Yeah, I'd sensed it.'

'He says you've got attitude. You're too headstrong. I'm guessing, during your time in uniform, you worked with the Tactical Aid Unit?'

The knuckle-draggers, thought Jon. The largest and most physical officers serving with Greater Manchester Police. Whenever local uniforms couldn't handle something, the TAU was called in to break a few heads, restore order and then disappear. God, he thought, it was such a laugh. 'I did, yes.'

Pinner smiled knowingly. 'Going straight in where others feared to tread, mmm?'

Jon started to say something, then stopped.

'What?' Pinner asked.

'It's nothing.'

'DC Spicer, we're speaking openly. What did you want to say?'

Jon tapped a foot, unsure how honest to be. 'You'll know my arse was kicked out of the MIT. For pretty much the same reasons that Weir finds a problem. But this unit didn't take me on for my tiptoeing skills. What's his problem?'

Pinner nodded his agreement. 'He has a different way of doing things. Perhaps more of a micro-manager? He gives orders, you obey them.' Pinner waved a hand. 'Listen, how you go about your business might ruffle feathers. But the way you two operate as a pair seems pretty damn effective. Especially for the situation we find ourselves in currently.'

Jon eyed the other man cautiously. 'Which means what, sir?'

Pinner's eyes shifted momentarily to the door. When he spoke, his voice was almost a whisper. 'I'd say we have a few hours, tops, before this investigation moves across to the MIT and a new SIO takes over. Before starting to make any decisions, that person will need to be fully briefed. It's time that Olivia's baby doesn't have.'

Jon waited, wondering where the DCI was going with this.

Pinner's eyes shifted to Iona and then went back to Jon. 'Continue with what you're doing and I'll cover you for as long as I can.'

Jon wasn't sure he'd heard correctly. 'You want us keep after whoever owns the phone?'

'Isn't that our best chance of finding the baby?' Pinner asked.

'It is.'

'So we're agreed?'

Jon turned to Iona. 'I'm up for it. You?'

She hesitated a second before nodding. 'OK.'

'Right,' Pinner sat back. 'What do we know about this fucker?'

Iona quickly explained how the phone number that had featured on Wayne Newton's records belonged to a handset registered with the Manchester Veterans' Helpline. 'That handset has been assigned to this person,' she concluded, laying down the sheets she'd just printed off.

Pinner studied them in silence. 'He's ex-forces, too?'

'All the people working at the helpline are,' Jon said. 'Seems he's using the phone operator role as a way of identifying potential victims. Our theory is that, if someone rings the number needing help and they fit his criteria, he calls them back and gets their physical location.'

Pinner lifted his chin. 'They're vulnerable, possibly incapacitated with drugs or alcohol ...'

'That was certainly the case with Wayne Newton,' Jon responded.

'Christ. Why do you think he has he taken it upon himself to start killing people?'

Jon shrugged.

'What's important, in our opinion,' Iona said, 'is that killing Olivia Farnham was a change of direction for him. I think we can assume that she didn't ring the veterans' helpline. So the killer couldn't have called her back and asked where she was.'

'Which means,' Jon said, 'he came across her by chance: taking Olivia's baby was never part of his plan.'

Pinner's gaze dropped to the printouts once more. 'Have you started looking at the building where he lives?'

'Not as yet.'

He glanced up. 'This ... this is great work. Both of you. I didn't realise you were this close.' He ran a hand over his mouth. 'Christ, we're way outside Counter Terrorism territory, here.'

'What do you want us to do?' Jon asked.

'Get everything needed to execute a raid on his flat. If the MIT are being too slow, be prepared that it might be you who crashes down the door.'

Jon waited until they'd entered the stairwell before he glanced at Iona. 'That was a bit unexpected,' he whispered.

'You think he meant it?' Iona looked worried. 'That he'll cover us?'

'What choice do we have?' Jon replied. 'We have to trust him.'

Iona still seemed troubled. 'I suppose if it's not yet officially MIT's case ...'

'Exactly. So let's get all we can about where he's living.' His phone started to ring as they entered the main office. Alice, again. 'I'd better take this.' He started towards an empty desk. 'Babe, can I call you—'

'Have you heard from Holly?'

'Holly? No. Why?'

'She's not called your phone?'

He came to a halt. 'No. Alice, why are you asking?'

'You need to come home, Jon.'

'What's happening?'

'I can't find her. She's not here!'

'What do you mean she's not there?'

'She's gone.'

'Gone where?' He realised he had lifted his free hand and was gripping his forehead.

'I don't know! That little rucksack she keeps in her room is missing.'

Jon needed something to anchor him to the floor. He turned round and sat heavily on the edge of a desk. 'Alice, slow down. When did you last see her?'

'Hours ago. Hours! I thought she was in her room. Oh God, Jon, where will she have gone?'

'Hours?' He checked the time. It would be dark soon. 'How many hours? Two, three, more?'

'Maybe three? I'm not sure.'

It took all Jon's strength to keep his voice slow and calm. To not let the panic in his wife's words infect his. 'Where's Duggy?'

'It's Sunday – at my mum's.'

'Right.'

'I asked her to hold on to him. Jon, something's happened. I just know—'

'Listen to me, Alice.'

'I mean, what if she's—'

'Listen to me!' Heads turned. People were watching him. His mouth had gone dry. He wanted to retch and gulp in air all at once. 'Alice, listen. I'm coming home. But start calling round her friends. Can you do that?'

'Yes ... yes, I'll do that.'

'I'm on my way.'

CHAPTER 37

Gavin wanted to stay where he was for just a bit longer. Sitting here cross-legged, safely anchored before his shrine, he felt at peace. So different to when he was high up, just after someone else had crossed to the next world. Then he felt a giddy sense of exhilaration. It was partly due to the adrenaline of what he'd just done and partly due to where he was. Standing on the edge of a large drop tended to monkey with your heart rate. So did hearing someone's cry of surprise or panic. The last noise they would ever make. Except, of course, the sound of them as they landed.

But here, in the quiet of his flat, he could control his breathing and reflect on things properly.

He gazed at their pictures. The happy smiles on their faces. It was, he knew beyond all doubt, exactly how they looked right now. Those smiles were ones of encouragement. Soon, they were saying to him, soon we'll all be together once more!

The candle let out a tiny crackle as something ignited in the wick. The flame shivered briefly. He let his eyes drift to the painting by Bosch. The pair of figures bathed in brilliant light at the far end of the tunnel. Claire and Sophie, of course. Waiting for him in that place of purity.

He focused on the sheer whiteness of the circle in which they stood. So clean and perfect. And the tunnel leading to it wasn't long. Not much more than a hundred metres. It wasn't far to go for an eternity of happiness.

That's how he thought of it for all those he'd helped. As they fell through the air, some – the ones he couldn't persuade otherwise – believed they were dropping to the ground. Those were the ones who gasped, cried out or kicked and flailed at the air.

But the ones who'd seen the truth, they kept quiet. Not a sound. Because they knew that, though their body might be dropping towards the earth, the part of them that lived forever was being carried swiftly upward. Leaving this world for somewhere better.

It was time to go.

He unfolded his legs and got to his feet. The holdall was ready on the floor, his wings folded neatly at the top. In the gap between them, he'd formed a little crater in the folds of his long black coat. Just right for a baby.

He blew out the candle and waited for the smoke to rise up so he could breathe some in. Was that the last time he would experience that aroma? He didn't think there would be such things as smoke where he was going. In the photo, his wife's and daughter's eyes were on him. It didn't seem right to leave them there staring out at their empty home. He contemplated packing them into the bag. But why do that when they would be together so soon?

Instead, he traced the tip of a finger over their faces then turned the frame face down. Doing that had the appropriate air of finality. There was nothing more for them to see in this world. Over at the kitchenette, he put a line through the final day. All done. He put on his tabard and zipped it up. At the window, he looked down on to the street below. Several parked cars, but no vans or other vehicles that might belong to the police. Knowing that wouldn't be the case for long, he went to retrieve his bag from the floor.

Maybe it was anxiety, but he needed the toilet. Cursing the fact it had to happen now, he skirted round the bag and continued quickly towards the bathroom.

CHAPTER 38

Jon looked round his daughter's bedroom, hands in his pockets like he was attending a crime scene. Idiot, Spicer. Why didn't you see this coming? Wiper appeared in the doorway, tail moving slowly from side to side. A hopeful wag. Jon knelt down and held out a hand. 'Come here.'

The dog trotted over and lent its head against Jon's thigh. He trailed his fingers across the animal's head, grateful of the calming effect it had on him. Think, Jon. Think what might have been going on with her. What was she planning?

The rucksack she liked to use for any trips out was missing from the hooks on the back of her door. He got to his feet and quickly checked she hadn't put it in her wardrobe. All the time, the mental barrier he'd erected in his head was threatening to collapse. He couldn't let that happen. Couldn't let all the despair and dread out. Every now and again, his mind would flash up an image. What a certain type of adult will do with a child, if given the chance. He had to shove the thoughts aside. Tell himself to shut the fuck up. That wasn't going to happen to Holly. It wasn't …

'That was Helen, Maisy's mum,' Alice called up from the bottom of the stairs.

From the shake in his wife's voice, he knew the answer already. 'And?'

'Nothing. I don't know who else to call, Jon. I mean, there's only Diane and Cheryl who haven't rung me back.' Her voice was starting to crack. 'Maybe I should drive round to their houses?'

He closed his eyes tight. He needed to think. And he couldn't think. Not with his wife's tormented voice ringing in his ears.

'Jon? I want to drive round to—'

'Hang on. Let's just ... pause a second.' He opened Holly's bottom drawer. The thick fleece wasn't in there. He went to the shelf above her bed. Fairy lights were strung along its edge. The tin can she kept her pocket money in felt light. He glanced in. Only coppers. There had been a handful of pound coins in there, he was certain. Oh, Christ. He couldn't help looking out the window. The streetlights were starting to come on. Half an hour before night, at the most. And she was out there, somewhere. Alone.

A text sounded. He took his phone out. A message from Iona. 'MIT took his address. On their way there now.'

They didn't hang around after all, Jon thought. So we're out of the investigation. It's over. He couldn't have cared less.

Alice called up to him again. 'Jon, surely we should just ring the police?'

'Ali, I know how it works: it'll be a while before a patrol car turns up. And then some officer a month into the job will spend the first hour asking questions from a list he was given back at base. Then he'll take our answers to his senior officer who'll put them to one side while he finishes whatever he was doing; we can do more ourselves.'

He checked the tiny desk Holly used for homework. Lying in the centre of it was a school exercise book. He recognised it: at the back had been that picture. The one of Pompeii. He turned to it again and examined the disturbing imagery. The abandoned baby. Smoke pouring from buildings. The end of the world. Familiar things, suddenly irrelevant. In the fields beside the road, a small flag hung from a chest-high pole. It stood next to what looked like a shallow pit of sand. A thought occurred.

He walked out of her room and trotted down the stairs, Wiper following close behind. 'She didn't say anything that sounded odd?'

Alice was sitting on the bottom step, hunched over as if in pain. 'No,' she groaned. 'Nothing.'

'OK.' He squeezed past. 'Has she been out to the shed?'

'The shed? I don't think so.'

'I want to check something. One minute.' He undid the bolt on the back door and stepped into their little courtyard. The previous summer, he'd bought a small shed. It was a useful place to store items like windbreaks, sunshades and deckchairs. Things for days out. He swung the door open, allowing light from the kitchen window to shine in. Top shelf: the little camping stove was missing. He felt a glimmer of hope. No sign of the purple picnic rug, either.

Back in the house, he checked the food cupboard beside the boiler. The lower part was where things like baked beans, ravioli, savoury rice and other quick and easy-to-make items were stored. There was a gap where, he was certain, several packets of instant noodles had been. Back in the hallway, he crouched before his wife. She looked ill. 'I have a feeling I know where she is, Alice. You stay here in case she shows up. I have my phone. Anything happens, call me.'

'Where do you think she went?'

'You know the bottom of the golf course? The little copse of trees. I made a camp there with her back in the summer, remember?'

'Why? I don't understand. Why look there?'

'I think she's taken a few things with her. Stuff to make food. It just makes sense. I won't be long. Keep your phone with you. Come on, Wiper.'

The group of officers made their way up the stairs. The apartment they wanted was on the fourth floor, to the right. They were a team of six: two were carrying Perspex shields and one was carrying an Enforcer. The men were incredibly quiet. Once in position outside the target apartment, they turned to the man who was hanging back. He nodded before whispering into a throat mike.

'We're all good.'

A few moments later, the ring of a phone sounded in the flat.

One of the officers at the door had what looked like a doctor's stethoscope pressed against the wood. His head was bowed, eyes shut. The phone rang for another thirty seconds before falling silent.

The man who was hanging back listened as the next step in the plan was given; if the person didn't answer the phone and comply with the instructions to leave the property with their arms above their head, the crash team went in. He was about to wave the officer with the Enforcer into place, when the one still listening at the door lifted a hand.

'Toilet just flushed and a door opened,' he whispered. 'Get them to phone again.'

The man who was hanging back relayed the request to command.

A second later, the phone started up once more.

This time, it reached its fourth ring before being picked up. A male voice said hello. Silence as the person inside listened to the serious voice at the other end of the line. A slight squeaking noise got closer. The lock clicked and the door began to slowly open.

The team began shouting in unison: a tactic designed to overwhelm and intimidate.

'Police, get out!

Out now!'

'Do as we say!'

'Out, out, out!'

One of them shoved the door fully open. The man, who had started to peer out, found his elbows grabbed. He was dragged from his apartment and thrown face-first onto the carpet of the corridor. A knee went into his back while hands grabbed his arms. Cuffs locked onto his wrists. He heard a crash as his wheelchair was shoved aside. Footsteps as they rushed into his flat.

The one who was still kneeling over him called out to his colleagues. 'Any sign?'

'No!'

'Bedrooms checked?'

'Clear!' someone shouted back.

A second later, another voice: 'Clear!'

The man tried to turn his head, but a hand pressed down against his skull. An instant later, he heard hot breath in his ear as a voice demanded, 'Where's the little girl?'

'Little girl? I have no idea what you're talking about.'

CHAPTER 39

Wiper's claws clicked against the tarmac as the two of them ran towards Peel Moat Sports Centre. The building was marooned in an expanse of asphalt that bordered Heaton Moor Golf Club. Once on the grass, Jon looked to his far left; in the distance was Mauldeth Hall and, behind that, the narrow strip of woodland.

As he jogged across the damp surface, he thought back to the Sunday afternoon they'd spent collecting large branches and propping them against the tree with the thickest trunk. Once satisfied the framework was secure, he'd led Holly to a nearby clearing that had been taken over by bracken. They spent an hour cutting off the largest fronds, carrying them back to their frame and weaving them through the network of branches to form a protective layer. Then they'd both crawled inside. The air was weighed down by the aroma of the dead wood and freshly cut bracken stalks. He'd cooked some noodles, which they ate straight from the pan. Holly had loved it.

The line of ancient-looking street lamps that bordered the road leading to the hall had now come on. To his side, the windows of the golf course's clubhouse also glowed. He could see several figures. Middle-aged men in sensible jumpers. The rain was coming down more steadily now, a fine Manchester drizzle that penetrated clothing in no time.

Rounding the hedge that bordered the hall, he could just discern the copse of trees. Please let her – and only her – be in there. While making the camp, he'd spotted signs that underage drinkers had also been using the area. Empty bottles of cider and crushed cans. He'd been half-expecting the wood to be discovered by a homeless person; the fact it was outside the city centre and mostly behind a perimeter fence was probably the only reason it hadn't been.

Wiper lowered his nose and started following a scent trail. 'Is it Holly?' Jon asked. Wiper glanced up. 'Holly. Find Holly! Where is she?'

They entered the outermost trees. Jon found a narrow path and stuck to it. Followed it. No glimmer of light showed ahead. He found the small clearing, bracken now dead and collapsed. At the other side, he paused to get his bearings. She wouldn't have come here, a voice said. Being alone in these woods at her age. Surely, it would be too terrifying.

He remembered the tree was somewhere off to the right. A darker, more solid patch of shadow caught his eye. He wasn't sure whether to call out. What if there was no reply? He felt like his heart was about to burst. He started to worry she might be able to hear his footsteps getting closer. The heavy tread of an adult. Not wanting to frighten her, he cleared his throat. 'Holly? It's only Dad.'

The only sound was drips falling from the branches into the mulch of leaves surrounding him.

He could make out the camp better now. The passing of months hadn't been kind. One side looked like it had started to collapse and the bracken, thick and green when they'd woven it into place, was now withered and brown. He had to not think about what he might see in there.

'Holly? It's Dad.'

Wiper bounded forward, tail wagging furiously. The animal shot through the opening and he heard a small squeal of surprise. His daughter's voice. He almost fell to his knees and cried with relief. The dog was whining with excitement as he bent down and looked through the low doorway into the gloomy interior. 'Holly? Are you OK?'

'Yes.'

'Can I come in?'

'OK.'

He crawled in, hands and knees instantly soaked. 'The roof's not working so well.'

'No. Are you angry?'

'No. I've bought a torch. Shall I see what's happening with the roof?'

'It's gone all patchy.'

He played the beam of light up. Flecks of rain were getting through what remained of the canopy. 'Needs a new layer.'

'I tried, but all the bracken was damp and it snapped too easily.'

As he lowered the torch, he let the light pass across where she was sitting. At least she'd thought to lay the picnic blanket out. Could do with a layer of cardboard, he found himself thinking. Keeps the cold off. She was sitting with her knees up to her chest, arms round Wiper. Her face was totally in shadow. 'Are you cold?'

'A bit.'

The little stove was standing in the middle of the floor, one of the packs of noodles beside it.

'I didn't bring any water,' she said.

'Oh. And what were you going to light the gas with?'

'I thought they might go soft eventually. If I had water.'

'So the stove was just to stand the pan on?'

'I suppose so. I took the matches from the drawer in the hall.'

Jon didn't know there were any in there. Kids. 'Are you hungry?'

'Yes.'

'Me too. I came straight here.'

'Where've you been, Daddy?'

Daddy again, he thought. It's been a while since she called me that. 'Stuck with work.'

'That's what you always say.'

Is it? A stab of guilt. How much am I to blame for this? 'Why didn't you tell anyone where you were going? Me and your mum, we've been so worried.'

'Is Mummy cross?'

'She's scared. But she'll be happy when I tell her you're OK.'

'You'd better ring her.'

'Yup.' He brought Alice's number up. 'Hi. She's here. Everything's OK.'

'Oh my God. She's alright?'

'Yes.'

'But what's she been doing?'

'Not sure at the moment. I'll see you in a little bit?'

'Just bring her back, Jon.'

'Will do.' He cut the call.

'I wanted to see if I would be all right on my own. Like, if you and Mummy weren't around.'

He thought about that picture of Pompeii again. The end of life as people knew it. 'That's a funny thing to do. You won't ever be on your own.'

'How do you know? Anything could happen.'

'What do you mean?'

'Things don't always stay the same. There's Covid. And climate change. The floods and the heatwaves. Things we can't control.'

'I saw a picture you'd drawn in one of your schoolbooks. You've been learning about Pompeii and the volcano there.'

'Yes. They were all killed by it.'

'But that was a disaster. Now, we know if things like volcanoes are about to erupt.'

'We've been doing it in school.'

'What?'

'Climate change. How it's getting hotter and hotter.'

He supposed the volcano was a bit like the sun. An enormous presence that suddenly turned vindictive. 'I noticed you'd drawn some things in the picture that are from now. A car, for instance.'

'Did I?'

'You don't remember?'

'No.'

That was more worrying to him. It suggested those thoughts were in her head all the time. They'd become normal. 'So you were practising, were you? In case something like Pompeii happens again?'

'It is happening again, Daddy. Just a lot more slowly.'

He tried to make out her face, but it was too dark. 'Holly, you live somewhere very lucky. Here, in this country, we have lots of things to keep us safe.' He tapped his chest. 'The police, for a start. And hospitals. And medicine and lots of food. Things they just didn't have in Pompeii.'

In the darkness, he could just make out her hand moving back and forth across Wiper's back.

'They might have had dogs, though,' he added. 'Or maybe cats.'

'The ancient Egyptians had cats.'

'Did they?'

'I want to go home now.'

'Good idea. Tell you what, shall we get some chips on the way?'

'Yes.'

'And shall I send a text to Mummy? Ask her to run you a nice warm bath?'

'Yes, please.'

Once they'd packed her bag, they crawled back out into the night. The lights of the golf clubhouse seemed to shimmer between the shifting branches. He turned to her and said, 'Shall I carry you?'

'Carry me? I'm ten.'

'So?' he replied. 'I don't think that's too old.'

'OK, then.'

She stepped in front of him with her arms raised, just like when she was little. He lifted her up so her face was level with his, hoping it would encourage her to rest her cheek on his shoulder. She did and he let her hair squash up against his face and nose and he tried not to cry.

They were home with two portions of chips twenty minutes later. Alice was waiting in the hallway with towels and Holly's fluffy dressing gown. He left her smothering their daughter with kisses. As he was dividing the food onto three plates, his phone went. Iona. He'd ring her back. Next, he put out ketchup, mayonnaise and salt then turned to the open kitchen door. 'Food's ready!'

Alice appeared with an arm still round her daughter. Holly's hair had been tied back and her dressing gown was wrapped tightly about her. For a moment, Jon wondered if Alice was going to insist Holly eat her food while sitting on her lap. But she allowed Holly her own chair, settling down in the one opposite to watch.

Holly put a dollop of mayonnaise on the side of her plate and then glanced up nervously. 'Am I allowed some ketchup, too?'

Ketchup and mayonnaise, Jon thought. It had to be a special occasion for that. He scooped up the squeezy bottle, reached over and criss-crossed red sauce across her chips.

'Daddy!' she gasped delightedly.

Putting the bottle back in the middle of the table, he caught Alice's smirk. As he wolfed his portion down, the urge to check on Holly kept pinging into his head. Every time he did, he saw that Alice's gaze was also locked on her. After a while, Holly sensed she was being watched. 'Mum, stop staring.'

She flinched. 'Sorry. I'm just so glad that we've got you here.'

Holly put her fork down, half her chips untouched. 'I can't eat any more.'

'Don't worry,' Jon replied. 'The portions are massive from that place.'

'They were really nice.'

'Your bath's ready,' Alice stated, starting to get up. 'I'll get you a nice fresh towel.'

'Thanks, Mum, but I know where the towels are.'

'Of course. Do you want anything else?'

'No, I'll be fine, thank you.'

Once she was upstairs, Alice turned to Jon. Her eyes were worried. 'She seems OK. Does she seem OK to you?'

Jon had already started on Holly's leftovers. 'Yeah.'

'Did ... what did she say? When you found her. Did she say why she'd done it?'

'Kind of. There's a picture of hers you need to see, upstairs. They've been doing climate change at school and then that volcano in Pompeii and I think it all got mixed up in her mind. She wanted to see if she could survive without us.'

'Without us? I don't understand.'

He pushed Holly's empty plate aside and then pointed with his fork. 'You eating those?'

She passed her plate across without a word.

'Like if something happened to us both,' Jon said, stabbing at an especially large chip. 'She'd taken the little gas stove from the shed and some instant noodles. Basically, she was giving it a dry run.'

There were tears in Alice's eyes. 'I don't understand why she wanted to ... that's not right. She's only ten, for God's sake.'

'Look at it this way: she's trying to develop a strategy. A plan. At least she's not just watching crap on the Internet. Obsessing over social media. I'll take her on a bushcraft weekend. You go out into the hills and learn how to make fires, skin rabbits, stuff like that.'

'Which hills?'

'There's one that takes place in the Peak District.'

'Really? You think that's a good—'

'I do. And I'd quite enjoy doing it myself.'

Alice reached across and stole a couple of chips.

'I knew you'd do that.'

'My chips.'

'Actually, you gave them up. You no longer can claim—'

'Oh, be quiet. I don't know about skinning rabbits. She wanted one as a pet not that long ago.'

'She'll be all right. Tougher than you think, that girl.'

Alice was silent for a few moments. 'What's going on with this case you've been working on?'

'I'm not sure of the latest. Iona left me a message just before. The person we've been trying to find has now taken someone else's baby. But we know his identity and where he lives. It'll be OK.'

'A baby? Whose baby?'

'That's ... complicated. Anyway, it's out of our hands. We did all the groundwork, but MIT have taken over. We get to offer support, at most.'

Alice placed her hands on the table. 'Hang on a second. A baby has been taken and it's still out there somewhere?'

'I don't know. As I said, it's MIT's job now.'

'But you're there to offer support?'

'In theory.'

She pointed to the door. 'Jon, go! You should be helping.'

'Ali, our daughter went missing. I think they'll understand why I rushed off.'

'Yes. And now we have her back. You found her; you should be helping to find the missing baby.'

'Why don't I see what Iona has to say?'

'You can do that in the car. Go!'

'You're sure?'

'If you can help, then help, for Christ's sake.'

Gavin knocked three times, then a couple more. He'd spent too long getting ready. The police must almost be here by now. Maybe they were gathering round the corner, getting ready to storm the building and smash down his front door.

He put the holdall down and was about to knock again, more loudly. Instead, he lowered his curled fingers and listened. He could hear her on the other side of the door, trying not to not breathe. What the bloody hell was the stupid cow up to? 'Miriam, it's me, Gavin.'

Nothing.

'Miriam? I know you're there. I can hear you.'

'The ... the baby's asleep. You should come back later.'

'Open the door, can you? I can't talk to you like this.'

'I don't want to disturb her.'

'You won't. We can talk more quietly if the door's open.'

A key turned and she peeped out. 'What is it? I don't want her to wake up.'

'I need to take her. For her mum. She wants her back.'

'You said her mum was ill. You said Sky needed to be looked after for a while.'

He looked off to the stairwell. Time was ticking on. What was the best way to play this? 'Her mum only wants to see her for a little bit. She says thanks, by the way. I'll bring her back soon.'

'I don't believe you.'

'Miriam, it's not your baby.'

'It's not yours, either. I'm going to close the door.'

He rammed the toe of his shoe into the narrow gap. 'No, you're not.'

She looked down, horrified. 'Move your foot! I want to close my door.'

They struggled for a second, both of them trying to force the door in the other person's direction; him to get it open, her to lock him out. Realising she was probably heavier than him, he dipped his knees and rammed his shoulder into it. The impact caught her by surprise and she fell back, one hand keeping hold of the handle, her arm a barrier to him getting in. He used his fist like a hammer on her forearm, beating down on her wrist until her grip broke.

She was on her knees, wailing. 'Leave her here, you've stolen her. I know you have!'

'What the fuck's wrong with you? I need to take her to see her mum.'

'You're lying. You're lying!' She lunged at his legs. Fingernails dug into the soft skin of his inner thigh. Pain, sharp and hot.

He kicked out and the side of his foot connected with her armpit. She lifted a few inches and fell heavily against the wall. He looked about. Where the hell would she have put it? The first door opened on a dark bedroom. The covers of the bed were neatly made. He moved to the front room. Stuffed fucking cats everywhere. He kicked a couple aside and saw the baby on the sofa, nestled on a folded blanket, cushions forming a raised barrier either side. On the arm of the sofa was a half-finished bottle of milk. He jammed it into a pocket and had only just lifted the baby up when he heard movement behind him.

She was wide-eyed and open-mouthed. Silently screaming, fingers like hooks, aiming for his eyes. Instinctively, he stepped back, lashing out with his free arm. His fist went straight between her outstretched hands and connected with the bridge of her nose. Her knees buckled and she started to topple into him, arms loose and ineffectual. He stepped away, turning his hips so she slid off him and down to the floor. Her eyes were barely open and she was groaning quietly as he stepped over her and made for the door.

CHAPTER 40

'Is she OK?' Iona asked, spotting Jon making a beeline towards her desk.

'Yeah. Cold and hungry when I found her, but – bless her – more worried about us being cross.'

She smiled. 'Thank God for that. And Alice?'

'A lot calmer now, that's for sure.'

'You didn't need to come in, Jon. I thought you'd take the opportunity to get some sleep; you look like you need it.'

'I'll be OK. So, what the hell's happening? I didn't really take in the message you left me.'

'Bring your chair round and I'll tell you.'

He wheeled it to her side of the workstation. Sheets of paper were lined up across her desk. Among them, he spotted a printout of a newspaper article.

'The phone number we'd obtained from Wayne Newton's records had recently been reassigned to a new volunteer,' Iona said, tapping the end of her biro against the list James Pearson had given them.

Jon closed his eyes for a second. 'Shit. They raided the wrong address?'

'Afraid so. Dragged a wheelchair-bound veteran of forty-six to the floor in the process.'

'Jesus. I bet the MIT bloody love us.' He could imagine the confusion and anger among the crash team. Nothing worse than shit intelligence. 'What did they say?'

'Well, they rang here pretty damn quick wanting an explanation. I called James Pearson and was able to work out what had happened.' She moved the phone list aside to reveal a personnel record from The Manchester Veterans' Helpline. 'This is who we really want.'

Jon scanned the fields of information. Gavin Conway, age thirty-three. Address: Flat 9, Pear Mill, Hawthorne Street, Failsworth. He continued down to a lower panel. 'Served in the army, then.'

'Yup. He came out in late September.'

'Pretty much a year ago.'

'Hold that thought,' she said, lifting up the printout of the news article and handing it to him. The headline at the top had been circled with red pen.

```
Gas heater tragedy of wife and daughter
```

'They died on the way to meet him on his return from his second tour. He was flying in to RAF Coningsby. They were in a mobile home he'd renovated. The plan was, according to Pearson, for them to go on a little tour of Britain before ending up back in Manchester.'

Jon put the report back on her desk. 'Are we talking carbon monoxide poisoning?'

Iona nodded. 'His wife had parked up overnight at a place near Skegness. Their bodies were found the next day. They'd died in their sleep, both cuddled up in bed.'

'How old was his daughter?'

'Six.'

'And they were on their way to meet him?'

'Yes. He touched down and nobody was there waiting.'

Jon was still feeling the residual panic of Holly running away. The thought of losing not only your child, but your whole family. His field of vision began to waver and he had to bow his head. He tried to wipe the tears away with the back of a forefinger before glancing up.

'You OK, Jon?' Iona asked gently.

He nodded. 'Fucking parenthood. It does something to your brain.'

She grabbed his hand and squeezed it. 'Hey: your daughter's safe, remember?'

'Yeah.' He sniffed. 'Just hearing about this stuff. Never used to bother me.'

'Shall I carry on?'

'Of course. I'll stop snivelling soon.'

'Snivel all you want. Conway had to identify their bodies and then deal with the funeral arrangements. Within three months, he approached the veterans' helpline asking to volunteer.'

Jon cocked his head. 'Pearson was aware of all this?'

'Yes. He vets anyone who applies to work there. Said he had his doubts about the bloke. As the anniversary of their deaths approached, he'd been trying to encourage Conway to take time off. Conway said he needed the work for a sense of purpose and routine. Pearson wasn't happy, but let things continue – but then he realised Conway was breaking their guidelines and contacting people who'd rung the number asking for help.'

'That broke the guidelines?'

'He said volunteers are only permitted to ring someone back if they believe that person is at imminent risk of suicide. Pearson had noticed Conway had made several calls to external numbers.'

'The other victim,' Jon strained his mind for the name, 'the one whose family knew something was wrong because he stopped phoning them.'

'McClennan,' Iona said. 'Conway rang him on the first of June. Pretty much his estimated time of death. I've checked Conway's call history on the nights other veterans died. Calls to a couple of numbers in the early hours. Got to be to phones owned by them.'

'So that's how he was selecting them.'

'Looks it.'

'I wonder what happened to their phones. You reckon Conway took them?'

She nodded. 'They're all probably at the bottom of a canal.'

'And now? What's the state of play?'

'There's an MIT team on the way to his house as we speak.'

Gavin swept his eyes over a sea of partially covered faces; only the eyes of the other bus passengers visible above their masks. He still found it so weird. He made his way past them towards the empty rows at the back and gently lowered the holdall to the floor. The zip was partly open to let in air, but he didn't think the infant would particularly care. She'd hardly stirred as he'd carried her from Miriam's flat, slept soundly as he'd run down the stairs, didn't even open an eye as he'd laid her down in the space between the wings and drawn the zip closed above her upturned face.

He pulled gently at his tabard. It was slightly too small for him and, whenever he sat on the bus, it seemed to constrict his breathing. The vehicle started moving again. Not long until he was back in his special place, looking down at the streets far below, hearing the sounds and savouring the smells that carried up to him.

Now the end was so close, he'd started thinking about the final moment. In his mind, he always imagined he'd look out across the city towards the far horizon. Then it would just be case of leaning forward, arms out at either side, wings spread behind him. He'd close his eyes. Definitely. The sensation of falling could be that of ascending, too. If you couldn't see the ground.

But now he had something else to consider. He glanced down at the holdall and pictured the little thing fast asleep inside. He couldn't just drop her and then follow on a moment or two after. They had to go together.

Perhaps it would be better to let himself fall backwards with the baby clutched to his chest? It meant not having his arms outstretched. And the air would be rushing past the back of his head, not his face. But he wanted to be holding her as they emerged into that radiant world where everyone they loved was waiting. He wanted to hand her across to the mother, who would be crying with happiness. And then, once the baby was safely reunited, he would turn to Claire and Sophie, who would be smiling as they lifted their arms, and he'd step forward and bring them both close and press their faces against his and they would—

A little splutter of a cough from near his feet. He checked the rows in front; no one else had heard it. The bus was slowing down. He peered through the window beside him to see where they were: approaching the junction with the A6010. To the right, lights along the top of Manchester City's immense stadium dotted the dark sky. A few hundred metres ahead was the edge of the city centre. The vehicle came to a halt and he watched with dismay as a throng of noisy people started climbing onboard, several with face masks hanging below their chins. If the stadium wasn't closed, he'd have said they were football supporters just emerged from a match.

A few clumped their way to the back and fell into the seats directly behind him. He heard the sharp hiss of cans being opened. Should he just grab the holdall and get off? But people had now filled the aisle in front. Better to just sit tight: another few minutes and they'd be in the city centre.

The bus started forward again as excited chatter about the match washed all around him. He tried to pick up where he'd left off. Falling backwards, that was right. Turning to face the clock tower, maybe looking up to the tip of the spire. Even though the traffic lights in front were on green, the bus started to brake once more. Conversations paused as the other passengers tried to see what was causing the delay. A siren, rapidly increasing in volume. Seconds later, a police car cut across the junction. It sped off along the A6010 and the bus began to edge forward just as the lights turned red. The vehicle lurched to another stop.

In the second between people sighing with frustration and their conversations resuming, a wavering cry rose up from the floor. He kept his eyes on the window. The people on the row in front looked round.

'Weird fucking ring tone,' someone commented lightheartedly.

People's eyebrows were buckling as they glanced about, unsure where the noise had come from. If it was a joke.

Another cry. Longer, more frustrated. He felt about for the bottle. Where the hell did I put it? The side pockets of his tabard were empty. Was it in the bag itself? Bloody hell, the little thing never woke up. It always slept.

He heard a voice directly behind him. 'Come on, own up. Who's smuggling a baby in their coat?'

He tried to join in the laughter while surreptitiously reaching down to check the holdall's side pocket. Another cry. This one lingered. It reminded him of Sophie when she woke up in the night needing to be fed. Knowing things were only going to get worse, he grabbed the holdall and got to his feet. The cry sounded again, wavering off into a pathetic sob. 'Mind your backs, please.'

Now the bag was at shoulder level for the people sitting down. They could tell where the noise was coming from. A woman with a pale blue bobble leaned across her boyfriend. 'Tell me that isn't a baby in your bag.'

He ignored her. 'Coming through. Move, please!'

People in front were looking over their shoulders, eyes immediately dropping to the holdall. Confusion. Concern. Suspicion. The bus started forward and he repeatedly stabbed at the red 'stop' button set into the vertical pole by his side. Then, using his shoulder, he started to barge his way forward.

Someone called out from behind him. 'Whose is the baby, pal? Why is there a baby in your bag?'

'Out my way, I need to get off!' He got to the driver's cab and banged a hand against the Perspex screen. 'Let me off, please!'

The driver looked uneasily to the side. 'At the next stop.'

He cradled the holdall in his arms. Tried to rock it back and forth. The cries were starting again so he forced his fingers through the gap in the zip. He felt the down of her fine hair, the curve of her little warm head. He traced his forefinger across a miniscule nose to the mouth. He didn't need to encourage her; wet little lips latched onto his dirty fingertip and the crying stopped. Behind him, people were discussing what was going on. Some were insisting the baby wasn't real. It was a prank. Others were less sure. No one, yet, had challenged him.

The bus eased to a stop and the doors folded in with a rush of cold air. He jumped down to the pavement and fled for the nearest side street.

CHAPTER 41

'Who've you been speaking to in the MIT?' Jon asked.

Iona checked her notebook. 'A bloke called DI Saville?'

Jon was grinning to himself as he took out his phone.

'Why's that funny?'

'Oh – I used to work with him,' he replied, keying in Rick's number. 'Hey, long time no speak.'

'Jon, bloody hell. How are you?'

'Good. And you?'

'Absolutely.'

'You been liaising with a colleague of mine over here in the CTU. DC Iona Khan?'

'Yes. It did cross my mind you might know her. Don't tell me you work together?'

'On and off.'

'Poor woman. What did she do in a past life?'

'Hang on, just give me a moment to stop laughing.' He paused for a split second. 'There, all done. You cheeky git.'

'So, what's the score, my friend?'

'That's what I was wanting to ask you. We did all the early groundwork on this. Just wondering if there's any way we can offer a hand.'

'Appreciated. But I think after that wrong address from before, folk over here aren't keen. Besides, your boss has already requested that we keep him up-to-date on any development.'

'DCI Pinner?'

'Yeah, that was him.'

'Who's handling it your end?'

'DCI Parks.'

Jon nodded. She was good. Really good. In fact, of all the DCIs he'd pissed off in the MIT, she was the one he felt most guilty about.

'I told your partner there's a team on the way to his place in Failsworth. They're due to go in any minute.'

'Where are you? Back at base?'

'Yes.'

'So, what if he's not there?'

'We've spoken at length to the person who runs the charity helpline: he informed us Conway works as a nightwatchman. The art deco cinema on Upper Brook Street that's being restored? His shift is due to start there at half six. Another team's heading there. We've got the desk jockeys working the usual stuff: tracking his bank card and all that.'

'ANPR cameras been given his car's regis—' He stopped himself. Of course they would have done that. It was the most basic of measures. 'Sorry.'

'As it happens, there is no car registered to him. Don't worry, Jon: Parks has committed enough manpower to bring this to a swift conclusion.'

'She better have. He's got that baby with him.'

'You think she doesn't realise that?' There'd been an edge of impatience in Rick's voice.

'Yeah – but the bloke is totally cracked.'

'Jon, your offer is appreciated – you know that. But I'd better go. Things are going to kick off. I'll let you know how it plays out; I appreciate it's a bastard to be closed out of things like this.'

'Too right it is. Speak to you soon.'

The line went dead. Jon lowered his phone and found himself contemplating the blank screen. It felt weird to have someone he'd helped train give him a very polite flick-off.

'What did he say?' Iona asked.

'In a nutshell: don't call us, we'll call you.' He let out a frustrated sigh. 'What a pile of bollocks.'

'That's the way it works.'

She was right, he had to admit. No point holding it against Rick. 'He said that Conway works as a nightwatchman on a construction site. Suppose he would have to be a night owl, the way he operated.'

'Which company?' Iona asked.

Jon shot her a questioning look.

'Which company does he work as a nightwatchman for?'

'He didn't say. That old cinema on Upper Brook Street. Cool-looking building: big arched roof.' He sent a glum look around the room. 'Should be a nice place to go and see a film once it's all done.'

Iona had started tapping away on her keyboard.

He reached for the little round tin beside her monitor. Vaseline lip balm. Apple flavour. 'Used to smear this over my eyebrows when I played rugby,' he stated. 'Not apple flavour, just the regular stuff.'

'Why?'

'Reduced the chances of needing stitches if you clashed heads with someone.'

'Except it didn't, did it?' Her eyes went to the scar that bisected his left eyebrow.

'Fair point.' He turned the tin on its side and started to roll it back and forth.

After a few seconds, Iona glanced impatiently in his direction. 'Jon?'

'Mmm?'

'That's really annoying. Why don't you sit at your own desk? In fact, why don't you head back home? This case is closed – to us, anyway.'

He looked at her from the corner of his eye. 'Not necessarily.'

'Come on. It's out of our hands. And I'm sure Alice would appreciate you finally being in the house.'

He pictured his wife. As he'd left, she'd been on the phone to her mum Reliving the ordeal, letting it all out. Holly was fast asleep in bed, totally exhausted. He looked at his phone, wondering if Rick would ring. Who are you trying to fool? It wouldn't be at the top of his priorities. Christ, he thought, this is shit. 'You're probably right.'

'You know I'm right.'

Reluctantly, he got to his feet. The thought of Conway somewhere out there with the baby; the jittery feeling inside him wouldn't subside. He contemplated heading to the gym in the basement and smashing the crap out of a punchbag. Was there really nothing they could do? 'It'll probably be on the bloody news before we get a heads up.'

'Here it is.' She nodded at her screen. 'Acorn Construction. They're the contractor Conway works for.'

'Acorn?' The name seemed familiar and Jon turned back to look at her screen. The company logo was shaped like an oak leaf. He'd seen that somewhere before.

Iona started tidying the paper that was strewn across her desk. 'God, I hope they find that little girl before he does anything stupid.'

Jon was still staring at the logo. Where the hell had he seen it? Somewhere recently. But he hadn't driven past the cinema for ages. He wheeled his chair back round to his side of the desk then logged on to the system. He spotted Iona's questioning glance. 'Just checking for any emails,' he said. 'You never know.'

'Jon, you're delaying. Go home. We've done all we could.'

She was right, but he scanned the messages anyway. Nothing significant. 'OK. How late are you staying?'

'Soon as I've filed this lot and sent it over to the MIT, I'm off.'

He looked at the paperwork; all their effort gifted to another team. When Conway was finally caught, the credit would go to them. 'Sure you don't want a hand?'

'No thanks.'

'Right. If we don't speak later, see you tomorrow.'

'See you tomorrow. Sleep well.'

He made his way to the aisle, glancing at Peter Collier's empty desk as he passed it. Need to thank him for all his help on this, he thought. The construction company's logo was still in his head. Why did it seem familiar? A phone started ringing behind him. He was halfway to the doors when they swung open and Kieran Saunders stepped through. Behind him, Iona called his name. He was still looking at Kieran. The logo ...

'Jon!'

He turned round to see Iona was now standing, the receiver of her desk phone in her hand. 'That was Pinner! Conway's flat was empty.'

'The baby?'

She shook her head.

He glanced back at Kieran. What, he asked himself, was I just thinking? Whatever it was, it had now gone. He hurried back to Iona. 'What did Pinner say?'

'Flat recently vacated. Candle wax still warm. A woman on the floor below claims he left about twenty minutes ago, with the baby.'

'Twenty minutes?'

'And he had his work tabard on and a holdall he normally takes with him when he leaves for a shift.'

Jon pointed at Iona's computer. 'Bring up iOPS: see what's happening round town; 101 calls, anything. He hasn't got a car – so he's most likely on foot. Twenty minutes, carrying a holdall and a baby? There must have been a ping on him, surely.'

He brought up the map of the city he kept bookmarked in his browser's tool bar. Twenty minutes. 'What was his postcode again?'

Iona called it out and he tapped it in. The map zoomed in on Failsworth, to the north-east of the city centre. From there to the cinema on Upper Brook Street was a good three miles. Why would he be heading to his place of work with a baby? It didn't make sense. He sat down and tried to imagine what was going through Conway's head.

'Pinner said there was a calendar in his apartment,' Iona announced from behind her screen. 'Today's date has a big cross through it. Nothing after.'

That was worrying. He recalled Conway's boss mentioning this was the anniversary of when Conway's wife and daughter had died. Please, Jon thought, don't be planning on taking that little child with you. 'He likes high buildings. Could he be heading back to one of the sites where he's killed before?' He scrolled the map back towards the city centre. Failsworth was just north of Ancoats and Piccadilly: the part of the city where several people had fallen to their deaths.

'Two-hour bloody delay!'

He looked up to see Kieran standing next to his desk. 'What's that?'

'Those Yanks flying back to the States. We had to sit around for two hours because their flight was delayed.'

He was talking about Alicia and her party. 'So they've gone?'

'Finally.'

The airport job seemed like a lifetime ago. 'Mate, do me a favour: have a look at the website on Iona's computer. For some reason, I connected it to you.'

'OK.'

Jon zoomed in on the network of roads. The NCP where Conway's first victim was found. Bendix Street where he struck again. The mill where another died. All the sites were in that part of the city. It was under a twenty-minute walk from Conway's flat.

'Jon!' Iona called. 'There was an incident on a bus! Came in eight minutes ago. Someone reported that a man was onboard with a baby in a holdall.'

Jon's head went up. 'Where was this?'

'Oldham Road. Bus was at the junction with the A6010.'

He examined the map once more. 'He's heading into the city. Which number bus?'

'89B. It's a service that goes to the Shudehill Interchange. But he got off when the baby started crying.'

'Which side of the junction with the A6010 was it?'

'The one closer to the centre of town.'

'Eight minutes ago?' He went back to the map on his screen; Conway could be at any of the sites where he'd killed before. 'I'll call Rick.'

He brought up his old colleague's number and pressed green. The phone took him through to the answerphone option. Fucking typical. 'Rick, it's Jon. He's not going to that construction site on Upper Brook Street. You need to get all your manpower to the locations where he's previously struck. They are all listed in the notes Iona supplied. Ring me if you need them again.' He put his phone to the side. 'Kieran, any joy?'

His colleague was looking at Iona's screen. 'Oh, Acorn. Yeah, I told you about that – it's who I used to work for. When I first came out of the army.'

It was like a lightning strike through his brain: a flash that fused everything together.

Escorting the Americans to the meeting near the Lincoln statue when they first arrived in Manchester. They'd driven past Albert Square, which was screened off because of the renovations taking place in the Town Hall. The construction company's logo had been on the hoardings. Kieran mentioned he'd mostly worked at the

Victorian Baths. Mostly. 'The company have more than one project going at any one time?'

'God, yeah. It's all heritage buildings, though. Couple of times they ferried me out to that National Trust house in—'

'And you could get into either site OK?' Jon was picturing the immense Town Hall. Its Gothic architecture. The arched windows and blackened statues. Its ornate clock tower with balconies and gargoyles that peered down on the very heart of the city.

'How do you mean?'

'You didn't need approval for a specific site.'

'No – it's all done on a fingerscan at the main entrance. If you're on the system, you can get in.'

Jon jumped to his feet. 'I think I know where he's heading.'

CHAPTER 42

In the shadows of a doorway, Gavin held the bottle to the baby's lips. The bloody thing had been in a pocket of his tabard all along. After a few minutes, he lifted it up to see how much milk remained. The level was barely a notch lower. How could she drink so little? He remembered how Sophie could easily polish off six ounces when she was this small. Actually, she'd never been this small. He held the baby away from him. Something wasn't right with her. She was so frail. He looked at her tiny face as it began to crease with discomfort. She let out a tiny gurgle.

Need to wind her, he realised. He placed the bottle aside and propped her chin up with the crook of his forefinger and thumb. Using the fingertips of his other hand, he tapped gently against her rigid spine. Funny the speed that memories of doing this stuff return, he thought. Sophie would often let out a dribble of milk which ran across the back of his fingers. He couldn't imagine this little mite managing that. She'd hardly swallowed anything. A second later, a bubble of air made its way up her windpipe. He felt her sag down into his hand. Fast asleep again. After he'd laid her back in the holdall, he reached for the bottle.

No need to bring that, he thought. They'd be at the Town Hall in no time. After that, it wouldn't take long.

He raised himself from the steps and set off once more. Somewhere to the side, he could hear laughing. People in a restaurant. He moved away from the voices, sticking to the poorly lit back roads that formed a network in this part of the city.

At the brightly lit Corporation Street, he hung back until a break in the traffic. Then he crossed the road quickly, head down, holdall swinging from his hand. No one knows, he told himself. You're just another worker going about his business.

The next main road was Deansgate, but that would be even busier than Corporation Street. Instead, he skirted round the back of the National Football Museum, aiming for the wide walkways and grassed areas that fronted Chetham's School of Music. No sign of anyone. As he neared the cobbled street leading past the cathedral, music began to swirl around him. Someone was playing the organ. The squat building's stained-glass windows were brightly lit. A service taking place.

A figure was slumped against the low wall that formed a border with the cathedral's pristine lawn. Gavin moved to the far side of the walkway, afraid the baby would give herself away once more. The man's hand was in his lap, a cup held loosely in his grip. His chin was on his chest and, as Gavin got closer, he could see the person wasn't conscious. The type of comatose state, he thought, only caused by chemicals. Probably Spice. Treading softly, he moved close to where the man was sitting, scooped every single coin from his pockets and poured them into the man's empty cup. It was a liberating feeling to know you no longer had need of money.

The sound of the organ continued to rise and fall and he took a moment to regard the building. Music written to honour God. He smiled. God. Didn't they see that God had given up on this world? How else could his wife and child have been allowed to die? There was no one above them keeping watch. Making sure things were fair. No one. Nothing. His gaze dropped to the holdall. No one to take care of this baby. No one to take care of him, he thought, glancing at the man passed out on the freezing flags beside him. This world is a cold, cruel world. God might be waiting in the next, and the sooner we move on from this one to where those we love are waiting, the better.

He strode on towards the middle of the city, the Town Hall only a few minutes away.

CHAPTER 43

Jon tore along Deansgate, blue light flickering behind the car's front grille.

Beside him, Iona was on her phone. 'No, sir, Jon couldn't get through. That's why I rang.' She listened for a moment. 'We're on Deansgate right now. We'll be at the Town Hall in a couple of minutes at the most. Yes, he's driving. OK, yes, will do.'

Jon kept his eyes on the road. About fifty metres in front, a couple of people were contemplating trying to make it across the road's wide lanes. He turned the siren on and set it to rapid pulse. Don't even try it, you fucking idiots. The car shot past them at close to sixty miles an hour. 'What did he say?'

Iona was looking worried. 'Well, he didn't sound convinced. He said we were to proceed to where workers check in and see what the security records show.'

'And then what?'

'Ring him again.'

'Even if we know Conway is in the building?'

She nodded.

'Fuck that.'

'Jon ...'

He slowed to forty when they reached the junction with Peter Street. A bus pulled to the side of the road, allowing him to cut across the junction without checking his speed. The car's tyres screeched in protest and, on the pavements, people with open mouths watched him pass.

'How did Kieran say it worked again?' he asked, straightening up and increasing speed once again.

Iona was gripping the sides of her seat. 'They work in three-man teams. One on the CCTV cameras, one on the radio channels and one doing a foot patrol.'

That was it, thought Jon, recalling how Kieran had explained that, because the company specialised in heritage projects, all nightwatchmen had been trained in monitoring and checking the various smoke and heat sensors positioned throughout the building.

'If access to the site is controlled by a biometric check—'

'You mean a fingerprint scanner at the turnstiles?'

'That's what I'm thinking. And if he isn't on duty, maybe he won't get past that point.'

'I get the feeling he has planned this too carefully to fuck up at the site perimeter,' Jon replied, swinging left on to Mount Street. Beyond the domed roof of the city's library, they could see the Town Hall's clock tower pointing up into the sky. He regarded the tall structure uneasily: it had to be where Conway was heading with the baby. Had to be.

'Jon, what if he's not here?' Iona asked quietly.

He shrugged. 'Then I'll look like a massive knob. Anyway, they'll have sussed he's not at the Brook Street site by now, so there's probably a team on their way here.' He followed the road into Albert Square. Concrete blocks now prevented any vehicle from mounting the pavement and entering the square itself; anti-terror measures implemented after attacks involving vehicles down in London. He screeched to a stop and glanced at the hoardings erected closer to the building itself. There was the logo he'd noticed before, stuck at regular intervals along the six-foot-high barrier. An entry point was a little way in front. 'There,' he stated, jumping out and hurrying towards it.

Iona appeared at his side. 'There was what looked like a separate gate for work vehicles,' she said. 'The corner of the square, at the top of Lloyd Street.'

Figures, Jon thought. There would be lorries coming and going all the time. 'OK, we'll need to check what security is at that point, too.'

A variety of signs were plastered to the outer perimeter. Health and safety messages, fire procedures, clocking-in instructions. No entry to unauthorised persons. The way forward was blocked by a wire mesh door. Jon tried the handle. Locked. No surprise there. He looked about and spotted an intercom and buzzer. Directly above it was a CCTV camera. 'This looks pretty secure to me,' he murmured, pressing the button and reaching for his ID.

'Is anyone even around?' Iona asked, peering through the wire. Directly on the other side was a ramp that led up to a Portakabin. A sign on its door read: Identification Cards To Be Worn At All Times. 'It seems so quiet.'

Jon crooked his head back. High above them was the tower's clock face. 'Ten to seven. The regular workers will have headed home. How high do you reckon that clock tower is? Seventy-five metres?'

'And the rest,' Iona replied. 'Nearer one hundred.'

Jon recalled the time he'd jumped off the ten-metre platform at a swimming pool in France. Measuring up the height of the tower, he guessed it probably was the equivalent of nine or ten platforms high. A long bloody way down, that was for sure. His gaze lingered on the ornate stonework of the pillars, narrow windows and spindly turrets. Angels standing on tiny ledges, imploring the world below with outstretched palms. The heads of grimacing gargoyles jutting out on every corner. 'Building belongs in a Batman film,' he muttered, turning to the intercom. He was about to try again when a voice spoke. 'Can I help you?'

Jon lifted his ID towards the camera. 'We need to come in. It's urgent.'

'Oh – hang on. Give me a minute to get to the Portakabin; I'm in the main building.' The intercom clicked off.

'Fuck's sake,' Jon cursed, pocketing his ID.

Iona's phone went. 'Pinner,' she announced, taking the call.

'See what he wants, then. I'll check the goods-in point.'

He walked back to the corner of the square. Sandwiched between the Town Hall and the city council building, Lloyd Street was narrow enough at the best of times: now the barrier of hoardings running down the side of the Town Hall meant the pavement on that side had disappeared. He turned round and examined the pair of fenced gates that allowed vehicles on site. Nine feet high, with three strands of dark wire at the top. They're probably coated in anti-climb paint, Jon thought. No way anyone was scaling that – not with a holdall containing a baby. He got back to Iona to find her still speaking on her phone.

'He's here, sir. Just been checking where they let lorries through the outer barrier. OK, I'll tell him. Speak to you shortly.' She lowered the phone and looked at him with a pained expression.

Beyond the gate, he saw the Portakabin's door open. A man clutching a walkie-talkie stepped out.

'It's unlocked!'

Jon stepped round Iona and turned the handle. 'What did he say?' he asked her.

'Conway's not at the Upper Brook Street site. Pinner's in contact with his opposite number at the MIT. People are on their way here; we're to stay put until they arrive.'

'OK.' He marched up the ramp towards the man waiting in the doorway. 'Evening. Are you in control of whoever gets on site?'

'Yes. Me or my two colleagues. Whoever is on the control desk in the main building.'

'When did your shift start?'

'Half six this evening.'

'Has anyone been let through within the last thirty minutes?'

'Thirty minutes? No.'

Jon looked around the narrow room they were now in. Behind the counter running down one side was a single monitor. At the far end was a turnstile with an orange console beside it. He took a closer look. White lettering spelled: MSite. The glass screen set into it was lit. Below an oval shape in the centre of the screen was a line of text: Place Finger Here. Flat. Firm. Central. 'This is how everyone clocks in?'

'Yes. During normal hours, this desk is manned. You don't come through if you're not on the system.'

'But it's not manned now. How long has that been the case?'

'Since we came on shift.'

'What's to stop me from just jumping over this counter?'

The security guy looked confused. 'Well ... nothing. But you'd have to have been buzzed through the outer gate first.'

'And, apart from us, you've not buzzed anyone through?'

'No. And there are the cameras, too.' He pointed to the unit behind the desk.

Cameras, Jon thought, are only any use if someone's actually looking at what they're filming. 'This is a massive building. Surely there are multiple doors in?'

'Yes. But they are all on an alarm circuit. That went active shortly after half six. We'd know straight away if any outer door is breached. You think someone might have got on site, is that it?'

Jon tapped a finger on the counter. Have I got this wrong? He licked his lips. 'Maybe.'

Behind him, Iona's phone went off again. 'Hello, sir. We're still at the perimeter, yes. We're talking to someone now. Is there any sign of Conway here? Erm, well ...' Jon could sense she was looking at him.

He turned to her and nodded. It's fine. Just say it.

'At this point, no, sir. There isn't. Yes, sir.' She cut the call and gave an awkward cough. 'He says the MIT lot are almost here. Soon as they arrive, we're to return to base.'

Where a headmaster's bollocking awaits me, Jon thought. Christ. The implications of it being a wrong call were sinking in. Because of him, attention had been diverted down a dead-end. They should have been checking Conway's previous kill sites. He nodded at the security man. 'OK, thanks for your help. Iona? We might as well wait out front.'

'It was worth it,' Iona said, pulling open the door. 'He could easily have been heading here.'

He brushed past her and set off down the ramp. 'Not sure upstairs will be so supportive.'

Iona called out behind him. 'Wait!'

He turned round to see her pointing at a sign on the door that read: Identification Cards To Be Worn At All Times. 'I just thought of something.' She stopped the door from swinging fully shut. 'Excuse me?'

The security man was now on the far side of the turnstile. He glanced back. 'Yes?'

'This is a biometric checkpoint. But you have identity cards, too. Are they swipe cards?'

'Yes.'

'What for?'

'Various doors within the building. To control who has access to certain parts of it.'

'And the system logs each time someone uses their card?'

'That's correct.'

She nodded at the monitor behind the desk. 'So, you can go on there and tell us who is currently on site?'

'I suppose so ... yes, it can show us that.'

'Please.'

They watched from across the counter as he sat down and logged in. 'Right, where will it be? Oh, yes. I head to this bit and select ...' He squinted at the screen. 'Odd.'

Jon leaned both elbows on the counter, vainly trying to see round to what was displayed. 'Go on.'

'Well, the security team for tonight is me, Rishi and Bruce.'

'And?'

'Well – I don't know what Gavin Conway is doing here.'

'Conway is on site?' Jon demanded.

'Six minutes ago, he used his card ...' The security guy looked to the side and his eyes narrowed. 'He's come in via the FM Services desk.'

'What's that?' Jon asked.

'Council offices across on Lloyd Street. There's a tunnel goes under the road to here. It's restricted access and you need keys: but that's no problem for us.' The man removed a key and started to unlock the turnstile. 'If you're coming on-site, you really should be wearing a face mask.'

'Fuck that,' Jon replied, vaulting the counter. 'Iona, call Pinner. Tell him I've gone in after him.'

CHAPTER 44

Gavin Conway swiped his pass for the third time: the last set of doors leading up from the underground walkway opened. He was now in the Town Hall's inner courtyard. Waist-high blocks of neatly piled cobbles, wrapped in cellophane and mounted on pallets, blocked his way. Yellow power cables looped along the soot-stained walls to free-standing floodlights, all of which were off. A large door led into the main building, but he knew there was a camera trained on it. Keeping to the shadows, he walked quickly towards an archway that led to another, smaller, courtyard. Dark, mullioned windows surrounded him. On the far side was a smaller door. He hurried straight to that one and quietly let himself into the unlit porch.

Chipboard had been erected around the statues that guarded either side of the door. The brass handrail leading up the shallow flight of steps was encased in bubble wrap. At the top, he eased aside an orange and white concertina barrier and checked the dimly lit corridor. A short distance to his left was the main lobby. Out of sight on its far side was the front desk. That's where the team who were on for the night would be. He listened. Faint music and, just audible alongside it, two voices chatting.

Directly in front was a short passage leading to the main stairs. He glanced at his watch. Whoever's turn it was to be doing the rounds should be on his way to the far wing of the building, where he'd start on the second floor before working his way down to the official function rooms on the first floor. Finally, he'd emerge at the main staircase in about fifteen minutes' time.

He checked the deserted corridor again. The intricately tiled floor had yet to be covered by protective sheeting; that meant walking along it would make less noise. He looked to his right. A succession of pointed arches led off into the distance. He knew that at the far end was a small lift. Should he risk that, or take the main stairway? That would be quieter, but more exposed. Plus, there was another camera positioned at the top of the initial flight. He would be in its view every single step he climbed.

He decided on the lift. All he had to do was take it to the sixth floor and then walk halfway along the corridor to the clock tower's door. Not so bad, considering all he'd been through to get here. Once he had that open, he could lock it behind him and no one would be able to follow. Glancing down at the holdall, he held a forefinger out. Shush now, he thought. We don't want to be making any noise.

'What's your name?' Jon asked.

'Andy.'

'Which way to your control room, Andy?'

'To your right,' he replied. 'Round the corner and up the steps.'

'Come on!' Jon ran down the ramp and onto the rubber matting beyond. The doors into the building were massive and heavy. He shouldered his way through and found himself in a lobby that still echoed with the sound of his arrival.

His first thought was how poor the light was. It took a second for his eyes to adjust. Stone pillars and pointed archways were spread out before him. Above, patterns on the vaulted ceiling were barely visible in the half-light. At his feet, a tiled floor. It was like being in a medieval banqueting hall. There was a reception desk to the side. Two blokes behind it, both looking at him in surprise. Behind him, he heard Andy coming through the door.

'Where's your CCTV?' Jon asked. 'I'm police.'

The two at the desk were still just staring at him.

'Gavin Conway's on site,' Andy announced, moving past Jon. 'Come in via FM Services.'

The older one of the pair behind the desk scratched at his beard. 'What's he doing here?'

Andy looked questioningly at Jon.

'Just help me find him,' Jon stated. 'Any camera picking him up?'

No one moved.

'Rishi?' Andy said, clapping his hands. 'Cameras?'

'Right.' He stepped into the rear room.

Jon looked around once more. Corridors branched off in several directions. He moved further into the main lobby. Through the largest arch, he could see a huge, curving stairway. Statues scrutinised him from dark recesses. Hanging from the ceiling above was an elaborate, unlit, chandelier.

'Can't see him,' Rishi announced.

'How do you get to the clock tower?' Jon asked.

Andy appeared at his side. 'Access to that is on the sixth floor. Little wooden door. He likes the clock tower, does Gavin.'

Jon regarded the other man. 'Why do you say that?'

'Any excuse, he sneaks up there.'

'Can you take me?'

'Yeah.' He pointed off to his right. 'There's a lift at the other end of that corridor. But it'll be fastest if we go up the stairs. I'm assuming we're in a hurry.'

'We're in a hurry,' Jon replied, setting off. 'And we need light!' he shouted back to the desk. 'Every bloody bulb in this building! I want them all turned on.'

*

'He's already gone, sir,' Iona said. 'I couldn't stop him.'

At the other end of the line, DCI Pinner sighed heavily. 'The MIT team will be there any second. He really couldn't wait?'

'To be fair, sir, no. Conway got on site almost ten minutes ago. He'll be in the main building by now. With Olivia's baby.'

'I understand,' he said more quietly.

Her last comment hit home, as she'd hoped it would. 'Shall I stay here?'

'Yes. Make sure the MIT lot can get in. I'll contact DCI Parks and let her know what's happening. And I'm heading there myself. See you shortly.'

'Sir.' She pocketed her phone. Pinner and Parks. Things were going to get lively. She leaned over the counter and spotted the release button for the outer gate on a console beside the keyboard. The bloody thing was too far for her to reach. Gripping the monitor, she slid it across and used its corner to press down on the button. Then she unhooked the fire extinguisher from the wall, hurried out of the Portakabin and down the ramp. The lock mechanism was buzzing. She opened the gate with a sense of relief and propped the fire extinguisher against it. Job number one complete. Next, she called for an ambulance. A precaution she hoped wouldn't be necessary.

What, she thought, should I do now? She turned round to examine the main building. Its lower floors were obscured by a thicket of scaffolding, at the top of which was a wooden walkway. Above that, was a steeply-angled roof. She let her eyes travel along its crest to the looming clock tower. Was that Conway's plan? To end it all up there? By tilting her head back, she could see some kind of balcony above the shining white clock face at the top. If he jumped off that, where would he land? She dropped her gaze. Somewhere on the lower roof. Perhaps straight on to the vertical poles of scaffolding. A shudder gripped her.

Keeping an ear out for the sound of sirens, she walked back into the Portakabin and hopped over the counter. Emerging through the door at the far end, she surveyed the area before her. All the scaffolding at the base of the building had been encased in yellow foam. A sign affixed to one of the poles said, 'Main Entrance'. The arrow pointed to the right. Looking in that direction, she saw a rubber walkway that disappeared round the corner of the building. Just beyond that were the gates at the corner of Lloyd Street. She turned her head in the other direction. About thirty metres away was a row of skips, several overflowing with empty cardboard boxes. Judging by the head-high stack of rolls directly before her, this area must be where lorries deposited their cargos for ferrying into the building.

She moved closer to see what the rolls were made of. Was it bubble wrap? The stuff she so loved to pop as a kid? She pressed her palm against the nearest one and felt the bumpy surface beneath the wrapping give slightly. Yes. Industrial-sized rolls of bubble wrap. Metres of the stuff.

She returned to her previous position where she could keep an eye on the perimeter gate. But the presence of the dark clock tower behind her was irresistible. She stared it once again. To her surprise, a series of floodlights positioned at its base started coming on. Bright beams of light shining upward. Then the turrets at the top began to glow purple. Next, the building's windows began springing to life. Row after row. Jon, she thought. He'll have told them to do that. With all the lights on, Conway would have nowhere to hide.

CHAPTER 45

The lift rose with a gentle rumbling noise. Gavin Conway looked about the confined space. Like the rest of the building, it dated from the century before last. Protective sheets of foam had been taped to the lower panels of wood. A thick plastic sheet covered the carpeted floor. The buttons were enamel, set into a panel of polished brass. The speed of the thing matched its appearance: slow and stately.

He thought about the rest of the building. It was, effectively, a museum piece. In the Banqueting Hall on the first floor, all the paintings were in the process of being taken down, ready for transportation to a storage facility somewhere in Cheshire. Even the courtyards were being meticulously taken up so each stone could be cleaned and, eventually, returned to its former position. It would be a shame to not see the building once it had been returned to its former glory.

The lift seemed to be even slower than usual. He placed the holdall on the floor and opened the zip. If it wasn't for the purple smudge on her eyelids, he would have thought the little thing had already died. Just to be sure, he checked her cheek with the back of his forefinger.

Still warm. He decided then that he'd go off the clock tower backwards, holding the baby away from him at arm's length, offering her up so the mother could claim her. His gift.

A gentle bump let him know the lift had arrived on the sixth floor. As the doors slid open, he froze. Something wasn't right. Cautiously, he stepped out. Why were all the lights on? They never had them on at night.

The lift was set into a recess and he edged his head round to check the corridor beyond. Empty. The door to the clock tower was halfway along. Low and made of thick wood, it had a single small window of frosted glass near the top. Nothing to indicate that, on the other side, one-hundred-and-seventy-three steep steps spiralled up to a narrow balcony that was littered with the shredded remains of dead pigeons.

He turned his head. Was that the sound of sirens? He edged round the corner and went into the first room on the right. Just a few weeks ago, this had been full of council employees. Now, it had been stripped. A few square patches of the carpet were still intact, discolouration revealing where people had once walked to and from their desks. The rest of the carpet tiles had been pulled up and tossed into an untidy pile in the centre of the room. Bare shelves stretched along the side wall.

He crossed to the windows. The sirens were much louder, now. Directly beyond the small glass panes was the wooden walkway of the scaffolding. Planks of wood prevented him from seeing down into Albert Square, but pulses of blue light were bouncing off buildings on the far side. So, the police have arrived, he thought. But not fast enough.

Iona could hear the cars' sirens long before she saw the vehicles themselves. Why have your sirens on? Now he knows we're here. She watched as three cars raced round the corner and pulled to a halt near their vehicle. She held up a hand as doors started to open. As the first detectives reached her, she readied herself to let them know what was happening.

'This the way in?' the first officer asked, hardly breaking step.

'Yes. Do you need me to bring you up to speed?'

'No, you're alright love,' he said. 'Just point me in the direction of the control room.'

Shocked, she moved aside. 'Right. Head into the Portakabin. You'll need to climb over the counter. Go through the door at the other end and you'll see the signs.'

'Cheers.' He turned to his approaching colleagues. 'Boys! Follow me.'

She watched in silence as they started to file past. All men, mostly wearing suits. A couple met her eyes for a second before looking away. Really? she thought. Not one of you is going to—

A bottleneck formed on the ramp. The last detective was forced to stop right next to her. He spoke at her from the side of his mouth. 'Is it true Spicer's already in there?'

The nearest detectives turned in her direction.

'Yeah,' Iona replied. 'He went in about five minutes ago.'

The one who'd asked the question shook his head before speaking to his colleagues. 'Can't fucking help himself, can he?'

As they continued edging into the Portakabin, Iona found herself staring incredulously at their backs. 'Well, I suppose if he hadn't worked this out, you lot would still be driving round empty NCP car parks in Ancoats.'

'Yeah,' the detective said over his shoulder. 'But how will it play out? It's Jon Spicer.'

'What's that supposed to mean?' Iona demanded.

'Usually, not very well.'

Another car came to a halt and a lady with curly black ringlets of hair and a large mole on her left cheek made her way quickly across. A female officer, Iona thought. Finally.

'You're DC Iona Khan?' she demanded in a cold voice.

Any hope for a more reasonable attitude instantly evaporated. 'Yes.'

'DCI Parks. You've been working with DC Spicer, correct?'

'I have. He went in after Conway about—'

'So, you have a number for him?'

'Sorry?'

'A number. You have his phone number.'

'Yes, I do.'

'Ring him and tell him to get out.'

'Pardon?'

'Ring him. This is an MIT operation. Tell him to get out. Now.'

Jon bounded up the stone stairs two at a time. As he ascended, he passed empty plinths that, he guessed, were once home to busts of serious-looking men. The historical figures who'd built Manchester into an industrial powerhouse. He got to the first floor and grabbed the handrail, immediately registering the layer of bubble wrap beneath his hand.

As he set off up the next flight, he checked the security man was keeping up. He was, just. At the third floor, the decor noticeably changed. Less grandiose, more plain. He guessed he was entering the functional part of the building; areas not designed for entertaining dignitaries and hosting official functions. By the fifth floor, he'd lost sight of the security man. He paused on the landing and glanced at the window. Blue lights were flickering in the square below. The MIT had arrived, then. He wondered if he'd have worked with many of the team. He wondered if many of them remembered him fondly. Maybe one or two, at most.

The security guard came into view, but he was puffing badly. Spotting Jon further up, he came to a stop. 'Thank God for that. You need the bloody key. I can't keep up with you.'

Jon immediately started back down. 'How will I know which door?'

'It's the only one made of varnished wood. About halfway along. The rest are white. You can't miss it.'

He took the key from the man's shaking fingers. 'Do you think he could have his own one?'

'Who knows. If he has, you better hope he hasn't locked it behind him.'

'Why?'

'The only way through that thing will be with a bloody great axe.'

Jon spun round and started up the stairs once more. As the final set of stairs came into view, he slowed his pace. Tried to make no noise. There was a corridor at the top. He edged up the final steps and closed his eyes to listen. Footsteps. Dropping to his knees, he kept his head low. Just as he started to peep round the corner, his phone started to ring inside his pocket. No! The noise echoed along the empty corridor.

CHAPTER 46

Gavin Conway stood before the wooden door to the clock tower. All the sirens had gone silent, which only made him more nervous. Hurriedly, he patted his trouser pockets, searching for the key. What the hell? It wasn't there. It wasn't there! Calm down, he told himself. Of course it's there. Try again. Take it slowly.

This time, he felt it.

His heart was pounding and he let the breath seep slowly from his lips. You're nearly there. It's all nearly over. You've done it. His fingers were trembling as he raised the key towards the lock.

A phone's shrill ring made his head snap to the left.

It wasn't a faint sound, floating up from far below. It was close. Really close. Further along the deserted corridor, something was coming into view. It was almost at floor level, where the stairs began. Was it the top of someone's head? He watched incredulously as a forehead and then a face came into view. Suddenly, the big bastard he'd seen outside the Veterans' Helpline office sprang forward and began sprinting towards him.

*

Jon roared the words at top of his voice: 'Do not fucking move!'

Conway's eyes were wide open and Jon saw him flinch. The key in his hand fell to the floor. For a moment, Jon thought his tactic had worked. The bloke had frozen. But then Conway stooped down, fingers scrabbling desperately at the carpet.

'Police! Stay still!'

Another quick glance in his direction and Conway snatched up the holdall and bolted in the opposite direction. He ran for a few metres then vanished through the nearest doorway. A bang as the door slammed shut.

Jon reached it moments later. The handle turned easily enough, but something stopped it from opening. He slammed his upper body against it. The thin wooden surface flexed, but didn't budge. He took a step back and kicked at the lower part with his heel. The panelling immediately cracked. He repeated the action again and again, watching it start to splinter, then come apart. Once the hole was big enough, he reached in and started snapping sections away with his fingers. The nail of his forefinger caught on an edge and was half-ripped off. He kept going until the hole was bigger. Dropping to his knees, he peered through. A chair, tipped back on two legs, the back of it wedged beneath the door handle. He reached through, grabbed the leg closest to him and threw the thing aside.

The door cracked against the wall as he stepped into the room beyond. Whatever it had once been, the place was now empty. He scanned for another door or exit. No side room or cupboards or anywhere to hide. Nothing. That left the line of windows on the far side. He ran across and looked out. A narrow wooden platform beyond the glass. He started checking the old-fashioned metal handles. All were pointing down, which meant the latch was engaged with the frame. All except the last, which was horizontal. He pushed it open and stuck his head out. Cool air washed over his face. Off to his right, Conway was stumbling along the walkway. Jon couldn't see the holdall. Had he left it behind? Then he realised he couldn't see the man's arms, either. He was clutching it to his chest. He still had the baby. Jon crouched down and squeezed himself through the narrow opening.

'No answer,' Iona announced, turning to the DCI. 'Want me to leave him a message?'

'Don't be bloody stupid,' Parks spat. 'That bloody man.' She retrieved her own phone from her pocket and selected a number. 'Evans, where are you? Cameras showing anything? Damn. OK, you know the score: divide up and start a sweep of the building. Soon as Spicer is located, tell him to retire from the scene, understood?'

Behind Parks, Iona could see another car pulling up. She watched as an overweight man with long straggly hair climbed out and lifted a hand. 'Evening! I'm Toby Bishop, the negotiator. Any ideas where he is?'

Parks swept a hand out. 'Somewhere in there.'

He surveyed the massive building with a look of dismay. 'Okay. Have we any means of contacting him? A phone?'

Parks ran a hand through her hair. 'I don't know,' she replied irritably, before glancing in Iona's direction. 'Weren't you sourcing that?'

'I was, but I was given the instruction to hand everything over to your team.'

She saw the negotiator look despairingly in the opposite direction. Parks appeared to be wilting. After a second's silence, she said to Iona, 'Where did Jon think he might be?'

Iona took a step back and raised a finger towards the clock tower. 'He reckoned that—' Up on the sixth floor, a figure was making its way along the scaffolding's walkway. Her eyes tracked back. Jon! He wasn't far behind – and the distance between them was closing fast.

*

With every step Conway took, the wooden boards flexed and bounced beneath his feet. He looked to his side: just a waist-high length of scaffolding acted as a handrail. Beyond that was nothing but the drop down to the hard stone of Albert Square. An ambulance was edging its way round a cluster of parked cars. He could see the number 43 on its roof. Beyond the perimeter hoardings was a group of people, all their pale faces turned up at him. Directly behind, he could hear the thud-thud-thud of the detective's footsteps. How had he broken through the door so fast? The bastard was relentless. He heard that same hoarse, gravelly voice.

'Don't be stupid, Gavin, for fuck's sake. Talk to me, mate. What are you trying to achieve here? Just talk to me.'

Talk to you? Gavin almost laughed. Why? Why would I give you even the tiniest chink? I've been trained in talking, you cretin.

There were only a few metres of walkway left. Where the gangplanks ended, a ladder had been lashed to the scaffolding. It was at a right-angle, slanting steeply towards the gutter of the lower roof. I could climb up, Conway thought, if I wasn't carrying this bag. He wanted to roar with frustration. He'd nearly done it! The tower was so close, it blocked out all the sky. But now, he realised, I'm not going to make it.

He whirled round and extended his right arm so the holdall dangled in the air beyond the handrail. 'Get back! I'll drop it. I will!'

CHAPTER 47

Jon raised both palms. 'Fine: I'm not coming any closer. But is this really what you want, Gavin? Come on, it can't be. Tell me what you want. I'm listening.'

'I want you ... I want you to sit fucking down.'

Jon was surprised at how ragged Conway's voice was. The man was close to collapse. It gave him hope. 'OK. You're in control here.' He lowered himself onto the planks of wood, quickly gauging distances as he did so. Too far to rush him. Take your time, he said to himself. Easy does it. 'I'm sitting down, see?'

'Cross your legs! Put your hands on your head.'

Clever, thought Jon. Making it as difficult as possible for me to get up fast. 'I'll try, mate. But my knees are knackered.' He lowered himself to a sitting position and bent his left leg in. But as he tried the same with his right, pain started stabbing into the knee joint. 'Best I can do. Honestly.'

'Hands on your head!'

'OK. Done.' He watched Conway bring the holdall back over the handrail and lower it to his feet. Thank God for that. 'The baby's in there, is she?'

Conway tore off the high visibility tabard. Now he was dressed only in black.

Jon didn't like it. 'What's the plan, Gavin?'

The other man's lips remained tightly shut. In fact, Jon thought, his whole face was locked down. Just the eyes – bright with distrust. 'Speak to me, Gavin.'

Conway dropped to a crouch and unzipped the bag. Checking on Jon every other second, he reached carefully in and started to lift something out. Jon expected it to be the infant, but what started to emerge was insubstantial. And black. Oh fuck, it's the wings. 'Gavin? What's going on?'

Conway raised them over his head and settled them on his shoulders. He pulled a stretchy band of material down over one shoulder and attached it to a clip beneath his armpit. After doing the same on the other side, he tightened both straps and shrugged his shoulders a couple of times.

'Gavin, you're making me uneasy here. Gavin?' The man didn't react. It's like, Jon thought, he's following instructions via an earpiece. Can he even hear what I'm saying? When Gavin stood, Jon's sense of panic increased. He started speaking more quickly. 'Tell me about your wife and child. I've got a daughter, too. She ran away from home earlier today.'

Finally, something sparked. 'Go on.' There'd been a flicker of anticipation in his eyes as they closed.

Jon used the opportunity to shuffle himself forward a few inches. The pain in his left knee was rapidly increasing. Spreading into his thigh. 'She's only ten years old. Some ways, she's a lot younger than that.' He saw Gavin's eyes open again and stopped moving. 'Just getting a bit, "I know best". As they do.'

Conway was now watching him intently.

'We didn't know where she'd gone. Me and Alice, the feeling – it's like someone's yanking your intestines out. I wanted to puke.' He could see Conway starting to work his lips. It was having an effect. 'Honestly, my legs felt like they were going to fold. I couldn't get my—'

'What happened?'

'With Holly, my daughter?'

Conway nodded.

'I found her in the local park, cold, but otherwise safe.'

The other man's face fell and Jon realised he'd been hoping for a worse outcome. The sick bastard. 'We'd made this camp back in the summer, among the trees. She'd gone there to try and be a grown-up. Live on her own.' He pictured her crouched in the dark, rain dripping on her head, dry noodles in a pan. To his surprise, his eyes filled up. This is good, a voice said to him. Go with it. 'It absolutely wrecked me, seeing her there.' He squeezed a tear out onto his cheek. 'So ... I can't imagine what it was like for you. To be told your wife and your daughter were both—'

'Shut up!'

He lifted his chin. Conway's finger was pointing at his face.

'I know what you're trying.'

'What am I trying?'

'You're ... you're so fucking obvious. Just shut up. Not another word.'

Now the only noise was the breeze catching in the stonework around them.

Conway looked off the side and Jon shuffled a bit closer. The pain in his knee was now more like a knife, stabbing. Am I close enough? Not quite. Just a bit more. Conway's head turned back in his direction. There was a deadness in his eyes and Jon knew he'd failed. He was going to do it.

Before he could move, Conway bent down and lifted the slack baby out of the bag.

Jon raised a hand, edging himself forward as he did so. 'OK! I'll level with you, Gavin. Join your wife and daughter. Isn't that what you want?'

The other man's head cocked to the side.

'I know it's what I'd want if I lost mine. So, leave. Go.' He flicked his fingers towards the walkway's edge. 'Launch yourself. But don't take the baby, for fuck's sake. She has a family. She has people to take care of her. Leave her with me. Please.'

Gavin flexed his shoulders once again. Clutching the baby to his chest with one hand, he tightened a strap with his other. Jon looked on desperately. Can I get to him? I don't think so. But if I don't try now, I'll miss my chance. He took another shuffle forward. Conway would have to climb over the handrail. That would take a second or two. 'Gavin! Are you even listening to—'

The other man started to turn away and Jon jumped to his feet. Both legs felt numb. Like they belonged to someone else. He swung his left leg forward but, as soon as his weight came down on it, the knee buckled. No, he thought, falling forwards. In front of him, Conway was climbing swiftly over the handrail.

Jon forced himself back to his feet and tried stepping forward again. This time, his leg stayed firm. He took a tentative step with his right. Even as he started to stagger forward, he knew he was too late. He stretched an arm out and tried shouting again. 'Give her to me! Give her!'

Conway's eyes were closed and there was a blissed-out smile on his face. Clasping the baby with one hand, he reached behind him and pulled on something.

Jon saw the wings snap out either side of his shoulders. He was almost within touching distance.

Conway began to let himself topple back, the baby raised towards the sky. The handrail bit into Jon's stomach as he lunged at her with his hand. The tips of his fingers brushed against her soft babygrow and then ... she was gone.

He had a freeze-frame image of them both falling away from him. He closed his eyes and heaved himself back from the edge with a cry of despair. Before he landed on the walkway, he clapped both hands over his ears. If he heard the sound of their bodies hitting the ground below, it would be in his head forever.

Lying on his back, he started grinding his heels against the wooden boards. She had been right before him! So close he could see the traces of veins beneath her eyelids. The little nostrils. The miniscule creases in her lips. If he ever needed more proof God didn't exist, this was it. 'You fuck, you fuck, you fucking fuck!' He knew he was crying, but he didn't care. It couldn't be true. Please, he begged, let me wake up from this. A tram let out a low hoot somewhere nearby.

He opened his eyes and saw the floodlit clock tower above him. The white face and black hands. Time hadn't stopped. It's real. Everything is real.

There and then, he decided he couldn't go on. He would leave the police and do ... something. Anything. He had his family. They were safe. What he had just seen, how would he ever get rid of it?

Eventually, he became aware of a new noise. The ring of his phone. Should he answer? He had to. Had to let them know it was over. The baby and Conway were both dead. It was Iona's name on the screen and he took a deep breath before pressing green.

'Jon! Are you OK?'

Below him, he heard the sound of a siren starting up.

'Iona. I'm so sorry, but—'

'You just disappeared. Are you still up on the walkway?'

How did she know where he was? He lifted his head. 'Yes. I fell backwards. You saw me up here?'

'Yes, you followed Conway out! I'm down in the square.'

Oh Christ, he thought. She saw it, too. She saw them drop. But her voice wasn't right. She sounded almost ... excited.

'Can you stand? Can you look down to where I am? I'm right below you.'

Next to their bodies? He didn't want to see that. 'Iona, what's going on?'

'I'm here. I'm waving. Where are you?'

He regained his feet. On the far side of the square, an ambulance with lights flashing was taking the sharp turn onto Princess Street. Tentatively, he looked over the edge. She was down there, one hand moving back and forth, the other holding her phone to her ear. Beside her, a scattering of debris obscured the flagstones. Cardboard boxes. Long strips of what looked like plastic sheeting. Several officers were standing among it all. He realised they were gathered around a motionless body in black clothing. 'Iona? I don't understand.'

'We built a platform, Jon!'

'What do you mean?'

'Empty boxes with layers of bubble wrap on top. Something for them to land on.'

He realised she was talking about a crash mat. 'Where's the baby?'

'The ambulance took her. She survived.'

He gazed across the square, listened to the rapidly receding sound of the siren. Oh, my God. Turning back to Iona, he asked, 'And Conway?'

Her head shook.

EPILOGUE

'All snug, then?' Jon asked, smoothing the edge of the duvet beneath his daughter's chin.

'All snug,' Holly replied.

'Good. You sleep well.' He placed a kiss on his daughter's forehead, began to stand, then changed his mind and sank back onto the edge of the bed. 'I was wondering. How do you fancy us two go on a weekend in the Peak District? We could learn how to create a proper shelter, forage for food, make a bow and arrows – that type of thing.'

She looked intrigued. 'Like Forest Schools, you mean?'

He briefly considered the short walks in woods her class did at school. 'Better than that. Much better. We'd be with a guide – but he'd be more like the man you watch on the telly; the one who goes into the wild and lives off the land.'

'Ray Mears?'

'Yes, him. They might even show us how to catch rabbits.'

'Really?'

He nodded, scrutinising her face.

'And what,' she asked uncertainly, 'would we do with ones we caught?'

'Well, not keep them as pets.'

'Would we cook and eat them?'

'I reckon so.'

'On a camp fire?'

'Yup.'

'Really?'

'Yes.'

'Just you and me?'

'Yes.'

'That sounds brilliant!'

'Great. I'll see about booking us in.'

Before heading down the stairs, he poked his head into Duggy's room. He was spreadeagled on the mattress, round belly pointing to the ceiling. If you came with us, Jon thought, you'd eat the bloody rabbit raw.

Alice was in the telly room sifting through a basket of laundry on the sofa beside her. When he came in, Wiper's tail started a lazy thudding against the floor, but the dog didn't stir from his place before the wood-burning stove.

'Anything else for the wash before I put this lot in?' she asked.

'No, thanks.' He slumped down in his battered armchair and glanced across at his wife. She was barefoot, in baggy tracksuit bottoms with one of his old rugby shirts hanging down to her thighs. Blonde hair had been messily secured with a large brown clip on the top of her head. She lifted a pair of his black combat work trousers and checked the side pockets.

'Why have you got this?'

'Got what?'

She scrutinised the small piece of rectangular card. 'Alicia Lloyd. Head of Operations. Why is her business card in your pocket?'

That's what happened to it, Jon thought, groaning inwardly. 'She kind of stuck it in there.'

Alice flipped it over in her hand. 'Oh yeah? That's a bit irregular, isn't it?'

'It was, actually.'

She looked at him properly. 'Why did she do it, then?'

'I don't know.'

'She wasn't making a pass at you, was she?'

He wasn't sure how to answer that.

'Jon?'

He saw Alicia in his head; the offer of a bath and a brandy up in her hotel suite. She made a bit more of a pass, he thought. 'She may have been. It was all a bit weird, to be honest.'

Alice left the card on the arm of the sofa to resume her sorting. But her lips were now tight and her fingers moved spikily.

Jon sighed. 'You're not upset, are you?'

She rested her hands in her lap. 'Look at me.' She plucked at her track suit bottoms, then caught sight of her toes and wiggled them. 'Look at the state of my nails. Varnish flaking off them like ... like scales off a stranded fish.'

'Stranded fish?' He laughed. 'Where did you get that from?'

'You know what I mean. I bet Alicia Lloyd's toes don't look like dead trout.'

'Dead trout?'

'A high-powered businesswoman like her? No bloody chance. Probably gets them manicured every other week, the bitch.'

Still smiling, he shook his head. 'I know she was entitled and arrogant and had all the charm of a dead fish. I know that much.' He got to his feet, plucked the business card from the arm of the sofa, hooked open the door of the wood-burner and tossed it onto the glowing embers. 'Ali, I'll take the battered toenails and baggy clothes any day, believe me.'

'Really?'

'Really.'

She smiled before lifting a pair of his threadbare boxer shorts up. 'Well, I won't: look at the state of these! Get yourself down to Marks and Spencer's, it's like being married to Worzel Gummidge.'

'Cheers, babe.'

'My pleasure.' She straightened out a tiny Thomas the Tank Engine sock. 'Still can't believe what Pinner did. What is it with people?'

He eased himself back into his seat, thinking of how his senior officer had left him dangling in the wind over entering the Town Hall alone. 'It's how he got to be a DCI. Plus, I think the mayor was sticking his oar in; I definitely wasn't his cup of tea.'

'Still no acknowledgement that you saved his granddaughter?'

'Ali, there'll never be an acknowledgement of that. And I didn't save his daughter, did I?'

She untangled the legs of a pair of Holly's tights. 'He's still a twat.'

'It's fine. Rick got in touch the other day.'

'Rick Saville?'

'The one and only. He knows what actually went on in the last few hours of the investigation.'

'I bloody love Rick. What did he say?'

'He's in line for a promotion. They're having a shuffle round, now DCI Parks is moving up the food chain. He said once things have settled over there to give him a ring.'

'Moving back to the MIT? Your old stomping ground?'

'Yup.'

'Working with Rick again?'

'Working under Rick, more like.'

Her eyes shone. 'Jon! Imagine that: Rick as your boss and not some slimy prick. Would you go?'

'I don't know. I'd have to ask Iona – we're kind of a team, as much as you can be with the silo system they operate in the CTU.'

'But you've never really liked it there, have you?'

Jon considered the shiny new building, the latest equipment and generous amounts of civilian support. Then he considered half the people who worked there. 'Not really.'

Alice went back to her sifting. 'Rick. Trust him to come to your rescue.'

'Greg Scott agreed to things, too. I spoke to Senior just before.'

'Your idea for him to become the groundsman at Cheadle Ironsides?'

'Well, part groundsman, part general odd-job man. But he'll live in that little flat that's joined to the clubhouse. I can't see any scrotes trying to break in if they know someone's actually living on site.'

'That's brilliant. Him and Senior will get along fine.'

'Oh, yes.' His mind went to the chat he'd had with Greg. They'd sat in the Burger King and he'd admitted that, for a while, he'd suspected the ex-soldier of being the Dark Angel.

'Thing is, Greg,' he'd mumbled. 'Would I have been so quick to think it if, say, you'd been living in a nice house, driving a car, going to and from an office each day? I think you being homeless made me biased and that really guts me.'

Greg smiled sadly. 'Hardly surprising. It was me with Wayne the night he was murdered.'

Jon hesitated a moment. 'And this woman who was out begging; she said you used to two-up with Luke McClennan.'

Greg looked genuinely shocked. 'Luke? About twice. Any young lads who'd been in the army, if they needed help, I'd give it. Any of them.'

You, Jon thought, are a Guardian Angel, not the Dark Angel.

'Talking of young lads,' Greg continued, 'I rang my son the other day. Nine years, Jon, since we spoke. He's not so young anymore.'

'What did he say?'

'Yeah, we're going to meet. Not sure when. But at least we're talking again.' He paused a second. 'I could never face it before. Not when, you know, I was living on the street. But now I'll be in that flat.'

'It's great you rang him.'

'Best thing of all, Jon.' He raised a forefinger. 'Doesn't matter who's in it, however big or small, never forget your family, mate. Never.'

Jon let his gaze drift in the direction of his wife. He thought about his two kids, fast asleep above him. Then he regarded his dog, stretched out on the floor. I am, he said to himself, so bloody lucky. He leaned back in his battered armchair and reached for the TV remote. 'Shall we see what's on the telly?'

She wrinkled her nose before sending him a wary glance. 'Not if it's one of your boring history documentaries.'

He feigned outrage. 'Cheers, babe.'

'My pleasure.'